*

This book is a work of fiction. Any resemblance to persons, locales, or organizations, whether real or imaginary, is purely coincidental

Silver Tyrant

ISBN-13:

978-0-578-67362-2

Library of Congress
Control Number: 2020915739

A One Tempest Book

*

*

For Stacy, the best big sister anyone could ever ask for.

*

*

Acknowledgements

This work could never have been made possible without the
generous help of others willing to share their thoughts while I tried to
refine the adventures of Darien and his friends into a story worthy of
the time they committed to helping complete this book. A big thank
you to Carolyn Labrie, Corinne Cohen, Andrew Shedden, Ben Ames,
Nate Richardson, Dan Lashomb and of course mom and dad for all their
help!

*

*

Silver Tyrant

*

Prologue

Bamaul silently fumed.

The messenger prostrated before him on the cold floor of the throne room droned on, oblivious to the fact that his king had stopped listening quite some time ago. Regam stood silently behind the man looking down on him in silent disdain. Deep creases marred Regam's dark skin despite the ritual black and red Makavai obscuring his facial features except for hard eyes tinged with suspicion. His most trusted of Bloodsetters, Regam was the only one not required to show absolute obeisance before his king; even the guards stationed along the walls and at the entrance of the throne room bent their knees in reverence. Regam had brought the messenger before his king as soon as the man had arrived, denying him even water after the hard ride back to the Castle of the King. And his most favored of Bloodsetters had another purpose as well.

"How exactly was the one man I specifically asked to be brought before me able to escape your grasp?" Bamaul sharply cut into the man's spewing of nonsense.

Falling silent in mid-syllable and visibly quaking in fear the messenger pressed his forehead even further into the floor.

"Sire, I-I was not part of the Bloodsetters that engaged your enemies! I," the man stuttered in terror.

"Enough!" Bamaul roared. The king of Katama had a hot ringing in his ears as his temper flared to life like an uncontrollable tempest. Absently rubbing the sliver of silver embedded in the large onyx bracelet he wore tightly bound to his wrist the enraged ruler slowly heaved himself from the throne. Purposefully covering the short distance to the cowering messenger his rage built with each echoing step as bells of fire rang hotly within the recesses of his mind. The ringing of bells grew louder and more intense as he approached the object of his ire. Despite his initial outburst Bamaul was able to keep his voice calm with some effort despite his mind being torn apart by the bells. It seemed an example must be made of this blind, ignorant fool.

"My enemies? Mine alone? These men are *our* enemies. The enemies of all Katama, bent on reducing this country back into obscurity and incompetence. This country shall not have it! *I* shall not have it!"

The bells in his mind began to clang even louder as he looked down with bloodshot eyes at the ragged man quaking in terror at his feet. The calmness of his voice seemed to come from a great distance, like from the far shore adorning the ocean of clanging bells inside his head.

Bamaul gently lifted the messenger's head with the toe of his boot and gazed fiercely into the quivering man's eyes.

"Could it be that this man escaped because you do not truly

believe him to be your enemy? You did in fact say *'your'* enemies and not *'our'* enemies did you not? I find that curious...What was your name again?"

The man swallowed hard before sputtering an answer. "G..Gelas sire."

"Gelas. Good. Now Gelas, as I was saying I find your verbiage to be most interesting during the course of our conversation. Have you turned on your king and country? Or is it that you were never on your country's side to begin with? Regam!"

Regam snapped to attention and all outward signs of his disapproval of Gelas vanished. Cold and wary eyes stared out from between the folds of his Makavai as he awaited his ruler's pleasure. "Sire!"

"Regam my friend, when did this....Gelas was it?...When did this Gelas begin his service in my castle?"

Bamaul could tell from the wrinkles forming along the Bloodsetter's eyes that a thin, cold smile had formed beneath his ceremonial garb.

"I believe him to be a hold-over my liege. One of the few who convinced the staff of his usefulness once your rule became secure. His ability to ferret out gossip among the old castle staff is what initially got him the position of messenger if I recall correctly."

Bamaul was positive that Regam recalled events exactly as they had occurred. The man had a memory like none other save one. If prompted he was sure that the man would be able to recall the journey out of his own mother's womb.

Nodding absently at Regam's words Bamaul continued to toy with Gelas' chin as he stared off into one of the large open windows lining the throne room. The central region of Katama was humid for much of the year, unlike the northern reaches where the air cooled under the shadows of the Breathwynd Mountains and the southern region where the sweltering heat ruled the borderline. These windows helped to serve as a twofold convenience for the monarch of Katama. For one, they provided an additional current of airflow through the throne room, allowing the ruler to preside over occasions just such as this in comfort no matter the weather conditions. Even rain posed little problem. Should it rain servants would swivel slatted swing gates into position to fill the empty space, effectively protecting the monarch from the offending weather while still allowing some air to flow into the room.

Secondly, and more importantly, they provided a convenient avenue of travel for any undesirable person that found his or her way into the presence of Bamaul. Both the commoners and nobles of the region simply referred to them as 'jump-holes' and those that were often seen flying out of them as 'jumpers'. The cost of cleaning and maintaining the yard below the windows tended to lean on the expensive side, but Bamaul had accepted this as no more than a minor inconvenience. Besides, having staff solely responsible for disposing of the bodies and blood of those who offended him was appropriate for a man of his station. There were none higher than he after all.

Out of the corner of his eye Bamaul could see this Gelas fellow staring in horror at the windows as understanding of Bamaul's intent slowly crept over him.

"Please, your kingship! I beg of you! I chose my words poorly and it will not happen again, I swear!"

"No," Bamaul said. The bells rang to a furious cacophony in his head as he bent down and used a single finger to guide Gelas gently to his feet, never once disengaging his gentle touch on the man's chin. "You will not. Regam."

Regam stepped forward and roughly took Gelas by the arm and began to forcefully guide him towards the nearest window. Bamaul's chief Bloodsetter expertly applied pressure to the sensitive nerve located within the crook of the elbow to prevent the man from escaping his grasp. The added pain inflicted was always an added bonus that Regam reveled in.

"Wait! I swear I am reliable! I serve you loyally! Please! I have a family!" screamed Gelas, tears streaming uncontrollably down his face.

Bamaul watched with detached interest as the bells rose to a fever pitch inside his head. His entire body felt like it was afire; it was as if lava had replaced the blood in his veins and was incinerating him from within. His hands began to lightly shake before he corrected himself. Maintaining his outward appearance was taking more and more of an increased effort as Regam continued his slow advance with the wailing man firmly in tow.

"I care not for the families of cowards and traitors. Regam, toss him and declare his position open," Bamaul said through gritted teeth.

"No! I didn't finish my report! There is more!" sobbed Gelas as Regam brought him to the very edge of the window.

Bamaul sighed heavily at the fool's obvious attempt at delay. He wanted this done with. The bells would go away then. The tempest of bells was resonating with a fury he had never experienced before and he instinctively clenched his fists so tightly that his nails dug deep into his palm. Bamaul gritted his teeth even harder and forced himself to close his eyes and concentrate all of his immense will into maintaining composure.

That brief moment of delay saved Gelas' life. "There was a boy among them! A boy with strange eyes. Eyes that shimmered and glittered in the night and colored like jewels!"

Bamaul went rigid and his eyes snapped open at the description this Gelas had just desperately blurted out. The torrent of bells intensified their assault and his body shook under the strain. Regam and Gelas blurred in his vision and he had to force his mind to subdue the bells slightly in order to focus on the pathetic sobbing visage of the messenger.

"Regam, I would hear more," he said more calmly than he felt.

The king even deigned to join the two of them at the precipice of the window. A slight breeze trickled past his face as he continued to maintain an uneasy balance between the raging inside his head and his outward demeanor.

He could tell by the Bloodsetter's subtle change in body language that he was disappointed in the sudden change of orders, but he acquiesced all the same. That was one of the best qualities of Regam and his Bloodsetters. Their unquestioned loyalty and obedience were necessary qualities a strong king needed to effectively rule a country and the Bloodsetters offered both to him in abundance. And for good reason.

Regam forcibly grabbed Gelas by the scruff of the neck and unceremoniously dumped him at the king's feet. Gelas wailed in terror as he wobbled on the very ledge between life and death. Gasping back a sob the messenger desperately tried to steady himself millimeters from doom. He knew one wrong word and he would be sent tumbling over the edge to his death.

Gelas immediately pressed his head into the floor again so hard that he looked like he was trying to become one with the stone. He began to stammer some sort of gratitude for sparing his life, but Bamaul wasn't interested.

"Cease this spectacle at once or I will fling you from this place myself!" Bamaul erupted.

Gelas cut off mid-sentence with a frightened whimper and remained silent and trembling at the king's feet.

Bamaul sighed as his outburst of rage subsided and he regained his tenuous balance of the clanging bells. An idle thought penetrated the ferocity of the bells as he passively gazed down at the wretch before him. *Patience ultimately yields rewards, wasn't that what the foolish old man used to preach all the time?* It was almost too much to separate such a coherent thought from the raging of the bells, but he willed himself to focus.

"Now...Gelas correct?...Now what was it that you were saying about a boy with eyes like jewels? Mind you I have not fully reconsidered tossing your pathetic carcass out the window as of yet. Your presence alone stains the honor of my floors. Please do continue your report. I am all ears to your words and rest assured I will be listening *very* carefully."

"Y-Y-Yes sire. As-As I was saying there was a strange boy among them. I saw him a second time again in Rowe once the Bloodsetters didn't return after the ambush on you...*our* enemies. Daras, the man in charge of the unit tasked with the assault, had commanded me to return to Rowe and wait to see if any surviving persons of interest returned there. It took the better part of a couple days, but Philip and three others returned to the Dancing Parrot. The boy returned somewhat after, although he caused a small spectacle when he did."

"Because of his eyes?" Bamaul cut in eagerly, a feverish glint entering his eyes with such ferocity that even Gelas could feel the king's gaze boring into the back of his neck.

Cringing even further into the floor, Gelas continued his report. "N-No sire. His eyes were nothing to make note of at the time. This was confirmed by our agent at the inn who dealt with them directly."

Bamaul could feel the waves of a vast ocean lapping up against the base of his skull, foreshadowing a total consumption of his being by the storm of clanging bells raging ever more furiously within his mind.

"Then what is this gibberish about his eyes glittering as jewels? If you are nothing but stalling then I swear to those Godlings of yours I will throw you twice!" Bamaul growled.

"N-N-No sire. That is only part of my report. After they left the Parrot I took it upon myself to follow them even so far as the Grove that cuts off that small village of Breathwynd in the north. I lost them in the darkness and as I pressed on through the night began to think they had eluded me. Seeking to return in order to make my report as soon as possible I heard riders approaching out of the darkness and hid myself among the dense growth despite my fear of discovery and the spirits that haunt there."

"How very noble of you," Bamaul murmured with disdain as he began to absently caress the thin sliver of silver embedded in his bracelet again.

Bamaul could hear the man swallow a lump in his throat and began to count the individual beads of sweat standing out on the nape of the man's neck to amuse himself until the wretch was done prattling.

"Th-Thank you sire?" Gelas managed while nervously fidgeting in his prone state. He could hear the metal clicking of the king's bracelet with each of Bamaul's movements and he wished fervently that he wouldn't discover firsthand if the rumors about that bracelet were indeed true. When he had been lifted to his feet by the king earlier he had seen first-hand the thin, blackened lines spider-webbing and spreading outwards from the King's wrist. The sight was enough to make him quake even more violently in terror.

"As-As I said I was in hiding as they passed, but I could see clear as day that the boy's eyes had changed drastically since the inn. They shone in the night like a beacon despite the lack of moonlight and the distance between us. I was able to clearly see the color and shape were none belonging to any human."

"What did these so very non-human eyes look like to you, my dear Gelas?" Bamaul asked so quietly that Gelas had to strain the limits of his hearing to catch the words.

Gelas swallowed hard again before answering. His clothes had become sticky with sweat and road dust still clinging to him after his long ride back to the castle and his throat was raw from terror and want of thirst. He squeezed his eyes tightly shut and tried to keep from trembling any more violently as his bladder threatened to fail him. Uttering a silent prayer to the Godlings above Gelas carefully framed his reply.

"Like the eyes of a feline, or a lizard of some type, sire. Glittering in the night like a demon!"

"Be more specific!" Bamaul suddenly roared at the man. The bells went berserk. There had been no acceleration in their intensity and pitch this time. It was as if a smith's hammer had suddenly and violently connected with each and every one of the thousands of bells that were trying to forcefully break his mind. He ceased stroking the bracelet and the bells rescinded ever so slightly, but it still took him a few moments to regain control of his faculties. Regam subtly glanced at his king in silent question, but Bamaul ignored him. Only Regam was aware of the presence of the bells and of what they foretold. The others who had known were long disposed of and long forgotten.

Gelas' bladder failed him. The stench of urine assaulted Bamaul's nostrils and he had to fight a momentary gag as the scent caused the bells to flare again in ferocity. He would soon lose himself to the ocean of pain flowing into his mind from the base of his skull if this wasn't wrapped up immediately. Slow, controlled breaths from the king and the rustling of the soiled and trembling man's clothing were the only audible sounds in the throne room for several minutes. Gelas took this as a sign that his life was forfeit if the king felt his report was a personal offense, but he was so panicked that he couldn't think of how to be specific enough to please the king.

Tears began to flow again onto the black and grey stone flooring that had once shone so brightly under the previous king, but had gone unpolished and untended since Bamaul's rise. It was rumored among the staff that this was so all those presented to the king would be reminded they were so far beneath him that they were nothing more than dirt in comparison. Thinking that the sight of the throne room floor would be the last thing he would see before being tossed to his death he quietly tried to qualify what he had witnessed. He hoped and prayed his wife and young son would be able to carry on without him and that Bamaul would not seek them out to deliver punishment for his failure.

"They shone with glittering hues of green, of orange, and of purple. Colors so defined they could be seen even within the darkness and shadows of the Grove. The pupils were thin slits of inky black. They were just like the stories describe..."

"Out with it!" the king exploded in fury. The ocean consumed the clanging storm of bells and merged into one as he gripped his bracelet so tightly that he thought it would shatter his very bones. As the ocean began to completely envelope his mind Regam calmly walked forward and struck Gelas in the ribcage so hard with his boot a lone whimpering word tumbled out of his mouth.

"Dragon," Gelas whimpered.

The bells vanished as if they had never been.

"Regam," Bamaul said quietly.

"Yes, your Majesty?" Regam replied, again snapping to attention.

"Bring this man to his feet so I may look at him."

Bamaul could tell Regam had arched an eyebrow under his Makavai in another silent question, a gesture that would have ensured death in any other. Such was the limit of disobedience Bamaul allowed from just this one man. Bamaul nodded. Regam hauled the still shaking and foul smelling Gelas to his feet. His ragged tunic stuck to his chest with sweat, dirt and grime. His leggings had been stained by the urine and a small puddle had formed underneath him. A worse wretch Bamaul had never before seen. The man looked truly pathetic and Katama's king twisted his nose in disgust at one so much lesser than he.

"Master Gelas," Bamaul began slowly in measured tones. "Were I even remotely capable of such petty emotions as pity I would simply draw my sword and run you through myself just to be done with you quickly and to remove your foul stench from my presence. However, there may be something that you can do for me."

"H-How may I serve, your Majesty?" Gelas stammered nervously.

Bamaul smiled, a thin venomous line accentuating the sharp angles of his cheekbones as he gently turned Gelas to face the open window.

"Why my dear Gelas, you can learn to fly."

Chapter 1

Darien panted heavily, desperately trying to catch his breath. Throwing himself up against the wall of the dimly lit corridor he frantically strained his inhuman eyesight and enhanced hearing for any sign of his pursuer. His dragon eyes allowed him to perceive more in the hazy corridor than other humans could see in daylight under a clear sky, but so far he hadn't been able to catch even a glimpse of his opponent. He was sure any other human would be mostly blind in the darkness only accentuated by lazy wisps of smoke wafting down from the torch back at the entrance. He was baffled how anyone could avoid detection in an environment where he should have such a distinct advantage. Water laboriously dripping from somewhere in the corridor echoed around him, only adding to his unease.

Cold sweat trickled down his back and gooseflesh prickled up and down his arms as a sudden chill wracked his spine. Continuing to strain his hearing and eyesight to their utter limits, he felt absolutely certain that his pursuer was watching him. He had no real basis for this assessment, but he could *feel* someone's eyes on him. It was an unsettling sensation to say the least.

Where is he? Darien thought furiously, trying to recall everything he had been taught over the last few months. A flood of information entered his mind while he tried to quickly assess what tactic would best keep him alive.

Crouching low, he slid his hand down to the stylized dagger tucked into the sash tightly wrapped around his waist. Worst case scenario he could always trade his own life for that of the unseen pursuer, but he'd rather avoid such a heroic tragedy.

It's never like this in the stories, he thought grimly. Growing up in the isolated and remote Village Breathwynd, Darien had loved spending time reading stories about travelers and the adventures they had, places they went, and people they met. There was never a situation the hero of the story encountered that he or she wasn't able to overcome or enemy that couldn't be defeated. The stories always ended in the hero's favor without fail, but Darien's experience in his own travels had been far, far different. He wasn't sure if *anything* had really ended in his favor recently. To make matters worse, if he made one wrong move here he'd be killed for sure; his opponent was the most dangerous he had ever faced in his young life.

Lightly trailing his fingertips along the wall he slowly worked his way down the hallway in a crouch as he tried to guess where and when his enemy would strike. Still trying to control his uneven breathing he attempted to get a feel for what his adversary might be thinking. His opponent was a master of subtlety and the art of assassination; able to land a lethal strike without a sound. Darien thought of several scenarios and summarily dismissed each one as he moved along the wall. It wasn't helping that his brain couldn't seem to latch on to any one thought before it was replaced by another. The sporadic and haphazard thoughts were enough to keep him on edge, but he did finally get his breathing under control with some effort. The echoing sounds of condensation continued its methodical and constant drip...drip...drip and the sound was beginning to grate heavily on his already frayed nerves.

Nervously rubbing at the hidden dagger with his free hand a sense of worry suddenly accompanied a gentle nudging in the back of his mind as he crept along the hallway. Ignoring the impulse to acknowledge the mental intrusion Darien instead tried to focus even more intently on his situation. '*Stop sulking*', he sent at the indignant and pouty sensation that his initial non-response had received. The nudge lessened with a vague sense of disappointment and the other consciousness in his head faded somewhat. He did feel bad about not acknowledging his sister dragon's concern, but losing focus now meant losing his life and that was something he desperately wanted to avoid.

His opponent could appear at any moment and he had to be fully prepared for that at an instant's notice. Intercepting his pursuer's attack at the critical moment when his location became known would be the crucial factor as to whether Darien would live through the day or not.

Trying not to inhale too much of the smoke he continued his slow advance down the hallway. It wasn't out of the realm of possibility that the smoke itself was a ploy on the enemy's part to hinder him. Truly anything within the confines of the narrow tunnel could be used against him, even the air or water. He stopped short too late as a sudden realization hit him.

The water! he thought. There shouldn't *be* any water down in this area, nor was there any type of drainage that ran through this particular part of the keep. Even the natural moisture found here shouldn't be enough to cause the steady rhythmic pattern echoing all around him. He slowly reached for his hidden dagger, but was stopped when a strong hand gripped his shoulder and forcibly pinned him against the wall. The cold touch of steel pressed tightly against his throat, preventing him from drawing the dagger in his sash or the short blade sheathed at his hip as it was now wedged between him and the wall. He was trapped with no options left. In that moment he knew his life was forfeit.

"You lose," came a soft whisper so close to his ears that his enhanced hearing seemed to give the words physical form.

Not only had Darien not heard any sign of his attacker's approach, but he had cost himself the chance to draw the short blade hanging at his hip by remaining so close to the wall. His free hand still rested on the hilt of the hidden dagger and his fingers flexed instinctively at the thought of using it despite not being able to draw it.

"None of that," came the sibilant whisper again as the blade pressed so tightly against Darien's throat he was certain it drew blood. Fearing that even swallowing meant having his throat cut Darien grimaced in resignation.

"Hells! You got me again!"

The man hanging upside down from the ceiling chuckled softly before quietly dropping to the ground, gracefully twisting in mid-air to land effortlessly on his feet without making a sound.

"Did you really need to draw so much blood? I thought my neck was gonna get cut open if I moved the wrong way!" Checking to see how much damage had actually been done his hand came away sticky with more blood than he was comfortable with. No permanent damage seemed to have been done, but the feeling was decidedly unpleasant.

The man crossed his arms and gave an electric smile. Combined with the deep darkness of his skin and the lack of light in the corridor he cut an imposing figure in the gloom. The man seemed to tower over him in the confines of the hallway, although he actually wasn't much taller than Darien. He just exuded a sense of being so strong that it was almost overwhelming.

"Did you really have to go for that dagger you have in your sash? Especially in such a predicament?" came the soft rebuke.

Darien's shoulders sagged in defeat. Tartas had a point. He should have known that the top disciple of the Order of the Fist would have noticed his intentions.

Tartas. Darien had met the man shortly after he and the others had arrived at the Order of the Fist, where his friend Jack had been raised and trained. He had taken a liking right away to the dark skinned and soft-spoken man who was always quick to smile and offer advice; but the gentleness with which he spoke belied a viciousness underneath that could spew forth like a raging storm when unleashed. At first glance one could make the fatal mistake of assuming Tartas was just like anyone else. They would be wrong. Very, very wrong. The man had a strength and skill that belied his whip-cord thin appearance and that few could rival.

Darien had since learned that Tartas' appearance was a trait common to many of the dark-skinned inhabitants of the Bowali, an area of swamplands in north-eastern Pajana. Tartas' skin was so dark that Darien nearly mistook him for a Bloodsetter at first, but not even that particularly nasty breed of men had tones deep as night like him. He was the only Bowali within the Order and Darien felt like somewhat of a kindred soul considering his own unique appearance. Over time and through various painful lessons, like the one he had just experienced, Darien had become very grateful this man was on his side and even more grateful that he had agreed to become one of Darien's teachers.

"I guess I need to work on that," Darien grumbled, absently scratching at the wound on his neck that was already flaking and crusting as it healed.

Tartas' grin widened. "That and many other things. You did well to notice that I was watching you, but you still haven't grasped many of the subtleties of the Order's philosophies."

Darien could only nod in agreement. There had been a time not too long ago that he would have been so frustrated by failure he would have wanted to give up, but the events of the past few months had served to forcibly change his mindset.

He knew every failure he endured during his training now would inevitably allow him to avoid making mistakes in the future that could get himself or one of his friends killed. That was something Darien had vowed to never allow ever again. He had already lost his home and family to the ruthless band of Bloodsetters that Bamaul had unleashed upon his adopted homeland of Katama. Memories of that night still haunted his nightmares; more than once he had shouted himself awake during late hours of the night in a cold sweat and with tears running down his face. He never wanted to relive any of those painful memories again and had vowed that he would do whatever he could to protect others from experiencing the same suffering.

Shaking off the black mood, Darien tried to focus on the here and now and began to analyze just where he had gone wrong during the exercise. One thing about his mistakes stood out in his mind. The steady, hollow sound of water had ceased once Tartas had 'killed' him and Darien couldn't figure out the secret behind the anomaly.

"Tartas, you had something to do with the sound of the water didn't you? I kept hearing it, but couldn't place exactly where it was coming from or what was causing it. It didn't seem natural and the sound stopped once you attacked," Darien said.

Tartas' smile broadened impossibly wider. The Bowali then made an oval with his mouth by sucking in his cheeks and plucked the side of his face with a single finger. The resulting sound mimicked exactly the hollow sounds that had confused Darien during the lesson. Even the timing between each pluck of the dark-skinned man's fingers evenly matched how long it would take for a drop to fall, reform, and drop again.

Darien was amazed. Even with his enhanced hearing he couldn't tell the difference between Tartas' imitation and the real thing. He scrunched his face in concentration, knowing that he would not only be expected to understand that this minor detail was important, but also *why* it was important. He mulled over each possibility he could think of and summarily dismissed each one as he struggled to find the answer.

Tartas continued his mimicry while Darien sought a solution to the riddle. As he continued to think, the hollow sounds started to become more and more of a distraction that he found harder and harder to ignore. As the sound droned on he found himself focusing on the sound instead of analyzing the lesson. In fact, it seemed like there was nothing else except for that steady, rhythmic beat echoing from somewhere within the hallway.

Wait, why does it sound like it's coming from somewhere else in the hallway?

Darien was confused until the realization hit him that the sound was *supposed* to draw his attention. Darien stared up at the ceiling, easily recognizable to his dragon eyes in the hazy gloom. He was certain that he would have heard Tartas' movements if he had concealed himself up above. Tartas had taken Darien's hearing into account and used the echoing sounds to not only mask his own movements, but to distract Darien as well. In addition, Tartas was able to throw the sound to a different location at will and the steady pattern had not only distracted him, but had lulled him into a state of vulnerability. Darien was amazed. Such a simple trick had fooled him and could very well have cost him his life had this been an actual fight. Add in the fact that Tartas was the most adept disciple of the Order of the Fist, the one closest to attaining the rank of master, and Darien could understand very easily how he had lost this particular exercise.

One of the constant lessons his teachers at the Order tried to impress on him was the ability to process everything around him, even if it seemed minor or unimportant, in order to grasp an understanding of the underlying and unseen. He was often told that his enhanced hearing and eyesight were of paramount importance since there were just as many ways for enemies to take advantage of these attributes as there were for himself to make use of. He had also learned that his abilities could prove to be a handicap since he relied on them so much. It had even become a detriment in some of his other training sessions, but he tried not to let that bother him.

However, there was still one thing that was bothering Darien as he finished his inspection of the ceiling.

"How did you follow along behind me from up there? There aren't any hand or foot holds that I can see," he said. That was the reason Darien had dismissed the possibility of an attack from above. It just wasn't possible for an enemy to attack from above in this space. At least that's what he had thought.

Tartas finally ceased his imitation and simply pointed up and to the left where the ceiling joined with the wall at a sharp angle.

Darien was puzzled. "What? There's nothing there."

Tartas sighed. "What do you think I did? Think it through Darien. You still have the bad habit of questioning everything and expecting an answer without trying to discover the truth yourself. Have you learned *anything* in your time here?" His tone indicated that Darien was a rather slow student who should have already grasped the concept that Tartas was trying to teach him. Darien tried to avoid blushing in embarrassment at the rebuke.

Tartas' words strongly reminded him of the man who had raised him; Oltan, the only family the orphaned Darien had ever known, had been missing since the raid on his home village of Breathwynd. So much had happened since that night, but he firmly suppressed those sudden memories and focused on what it was that Tartas was trying to teach him.

Still gazing upwards Darien began to sort through the possibilities about how Tartas had accomplished such a feat. Without hand or foot holds the only way to move about the ceiling would be to...

There's no way!

Darien's jaw dropped in awe. The only way to move up above was that Tartas would have had to wedge himself into the spot where the ceiling joined the wall and use his hands and feet to push and pull himself along the ceiling; all the while maintaining, and throwing the location of, the illusion of sound! With such immense strength it was no wonder Tartas had so easily been able to hold him in place with one hand while 'killing' him, upside down no less!

Darien shook his head in amazement at his teacher's endless supply of talent and insane strength. Not even Jack had displayed abilities at the level that Tartas possessed. It was overwhelming.

"I guess I still have a long way to go," Darien said sheepishly.

He knew he didn't need to explain that he had figured it out. Tartas would already know by the subtle changes in Darien's voice and facial expression. It was another uncanny aspect of Tartas' abilities that Darien sometimes found unnerving. Especially since he was terrible at concealing his emotions.

Tartas' familiar grin flashed back to life instantly. "That you do."

Darien sighed heavily in defeat. His strength training hadn't been going as well as he had hoped and he had run into so much trouble learning the sword that his lessons had been shifted to mastering what the Order referred to as the art of 'Tankuto'; a series of small blades and daggers used as extensions of the body. Hand to hand fighting without a blade was also being hammered into him on an everyday basis. The daily beatings were taking their toll, but thankfully his ability to heal quicker than most was keeping him mostly upright. Some of his more zealous instructors even used this as an excuse to go after him even harder, but he tried to endure the arduous training the best he could.

However, not everything had become as hopeless as his training with the sword had turned out to be. Training his aura had progressed faster and more easily than his physical strength training by far. It had not only strengthened his recently formed bond to his sister dragon Koseki, but had helped them both better understand the invisible link connecting them over such a vast distance. Apparently part of linking with Koseki manipulated a portion of their 'auras', or the invisible essence of their being that only a few in the world were capable of utilizing at will. In fact, there were only two other people at the Order who were capable of the feat.

Kuldari, Headmaster of the Order and one of these people, had explained that aura training was different from the use of magic in that it was the manipulation of something already existing within the natural body rather than manipulating the intangible energy of the world. Although the Headmaster was certain magic had played an extensive role when Darien had joined with Koseki as a Ryudojin, he was adamant their auras had also been involved and that they were indeed separate concepts. "Although in your case one may perhaps be able to support the other in various ways given appropriate time and training since your joining was apparently so unique. It's quite exciting to have you here Darien, but you need to concentrate and work harder for both of your sakes. Your lives depend on it, especially since dragons mature physically much slower than mentally so you need to make up the difference as Koseki's human equivalent until she is capable of protecting herself. She won't be at her mother's side for long," he had said early on in Darien's training.

Despite his struggles, his training with Kuldari was something that he most looked forward to each day aside from his private conversations with Koseki that they ended each night with. They were progressing, but he was finding that with each step there was always more to learn. It often felt like those nights he would spend studying back home before his world got turned upside down.

Unlike normal people Darien and Koseki's auras were constantly intertwined and occupied what Master Kuldari referred to as 'another space separate, but connected to the world.' Darien's head hurt just trying to think about it, but he had to admit he had grown much closer to Koseki in the time they had spent at the Order thanks to the instruction of those like Master Kuldari. He was thankful he had been able to meet someone who could guide him in the right direction where the human side of his newfound abilities was concerned.

It seemed like forever ago that Darien had found Koseki and her mother Hosroyu back in the legendary Grove during his early travels. Deep within the confines of the Grove, he had been lured by Hosroyu's entrancing song of mourning and found the Elder black dragon in the throes of giving birth to a stillborn infant. In contradiction to every story about dragons giving birth via hatching an egg, Darien had watched as the unmoving infant dragon tumbled out of her mother with a long black umbilical cord tightly wrapped around her elongated neck. Darien had mustered enough courage to save the baby dragon's life and had accidentally inherited the abilities of a 'Ryudojin'; one of the legendary people psychically and physically connected to a dragon and not seen on the world of Taulia in generations. His life had taken an interesting twist since then.

Darien started as a chime reverberated loudly throughout the hallway.

Tartas gave a soft chuckle. "Dinner chime. Let's get you fed so that you'll have plenty of energy for your lessons with Kuldari."

Darien grinned at the soft-spoken man. The dinner hour was his favorite part of the day. Compared to the disciplined and exhaustive training and studying the Order expected of its students and guests alike, the dinner meal was always boisterous and rowdy. Calling it a free-for-all wouldn't do it justice. It wasn't uncommon for food, plates, silverware, and fists alike to be thrown about in reckless abandon. The meal hall was always filled with song, music, heated arguments of dubious origin, and boastful declarations of one variation or another. Even Darien had often found himself caught up in some kind of shenanigans when it came to the dining hall at the Order.

He had been shocked when he had initially been exposed to the chaos, but it had been explained to him the Order's general rules of conduct were relaxed not only as a way for the residents to blow off steam, but for its widely varied students to bond as well. This was one way the Order built trust among its members that was intended to translate when its students encountered hardships outside the walls of their home.

That first night, it had taken some not-so-subtle prodding from Jack and getting over-served on the Order's particularly dark and bitter ale for Darien to become fully immersed in the cacophony encompassing the dining hall. The Order's residents of course, were more than happy to indoctrinate a new arrival to the general melee. He had survived that first meal with no more than a blackened eye after becoming drunker than he had ever been in his life. He still had no recollection of who had punched him or why, but he couldn't shake the feeling that it had probably been Jack.

Thankfully the proctors in charge of the hall didn't permit any weapons for safety reasons or things could have been much worse. It even surpassed the incident with whiskey back in Rowe when Jack and Geru had gotten him drunk on the stuff in order to stitch up a wound he had received in the back of his skull. He had been so useless during his aura training that Kuldari had sent him off to bed in disgust and with a stern warning that he would only ever receive this one free pass. Darien had appreciated Kuldari's leniency, but his hangover in the morning had been more than just punishment. Jack appearing just as the sun broke above the horizon to drag him out into the stabling yard for Tankuto didn't help either.

However, tonight Darien had a surprise for everyone that would show just how far he had come since that first night in the Order. He and Koseki had been practicing this surprise in secret, keeping it from his friends and instructors for months under Hosroyu's careful watch and instruction, and they were both excited at the prospect of showing off a little.

The original idea for their surprise had been the result of a conversation with Koseki's mother. The connection he shared with Koseki was singular in nature due to the abnormal circumstances surrounding how the link had been formed, allowing Hosroyu to 'intrude' on their bond to share much needed guidance and advice. Over time, and due mainly to their training with Kuldari, Hosroyu had been having a harder and harder time breaking into the link.

Although she had assured him this was a good thing and often reminded him that she had spoken of this inevitability before, Darien often worried about their ability to survive without her guidance.

Despite his reluctance to lose Hosroyu's wisdom, both he and Koseki were nervously eager for the opportunity to have full control of their unique bond. When Darien had first bonded with Koseki, there had not only been the physical ingestion of the young dragon's blood and birthing fluids, but an intense amount of emotional exchange that neither had been aware of at the time. He suspected that Hosroyu knew more about their abnormal circumstances than she let on, but he had decided not to press the issue. From his conversations with the Elder dragon he had learned that the normal process for a human to become a Ryudojin was an intense amount of meditation and emotional bonding with an unborn fetus as it grew within a consenting adult dragon. During the dragon's gestation period specialists would withdraw fluids directly from the fetus as it grew and inject them into the human initiate to speed along the bonding process. Once the infant was born directly into the initiate's hands a link would usually form between it and the newly christened Ryudojin. However, it was not uncommon for a link to fail for reasons that were never clear, which made the existence of a Ryudojin that much more exceptional. Especially since those that failed to form a link generally went insane due to the strain placed on both their minds and bodies. As far as he was aware, the circumstances where he had become a Ryudojin by saving Koseki's life was unique in history and that there were bound to be unknown surprises and complications both.

It had been within the first month of his aura training, after a particularly grueling session, when Darien had asked Hosroyu if physically altering or touching the things he could see when he was fully connected with Koseki was possible. Since whenever he or Koseki initiated a complete link he could see his little sister and her surroundings overlaid over his own, much like an incorporeal double image, he figured such an ability could prove useful. He also wanted to know if it was possible to manipulate the overlay so that others could see it as well. Darien had been doubtful of the chances, but had been surprised by what Hosroyu had said.

'It may indeed be possible young one,' she had begun in her deep velvety voice resonating within the confines of the link connecting him to Koseki. Darien had actually *felt* the peripheral of the link slightly vibrating in response to the elder dragon's words. The sensation never failed to make his shoulders itch and he wondered if he would ever get used to it.

'There is a process that could allow you to eventually manipulate the bond betwixt you and Koseki in a unique way, but none of our brothers and sisters, ones that the humans refer to as 'Ryudojin', have ever been able to master the ability in such an extreme manner. I believe the path the two of you have undertaken is truly yours and yours alone among our kind. Only the actions of you both will determine whether or not your efforts bear fruit. There are also other abilities both of you may be able to master, but for now you have much more to learn before you become able to wield the power you seek.'

Darien had been encouraged by Hosroyu's words, especially since new information regarding the topic of their conversation seemed to bubble to the forefront of his consciousness as if it had been there all along. He had discovered early on there was knowledge about being a Ryudojin locked away in his mind until it was ready to be used and he figured it must serve as some sort of safety mechanism to help him learn slowly over time. He also got the impression that it was also a way to keep his sanity intact. This had been a recurring theme since the night he had first bonded with Koseki, but Darien had still felt surprised to find that they could be capable of even greater things. For now he decided to focus solely on how to make his question become a reality and leave the mystery of how much information was locked away inside his head for another time. Tonight would be the first test of their secret training and he and Koseki were both eager to display the results.

The dining hall was already as raucous and chaotic as ever when Tartas and Darien arrived. After giving a perfunctory greeting to, and being scanned and examined by, the two proctors at the hall's entrance Tartas flashed a bright smile and ducked into the raucous din with the ease of someone who had been attending the chaotic meals for years. Easily weaving through punches, flying crockery and whatever else that found itself airborne, the Bowali fluidly made his way to the buffet tables laden with food.

Thankfully the denizens of the Order had enough sense to not disturb the area of the hall containing their actual meal; no one wanted to incur the wrath of the head cook Mellor and risk getting banned from the hall to be fed in his or her room. Taking a deep breath Darien prepared himself for his own journey to the bountifully laden tables. Mouthwatering aromas wafted through the air and mingled with the sounds and smells of the cacophony of the Order's residents, making Darien's stomach rumble in anticipation; Mellor *was* a phenomenal cook.

Ducking into the hall, he snatched an errantly thrown bread roll out of mid-air and began to follow in his mentor's wake. Although not nearly as adept as Tartas at effortlessly evading the maelstrom around him, Darien was still able to make it to the safe zone of the tables unscathed and eagerly helped himself to what had become his favorite food during his stay; Mellor's sticky ribs. The ribs themselves came from some unknown animal kept secret by Mellor and his staff, but Darien was far less interested in where it came from than how it tasted. He bit down into the soft, sweet flesh of the rib and closed his eyes in glorious appreciation of Mellor's efforts. As usual, the ribs were cooked perfectly, the sweet and sticky meat disintegrating in his mouth and Mellor's secret glaze caressing his taste buds with each bite. The glaze coating was by far his favorite part of the dish. The secret sauce was sticky to the touch and so sweet that it almost made the back of his teeth hurt, but in a good way. He loved the sticky crunch of the first bite and it never failed to deliver on his expectations. Sucking the excess glaze between his teeth before devouring the rest down to the bone he quickly grabbed another.

Trying to stay out of range of the flailing arms, legs, and occasional noggin' that came just a bit too close to the safe zone, Darien was only able to enjoy a few of the ribs he coveted before inevitably being drawn into the chaos.

"Hoo-hoo! There do bein' a sight for sore eyes!" came a familiar hooting loud enough to be heard above the din. It didn't take long for Darien's dragon eyes to make out the spindly form of his friend Jack. Seated casually amongst the rafters and leisurely enjoying a plate heaped high with food balanced impossibly on one knee, Jack lazily waved a free hand in Darien's direction. A large mug of ale sat precariously atop his head and Darien wondered how he didn't end up spilling all over himself.

Jack, or Lantern-Jawed Jack as he was commonly called, was the first person that Darien had met after his village had been left in smoldering ruins by Bamaul's Bloodsetters. Jack had proven himself to be a strong and loyal companion on their journey together, but he had also proven to be a consistently irritating pain in the backside.

Sarcastic, condescending, and eager to provoke, Jack was a singular character that took great delight in aggravating those around him, especially his friends. Most especially Darien. But despite these shortcomings and the aggravation that came with them, Darien was glad that Jack was on his side since he was still alive thanks to Jack and the others he had met during his travels. Jack, Geru and the furtive Squirrel had become much like family to Darien and he was grateful for their companionship and guidance. Even their leader, the hard and determined General Lockhart, had become part of these feelings. The General still tended to give Darien chills whenever he looked at him, but he had been slowly acclimating to the man's serious and demanding nature over time.

Jack, on the other hand, was affable and approachable despite the acidity of his tongue. There were definitely times when Darien questioned just *how* grateful he should be, especially at moments like this. Being hailed by his 'casually out of the way' friend had attracted the attention of several of the others in attendance. A sinking feeling began to grow in Darien's stomach as his eyes picked out an ugly grin spreading across Jack's face.

A small group of people had finally noticed Darien's arrival thanks to Jack's not so subtle greeting and began to weave their way through the throng in his general direction.

Darien sighed and tensed his body while relaxing his mind as he forged a complete link to Koseki. Part of their training with Kuldari was to strengthen and improve their ability to solidify the ever-present link at any time, even under the most stressful of conditions, and he couldn't think of a more stressful group of people than the ones making their way towards him now. He had planned to use what he had learned from their training as part of the surprise he and his sister dragon had on their agenda for that evening, but it looked like they'd be unveiling that surprise earlier than intended. He hoped that would deter those approaching from any of their usual harassment.

The group none too gently wending their way through the chaos was led by another figure that had become very familiar to Darien during his stay. The lithe form of the beautiful Lady Liana, with her alabaster skin and light red hair swept back by an oddly designed ringlet of gold, was always easy to spot. Walking arrogantly on either side of her were the De'Segua siblings Marco and Mari, who had attached themselves to her shortly after Liana's arrival and accompanied her everywhere she went.

Arriving at the Order shortly after Darien and his friends, Liana had quickly decided Darien would be her rival for reasons that continued to baffle him. Unlike the reason behind her motives however, there was one thing he knew for certain. When it came to Liana it always meant a confrontation and she often chose meal times as a convenient excuse to pick a fight with him. Personally he'd rather not have anything to do with her, but she seemed particularly obsessed with him and the determined look on her face made it clear he wouldn't be getting a reprieve today.

When Liana had first arrived at the Order Darien had heard from both Jack and Tartas that many of the instructors were eager to work with her. Apparently her latent aura was not only unique, but also held a massive amount of potential unseen in a very long time. Darien had been given the impression it might even surpass his own, although that fact didn't particularly bother him all that much. However, rumors quickly began to spread that Liana and her instructors both, even Kuldari, were having great trouble tapping into that potential.

He had overheard Kuldari say once that her aura seemed diluted as if it wasn't able to manifest itself in its purest and strongest form. "It is most certainly there. She tested amongst the highest percentile I've ever seen, even higher than Darien, in terms of strength and potential. There is something within her holding her aura back, or more accurately drawing strength away from it as if something else needs the energy more. Not to mention that *other* anomaly," he had commented to another instructor.

Darien hadn't given much thought to the rumors as he didn't have time to worry about someone else's training; he was having a hard enough time with his own. And he definitely didn't have time to worry about it now as Liana's followers cleared a path for her. Not surprisingly the two were absorbed into the general melee rather quickly, but this was by design as their efforts ensured their mistress' path would be unimpeded. It also didn't hurt that she had a reputation of being aggressively violent more so than most so people had quickly gotten the message that she wasn't someone to casually mess with. Locking eyes with Darien Liana suddenly launched herself through the air quicker and with more grace than should have been possible. A scream of unadulterated rage escaped from her lips as she swung a fist at the side of Darien's head meant to cave in the side of his skull.

Darien was stunned that Liana would launch an assault against him while he was still so close to Mellor's spread, but he didn't have much time to be surprised. Barely dodging the enraged woman's blow Darien finally abandoned the safe zone and entered the chaos around him. Thinking of how to escape Darien wondered why this woman he had never met held such disdain for him. He was sure he hadn't done anything to earn her ire during the few brief interactions he had with her after her arrival. She always seemed to somehow know exactly where within the Order he was and often took advantage of that in order to pick a fight with him whenever and wherever she could.

After one particularly nasty encounter on the roof of the Order that had left him gashed and bloodied he had come to the realization that this woman actually intended to kill him. If one of the guards hadn't come around on his rounds when he did Darien may very well still be lying on the Order's rooftop. His fears and warnings had gone largely unheeded however. It seemed the general consensus among his companions and the Order itself was that Liana had complicated feelings for him and was trying to get his attention in the only way she knew. How anyone could interpret her actions in such a way he had no idea, but he had resigned himself to having to deal with this situation on his own. If he stayed alive long enough to do so.

Snagging a boiled egg hurtling through the air and stuffing it into his mouth Darien tried to elude Liana to the best of his ability.

As the hot spices from the egg created a slow burn in his throat he partially shifted his focus to Koseki, who had eagerly been awaiting Darien's instructions at the far end of their link. The overlay of his sister dragon's surroundings had sprung to life and Darien was now trying to maintain a delicate balance of focusing on Liana, Koseki, the dining hall mob, and the overlay of the Birthing Circle all at once. If it hadn't been for the training he had been undergoing with Tartas and Kuldari he knew the concentration required for such a task would have been impossible. Albeit, it was still a challenge that he was finding difficulty coping with.

This is definitely not going the way I had imagined it, he thought as he instinctively dodged an errant elbow. *'And stop that!'* he irritably chastised Koseki. She apparently was finding great delight in Darien's situation and sat placidly watching his flight with her tongue lolled out in a dragon smile. Her tongue only lolled out further at his words and Darien got the sensation that she was thoroughly enjoying things. Swirls of deep blue and silver mingled with each other as they flowed through the link from Koseki to Darien, confirming his suspicions that she was indeed having a great time at his expense.

He sighed. Initially they had planned to use what they had learned to allow as many people as possible to witness the creation of the overlay. But since doing so required an intense amount of focused concentration and a dispersing of his own aura in a way that touched upon the auras possessed by the others within the Order, he decided his only option was to use it on Liana and bluff that it could do actual harm. He was sure there would also be unexpected side effects that came with it he wouldn't be able to properly prepare for, not to mention how much rest they would need to recover afterwards, but there was no helping that. They had also been training somewhat for something far more difficult, and by extension far more dangerous, but he wasn't willing to go that far with something so reckless.

Maybe I should have waited until I could physically manipulate things before I tried this. He dove under the nearest table and popped up on the other side, grabbing a coney leg off the plate of one of the diners.

"Hey!" the man yelled as he pushed his chair back to stand and give chase.

"Sorry," Darien mumbled over his shoulder with a mouthful of meat. Behind him, Liana sprung atop the same table on one foot and catapulted herself forward, thrusting her other boot into the man's chest to send him tumbling backwards over his chair into another group of students. Whatever thoughts of giving chase the man had vanished as the collision caused another brawl to erupt within the general melee.

Dashing through the crowd of churning bodies mixing with the images of the overlay was threatening to make Darien nauseous. He couldn't afford to close his eyes nor could he sever the link in such a state without causing harm to both Koseki and himself so he was stuck trying to stave off waves of dizziness as he ran.

'*I promised we would do this tonight, didn't I?*' he sent in response to what he was getting from Koseki. He could feel Koseki's eagerness and impatience grow as he ran. Pink and purple mists assaulted his mind and almost caused him to lose his balance. '*Yes, yes, I know, but right now we have to concentrate!*'

It didn't help that the young dragon was still laughing at him and the brief glimpse he stole in the direction of her image confirmed what the mists were telling him.

'It's not funny!' he almost shouted in exasperation.

'Pretty girls always chase you', Koseki's reply echoed inside his head.

He gritted his teeth. She had a point; he did tend to get chased by pretty girls rather often. The only problem was that they were usually trying to bully, threaten, or murder him. Koseki opened her mouth wide in silent dragon laughter, revealing row upon row of sharp needle-like teeth that someday would grow to be the size of long swords like her mother.

'Stop that! Do you want to do this or not?' he sent more sharply than he intended. Darien knew snapping at his little sister would hurt her feelings and he would have to apologize later, but he was exasperated. Hopefully the prospect of doing something she thought fun would overshadow any hurt feelings on the young dragon's part.

And if matters weren't bad enough Darien's enhanced hearing could pick out Jack's distinctive hooting emanating from amongst the rafters.

"Maybe the lass do be just wantin' to be givin' ya a kiss me lad!" Jack followed this up with some descriptive and in-depth suggestions about the intimate usage the male and female body allowed that made Darien's ears burn. Even Koseki seemed abashed at Jack's words. The young dragon didn't understand exactly what Jack meant, but the feelings and impressions she received from Darien were more than enough to get the message.

He finally ran out of space to scramble as he came up against the far wall of the hall where many of the calmer and more experienced of the Order's members dined on the outskirts of the madness. Sucking wind through his teeth, Darien whirled around and braced himself for the coming confrontation with Liana.

"What trouble are you causing now?" Tartas' soft voice registered in Darien's ears. Tartas and the others around him were calmly eating their meals with plates resting on small tables and mugs of ale in hand. Normally, unattended plates of food were fair game for theft and destruction, but it was an unspoken rule that messing with Tartas and those around him was something to best be avoided for those interested in maintaining their own health and safety. Darien wished he had the same kind of immunity when dealing with situations such as this, but he knew that was a false hope where Liana was concerned.

Risking a glance over his shoulder Darien gave his instructor a pained look before returning his attention to Liana, now stalking him with murderous intent etched into her delicate features. Darien could almost feel Tartas grinning as the man's light chuckle tickled his sensitive ears. He resisted the urge to shake his head in irritation.

I don't know why everyone thinks this is so entertaining. I'm positive she intends to kill me right here! What in the Hells is wrong with everyone?

'*Show now?*' came the dulcet and childlike voice of Koseki.

'*Now or never I guess*', he replied grimly. Darien could feel the excitement almost oozing off his sister dragon. The swirling mists spiraling through the link coalesced into a single deep blue, indicating Koseki's excitement was at an all-time high. They had discovered through experimentation that the mists that often appeared within their link, the presence of which had baffled them at first, were a physical manifestation of the aura of emotions they shared with each other. Over time they had also learned how to see those of others and how to keep those mists from springing up uncontrollably when he or his young sister dragon became distressed.

Some people were much easier to fully read than others and Kuldari had taught them that the stronger a person's aura, the harder it would be to read them until he and Koseki matured in the practice. Right now reading the majority of the residents of the Order had proven to be of little problem, but reading someone like the General or Kuldari himself was like trying to pull teeth. Darien had referred to the sensation as literally trying to 'tug' the emotions out of them and Kuldari had laughed at the description.

"I admit I cannot fully comprehend what you mean, but I understand the concept. With time, patience and dedicated practice I am sure you will eventually have little trouble no matter who you read," the aura master had said.

There *were* times when mists would 'leak' from someone strong like the General, but such an occurrence had proven to be rather rare and Darien wasn't sure he even wanted to start getting involved with any emotions the General may or may not have.

As for those in far less control, once they had discovered how to evoke these auras it had taken some time for them to learn how to lessen their intensity so they wouldn't be overwhelmed, but eventually they had discovered how to suppress them unless they willed it otherwise or their concentration was broken. In times of extreme stress or turmoil when their control was at its weakest the

mists still had a tendency to erupt around them in a dizzying
display, but they were trying their best to lessen the chances of that
happening. They both had vivid memories of those earlier days
when they could barely function after even a short amount of
exposure and neither of them wanted to go through something so
intense again. Despite what setbacks they had faced, Darien found
this experience very helpful in getting to understand Koseki better
and hoped that their efforts wouldn't be wasted since it would
probably end up very badly for them otherwise.

Taking a deep breath Darien began to focus more intently on
strengthening the link he held with Koseki and tried to assess how
big of a threat Liana posed as she continued to stalk him. Weapons
were not allowed within the dining hall for safety reasons, but
Darien wouldn't put it past the enigmatic woman to have somehow
snuck something past the proctors that were responsible for
ensuring everyone followed the rules.

Diluted colors of red and yellow misted about Liana's head and
shoulders. He had never tried to read Liana and had never noticed
any 'leaking' from her before so he was at first surprised by their
appearance. The dilution of colors also confused Darien, but after
a moment he realized this must be what Kuldari had mentioned
about the strangeness of Liana's aura. The auras belonging to the
majority of the Order's students were like a candle's flame, but
always produced a solid mist to Darien's dragon eyes when evoked.
The size of the mists about Liana indicated that she had a major
aura like him, but the colors were almost translucent, like they had
been painted over her with watercolors.

As he continued to concentrate on his pairing with Koseki he
noticed Liana making some odd movements around the hall and

through the overlay as she advanced. It looked like she was avoiding the obstacles in her path both real and illusionary.

What the Hells? He had little time to ponder the matter as Liana suddenly quickened her pace and launched herself in an impossibly high arc in Darien's direction. With a soft metallic 'click' that only one with Darien's ears could hear a thin metal blade extracted from the leather brace Liana always wore on her forearm.

How in the Hells did she get that past the proctors? He tried not to panic, but was struggling with so many things happening at once.

'Taya!' Koseki whined through the link, orange mists of frustration beginning to overlap and mingle with the deep blue. A short time ago, the impact of Koseki's rapid change in emotion would have overwhelmed his senses, but his time at the Order had honed his skills enough to where he could withstand the strain on both his body and mind for a short time. He knew this was the first real test of what they had learned during their time at the Order and that it was a perfect opportunity to display the results of the secret training he and Koseki had been practicing.

'Let's just hope this works!' He took a calming breath as Liana descended on him. Darien felt as if time slowed as he mentally 'reached' through their link to form an image of a physical connection to Koseki in concert with their emotional one. He imagined creating a mirror image of the link they shared, one hovering just above the other and thrumming in an unbalanced rhythm. The sensation of handling the new link was much like handling wet soap, slippery and difficult to grasp, but Darien pressed on and slowly began to merge the two links together with Koseki's help.

Koseki opened her mouth impossibly wide in response to Darien's invisible touch and let out a small soundless roar that lightly reverberated through the link, but struck Darien like a thunderclap. Shuddering in response to his sister's cry he almost lost control of both links, but holding on for all he was worth Darien forcefully began to 'push' Koseki's roar to the area between himself and the airborne Liana. Using his aura training to mold the image of the roaring Koseki into what appeared to be physical form they slowly completed the process.

The image of the roaring head of Koseki projected a few feet out in front of him just as they had expected. What Darien didn't expect was that in the same instant he could feel the unpleasant sensation of bone, muscle, and sinew beginning to mold and expand with audible cracking and popping that made him feel like his face was tearing apart. He gasped at the intense pain coursing through his face as it transformed and sweat beaded on his forehead as he willed himself to deal with the discomfort. The process took only a few moments, but the end result was Darien's visage having changed from that of a boy of seventeen summers to a hybrid of his and Koseki's own features. To the stunned students of the Order he looked like an odd combination of human and reptile as patches of scales replaced skin and thick ridges grew where his eyebrows had been. He could feel his tongue and teeth forcefully twist, mold and reshape to where he had to be careful not to bite the inside of his partially still-human mouth. Breathing heavily, he thought of Hosroyu and how she had hinted at what more could be accomplished with their bond as they both grew in strength and experience. He wasn't sure if this was something she had been referring to, but he was in too much imminent danger of being skewered like one of Mellor's meat and vegetable kebabs to dwell on it overly long.

Although he wasn't able to make the image of Koseki tangible yet or transmit sound the produced image had the desired effect. Roaring in unison with the soundless image Darien forcefully uttered a single word. "Enough!"

It wasn't the most eloquent and came out with a lisp due to his newly sharpened teeth, but it produced the results he hoped for as Liana immediately dropped to the ground like she had been violently pulled by an invisible string. In fact, the spectacle had an even greater effect than he or Koseki had anticipated. The entire hall went still as the image of Koseki faded and his face painfully reverted back to normal. He doubted anyone else in the hall besides he and Liana had seen Koseki or the overlay, but everyone definitely saw the change in his face and had felt the impact of the silent roar. Still panting heavily, Darien doubled over at the waist and pressed his hands firmly into his knees to keep from passing out. He worked his jaw several times to ease the soreness and pain enveloping his head and could taste blood in his mouth.

That was more exhausting than I thought it would be. And what in the Hells was with my face? That shouldn't have happened unless we were doing the other thing! During their experimentation he had always felt drained afterwards, but never to this extent. He supposed it had to do with the extra stress involved in dealing with Liana, but he still found the experience unpleasant.

Remembering that Liana had been attempting to impale him he warily raised his head and was shocked at what he saw. The entire hall was staring at him, their own distractions forgotten. Even Jack only gave a low whistle of amazement from his place up in the rafters.

The most amazing of all was Liana. A moment ago she had been airborne and intent on skewering Darien with all her might. Or at least he was reasonably sure that had been her intent. Now the mysterious woman knelt lightly trembling on one bent knee and bowed head before him, her blade retracted back within its protective sheath. The proctors were hurriedly shoving their way through the crowd in their direction, but when they saw Liana they stopped in confusion. Her companions rushed to the scene to offer their aid, but were stopped in their tracks by a single raised fist from their mistress.

Darien took a tentative step forward and Liana, with shoulders heavy, immediately inched back. Her followers exchanged confused glances, but mimicked her movements.

"Liana…" he began.

An audible gasp escaped from her lips and her shuddering increased in intensity, causing her entire body to convulse uncontrollably.

Darien was utterly confused. He and Koseki had both wanted to surprise and impress everyone, but Liana's actions were bewildering. Darien thought it might be best to sever the link to Koseki at the moment and silently said his goodbyes to the young dragon. Perhaps they had gone a little too far.

'*Maybe?*' came Hosroyu's echoing reply before the link severed. Darien blushed a deep crimson. He had been so engrossed that he hadn't even noticed the Elder dragon patching in to their link. To make matters worse, he couldn't help but feel his sister dragon was still somehow laughing at him.

A hand fell lightly but firmly on his shoulder and he glanced up at the dark form of Tartas quietly analyzing him.

"Lockhart was right about you. You really are full of surprises. Perhaps you should call it a night here?" the Bowali quietly spoke.

Darien knew from experience that it wasn't a request and nodded. He could feel every eye on him as Tartas slowly led him out of the nearly silent hall with the only sound heard being Jack cackling with glee from up above.

Chapter 2

Liana knelt trembling in the spacious quarters provided for her by the Order. Cold sweat dripped from her dampened hair and stung her eyes as chaotic rivulets ran down her slender shoulders to pool in the small of her back. Her eyes were red and swollen and had anyone seen her they would assume that she had been crying, but Liana did not cry. She was incapable of such emotions as sadness, fear and confusion. At least, that was what she had always believed. However, what she had just witnessed had annoyingly brought those unnatural and suppressed emotions to the forefront. She was appalled with herself; it appeared she had made some mistakes with her preparations before she had left her home. Next time she would have to choose her migrations more carefully if such incidents as this could occur, but that would have to wait for another time.

I may have made a slight blunder, she begrudgingly admitted while her dedicated followers had escorted her back to her elaborate suite after the stunt the brat had pulled.

The Order had honored her presence as they should have by placing her in the most luxurious quarters possible, with blankets of red silk and velvet pillows of every eye pleasing color piled high in abundance for her comfort. Fine carpets of a soft material pleasant to the touch of her bare feet adorned the room from wall to wall and a large canopied bed draped with sheets of sheer silk dominated the center of the chamber. The mattress was stuffed not with straw, but feathers that allowed for a more comfortable sleep than most would ever receive. Intricate tapestries lined the walls depicting all kinds of silly things that others might find interesting, but not her. No doubt the Order felt it was offering her the best they had for her stay. As it should be for one of her stature. It irked her to even have to stay in such close approximation to those she contained so much disdain for, but it couldn't be helped. She had a mission to complete and nothing would stop her from getting what was stolen from her. Even if she wasn't exactly sure what that was.

She had followed the boy for what felt like halfway across the created world in pursuit of what he had taken. Or at least what she *thought* had been taken. She had been determined to kill the boy no matter what and return home with what had been stolen in order to restore it to its rightful place, but she had never considered any alternate possibilities.

That brat didn't steal anything! He was Selected! She ran through the idea again before clearing her mind with a violent shake of her head. *Impossible!*

The thought of a human child being Selected by one of the sovereign entities such as the Elder black that ruled her home confused Liana to the very core of her being. The last of the great blacks that frequented the inner confines of that place would *never* associate with humans, let alone Select one to wield power associated with their kind. But the imagery the human had produced and the physical change as he bonded couldn't be dismissed as anything but proof of that fact.

Why that *brat?*

The question tumbled around her mind time and time again as she lightly shuddered within the circle of light created by the finely made candelabras generously allocated throughout her quarters. It made no sense to her. There *had* to be another explanation for this anomaly. No matter how many times she replayed the incident from earlier in the evening she could not come to any conclusion other than the boy had been Selected to wield a magic that hadn't been willingly passed to any human in generations. Biting her lower lip in concentration she again tried to consider the implications of what such a thing could possibly foretell.

Why would the Elder choose such a weak and useless child for one of the Selected? she wondered again. For the first time in her existence Liana was baffled by the circumstances surrounding her. No matter the obstacle she had encountered in the centuries since her creation Liana had always acted with absolute conviction that her choices were always correct. There had never been any remorse, regret, or consideration for almost anyone but herself, but now she found herself confronted by uncomfortable emotions that were both annoying and frustrating. It felt like the one she had chosen for her last migration was trying to exert influence over Liana's current incarnation, but she was sure she was much too strong to allow such a pitiful thing. Once she was back within the confines of her home and could again use her own essence to the fullest such a hindrance would no longer be a problem.

She let out a light sigh as she thought of her home. Her time here at the Order of the Fist had not gone according to her wishes, but there had been other benefits attributed to her stay. *This 'aura' training they speak of has been somewhat beneficial. I do wonder how much more powerful I will be once I am able to return and am no longer shackled by restraints.* She frowned at the positive thought forming about her time with the humans.

Such thoughts will only serve to weaken me. I must discover the truth of this issue without dwelling on these changes overlong. Even if the truth remains hidden it will be much simpler to just kill the boy and drain the magic from him. He is only human after all, isn't he? Her frown deepened; her thoughts were coming unexpectedly and unbidden from within the recesses of her mind. She chose to ignore the cause of it for the time being, there was too much else to do. Taking a deep, shuddering breath she composed herself and prepared for what was next to come.

"Lady Liana! Is everything alright? Is there anything we can do? What happened back there?" came a frantic feminine voice from just beyond the door.

The incessant voice belonging to one of the De'Segua siblings was muffled by the great wooden door serving as the entrance to her suite. She was thankful for the baffling the door provided since both of them had been jabbering continuously from just outside ever since she had returned. Their constant presence was an annoying necessity that she could hardly wait to rid herself of at the earliest opportunity.

Liana inhaled deeply, now more in control of herself and shouted at the useless creatures 'guarding' her door.

"Cease!" she roared with a ferocity that belied her delicate appearance.

Her followers obediently fell silent although she could still hear one muttering sullenly under his breath. No doubt he assumed she couldn't hear him and thus would receive no punishment for his insolence. How wrong he was.

Liana slowly moved from her kneeling position, the very picture of grace and elegance as she sibilantly rose and quickly regained her regal bearing. Quietly gliding across the room to the large wooden door she lightly pressed her forehead against the cold grain of the wood and closed her eyes. Reveling in the earthy smell of wood and iron she took another breath and let the familiar sensation of the scents of the natural world calm her.

"Marco," she murmured, "If you don't shut your mouth immediately I'm going to kill you this instant."

The muttering from the male De'Segua, the aforementioned Marco, ceased immediately without even offering a hint of apology.

Liana's eyes snapped open and narrowed. She had expected him to begin apologizing and therefore ignore her command. She had hoped to vent her anger and frustration on him as she killed him, but apparently he wasn't always as clueless as he seemed. She let out another light sigh while she continued breathing in the intoxicating aromas. Still, he *was* useful at times just as the other human that followed her was. Otherwise they'd already be dead.

Liana continued to silently revel in the magnificent scent of the door's natural construction as she meditated. Slowly a plan began to form in her mind. If all went well it would verify what exactly was going on with the brat and what the truth was behind his connection to her home, the place humans referred to as 'The Grove'.

Darien fidgeted in his seat under General Lockhart's scrutiny. Philip Lockhart, the taciturn and intense man with the icy blue stare that still made Darien squirm in discomfort, was the leader of the group of men that had found Darien alone in the Grove when he had first set out on his journey. He had just begun his search for the Bloodsetters responsible for the destruction of Village Breathwynd when Jack and Geru, Lockhart's top subordinates, had found him terrified and bewildered within the mystical Grove. Having been taken under the group's wing Darien had learned that these Bloodsetters had been acting under orders of the king of his adopted homeland of Katama and that they were seeking to oust the tyrant from his throne. He had had a myriad of adventures and trials in the short time he had been with them and Darien was very thankful for the care they had given him. But right now none of that seemed to matter as he stood in judgment for his actions and wished desperately to be anywhere but standing in front of the General.

To make matters worse Kuldari, his aura training instructor, was also in attendance along with Geru, Jack, and Tartas. Squirrel, the other surviving member of the Bloodsetter night raid that had wiped most of them out, was nowhere to be seen.

Darien wished that the rodent faced man was in attendance; Squirrel always exhibited a knack for perceiving underlying issues behind controversial and stressful situations and Darien felt like he could use all the help he could get at the moment.

Lockhart slowly let out a breath, air calmly escaping through flared nostrils the only sign the stoic man was vexed. The General was an unnervingly iron wall against emotion. A constant bulwark no matter what trouble or chaos erupted around him and Darien was more than aware of the fact he was often the cause of that trouble.

Lockhart steepled his fingers together and leaned forward intently, his piercing eyes holding Darien's gaze.

"How many more surprises do you have in store for us Darien? First it was the business back in the Grove, then the revelation of you being a Ryudojin while we spent time among the Jarabin, and now this. I had thought after the time spent here at the Order you had finally exhausted your allotment of surprises, but now there's this...whatever that was," he said.

"But...," Darien began.

Lockhart held up a hand for silence and Darien snapped his mouth shut.

"I needn't remind you once again what will happen should we lose our trust and faith in you Darien," the General said slowly for emphasis. "I *will* leave you behind. Despite your abilities and the progress you've made if you still can't bring yourself to trust in us to understand what you're going through then eventually that lack of trust will lead to either your death or ours. Most likely both. I understand even now you're still learning to cope with your abilities and your aura training must also put quite a strain on you, but in the name of all the Godlings above please share this type of thing with us before you unleash something like that on an unsuspecting public. Lady Liana still hasn't emerged from her quarters yet. She seemed extremely distraught about what occurred."

"Is no one going to comment on how she just tried to skewer me in public?" Darien muttered.

"Be quiet!" the General ordered.

Darien furrowed his brow. He was more than annoyed at the General's comments. Up until now he would usually mumble some sort of apology and pray that he wouldn't actually get left behind by the only people he could call his friends. He had made plenty of mistakes on their travels together, but this time things were different and the General's comments about Liana rankled him.

Clenching his fists Darien pushed back his chair and stood, anger coloring his face. He briefly brushed aside Koseki's worried mental touch at his sudden change in mood and faced the General.

"That's wrong!" he shouted with more force than was probably necessary.

"And why is that?" the General said evenly, his eyes narrowing at Darien's outburst.

Darien tensed. He felt fearful of proceeding and nearly melted under the pressure of the General's intensity, but if he backed down now he knew he would never find the courage to speak his mind. Past events quickly cycled through his memory one by one as he thought furiously of what he should say. Thoughts of his friend Corly, who had been becoming more than a friend before everything happened, and his caretaker Oltan were foremost among those in his thoughts. He thought about the memories of the night he met Jack, Geru, and the rest of the company and their adventures so far. Everyone he loved and cared about made an appearance. Wochisa, the woman he had quickly fallen in love with back on the Jarabin Plains, was the final face that flashed through the images in his mind. Her dark and exotic eyes lingered in his memory for a brief moment and he again saw the tiny white sparks deep within them that had so captivated him.

Being reminded of everyone important to him made Darien realize that the General was right. He did have trouble revealing things to the people around him, especially concerning his transformation as a Ryudojin, because he was afraid it would drive them away and that he would lose them just like he had lost his home. But what had occurred in the dining hall was beyond his control and an act of self-defense. If he didn't state his concerns and speak his mind now he was sure he would never be afforded the opportunity again.

"I said that's wrong! This isn't right!" Darien almost shouted.

Geru made to move, but a subtle gesture from Lockhart sat him back down. Kuldari and Tartas for their part remained silent while a large grin split Jack's ugly mug.

Darien took a calming breath to steady himself. It was time to deliver as the stories say.

"I fully admit I have made my share of mistakes," Darien began slowly. "And I take responsibility for them. But this time I refuse to accept all the fault. Liana was trying to kill me! Yes, Koseki and I wanted to surprise everyone, but not so suddenly or shockingly. We didn't even know about how I would change or how painful it would be. If Liana hadn't tried to gut me it wouldn't have happened that way!"

"Darien…" the General began.

"I know what you're going to say!" Darien cut the General off. He was fuming now, angry at General Lockhart, at Liana, at his friends, the Bloodsetters that had destroyed his home, angry at everything. His pent up emotions and frustrations had reached past his limit and now they were flowing like magma as he vented his anger. Deep red mist began to roll off of him and he had to take a shuddering breath to tone down its intensity before continuing.

"Everyone seems to think it's some sort of game. That there's no real harm, that it's just some kind of rivalry between students who happened to arrive at the same time or that it's just a way for her to vent her frustrations. Some even say it's because of other idiotic reasons with a stupid grin on their face! It's not! Liana has tried to kill me more than once and everyone wants to overlook it! The Order thinks it's training. My friends think it's because she doesn't know how to approach me. It's neither! For whatever reason that woman wants me dead. I've been running from her this whole time just trying to stay alive! No more! I defended myself the best I could and I won't regret it or apologize! Hells, Jack you were there! Did it look like she was playing games to you? She snuck a weapon past the proctors! How is that even possible?"

"Well, that do be…" Jack began.

"Shut up!" Darien roared, taking everyone by surprise. Even Lockhart arched an eyebrow. There was a slight reverberation in the air after his explosion and Darien felt an odd vibrating inside his skull, but he shook it off and pressed on before anyone could stop him.

"I don't understand why everyone overlooks and excuses her actions," Darien continued. "I'm tired of it! I'll say this now, if she comes after me again I'll do more than that! I swear on the Godlings above I'll kill her! If that's a problem then just leave me here and I'll figure out the rest later! I'm not running away anymore!"

Darien was panting heavily as he concluded his rant. He felt flushed and drained of energy as an overwhelming urge to curl up and sleep washed over him.

Lockhart's icy stare cut through Darien like a knife.

Maybe I said a little too much. Maybe the General really will leave me here. Darien began to worry. He had talked big, but how exactly *would* he deal with things if the General decided to cut ties with him?

Darien swallowed hard, but now that he had spoken so fervently he knew he had to force himself to maintain the General's gaze no matter how terrifying such a simple task could be. He had made bold claims during his tirade, including the first time in his life he had threatened to kill someone, and he could feel General Lockhart weighing his words and his worth with those piercing blue eyes. He knew he had to be prepared for any consequences that would come from his actions, both from earlier in the evening and now, so he steeled himself for whatever they may be.

Lockhart began tapping his fingers on the arm of his chair in a rhythmic staccato, the only minor habit Darien had ever seen from the man in the time they had been traveling together.

The silence in the room was deafening. Darien found himself holding his breath as he desperately tried to hold onto the General's gaze. His heart was thumping so loudly in his chest that he was sure everyone in the room could hear it.

"I think it's best if you cooled down for a bit Darien. Why don't you retire to your room for a bit while we discuss your concerns?" Lockhart eventually said in measured tones.

Darien was momentarily stunned. Not so much by General Lockhart's words, but by what he saw as the meaning behind those words. For the first time since he had joined with the General and the others he had not been given a direct order; he had been given a choice. He wasn't sure how he knew, but he knew his interpretation of what the General had said was right.

Feeling as if he was at an important crossroads on his journey, Darien knew he had to make the right choice here or else nothing would ever change in how everyone viewed him. Should he return to his room he knew he would never earn the trust and respect from his companions needed to stand shoulder to shoulder with them, fight with them, and even protect them. Up until now he had always been the one protected and watched over. Always the one making mistakes and running for his life. He would never achieve what he wanted most in this world should he continue on his current path. Darien knew his time with the General, as well as his time spent in the Order, had strengthened him, but the time had come for him to show some indication of that strength so he could proudly stand as an equal among them.

Still straining to hold the General's gaze Darien uttered the single most terrifying word he had ever spoken.

"No." He tried keeping his voice steady and almost succeeded.

Jack's grin impossibly widened and Geru audibly sucked in air through his teeth. To their credit, and much to Darien's relief, Kuldari and Tartas continued to maintain their silence.

"Say again?" Lockhart's voice cut through the silence of the room like a sharpened blade eviscerating the opposition to his will.

Darien flinched at the strength inherent in the stern man's words, but held his ground...albeit barely.

Darien felt like he was about to falter, but reminded himself that he had made his decision and that he would need to adhere to it no matter the consequences. He swallowed hard again before answering.

"I said no," he repeated, this time with more resolve. "I am as much a part of what we are trying to accomplish as much as anyone else here. I am just as much a member of our party as Geru or Jack...or you."

Darien was sweating profusely as he made his assertion, but he needed to follow through with his newfound resolve before he lost the strength to do so. He felt weak in the knees and like he was going to throw up, but forced himself to push on. He would never forgive himself otherwise.

Darien took a breath and plunged ahead. "I recognize I really haven't been doing my fair share and have kept things about what happened in the Grove that turned me into a Ryudojin secret. I know that any excuses I make for that won't absolve me of my past mistakes, but if I'm going to be of any real help I know I need to prove I'm worth an equal standing. I won't simply run and hide anymore, nor will I keep things secret from the rest of you. I intend to see things through all the way to the end and I can't do that being sent to my room like a child. My complaints about Liana are not tantrums, but are valid concerns. If you have matters to discuss then we can discuss them right now. I'm not going anywhere."

Darien finished and found himself clenching his fists in anticipation of General Lockhart's response. The excess perspiration had made his tunic clammy and stuck to his skin as he fought the urge to adjust his clothing. He had said what he needed to say, but that didn't alleviate the terror he felt at standing up to someone as intimidating as the General.

For a moment, no one moved. Then slowly and with measured purpose Lockhart moved to his feet. The man rose like a viper uncoiling as it began its strike, his piercing gaze never ceasing its attempt to penetrate Darien's soul as Lockhart approached him.

Darien gritted his teeth so hard they ground together. The cold clamminess of his tunic made him shiver and he was pretty sure he had to have a bowel movement, but he somehow was able to stand his ground at the General's approach.

The General's long legs took only a few powerful and determined strides to reach him. Darien watched as if in slow motion as the General raised one hand to strike him with a powerful blow from which he was sure he would never recover. His eyes followed the arc of Lockhart's arm and Darien winced in anticipation of being punished for his outburst.

Instead of the furious blow he had expected, the General's hand fell to lightly rest on his shoulder. Darien risked a glance up at the General and was surprised to find a look of approval on the usually stern man's face.

"Well spoken Darien," Lockhart said with an approving nod. "Standing your ground and speaking your mind must have taken a great amount of courage. None of us can truly understand the changes you've undergone, but all of us here can understand loss, grief and the need to see justice. We may not have seen things about the Lady Liana as you have, but I promise you going forward we will heed your words and try to come to a conclusion that satisfies everyone. However, I must also say the words you just spoke apply two ways. You said you want us to include you as an equal and that we can trust you to not keep secrets from us. In order for that to happen *you* need to trust *us* as well. I believe we've had a similar discussion before, but it seems you only now finally understand what I meant back when we camped within the Grove. Very well. We will listen to all of your concerns about and interactions with Lady Liana since coming to the Order. Should we decide that your accusations are accurate then we will work with the Order within their protocols to find a solution."

"But…" Darien tried to protest.

The General's grip tightened on his shoulder.

"We *are* still guests in the Order's home after all. We should be respectful about how they choose to do things here in the short time we have remaining," Lockhart said.

Darien sighed in resignation. "As long as their way of resolving things doesn't get me killed," he muttered.

The others laughed, finally breaking the ominous tension in the room. Even Tartas lightly chuckled. Kuldari, who had not spoken nor moved from his position of meditation throughout the meeting, merely gave a small smile.

"I am happy to see such growth in one of my students, but I believe we still haven't resolved the issue that led to us gathering here in the first place. Isn't that right Darien?" Kuldari said, cutting off the laughter.

Jack hooted. "You no be thinkin' you did be avoidin' that now did ya boy?"

Lockhart nodded at Kuldari's reminder. "Yes. There is that," he said.

Darien sighed again. He had gotten so wound up he had almost forgotten what had caused this impromptu meeting in the first place. He knew that in order for them to listen to what more he had to say concerning the issue with Liana, he would need to be completely honest and forthright about the secret training with Koseki and his reasoning behind doing so.

Taking a deep breath, Darien began to explain in detail how he and his sister dragon had devised such a dramatic strategy and what they hoped to accomplish with it.

When he had finished Kuldari nodded in understanding.

"As I said earlier," Kuldari began. "Your growth in the time you've spent here is impressive. Your ability to stand toe to toe with Lady Liana and the abilities you demonstrated during the dinner hour is more than enough proof of that. I wish you had requested both my assistance and advice in the matter, but I can understand your reluctance to do so. In the future I am going to make it a mandate that you inform me at the least of any Ryudojin specific training you wish to pursue."

Kuldari gave a sidelong glance in General Lockhart's direction. "Although I think the attention and gossip this incident has caused may have scratched the itch that the General has had for some time now. Do not worry about Lady Liana; we will investigate fully into the matter even after you have gone. I also wish to apologize, Darien. I should have made it clear to you that there isn't many ways for one person to take the life of another within these walls due to both the nature of the place and other reasons I will not go into at the moment."

Darien arched an eyebrow in question at Kuldari's words, but chose to remain silent; he had probably said too much already.

Lockhart nodded curtly. "Your intuition is correct as always. I think we should be getting to be moving on. We only spent so much time here in the first place for your benefit Darien. Hopefully you make good use of our stay here and will become more confident in trusting both your own abilities and to truly trust us with the knowledge of those abilities. Both will be needed when we encounter our enemies again. I count it a great stroke of luck that Bamaul hasn't assaulted this fortress in the time we've spent here. He might be insane, but it's implausible he hasn't discovered this is where we were headed by now."

Geru spat. "That bastard isn't crazy enough to make an enemy out of the entire Order of the Fist. That's as good as suicide."

Lockhart nodded. "Perhaps. But he's not the kind of man who's known for rational thought. As for Lady Liana, perhaps leaving her behind here now would be best regardless of her true intentions, whatever they may be."

Darien opened his mouth to again protest his case, but quickly closed it. He didn't want to risk dispelling the trust Lockhart had just placed in him so continuing to keep silent seemed like his best option.

Kuldari nodded at the General's words. "As far as your concerns about Lady Liana, we will take appropriate measures in our inquiries to verify the veracity of your claims. However, we will not impose any sanctions on the Lady without definitive proof of your accusations."

Jack hooted again. "I do be wonderin' what your response be if she do be lovin' you!"

Darien glared at his grinning friend and fought down an uncontrollable urge to punch him in the face. Then again Darien *always* wanted to punch Jack in the face. He knew for certain that for whatever reason Liana wanted him dead. Being in love with him was out of the question. There was only one woman who fit into that category.

Wochisa, the daughter of the Jarabin chief Atsadzil, had captivated him from the moment they had met and he had been shocked at how quickly a romantic connection had sprung up between them. Despite a rocky beginning she had reciprocated his feelings in the most intimate way possible before he and his friends had left the Jarabin encampment to continue their journey to the Order of the Fist.

Memories of the deeply tanned woman with deep black eyes that Darien found exotic and captivating flooded through him and he turned a deep crimson as memories of the night in a shared tent dominated his thoughts.

Jack hooted even louder at the change in Darien's complexion.

"Mebbe I did be hittin' a sore spot, eh lad?" he said.

Geru let out a deep sigh. "Let it go Jack, the boy's got enough troubles without you poking at him all the time."

"Ah Geru, me gigantic friend, pokin' at people do be what I be doin' best!" Jack replied with his usual grin spread across his wide face.

Geru rolled his eyes and balled one large, meaty hand into a fist and shook it menacingly at Jack.

"I'm going to poke *you* with my fist in a minute," Geru said.

Darien smiled at the familiar interaction between the two friends. Their banter was one of the few constants that had accompanied them on their travels and Darien was grateful for the level of familiarity it provided. Both of them had a unique personality that defined who they were, especially Jack, and Darien wouldn't trade either of them for anything.

Geru was as stalwart as they came. A solid and calming presence no matter what kind of storm raged around them, he always gave everything he had in their travels and he expected others to pull their own weight as well. Time and again he had proven himself more than capable and reliable in tough situations. Darien had to admit to himself that out of everyone he had met since he lost his home Geru was the one person he least wanted to disappoint.

Jack was as different from his much larger friend as could possibly be. There was no compromise when it came to Lantern-Jawed Jack. The spindly man with the large jaw was never going to change who he was no matter how much others complained. Not that that was necessarily a bad thing, but the man *was* extraordinarily irritating.

Well, maybe I'd trade in Jack, but it would still have to be a pretty good deal, Darien thought.

"Enough," Lockhart cut in curtly before their banter could escalate any further. "As I said, Kuldari is correct. I feel it best we move on and continue our efforts to regroup and consolidate the strength we have left for the coming struggle. Because of the ambush that I carelessly led us into a while back we suffered massive losses and what I had once hoped to accomplish through strength of arms has now become a mission of stealth, subtlety and guile. We will still adhere to the rule that we won't turn anyone away who wishes to aid us, but if they can't prove themselves invaluable to our cause then I will find use for them elsewhere. Is this acceptable to you?"

Lockhart turned to Tartas and the Bowali smiled.

"Sounds good," the dark skinned man replied in his soft falsetto.

Darien was taken aback. His surprise must have shown as Tartas' smile widened even further. "I've decided to join you at the Master's request."

Darien shook his head in amazement. "I'm happy you're coming along, but why? I didn't realize you had some personal stake in seeing the king of a different country dethroned."

Tartas' smile vanished. "The Order is my home. I've known Jack nearly my entire life and we owe him and the General both for much during Bamaul's reign. Things haven't been easy even this far away from the center of Katama. Bamaul's ascension to the throne of your country has had massively far reaching effects. The Order's own sustainability has even come under jeopardy so..."

"Tartas!" Kuldari broke in with a disapproving look.

Tartas held up a palm in token of apology.

"Sorry, Master Kuldari. I got carried away. I apologize."

Kuldari merely nodded in acceptance of the quiet man's apology.

Darien was shocked. *That* was Tartas getting carried away? His demeanor had barely changed! Although his curiosity was piqued as to what Tartas was going to say he knew better than to ask. He had to just be happy someone as strong as Tartas had joined them, no matter what the reason.

Lockhart folded his arms. "Now that that's settled, make sure you gather all that you need and say your goodbyes. We'll be leaving before first light and I expect everyone to be prepared," the General said sternly.

Darien groaned. Why did the General have such a fascination with giving them as little sleep as possible before setting out somewhere?

I suppose it doesn't really matter. I don't have much anyway and there should be ample time to say goodbye to the friends I've made here, he mused.

"So where are we headed from here then?" Geru asked, knowing the question was on everyone's mind.

"My, my, are we all going somewhere?" a new voice intruded into the conversation from behind them.

Everyone turned to see who had snuck into their private conversation unnoticed. Standing in the doorway with her head languidly resting upon one slender arm elegantly draped up against the framework of the door was the last person Darien wanted to see. Two others huddled behind the woman with accusing glares boring intently into Darien.

Darien's breath caught in his throat and an ominous feeling manifested in the pit of his stomach.

"Liana," he quietly breathed.

Chapter 3

It was an unsettled party that left the Order of the Fist early the next morning. The land of Pajana itself even seemed to share in the somber mood. Even with his enhanced hearing Darien couldn't pick up any of the waking sounds of nature that normally accompanied the approach of dawn. The grey sky above was like an ominous cloak buffeting them from the sounds of the world and Darien fervently urged the sun to rise and relieve them of the pall. He shivered against the cold, grey chill of the morning and pulled his riding cloak that had been gifted by Kuldari tighter around him as he led the column of riders away from the Order.

Despite being 'voluntold' as Geru had put it, to lead the way Darien couldn't help but nervously glance over his shoulder at the unexpected members of their party. Everyone, even General Lockhart, had been stunned when Lady Liana announced she would be accompanying them.

"My time here is at an end. I'm sure the Order will have no objections to my leaving despite the lack of progress your teachings have been able to elicit?" she had told Kuldari.

Darien had been furious at the implied insult, but Kuldari had merely given a slight nod of acquiescence.

"Your training is far from complete, but you have shown more talent and potential than any other that I can remember in the Order's long history. I would advise you to stay so that we may continue to determine what is diluting your latent abilities, but we here at the Order do not keep anyone against their will," the aura master had said.

Liana had smiled as she turned to face Lockhart. "I take it your honor won't allow a helpless woman and her inept entourage to travel unprotected through unfamiliar and malicious lands my dear General?"

Lockhart's lips had tightened in a subtle sign of irritation, but he remained silent as Liana continued her faux appeal of helplessness.

"Besides," the regal woman continued. "There are *many* things I am capable of that are sure to be of use to you. You *did* state earlier that you wouldn't turn away any useful people did you not?"

Everyone in the room understood Liana wasn't exactly asking the General if she could accompany them. Her tone and demeanor indicated she was most definitely coming with them and that they should be grateful for it.

Despite what Liana had said Darien had been sure General Lockhart would still refuse her. He had been shocked when the General acquiesced without argument.

He was more than a little confused as to why the General hadn't turned her down. The woman had been a constant thorn in his side since the day they met and he wanted nothing more than to leave her behind somewhere and never have to think of her again. A mournful feeling settled over him as he slowly led his sturdy mount Rosy down the winding path from the Order's stronghold. Riding the horses nonstop down such a sloping and winding course had been deemed too stressful by the Order's stable master so they were obligated to remain on foot until at least reaching the bottom of the convoluted pathway. Even the uncompromising Liana and her followers had agreed with the stable master's request. In fact Liana had seemed more concerned about the horse's well-being than that of her own retinue. It was almost like she was genuinely concerned for their safety. The Lady Liana was an enigma and Darien was certain she would prove to be more than troublesome once all was said and done. Mulling over the implications of General Lockhart's surprising decision Darien took one last glance at the forbidding structure that had sheltered them up until now.

The first time Darien had laid eyes on the Order he had been surprised at how bare and foreboding the fortress looked. Built entirely of hard, grey stone and heavily fortified to defend against a prolonged siege, the Order gave off a much gloomier vibe than Darien had expected based on Jack's colorful descriptions of the place. Various crenellations, walkways and murder holes dominated the upper reaches of the Order's exterior and Darien shuddered at the thought of attempting an assault on such a forbidding structure. It seemed so bleak and oppressive that Darien wasn't sure Jack had been all too truthful in his stories. When he had commented on this the square jawed man had just

laughed uproariously and rode away without comment. Squirrel
had shaken his head and smiled.

"Sometimes it's not the place, but the people in the place that
make it what it truly is lad," the rodent faced little man had said.

Darien hadn't understood what Squirrel meant at the time, but
once he had spent some time within the Order's walls he had come
to understand the words of the scout and tracker. The people who
inhabited the Order were as varied as the members of his own
party; each with their own unique personality and outlook on the
world. Despite the variety in nationality, heritage, gender and race
those within the Order were bound together by an unspoken bond.
It was common for those within the Order to argue, fight and cause
general chaos during the dinner hour, but there were never grudges
held or much continuation of an altercation afterwards, his own
problems with Liana notwithstanding.

Darien had often seen people who had brawled during dinner
walking the halls together in a friendly manner or calmly discussing
one matter or another over mugs of ale after the dinner hour had
concluded. He had been confused by this dichotomy at first before
Geru had explained it more clearly to him.

"Things can be like that because they consider each other to be
family even though they may not be related by blood," the larger
man had said one evening. "As such they get out their aggressions
while they can and try just as hard to understand each other
afterwards. They live, train, eat, drink, fight, and breathe life
within the walls of the place that took them in and gave them a
home when no one else would. In the end each other is all they have
so this group of people who may be seen as being at odds on the

surface is in fact a very close knit family. Jack once told me the Order calls this concept 'Tantai'.

"Tantai? I'm not sure I understand," Darien had replied.

Geru sighed. "Suppose it was the dinner hour and two people began to argue and started brawling. What do you think would happen if you tried to break it up?"

Darien had thought for a moment as he considered Geru's question. "I suppose they'd both get angry at me for getting involved."

Geru had nodded in approval. "That's correct. It's their business and they'll settle it as they see fit. No matter how upset they may be with each other in that moment they'd be much more upset, and probably very insulted, if someone else stuck his nose in their business."

Darien had thought he understood then. It was much like the relationship he had had with his caretaker Oltan, who had gone missing after the Bloodsetter raid that had destroyed his home village of Breathwynd. He had been raised by the old man as if he was his own son despite having no blood relation. No matter what differences arose between them, Oltan was his only family and Darien admitted to himself that he would have gotten very upset if anyone had tried to interfere in he and Oltan's personal struggles; Corly probably being the only exception.

Corly was the diminutive girl from his village who had been his best friend. The two of them had just begun to explore new and confusing emotions with each other right before the raid and Darien would never know what might have been. Looking back, it was possible he had been in love with her, but the village's destruction prevented him from exploring those feelings any further. Corly had sure made her own intentions clear when she kissed him though! But that was in the past and Corly and the others of his village were gone forever. Thankfully Wochisa had stepped in and filled that particular void, but he still thought of the small and fiery tempered girl from his home often.

He sighed and let his glance linger on the Order of the Fist just a moment longer. The Order had provided the only safety and stability he had experienced since the night he left the ruins of his village. He wished they could have spent more time there, but the General was a driven man and Darien had to be thankful for the amount of time Lockhart had allotted for them to stay.

They had stopped to rest the horse's legs for a few minutes when he was startled out of his reverie by a familiar, although unwelcome, voice.

"Does the brat feel sadness at leaving such a *very* safe place behind? Do you truly fear the world around you *that* much?" the melodic voice intruded.

Darien's hand immediately went to the short blade sheathed at his hip at Liana's interruption. Liana smiled in amusement as Darien instinctively stepped back warily before answering.

"Of course I'm afraid. A short while ago I was a villager living beneath the Breathwynd Mountains. I had never thought of being anything else, but now things have changed. The Order has taught me much that I appreciate and will be forever indebted for. Is that so wrong?" he said cautiously.

"And now? What are you now?" the regal woman replied.

Darien was puzzled by her question.

"Wha...what do you mean?" he stammered.

Liana's smile brightened dangerously as she stepped lightly towards him. Darien blinked in surprise at the movement; for a moment it seemed she had shimmered and floated from one spot to the next.

What in the Hells was that? he thought in confusion. Liana continued her slow advance, but for each step she took Darien took one back.

Darien never took his eyes off Liana for a moment during the peculiar dance they had created. Despite knowing full well her ill intentions he couldn't deny that Liana was an exceptionally beautiful woman. In fact, it was difficult for him, as well as most of those within the Order, to take his eyes off her even under normal circumstances. Both men and women alike in the Order had been more than open about their admiration and desire for Liana's company despite what Darien saw as an egregious flaw in her character.

With large, seductive green eyes set symmetrically within a delicate face above a small nose and pouty lips of a faint pink she no doubt could have her pick of many men or women should she so choose. Her light red hair was swept royally back with an intricate ringlet of gold which gave her a regal bearing that could be overpowering; evidenced by her entourage that stood by nervously watching their Lady interact with him.

"Why do you always run away?" she quietly asked, her tone slightly mocking.

Darien refused to answer. *Maybe because you're always trying to kill me! Why aren't the others stopping her? I already told them what she's been trying to do to me!* he thought in a panic. Darien wanted to risk a glance in General Lockhart's direction, but knew that doing so could prove to be a fatal mistake.

Seeing no end to Liana's harassment Darien sought the link to Koseki. She had been insisting on connecting since Liana had first approached him and finally Darien opened himself up to bridge the vast distance between him and his sister dragon. The completed link formed instantaneously and Darien steeled himself for Liana's next move as the manifestation of Koseki's surroundings sprang into view. This overlay of images was supposed to be visible only to himself unless he willed it otherwise by carefully manipulating the aura of another, but just like the other night Liana gracefully leapt back at its appearance. She released her hidden blade from within its protective sheath and for the first time since Darien had known her seemed unsure of what to do. She didn't kneel this time either. The turmoil on her face was evident, but he couldn't be sure if it was genuine. After a few moments of apparent indecision she slightly bowed her head and placed one hand over her heart in the same gesture she had used the other night. Darien noticed that she still tightly held on to her weapon however.

Geru moved to intervene, but was halted by a short gesture from General Lockhart. The Lady's attendants also began to panic, but backed down after a low growl from their mistress.

Darien was confused. Not only by Liana's reaction, but by Koseki's current surroundings. Up until now Koseki had always been safely located within the Birthing Circle located deep in the Grove where Darien had first encountered the baby dragon and Hosroyu.

Now she was romping about an unfamiliar and rocky terrain, barren except for sparse vegetation clinging sporadically to the rocks and dusty earth and he wondered at the sudden change in location. He hadn't gotten any sense of time or movement from Koseki at all, but his sister dragon's excitement as she explored her new surroundings flowed through him so he figured he'd ask about it later. If there *was* a later.

"What are you doing?" Liana hissed furiously as Hosroyu's immense head slowly swung into view.

'Hello young one,' Hosroyu spoke. Her words softly caressed the outer edges of the link he shared with Koseki and sounded muffled as if spoken from a distance. It was a vast departure from the night he had formed his bond with Koseki after saving the baby dragon from stillbirth. Back then Hosroyu's words had been so loud and dominant that he thought his ears would bleed, but as he and Koseki trained together and grew stronger her ability to intrude upon their link had progressively weakened. She had instructed them both numerous times that soon she would not be able to break into their link at all and that this was a good thing. The fact that she had been able to do so in the first place was a singular event due to her part in the unique pairing of the two and Darien got the impression it probably wouldn't ever happen again. She often chided the two of them to listen well to both her and their instructors at the Order so they would not be ill prepared for the day when she could no longer use this method to provide them with guidance. Now her words were like a soft caress lightly pressuring the outer shell of the link.

'This one intends us harm,' Darien 'pushed' the thought through the link to Koseki and Hosroyu.

'Does she now?' the great black dragon spoke with wry amusement. Koseki, who had stuck her head into a crevice to

search for something tasty, pulled back and swallowed whatever unlucky critter she had discovered. She lolled out her tongue in her dragon version of a smile in his direction. Darien frowned. He was starting to find that habit of hers extremely annoying.

Darien knew he was right to be cautious of this woman who had already tried to kill him several times, but he had to admit at the moment Liana seemed to pose no threat. She looked like she was deferring to royalty with the way she bowed with one hand over her heart. She was even slightly trembling. Liana. *Trembling.* It was the same as the incident in the dining hall. He had been relieved to have survived another assault at the time and hadn't thought too deeply about her reaction. He was beginning to think there was some deeper meaning to how Liana reacted to his link with Koseki than he had initially thought.

What in the Hells is with her? I don't understand any of this! he thought.

'Is that so young one?' Hosroyu asked with amusement still evident in her tone. He could no longer gain an impression of Hosroyu's emotions as the great black had become less able to intrude on the link, but she was powerful enough that she could still sense his own without issue.

Darien winced. He had a bad habit of forgetting how powerful Hosroyu was and that she still had the ability to interpret his emotions. Especially since perfecting this emotional exchange was something that had been a central focus of their training with Hosroyu's guidance. Kuldari had helped of course, but even the aura master had admitted a limited knowledge of how auras could be used within the bonds of the Ryudojin. He had learned early on that they would first be able to communicate with emotion before being able to 'speak' with each other. The more they interacted and trained the closer they would come to understanding all the complexities contained within their emotions. Darien had been confused by this. It had seemed redundant at the time, but now he thought he understood a little better. There were thousands of minute complexities and variations within humans and the emotions they displayed. Part of his training and experience with Koseki was leading them to a path where they could separate and define all of the intricate threads that wove those emotions together. It had been a revelation that opened more possibilities than he could have ever imagined, but right now he had a more immediate problem.

Darien's eyes narrowed as he studied Liana. Her attendants still hovered nearby with looks of worry and confusion while they watched the unnatural exchange. To them Liana had suddenly become submissive and seemed to be bowing before Darien. Marco in particular looked ready to explode.

Darien took a deep breath. *That's right, they can't see the overlay. But why can she? And why does it affect her so much? It's like she's a completely different person!*

Still, no one seemed willing to interfere and disobey orders from either group's leader. Lockhart stood rigidly in place with his arms folded sternly across his chest and an unreadable expression on his face. The General seemed content to observe the situation and see how it all played out for now.

Darien knew he was on his own. Just a few hours ago the General had placed faith and trust in him to not only share information about his abilities as a Ryudojin, but to be capable enough to handle matters that arose in connection with them if need be. He just hadn't thought that trust would be put to the test so soon.

Taking another steadying breath he began to focus on the aura of his link to Koseki in order to study Liana more in depth. He had discovered during his training with Kuldari that the mists of color often randomly appearing about the people around him were in fact a physical manifestation of their emotions. Each color represented a different emotion across the wide range of the human spectrum with varying hues, shades, and mixtures creating a dizzying variety of complex emotions to dig through. Learning the subtle differences in shades and hues of the mists was an exceptionally difficult task, but eventually with time and practice he and Koseki would be able to discern these variations and interpret those emotions even more accurately.

He had also found if he wasn't careful these emotions could influence him on a visceral level as well. It had been unsettling to share in the anger, fear and even happiness and joy of others, but thankfully learning to 'block' that aspect of their abilities had been something prominent in his lessons with Kuldari. It had taken time, but Darien was grateful he had at least experienced it, as it was one of those things he had been warned about when it came to the ways his own abilities could be used against him. He hoped it would never come to that and that he and Koseki would master their abilities sooner rather than later. Hosroyu had even once said they would be able to interpret the true emotions of someone even if that person himself was unaware of what he was truly feeling. And should they progress further they may even be able to manipulate and bend the emotions of others with weaker auras at will.

The thought of attaining such an ability to affect others to such an extreme degree somewhat terrified him, but that was still a very long way off. Darien was also wary of this since it was so closely related to the problem of other emotions affecting him and it had taken a significant amount of time for him to simply learn how to suppress the mists while he was linked to Koseki to keep from having his senses overwhelmed. The Order *did* have some very strong auras among their ranks after all. In fact, the last time he had been helplessly and completely overwhelmed by the mists was when he and Wochisa had shared their special time together before he had departed for the Order. However, that had been a *very* pleasant experience so he supposed the mists may not be so bad all things considered.

Reverting his full attention back to Lady Liana, he ignored the low rumble of a chuckle from Hosroyu and the widening grin from Koseki at his thoughts of Wochisa. A brief pang twisted his stomach and a vile taste entered his mouth as he intensified his concentration. Both he and Koseki paused at the shared sensation and Darien's face twisted in confusion. *'That was new,'* they said in unison. Shaking off the odd feeling Darien hoped Koseki would be attentive enough to understand what he was doing.

Thankfully, Koseki picked up on what Darien was trying to do and ceased her romping about to sit with wings folded and eyes closed like she had been trained. He could tell that it had been a close choice between acknowledging him or searching for another critter, but thankfully she decided to pay attention. Darien couldn't help but smile at his sister dragon's response. It had taken some time for the usually distracted dragon, still an infant by her kind's reckoning, to gain the focus and attention needed for an aura reading.

There had been plenty of times when Darien thought it would be easier to leave it to random and uncontrollable chance, but Koseki slowly came to understand how important it was to strengthen the bond to her brother and their abilities. Plenty of admonishment from Hosroyu and frustration on Darien's part had played no small role in pushing Koseki into learning to focus when necessary. The process was by no means perfect, but she had made significant strides compared to when they had first begun their training.

Taking several more calming breaths Darien began to concentrate not only on the link with his dragon sister, but on Koseki's physical self. Tuning his own breath to each exhalation and inhalation of Koseki's lungs they began to breathe in unison, sending the subtlest of silent communication between each other. Their thoughts ceased to be a two way connection and melded into a singular line of thought, connecting the two on a level indescribable to the common person. Darien felt like he *was* Koseki and vice versa. A single entity capable of individual thought shared simultaneously by two parties. It was an exhilarating, and somewhat frightening, experience.

This was the level of connection they were working towards one day achieving without effort so that every link would connect them as such, but for now maintaining their current state for more than a minute or so took a considerable amount of effort and concentration. Kuldari had warned them during the course of their studies that right now pushing their physical and emotional limits too far could cause them irreversible harm so they were both well aware they couldn't stay in this state for long. Not to mention there was a terrifying sensation of losing one's sense of self that accompanied their combined state. The first time they had attempted an aura reading Darien had burst into tears from the strain and Koseki had wailed in confusion. Thankfully Kuldari and Hosroyu had stepped in to help them, but it was an incident that neither of them would ever forget.

Once they achieved the connection they sought, they 'pushed' their singular consciousness into the area around Liana, trying to sense and fuse its way into her individual aura. For the briefest of moments they were successful, until a bright kaleidoscope of indescribable color exploded within their shared consciousness and shattered their link. Koseki and Darien silently screamed in pain at the brief glimpse of the intensity of Liana's aura and the violent sundering of their one mind. Darien sank to his knees, grasping his head and desperately gasping for air. His mind felt like it was unraveling and he was nearly overwhelmed by the immense sensation of sorrow, pain and confusion they were experiencing. For a brief, intense moment Darien felt like they were both about to lose their sanity as their connection was severed without warning.

Reeling from shock, he forced himself to painfully open one eye at Liana. She no longer bowed, but stood affixing him with a stern and slightly bewildered expression that he was sure boded none too well for him. Perhaps in his immediate future.

"What...What in the Hells was *that?*" Darien sputtered in a whisper as aid finally arrived in the form of Geru, who draped one of Darien's arms easily over his shoulder for support.

Liana's eyes narrowed. "I know not what you mean brat," she said. Turning deliberately on her heel Liana stalked past her retainers, snapping her fingers in command for them to follow as she distanced herself from the rest of the group. Marco still looked

like he was about to explode in rage and fervor, but he silently
obeyed his mistress' will.

"You okay there?" Geru asked quietly.

The concern in the muscular man's voice was genuine, but
Darien couldn't give a straight answer to the simple question.
Through the slowly receding haze of pain and nausea he was able to
absently decide he should alleviate the immediate concerns of his
friends first. A more detailed explanation could come later, if
whatever it was that had just happened could even *be* explained.

Taking a shuddering breath and trying to steady himself with
Geru's help Darien slowly stood. After a few wobbly moments he
disentangled himself from Geru and tried to clear his mind by
taking slow and controlled breaths. The pain continued to slowly
recede as his body acclimated to its normal constitution. Looking
General Lockhart's way he sighed, knowing full well he would be
required to speak with the General in private later on. It couldn't
be helped, although at least his friends knew about his aura reading
so he hadn't violated the trust that had been placed in him just yet.

Not that he could fully explain what had happened. The
explosion of color was not only painful, but confusing as well. And
not just because they had had their shared senses overwhelmed.
Once the consciousness he and Koseki shared had touched Liana
there had been the briefest flash of swirling colors of shades and
hues and shards of form that he had never even considered the
possibility of existing. Not only that, but from that brief glimpse
they saw Liana had within her not one, but *three* separate and
distinct emotional auras comprising her whole. It was both
fascinating and disturbing, but it also spiked a curiosity in Darien
that he tried to stamp out; it was becoming more and more evident

being anywhere near Liana was detrimental to his health and safety. As if she hadn't made that apparent enough already.

However, the look she had given him after the reading failed had the faintest signs of an emotion he had never seen Liana exhibit before, worry. He had a *very* bad feeling his involvement with the regal Lady Liana was about to get even more complicated.

Rosy whickered nervously and gently prodded Darien with her snout. Patting her gently Darien allowed himself a small smile. The relationship he had with his mare had improved dramatically since they had first arrived at the Order. He had Kuldari to thank for that he supposed. An unforeseen benefit to his aura training had been that he had become more attuned to how Rosy reacted to his own actions and their relationship had improved steadily during their stay.

"At least I understand you," Darien mumbled, staring off in Liana's direction. Rosy snorted, but affectionately licked his face. "Okay, *mostly* understand you," he amended. Rosy licked him again. This familiarity was a far cry from their first encounter and he was thankful that at least one relationship he had with a female in his general vicinity was amicable.

The peculiar grouping of travelers continued their trek through the wilderness of Pajana for the remainder of the day. Unlike Darien's adopted homeland of Katama, Pajana was much less developed and full of dangerous wildlife and wild men and women alike. According to Jack, surviving childhood in Pajana served much like a natural selection; you either learned to survive and grew up strong or you died. It was that simple. And that brutal. Darien was grateful that his caretaker had brought him to Katama as an infant and not to such a volatile place as Pajana.

Jack had emphasized that the dangers of Pajana were a major factor in his parent's decision to send him off to the Order in the first place. Being the eldest of nine children, they felt like he would have a better chance of survival by training within the Order rather than being sent off on his own.

Darien had been curious as to why everyone else in the region didn't send their offspring to the Order if it was such a hospitable and valuable place. When he had asked Jack had responded by cackling with his usual glee.

"The Order do no be trusted by most me lad," Jack had said. "Pajanites do be a most suspicious lot of anythin' and everythin' that do be outside their own circumstances. Me ma and da did no be thinkin' there be any other option at the time. I did be even lucky they be doin' that much, many others that did be like me got sent runnin' off on their own." Jack had paused for a moment as an odd look briefly crossed his face. "Low survival rate they did be havin' me lad," he had said quietly.

Jack had quickly masked the oddly contemplative look.

"Me and the other lads at the time that did be findin' our way to the Order did be surprised at how welcomin' and helpful they did turn out to be, especially when those bastards be doin' in my fam."

Darien could understand how Jack felt. He knew that Jack's entire family and steading had been wiped out by bandits shortly after he had left for the Order. His father and brothers had been mutilated and his mother and sisters had been brutally raped and abused before having their throats cut. It was a brutal massacre with no motive and no goal. Just horrific wanton violence. Despite his own circumstances Darien had never felt comfortable enough to ask Jack about the incident or the aftermath in detail. To hear

Geru tell it, Jack's vengeance, aided by the friends he had made within the Order, had been so furious and brutal that Darien was better off not knowing too much about it. When he had asked why not, Geru had just shook his head and said "You don't want the nightmares."

Darien had shivered at the tone in Geru's voice and decided then and there that he definitely did not need any additional fuel for nightmares than he already had.

It was a cold camp that night per the General's orders. Apparently the man had as much of a fascination with cold camps as he did with leaving before sunrise. Darien wished more than anything for his comfortable pallet back at the Order that was tucked into a small, but warm and cozy room.

Sighing, Darien crossed his arms behind his head and lay back against his saddle as he waited for the thick blanket he wrapped around himself to ward off the night's chill. Looking up at the starlit sky Darien was struck by a sense of awe.

So many stars. A brief wave of nostalgia washed over him. His home under the Breathwynd Mountains had often allowed him a similar view on many a clear night. The stars above were slightly off from where they should be, but they were still there keeping watch over him like always. Taking in the glittering night sky he was reminded he himself was much like those stars in that although he might feel much as he always had, he was now different as well.

It wasn't just his surroundings and friends that had drastically changed, but his appearance as well. Even now his eyes shone like glittering gems that had been mined from deep in the earth and polished to a mythical shine. Indescribable hues of purple, orange and green mingled intermittently throughout an iris conforming around an oval pupil of inky black. Eyes that could see further and clearer than any human being. The eyes of a dragon. The eyes of the Ryudojin. His ears had not undergone any notable transformation like his eyes, but he could hear much clearer and with greater precision since the night he had bonded with Koseki. Even now he could pick up the tiniest sounds of his companions down to the differences in their breathing and was able to tell what each of them was doing based on the sounds of their movements and captured nuances of their voices.

Glancing over at Geru and Jack he quickly gave a small prayer of thanks to the Godlings above that he had been lucky enough to meet people such as them so soon after leaving the ruins of his village. After having traveled what seemed like halfway around the world Darien had no doubt he never would have made it very far if it hadn't been for both their friendship and General Lockhart's leniency. Who could foretell what might have happened had Jack and Geru not found him camped within the Grove along the Travel Road? He closed his eyes and silently gave thanks again for all the people he had met over the course of his travels.

"Asleep already are we?" a melodic voice cut into his reflection.

Of course, not *all* the people he had met were pleasant to be around. He grimaced as he swiftly rolled to his feet to face the Lady Liana. He sighed again. The blanket had just started to warm him up too.

"My, for whatever reason are you so on edge? Did you not get enough warm milk before bedtime?" Liana asked with a delicate eyebrow arched in ire. Her mouth had formed its usual pouty expression and despite the musical quality of her voice her tone was blatantly mocking as she appraised Darien under the moonlight.

Darien's hand hovered over the hilt of his short blade in case he needed to quickly defend himself and he shifted his balance to the tips of his toes. He had learned through harsh experience that Liana was as quick, violent and unpredictable as she was beautiful and to always be prepared for the worst.

Liana's lips morphed from a pout into a smile as if she was amused.

"My, why are you so excitable? Do you perhaps have to relieve yourself, but are too afraid to go alone into the deep dark wilderness? Perhaps you would like me to escort you in private?" Liana let out a small laugh that was even more melodic than her voice. It felt like his ears were being massaged by a tingling, complex melody enticing him and promising him more. It was a beautiful sound. Darien was confused how something so mesmerizing could come out of someone so violent.

Realizing he was becoming distracted, Darien tried to focus. Liana's smile widened and he was struck by an unsettling feeling of a viper slowly coiling about its prey and waiting for the perfect moment to sink its venomous fangs into his neck.

"Or is it you're so nervous about being this close to a real woman that you're unaware of what to do? Hmmmm?" Liana purred in her mocking tone.

He could feel the eyes of the others watching their exchange. The hatred emanating off of Liana's supporters was so palpable that even with his training he couldn't entirely suppress the clouds of black mist from forming around them.

"I probably wouldn't be so nervous if you didn't spend so much time trying to murder me," Darien retorted as he warily observed Liana for any sign of sudden attack. "And I do know what to do when close to a woman so you're wrong there too," he added defensively, thinking of Wochisa again.

The sound of Geru and Jack spitting out mouthfuls of ale barely registered on him, although he was painfully aware of the intense amount of questioning that was sure to follow. But right now he needed to focus entirely on Liana. He had half hoped his response would throw the normally self-sure Liana off balance, but he had no such luck. In fact it seemed to encourage her to antagonize him even further.

"Oh, is that so," Liana murmured, stepping even closer.

Darien tried again to create distance between them much as he had done earlier in the day, but found it difficult to move with his eyes locked in Liana's gaze. A scintillating chill erupted along his spine and a strange woodland scent filled the air that instinctively made him reach out to connect to Koseki. Darien frowned as Koseki shied from his contact. A sense of wariness flowed through the connection and he mentally coaxed her into slowly establishing a full link. A stuttering image of the overlay winked in and out of view before stabilizing with a shudder and Darien breathed a sigh of relief. He knew Koseki was tired from earlier and he promised her that she could rest soon.

Liana paused as the overlay once again sprang to life around them. He had hoped that this itself would be enough to cow Liana much like it had before, but this time it only emboldened her.

Instead of dropping to one knee or bowing Liana began to weave an intricate sign with her hands and lightly began singing under her breath. The strangely haunting and beautiful melody tugged at a familiar memory within Darien. For a moment he was transported back to the night he had first encountered Koseki and Hosroyu within the Grove. Entranced by Hosroyu's song he had followed the Elder dragon's melody in a daze until he had discovered the Birthing Circle deep within the Grove where Koseki had been born.

The words flowing in an enchanting rhythm sounded similar to back then, but there was a distinctively different intonation and feel to it than there was to Hosroyu's song. Hosroyu had been singing of both celebration and mourning as Koseki had entered the world nearly still-born and only Darien's timely arrival had prevented a tragedy. Liana's melody had a similar feel, but the message within was indecipherable. He tried to discern any meaning as she sang, but the words slipped off the sides of his mind whenever he felt close to gaining an understanding.

Confused and transfixed, he desperately tried to think of a way to defend both he and his sister dragon. To his shock the skittish Koseki suddenly recoiled and violently severed their link. The only emotion he received before the link snapped was one of pure terror. The mental whiplash of the link being severed so suddenly a second time hit Darien so hard that he felt like his skull was cracking. The sudden pain was so intense all thoughts of defending himself vanished and he dropped to his knees in agony. He gripped his head in both hands and had to bite into his tongue so hard it drew blood in order to keep from screaming. His mind and insides alike felt as if they were being liquefied and his lungs constricted so tightly that he thought he would suffocate.

Squirrel was there in moments, supporting him as Darien sagged against his side.

Lockhart had silently drawn his sword and strode to cut off Lady Liana. Jack and Geru, unaware of the silent exchange between Darien and Koseki and assuming Liana was the source of his discomfort, drew their weapons and faced off against her retainers to prevent interference. Mari quailed slightly and shrunk away from the two mercenaries, but Marco snarled in rage and spit into the dirt as he drew his own sword.

Liana stopped her slow approach and her singing when Lockhart placed his sword between her and Darien. "I think it's best if you keep your distance from him for now on Lady Liana," the General said with steel in his voice. "You are proving to be a distraction and a danger already. You claimed to be of use to our cause, but so far all you have done is harass and antagonize the boy and it is only the first day of many. I cannot and *will not* have whatever vendetta you have get in the way of what he is trying to help us accomplish. Back at the Order I was content to let Kuldari handle things as he saw fit, but now that I have a better grasp on the nature of Darien's complaints I will not tolerate any more of this foolishness. Another incident such as this and we *will* part ways no matter the circumstance. Am I clear on this?"

Darien had seen such fire in the General's eyes before. It had been when he had been first introduced to General Lockhart and Darien had revealed himself to be from the destroyed Village Breathwynd. It was just as intimidating now as it was then.

To her credit Liana refused to be cowed by the steel in General Lockhart's voice and in his hand. "But he's so much fun," she purred with a longing glance at Darien.

"I asked if I was clear on this?" the General growled with such intensity that even Liana finally hesitated.

"Oh my, you're as scary as they say," Liana said, raising her hands mockingly in the air before turning it into a languid stretch. "But it wasn't me that caused this weak child such distress."

"Like the Hells it wasn't," Geru growled.

Darien's head was swimming from the shock and pain of Koseki's forced disconnect. At the sound of his friend's voice he turned his bleary gaze towards Geru. He would later blame it on his disorientation, but at the time Darien thought he could barely make out the intricate tattoos wrapping around Geru's thick, muscular arms twisting and writhing in agitation.

What in the Hells...? But his confusion was quickly forgotten when he suddenly began throwing up.

To Squirrel's credit he didn't drop Darien or push him away. The rodent faced little man helped Darien down into a sitting position despite being in the line of fire and wrapped the boy's blanket around him while he retched.

"I agree with Lockhart. Despite what you said back at the Order you haven't exactly been helpful and seem overly obsessed with Darien. There's already been too much out of you that screams liability, right?" Squirrel turned to address General Lockhart directly. "Perhaps we should reconsider our arrangement. It's just too dangerous to let them tag along," he said.

Lockhart stood silent for a few moments. His ice blue eyes were so intense that Squirrel had to look away and return to administering what aid he could to Darien.

Finally, after what felt like forever the General spoke in even, measured tones with iron finality to them that brooked no argument.

"Jack, Geru, sheathe your weapons. Lady Liana, instruct your sycophants to do the same. You and I will have a private conversation tonight. Right now it is too dangerous to leave you to your own devices, but just as dangerous to have you near the boy. We will reach an accommodation. I am no longer asking for your cooperation. I am demanding it," the General said.

For a moment it seemed Liana wanted to argue. Her retinue had reached an indescribable fury at the General's words and Marco took a menacing step forward. To their credit Jack and Geru heeded the General's instructions and sheathed their weapons. Finally Liana gave a slight shake of her head and twitched a small smile.

"As you wish, dear General. Marco, Mari, do play nice with our new friends hmm?" she said lightly, regally sweeping past him and motioning her followers to stand down and stay put.

Her followers obeyed as they had been commanded, but were visibly upset at the sequence of events. Marco's face twisted in an ugly fashion and he looked ready to erupt in fury.

Liana paused a moment as she passed the General. Lightly placing a fingertip on Lockhart's half raised sword she again spoke of her innocence. "Please understand dear General, I meant this pathetic child no real harm in accordance with our arrangement. Maybe you should ask him yourself instead of assaulting me with accusations?"

Lockhart silently sheathed his sword and glanced askance at Darien. Even in his dazed state Darien could feel the man's gaze weighing heavily over him like a pall.

"Well, lad?" Squirrel whispered quietly.

Even at such reduced tones, Squirrel was so close to Darien that his enhanced hearing made the words deafening in his ears. Darien whimpered at the impact of Squirrel's voice, but managed to eke out a response.

"Wasn't..." he took a deep breath as a wave of nausea swept over him. "...her," he gasped as the effects of the severing finally overwhelmed him and he slumped unconscious against Squirrel's shoulder.

Squirrel met the General's steely inquiring gaze and gave a slight shake of his head.

A tightening around Lockhart's eyes was the only outward sign of agitation as he walked back to his seat and sat down heavily. He began to drum a rhythmic tattoo against his leg in what Squirrel and the others had come to know meant he was deep in thought.

Liana, for her part, sauntered off on her own, leaving her followers in an obvious state of distress.

Marco still looked about to explode, but was cowed by an emotionless stare and a single soft spoken word from his mistress just before she walked away. The others in the camp couldn't hear what was said, but the mysterious woman's intent was clear. Marco immediately fell into a sullen silence and sat at the base of the nearest deformed tree, ignoring the muck and detritus beneath him while staring menacingly at Darien's unconscious form.

Liana slumped down behind a gnarled and twisted tree out of sight from the others. She had instructed Mari that she was not to be disturbed, but she was sure the pathetic human creature known as Lockhart would seek to accost her at some point in the night. Lightly exhaling into the night air she dismissed that as insignificant compared to what she had seen when the boy had contacted the great Elders. A vexed sigh softly escaped from her lips as she glanced upwards at the tree providing her with scant shelter. The moon shone much bigger and brighter than she could ever recall during her time inhabiting her home back in what the humans referred to as 'The Grove'.

"Perhaps this region too is affected by the last vestiges of magic left behind by the Fallen Great Gods," she mused. She reflected briefly on her tiring journey across the Jarabin Plains in pursuit of the boy and the magics he had stolen. It had surprisingly rejuvenated her, but that benefit had proven to be short lived. That last thought gave her a moment of pause.

She had set out after the thief fully intent on ripping the magic violently out of his very being as soon as she discovered what exactly it was that had been taken and the method used to steal it, but surprisingly had been unable to do so. There had been simply too many protections in place over the boy and her own powers were greatly weakened so far from home. It was like whatever had powered her as she moved across the Plains had run out of fuel. It had been disorienting at first, but she had been able to use that to her advantage once she reached the Order of the Fist. A place such as that was more than willing to take in a lone female traveler who was *so* very frightened and weakened by her journey and *so* very much in need of assistance. It was almost sickening how stereotypical the people there had reacted when she had put on that particular display.

Once she had been accepted within the Order's walls, her next tactic had been to simply kill the boy in the hopes it would release the magics back into the world, but the wretched human showed a discomforting penchant for staying alive. However, her last attempt on the boy at the Order had given rise to yet another avenue of approach. And to questions she decidedly needed answers to.

Her first attempt after leaving the Order had not gone as smoothly as expected. In fact it had the exact opposite effect than what she had intended. She had waited for the brat to connect and tried to sever his connection to the Elders so that he could not contact them again, but in doing so she had terrified the young Elder and caused her some distress. She had found then that their connection was shared between the two instead of coming directly from the brat as she had assumed. Then there was the fact the boy had somehow become broken in the process and that path was no longer a viable option at the moment; at least not until she got a better grasp of what was occurring between him and the great Elders. She still refused to fully believe he had been Selected, it was inconceivable someone such as he could be granted such favor.

This was especially true due to whatever it was that caused him to attempt to infringe upon her essence. An act that had infuriated her. No creature in this world had been allowed to live after invading her privacy in such a manner, but it seemed that to harm the brat would also bring harm to the young Elder. *I could never forgive oursel...myself for being responsible for such a thing.* She decided to exercise more caution than she would normally have expended from here on out.

She closed her eyes and exulted in the natural light of the world cast by the moon above. Despite not having any evidence to corroborate her feelings, she had always felt there was something akin to the magical about the great white sphere rising above the world of Taulia each night. It was one of the very few whims she allowed herself. Especially since glimpsing the moon through the thick, lush canopy of the Grove was an extremely rare occurrence.

Her lips formed a thin line while she mused on what had happened earlier when her latest attempt to unravel the mystery of the boy had gone awry.

It seems yet another change in approach to the human is necessary. She was surprised to find that she was annoyed. Never had an adversary been so vexing as this one miserable human child. *No,* she amended silently. *He has become more than human. But why? Why such an unexceptional brat? What does he have to offer? Or is he somehow binding the Elders to his will?* She shook her head in disdain at the thought. *There is no chance those such as the great Elders would ever be bound by a weakling like him. There must be something that I have yet to discover. Something I am somehow missing, but there is still plenty of time yet to accomplish my goal.* Liana deeply inhaled the intoxicating smell of the natural world around here and used the distinct scents of the land of Pajana to center herself. The scents of this harsh and unforgiving land were murkier and more stale than those of her home, but she enjoyed them all the same. Even the tinge of blood accentuating the land didn't change her thinking. It was a part of the land itself and she felt blessed to be able to revel in the essence of another portion of her world. It reminded her of times long past that she desperately longed to return to.

Taking smaller controlled breaths she glanced at the barely visible and slowly undulating golden trail glittering along the ground and vanishing off into the distance. It felt like it had been so long since she had seen her tether in a healthy and vibrant state that she almost couldn't recall what it looked like in its natural form. If it hadn't been for the strange magical properties revitalizing her as she crossed the Jarabin Plains she might have had to risk losing the tether altogether. Liana shuddered at the thought. There was nothing in the realm of humans that caused her worry, but losing her tether was the one thing that absolutely terrified her.

"After all," she lightly whispered, her breath forming a slight mist on the cool night air as she watched the tether writhe and undulate in all its glory. "It's all that's left."

She gently traced the golden trail with one long and graceful finger, phasing out just her hand as she did so. Looking at the clear, viscous form of her hand she thought her journey so far had not been without some benefit. Before coming to the Order of the Fist in her pursuit of the boy, phasing out a singular part of her body at such a distance from home would have been an impossibility. However, despite all the obstacles in training the instructors at the Order ran into with her inability to improve in a way they expected, she did learn something important that she held in reserve.

By correctly applying certain theories taught within the Order and through her own experimentation she was now able to convert a portion of the tether's essence into her own aura energy. By concentrating this borrowed essence on a single part of her body she was able to phase it out without the pain and fatigue doing so prior had caused. She was apprehensive about phasing her whole body out so far from home, uncertain as she was about the strain on the tether, but using and recycling the energy back into the tether seemed to work in small doses. She just had to be careful about how much she 'borrowed' and ensure the same amount was returned if possible. It was a delicate balance, but she was managing it well and would soon perfect it.

It was a far cry from when she had first started to experiment. Unbeknownst to anyone she had spent countless hours writhing in agony within her chambers before she began to see the fruits of her efforts. Now the act only brought on a minor discomfort that she was confident would fade with usage and time.

She brought the nearly invisible hand in front of her face and smiled as she turned it this way and that; admiring the fluidity of the limb. Soon she would be able to return home and phasing her entire being would once again be no more than an afterthought. Her time with the brat and the others would be no more than an unpleasant memory better fit for a lower circle of the humans' Hells.

Her smile broadened wickedly and her wide eyes glinted in the moonlight as she thought of all the nuisances she would also like to send to those Hells.

She sinuously rose to her feet. "In fact, here comes one now," she said softly in lightly mocking tones.

The human Philip Lockhart strode towards her with purpose and without fear or trepidation. She was mildly surprised one of her sycophants hadn't tried to stop him per her instructions, but with how easily humans were cowed by the strong she wasn't all that surprised.

The man came to stand before her, standing confidently with one hand resting on the pommel of his sword. Not that the sword posed much of a threat to one such as her, but she did begrudgingly admit that for a human he did make a striking figure standing under the moonlight. The contrast between the midnight black of his tunic and trousers to the shafts of moonlight glinting off the steel of his sword served to enhance the ice blue of his eyes. The gold sash holding his scabbard added a proud touch to an imposing figure she was sure would cow most humans. Mist coiled around their feet and the unfettered moonlight streaming down gave the man an ethereal look while he appraised her with unabashed scrutiny.

Liana smiled and arched one of her thin and finely groomed eyebrows in silent question.

"You and I need to have a conversation," Lockhart said in measured tones.

Chapter 4

The clicking of Bamaul's boots echoed ominously in the otherwise silent corridor. Guards posted in the hall knelt in reverence to their lord as he passed and would remain so until he vanished from sight. Regam strode purposefully a few steps behind the king, not bothering to hide his disdain for the guards. Bamaul knew Regam considered any assigned to the halls to be cowards too frightened and weak to hold any value to the Bloodsetters that he led with such pride.

Bamaul felt even that much of a concern was too much effort wasted on the insignificant creatures. Had he not been aware of Regam's feelings on the matter he would not have even noticed the kneeling wretches. They were simply dressings to be ignored. There were far greater matters requiring his attention than a few fragile ornaments serving only as a testament to his position.

Clasping his hands imperiously behind his back he quickened his pace. He began to lightly caress the silver filament embedded within the hard and ornate onyx bracelet that had recently begun to fuse with his wrist. The blackened lines of infection spreading outwards from the bracelet had slowly grown in length and severity so much so that they now crept halfway up his arm. If not for the retinue of healers and shamans constantly at his beck and call they may have grown even further, but not even the threat of being overwhelmed by the filaments' side effects could dissuade him from his purpose. Although there were other, more pressing effects that he had to deal with as well.

In response to his thoughts the bells in his mind slowly began to ring in agitation and he reluctantly ceased his ministrations. Lately the ocean of bells had been coming to life faster and with more ferocity every time he placed so much as a fingertip on the small filament of silver. No one but Regam knew about the presence of the raging ocean of bells ravaging his mind, but their existence made his current objective that much more of a priority.

He was, as he always was at this time of day, on his way to the 'interrogation internment chamber', or what the peasants of his country called a dungeon.

As he continued down the hall he could feel his excitement rising. Finally he could put plans he had held off on for so long back into motion. The sound of his boots continued to echo eerily off the walls of the corridor as his fervor mounted. Not even the various banners and tapestries so much as fluttered at his passing; it was as if even those inanimate objects were holding their breath in fear of angering the king of Katama.

Even Regam became unusually tense as he matched the pace of his lord. Bamaul could feel the subtle tension emanating from his chief Bloodsetter while they walked. A lesser man would have mistaken Regam's tension as a sign of fear or worry at his master's sudden change in disposition, but Bamaul knew it was more anticipation than anything else. Regam had been waiting just as patiently for their targeted prey to begin moving again and their patience had finally been rewarded.

He resisted the urge to caress the bracelet again as the bells receded far back into the base of his skull, but instead occupied his hands by lightly massaging the aching webbing of infection to alleviate the dull throb constantly plaguing him. A weaker man would have been overcome by such inconveniences by now, but Bamaul was more than anyone could imagine. He considered it a minor irritation to be endured until he could fulfill the purpose that had been entrusted to him.

When my promised time comes, all of this will be a fleeting memory left in the wake of my rebirth and the rebirth of this nation, of this world. Bamaul grinned at the thought and his dark eyes sparkled with the glint of madness as he envisioned the future where he would stand above all, and rightfully so.

He paused when he came upon an old wooden door weathered and stained with age. Regam stepped forward and opened the door with a slight bow and Bamaul entered the unlit staircase with a confident step. Despite the lack of light he was more than familiar with his current route since he had been coming this way every day, and some nights, for some time now. Every stone step covered in grime and lichen in the damp stairwell was as familiar to him as if they were part of his own brood. He knew twenty-two steps to the bottom he would face another corridor, as dark and foreboding as the stairwell descending into the darkness before him, with a single torch illuminating a lone door at the far end.

Hurrying to the bottom as fast as his dignity would allow Bamaul smiled as he approached the final door. Pitted and rusted, the metal door before them was unique to any other upon the world of Taulia. New hinges had recently been installed and Bamaul had had to turn the worker involved in their installation into a 'jumper' when he suggested that the entirety of the door should also be replaced.

Fool, Bamaul thought with a sudden surge of anger. *Such relics as this were to be carefully guarded and preserved; and put to more...practical uses within the world of Taulia.*

Within my *world of Taulia*, he amended. Soon he would be more than just ruler of a nation. He would be so, so much more. Unconsciously stroking the bracelet again he could almost see the fruition of his journey coming to pass as brief images of the future he imagined, but was not quite yet set in stone flickered through his head.

The corners of his mouth twitched in the briefest instance of a smile, but quickly turned into a grimace when a single bell among the ocean in his mind began to ring. Tearing his hand away he took deep, calming breaths as his powerful strides brought him to the torch lit door. His fingers spasmed involuntarily in anticipation. He knew stepping through this door would make his desire to caress the silver filament become too strong to ignore. Then the bells would thunder in an unabated cacophony once more.

Regam silently stepped forward and began unlocking the mechanism that would allow them access. Removing a strange looking key hanging from a leather cord around his neck Regam forcibly jammed it into the nearly invisible keyhole, turning it with such ferocity it seemed the key would break. Bamaul said nothing while Regam worked; the key had as much chance of breaking as Philip Lockhart had of appearing before him and offering his head. Bamaul smiled inwardly at the loud and metallic thud sounding from within the door. The addition of a key had been Regam's idea and it had taken no less than three shamans several weeks to figure out how to incorporate it into the door's locking mechanism.

He mused about the pros and cons of worthwhile and necessary expenses such as this while Regam continued his work. And throwing the three shamans from the throne room to the courtyards below had proven worthwhile as well. It instilled the proper fear into those that had once thought themselves untouchable to see their peers turned into broken piles of flesh and bone. Some would consider it wasteful to eliminate the best talents in a vital position to a country's infrastructure, but Bamaul saw it as a justified expense. In fact, he saw it as absolutely necessary since any shaman could be trained and replaced, but treasures such as the door must have its secrets preserved no matter the cost.

Regam tucked away the key and placed a hand on an elegant and complex insignia etched into the door. Strange patterns and designs came to life and a soft blue glow pulsed underneath his calloused hand. Moving the soft glow from one insignia to the next in a complex pattern only Regam knew he used his free hand to select a second insignia from among the multitude of glowing designs. He continued to weave these insignias until the Bloodsetter's hands were a blur of motion that Bamaul could barely follow.

Seconds later, the glow from Regam's hands vanished and the door emitted a series of echoing clicks before silently swinging open to reveal a dank chamber bereft of light and in a pitiful state of disrepair. Bamaul intentionally left the stairwell, hall, and chamber unkempt in order to preserve a feeling of despair and confusion upon those souls guesting here. The lone exception being the bars and locks on the cages. He knew that keeping his 'guests' as secure as possible would only further his designs for them.

The cramped room contained four separate, tiny cages with two to either side. The stench of mildew and unwashed flesh assaulted his senses and seemed to seep into his very clothes. Rotten straw strewn about the dirt floor rustled underneath his boots as he stepped into the room. Bamaul ignored the smell; he had far more important matters to attend to.

Regam lit the lone torch from the wall and strode forward with a confident step. The maddening clacking sound and the flickering shadows of the torch combined to give an ominous feeling in the hazy gloom. As they quickly made their way to the predetermined cell, Bamaul immediately submitted to the uncontrollable urge to caress the bracelet's filament.

Just as they arrived at the cell where his favorite 'guest' was being held the bells sprang to life with such intensity that Bamaul paused in his step to keep his composure in check before visiting his old friend. A haze of red clouded his vision and he fought fervently against the familiar tide of pain washing over him.

Regam, ever the consummate professional, gave no indication he had noticed his master's delay. Exhaling a long, slow breath and clenching his teeth against the onslaught of the bells Bamaul stepped to the cell weakly lit by the small flame of Regam's torch. As the torch's light fell across the wan face of the man hanging listlessly from the wall the bells began a furious uproar that threatened to consume all that he was, is and would come to be.

While the intense pressure mounted in his head Bamaul clenched his teeth even harder until blood spurted from his gums. Each visit always caused the same response, but the gain from seeing one brought so low outweighed any amount of pain the bells caused.

Licking the blood from his teeth Bamaul relished in the iron taste on his tongue. It was unclear if the shackled husk of a man before him had anything to do with the ringing of the bells, but he liked to think so. It made every meeting that much more exhilarating.

As if reading his thoughts the bedraggled and emaciated thing softly moaned and weakly lifted its head. Eyes that had once sparkled a bright blue with mirth and knowledge stared back at him yellowed and bloodshot from behind red-rimmed and crusted eyelids. Bamaul smiled at such a drastic dichotomy. It was not that long ago those eyes had stared hard and unforgiving in disapproval and judgment during a critical point in Bamaul's life. In fact, it could be said all that had come to pass since then could be attributed to that day and this man.

Bamaul held his smile tight against the clanging of the bells. He knew maintaining his composure would soon become more than a trial and that he must conclude this visit quickly, much to his chagrin.

"Hello Oltan, my old friend," Bamaul whispered.

Bamaul couldn't help but feel an intense feeling of satisfaction at seeing the old man he so despised brought to such a state of anguish. This man had hindered and derailed his plans for years and had played a major part in Bamaul's exile from Katama. An act for which he would forever curse the old man's name.

Bamaul paused for a moment as he thought that he *did* somewhat owe Oltan a debt of gratitude for his persistence in the matter, considering the result. Although his exile had been far from pleasant at first, things had decidedly and definitively ended in his favor. Those first few years however, had been no less than brutal. He inwardly winced as the corners of his tightly controlled smile twitched in pain at the memory of his initial exile.

His prisoner softly muttered something unintelligible and Bamaul had to force himself from laughing maniacally as the ringing of the bells resonated with each sound Oltan made.

Bamaul gripped his arms tightly behind his back in order to maintain a calm demeanor despite the raging bells reverberating against his skull. One finger still lightly caressed the silver filament without cease and Bamaul could feel his infection beginning to spread even further. He would have to have his healers and shamans visit him again that night, but that would have to wait.

"Sorry my old friend and treasured guest," Bamaul spoke in measured tones. "I am afraid I didn't quite catch that. Could you speak up perhaps? And maybe a tad more eloquently? It would be much appreciated. After all, shouldn't one present a dignified and knowledgeable front in conversation with his companions? Isn't that something you used to say quite often?"

Oltan merely dropped his gaze and sagged back within his chains with a meager rattling.

"Oh? I had thought you'd be up for more conversation than that, being that you spend so much time in isolation," Bamaul taunted.

Bamaul pressed his face between the bars of the cell in order to drink in Oltan's helplessness even more and sighed.

Never taking his eyes off his favorite trophy Bamaul continued to mock his prisoner. "Regam, it's so hard to hold a decent conversation these days is it not?"

Regam remained silent, but Bamaul could feel the man's emotionless grin forming behind his Makavai. Bamaul knew that his chief Bloodsetter enjoyed these little excursions just as much as he did. The man was fanatically committed to their cause and Bamaul could sense Regam's bloodlust behind the grin. He shuddered in ecstasy at the thought of once again releasing that bloodlust into the world, but he needed to conclude this meeting first.

Bamaul exhaled slowly and refocused on what he had come down to this miserable corner of his castle to accomplish.

"Now, now Oltan! It is hardly the time for a nap! We have so much more that we need to discuss," Bamaul said as a small rivulet of blood eked out from the corner of his mouth and ran down the side of his chin.

Another slight sigh escaped from the lips of the hanging man. Bamaul frowned. The man may be bowed, but it seemed he had yet to be broken even after all this time.

His patience was wearing thin and there was no end to the bells ringing ceaselessly in his mind. However, the blood from his gums burning as it ran down his throat allowed him to focus on his task without losing himself too far.

"Oltan, how many times are we going to have this little conversation before you realize it's in your best interest to cooperate with me?" Bamaul asked in conversational tones. He paused to see if he would receive an actual response before continuing on.

"Maybe you will feel slightly more invigorated if I inform you that our young friend Darien has finally moved out from within the confines of his protective bubble? It is now only a matter of time before I have him working under my command or hanging in the cell next to your own. You should at least show some gratitude that I am even allowing him such a choice. Most are not even offered that much. But I guess you would know that from experience wouldn't you?"

At the mention of Darien Oltan weakly clenched his fists and with considerable effort raised his head to lock eyes with Bamaul. For the first time since his incarceration signs of vitality flashed within Oltan's eyes. The former advisor to the crown and chief liaison of Katama's fledgling inter-species relations development department - Mythical Division was a tough man to break, but break him he would.

Bamaul parted his lips in a grotesque facsimile of glee at the despised man's reaction. "Oh, did I finally pique a modicum of interest? Do you truly have such a strong bond with that child? Even if you have no blood claim to him? Or could it be you thought that one day this boy might become something much more, something much akin to what Aplesi and Elze lost their lives pursuing? Tragic that was I must say, wouldn't you agree?"

Oltan's tired eyes widened slightly and Bamaul found himself pleased the old man was still cognizant enough to grasp what he was inferring. Although his suspicions had yet to be confirmed there had been ample evidence left in the boy's wake to make an educated assumption. The initial report from that Gelas person had only been the beginning of a multitude of reports concerning the boy and those he had befriended. The fact the boy was in the company of Philip Lockhart and his band of misfits had made things slightly more difficult, but Bamaul would rather deal with both problems at once. It was just as well if he could eradicate Lockhart and his fools while ensnaring Darien at the same time. It still irked him that the Bloodsetter ambush from a few months ago had failed to wipe out Philip Lockhart and his men completely, but for now he would enjoy sharing these tidings with Oltan and reveling in the wretch's misery. Plus the information had the rather pleasing effect of infuriating the old man, which Bamaul counted as a bonus.

"Oh that's right, you were unaware we had been tracking their son since you decided to relocate from that rustic outpost of Breathwynd to your current lavish locale weren't you?" Bamaul pressed in mocking tones.

"Even now," Bamaul continued. "We have several excellent surprises in store for the young man. But fear not my dear Oltan! I have no desire to end the boy's life for he will be able to fulfill a vital role in my ascension. Only then will he become no more than a useless husk like you yourself have been for quite some time. Worry not! It's for the good of Katama, no, all of Taulia itself!" Bamaul was ranting, his words punctuated with several heavy breaths while the bells continued to threaten to consume him.

Bamaul pressed his face even further into the bars of the cage and used the cold, damp feel of the iron pressing into his skin to focus. His vision blurred even further and jumbled images of his past began to flash haphazardly through his mind. Sorting reality from illusion would soon become an issue if he tarried much longer, but he continued on with his tirade.

"Isn't that something you used to say often? For the good of Katama? Isn't it!" Bamaul shouted. With each word his fervor increased as the ocean of bells rose in a tidal wave and were attempting to burst through his skull. Sweat beaded on his forehead and the fever in his infected arm caused a wave of confusion and nausea to wash over him. He was at his limit and needed to conclude this interview immediately lest the old man witness him overcome. Before he could utter another word Regam was suddenly at his side.

"Your majesty, we must not tarry any longer. There are many more important matters to attend to before days' end. There is also that 'other' surprise that must be attended to," Regam whispered loudly enough for the prisoner to hear.

All Bamaul could do was nod his assent and stiffly follow Regam from the room, unable to even give the old man any parting words.

The king of Katama woodenly followed Regam back through the doorway and into the corridor beyond. He was finally able to pull his hand away from the bracelet and the bells receded instantly, although it would be some time before they vanished completely. Bamaul stretched and tried to calm his mind. *There will be ample time to spend with my old friend in the days to come. An eternity even.*

Regam closed the door and began rearranging the insignias in a complicated order only he understood. Bamaul took a deep, shuddering breath and regained control of his faculties. Regam finished with the door as his special key completed the locking process and a new series of clicks echoed in the hall. Squeezing his eyes shut for a moment, Bamaul could feel Regam turn his attention to his master should the need for assistance arise, but

Bamaul refused to show any more weakness even in front of his most trusted servant.

Licking the last vestiges of blood from his teeth Bamaul again resisted the strong impulse to caress the bracelet. He would need some time to recover from his latest encounter and another surge so soon after the intense wave he had just endured was not something he wanted to test. At least not yet.

Taking a moment to compose himself Bamaul again clasped his hands behind his back, this time avoiding the bracelet, as he regally stalked back towards the upper levels of his domain with Regam following closely. Thoughts afire of the old man and the boy Darien, who would certainly prove vital to his plans, Bamaul began to feel the pangs of anticipation course through his body.

It's only now that things will truly begin to come together, Bamaul thought with a malicious smile.

Oltan sagged back into his chains, the cold and unforgiving iron chafing his raw wrists and ankles. He had long since gotten accustomed to the pain and fatigue associated with his imprisonment, but he had always taken solace in the fact that Darien had survived the destruction of Village Breathwynd and escaped from Bamaul's grasp. His locking Darien within the library that night had been a contingency for that very purpose. His only regret was that none of the others in the village had heeded his suspicions of the strange visitor that had turned out to be an advanced Bloodsetter scout. As a last resort he had offered himself as part of a negotiation that he knew would be one-sided, but he had not anticipated the extent of the mad tyrant's orders the Bloodsetters carried with them.

If only I had been more forceful in my warnings to the other villagers. If only I had been more prepared, Oltan thought ruefully. He had assumed incorrectly the scout would eventually leave as long as there was nothing in Breathwynd that aroused suspicion. Oltan cursed himself for a fool. His misjudgment had gotten everyone in the village killed, save Darien, and gotten himself captured by the same man responsible for the wound that caused his painful limp.

The worst part was that Darien's first love had also been a victim of his poor decisions and he would never forgive himself for that. Oltan hung his head sadly as he reflected on what could have been between Darien and the young girl Corly. The two of them had been inseparable since they were small and she had set her eyes solely on him since an early age, although Darien had been oblivious of that fact until just before everything in their lives had been ripped away from them. The girl had been stubborn, forceful, and full of fire, but had also been caring and compassionate; Oltan had cared for her as if she had been a child of his own. Everyone in the village had looked forward to the day the two of them were old enough to officially court, but now that was a distant and bitter memory.

I don't know if I can ever apologize to you enough boy, but please for now just stay alive! Tears ran unabated down his haggard and drawn face that once had been robust and full of vitality. Oltan was never one to ask the Godlings much for anything, but he fervently prayed the boy would get as far away from Katama as possible and never look back. But he doubted his prayers would do much good. Darien was much too stubborn and foolhardy most of the time. He was like his parents had been, always needing an answer or explanation and constantly seeking more information. Oltan hacked a throaty cough and forced a heavy sigh as his tears ran dry.

Bamaul usually alluded to the boy in some variation or another during his frequent visits, but for some time it seemed the boy had been able to stay out of the madman's clutches. Oltan had not been able to glean a clear understanding from the tyrant as to how he knew Darien to be the son of Aplesi and Elze or why he was so obsessed with the boys capture, but Oltan was wise enough to make the assumption that *something* significant had happened; Godlings only knew what.

What have I gotten you mixed up in boy? Oltan thought heavily as he began to use his tongue to press heavily on his back teeth. *I've failed in my promise to your parents to keep you safe and failed in my promise to myself as your guardian to shield you from your forebears enemies should they seek you out. Please forgive me.*

Oltan closed his heavy eyes and began to meditate as he often did while hanging from the wall and working to loosen his molars the best he could. He knew it would be an indeterminate amount of time before Regam would return to release him from his shackles and then the sadistic Bloodsetter would wait until his wounds had almost healed before returning to chain him once more. For the moment he began a series of calming breaths as he continued to work his teeth loose and sought solace within his own mind away from the pain and misery of his imprisonment. Despite his best efforts he couldn't shake the vivid image of a mewling infant cradled in his arms with the final, desperate pleas of Aplesi and Elze echoing in his ears. As his meditation shattered at the memory

Oltan weakly struck the stone behind him with the back of his head.

"How did something so routine become such a tragedy?" he asked himself for what must have been the thousandth time. He still clearly remembered the day he and the boy's parents left on their errand for Tammaz, the previous king Bamaul had overthrown in what was known throughout Katama as the 'Tyrant's Revolt'.

They had set out on an exciting expedition based on information found amongst the countless relics and copious amount of knowledge found deep within the royal library. A conglomeration of centuries of knowledge and history compiled by Oltan and his predecessors, the royal library had been the pride of Katama's royal family until Bamaul's uprising shook the country to its core.

If only he had anticipated Bamaul's true intentions and the scope of his power and influence over those people who had thrown away their souls to become his Bloodsetters. Perhaps then he could have done more than simply move a large portion of the royal library's contents in secret before Bamaul's advance reached the castle walls. Perhaps he wouldn't have had to abandon the precious item hidden away in his secret study that he prayed would remain undiscovered.

He did count denying Bamaul most of the library's knowledge a small victory within the larger conflict. It had taken some time for the tyrant to make his way to the Castle of the King after his surprise assault on the Kataman embassy located a few leagues within the border of Het Tapas. Despite their expedition's token forces being quickly overwhelmed by Bamaul and his followers, Oltan had been able to successfully flee due to the heroic efforts of

Darien's parents and those few soldiers who had served as their escort. He had suffered a major injury in the process, but he had succeeded in getting the infant boy out of immediate danger. Being an envoy of a foreign kingdom had allowed him to secure swift passage back to Katama and the castle, but he had underestimated the brutality of Bamaul and his men. To Oltan's trained eyes there must have been a strict timeline the man had been working under. And he certainly hadn't anticipated the power the man had displayed either. Just the thought of those events were enough to depress Oltan to his core. There was something terrifyingly unnatural about Bamaul and the odd bracelet that he couldn't keep from polishing all the time.

"I do wish I knew what the artifact's true purpose is," Oltan wondered aloud. He was certain it had been no mere coincidence Bamaul had appeared at the same site he and the boy's parents had located. However, if that were true then that meant there had been a traitor in the palace and Oltan didn't like the implications of that line of thought. It meant that Bamaul had thoroughly sowed his seeds even before he was removed from the court, as if he had anticipated his forced exile. It was possible the man had even *wanted* to be cast into exile in order to bring about the events that unfolded afterwards.

It may be that even his failed courtship with Princess Hylain was also part of his machinations, Oltan mused. If that were true then it would provide a modicum of insight as to why Bamaul had so desperately pursued an unattainable bride such as Princess Hylain. Perhaps he knew such a brazen attempt at the hand of someone so far above his station would hasten the process of his impending exile.

However, that didn't explain the sudden expulsion of the Princess from the castle once Bamaul had assumed power. Oltan had expected the man to force her hand in marriage, but instead had cast her out of the castle much as he had been; albeit he had left her with no coin, no possession, nor even clothing while forbidding anyone from providing her with aid under penalty of death. Despite Oltan's best efforts over the years, limited as though they had been while operating out of a quiet and remote location such as Breathwynd, he never did find any information on the Princess' whereabouts. In fact it had been startling to him how there was absolutely no information at all. Even foreign dignitaries that he secretly communicated with had no working knowledge or rumor of her whereabouts or fate. Oltan had assumed the girl would seek asylum in a friendly country before word of Bamaul's ascendancy reached foreign ears, but he had come away empty time and time again without any tangible lead. Princess Hylain had simply disappeared without a trace. It was like the world itself had absorbed her very being.

Oltan weakly flexed his fingers and toes to keep his blood flowing and to prevent losing feeling in his limbs as he pushed the extraneous thoughts of Princess Hylain from his mind.

He exhaled slowly and again shifted his thoughts to why Bamaul was so interested in Darien. It wasn't as if Darien had any working knowledge about his parents or their profession. Oltan had purposefully kept Darien ignorant of that particular part of his family in order to raise him as normally as possible. For the most part he felt he had succeeded in that so Bamaul's apparent obsession with the boy confused him.

I can say that at least he was normal the last I saw of him. It seems his penchant for finding trouble, or more accurately trouble finding him, may have changed that. Otherwise this madman would show no such interest in him. Still, thank the Godlings he's at least in good company if he is indeed with Philip. Maybe he's just the figure Darien has always needed to show him how to grow into a man of conviction and purpose.

If Oltan's hope came true then it would lessen a burden he had placed on himself long ago. He had early on in Darien's life made the decision to keep the fact he was with the boy's parents right up until just before they passed a secret in order to dodge any difficult questions, but now he felt that may have been a mistake. It appeared the fates themselves were taking a hand to force Darien into the middle of the chaos that Oltan had always tried to shelter him from. He only hoped the boy would prove to be worthy of the task as his parents had hoped. Thinking of the dark haired boy he had always raised as his own, Oltan couldn't help but smile weakly in the darkness.

Chapter 5

Darien was worried. A few days had passed since the incident with Liana and he was still unable to get Koseki to respond to his gentle prodding. He could feel her presence like always, but her emotions were distant and vague like they were being kept locked away behind a membrane of resistance. Even when he concentrated and focused all of his aura energy into trying to coax her to speak to him all he could get were thin, wavering colors and images he couldn't decipher.

He had been constantly trying to get his sister dragon or even Hosroyu to respond in any way he could without any luck. His fears as to what that could mean formed a hollow feeling in the pit of his stomach. In all their time together Darien had never felt such abject terror from Koseki as he did when Liana had attempted to...do whatever she had done.

Swaying slightly in Rosy's saddle he frowned while she stumbled in the sucking muck that formed a good portion of the trail.

At least she's left me alone since then. He glanced over his shoulder at the woman who had become the bane of his existence since the moment they met and again wondered just why she had such a singular obsession with him.

As if she could sense his gaze the Lady Liana lowered the hood of her finely woven riding cloak and locked eyes with Darien before giving him an affable smile. Darien shivered. He wasn't sure which was worse, Liana outright trying to murder him or the overly congenial demeanor she had adopted over the past few days. At least when she had been trying to obsessively kill him he knew what to expect. He fidgeted in his saddle and Rosy snorted at her rider's sudden change in posture. His frown deepened in worry as he patted Rosy's mane to assure her everything was ok. Although he wasn't exactly sure which one of them actually needed the reassurance.

Liana hadn't actually spoken to or approached him, but her attitude and actions had changed considerably so he supposed he should be thankful for the reprieve. He sighed. If he could get anything tangible out of Koseki he felt like he might actually be able to sort out some of his recent troubles, but as for where Liana was concerned that might be asking too much.

"Halt!" came a sudden and intense command from General Lockhart as he wheeled his new charger gifted to him by the Order to face the rest of the party. Striker, as he had been named, snorted and pawed anxiously in the muck at the sudden stop. Darien was amazed the General was able to control such a temperamental mount, but he supposed that for the General it probably wasn't anything out of the ordinary.

Darien thanked the Godlings above that Rosy didn't have such an extreme temperament as he reigned in his gentle mount. The

only protest she offered was another nervous whicker, but Darien
assumed that had to do more with her close proximity to Striker
than anything else. Continuing to pat her gently Darien waited for
everyone to settle their mounts and hear what the General had to
say.

"Darien, come here a moment," Lockhart said with iron in his
voice. Darien quickly dismounted and gave Rosy one last pat
before stumbling through the mud and muck that seemed to cover
the entire land of Pajana to stand as close as he dared to Striker for
fear of getting kicked.

"Look as far ahead of us as you can and tell me what you can
see," the General said in even, measured tones from atop his mount.

Darien blinked at the casual order. He glanced at the General to
see if any explanation as to what he should be looking for was
forthcoming, but the man sat rigidly still in his saddle, never taking
his eyes off the path ahead despite Striker's anxious pawing and
snorting.

He shifted nervously as he acquiesced to the General's
command. Even now he was still uncomfortable in the man's
presence, although he did feel some strides had been made since the
night they had met when Darien had been so terrified he almost wet
himself.

Shrugging off unpleasant memories Darien peered through the
gloom permeating the countryside and concentrated on finding
anything of note.

He quickly discovered what it was that must have alerted the
General; a small column of smoke was rising in the distance, almost
indiscernible from the rest of the fog and mist that coiled lazily
around them. In Darien's estimation it probably wasn't anything

more than a campfire and he couldn't understand how the General had even noticed it. There was no way for the man to see that far and Darien doubted the General could pick the meager smoke out from the rest of the gloom, but he quickly put those questions aside. Dwelling on the General overly long tended to give him a headache.

Darien narrowed his eyes to get a clearer view of exactly what he was seeing. A lone campfire usually wouldn't herald much of a threat to their group of experienced travelers and fighters, but he knew the General was highly averse to taking chances in even the best of circumstances.

Tracing the wisping smoke back to the ground his intuition proved correct as a small and weakly burning campfire showed to be its source. His satisfaction at correctly guessing the smoke's origin proved short lived however, as two figures hunched over the fire became clear to his dragon eyes. His mouth dropped in disbelief and he had to blink rapidly in order to convince himself that what he was seeing was real.

"Well?" Squirrel muttered nervously from nearby, anxiously picking at the covered string of his bow. Normally the furtive man would be the one to scout the trail they were following for potential dangers such as this, but Lockhart had prohibited him from leaving the main force for the time being. It was left unsaid the volatile Liana and her retinue had played no small part in this decision. It wasn't surprising to him that Squirrel felt so nervous, but Darien was too intently focused on one of the two figures hunched over the meager fire to dwell on his friend's mood.

A smile of disbelief crossed his face as Darien confirmed a recognizable figure.

"It's Wily!" Darien said excitedly.

"Are you positive?" Lockhart asked sharply.

Darien winced at the severity of the General's tone assaulting his ears, but nodded in response. Wily had been a member of their party that had nearly been eradicated by the Bloodsetter ambush that had left only himself, Squirrel, Geru, Jack, and the General alive. Or so they had thought.

Darien had interacted with Wily infrequently during their short time together, but the man had been helpful and informative, if not overly friendly. Still, it made Darien smile to see another member of their group had made it out of that nightmare alive.

"There's someone else with him, but he's unfamiliar to me," Darien added quickly. He assumed it was probably another one of the General's men that he had yet to meet. The General *had* mentioned in the past there were other allies scattered all over and part of their current objective was to group together as many of them as possible.

"Jack," Lockhart said curtly, spurring Striker forward so hard mud splattered all over Darien's trousers.

Jack, his usual grin plastered across his face, quickly followed in the General's wake.

"Good on ya boy! It do be good to know yer vaunted eyesight do no be deterioratin' as much like yer appearance!" Jack shouted as he rode past.

Darien stuck out his tongue and muttered "Shut up Jack," at the impossible man's backside. He knew it was childish, but seeing Wily alive had put him in a good mood so he didn't particularly care.

Squirrel shifted nervously in his saddle again. "Are you sure it's Wily?" he asked.

"Mm-hmm," Darien answered, still watching the familiar figure of Wily and the other unidentified man stand at the sound of the approaching horses. He was so engrossed in watching the scene unfold that he was barely aware of Geru as he rode up from where he and Tartas had been keeping an eye on Liana and her group.

"Wily, huh? Don't let it bother you Ven. You didn't have a choice about scouting this time around, especially when that man decides to be stubborn," Darien vaguely heard Geru say.

At the sound of Geru using Squirrel's real name Darien shifted his attention to his more immediate surroundings. Squirrel continued to fidget in his saddle and Darien realized just how out of sorts the little man must be after being ordered to remain with the main party. He knew that in Squirrel's mind he had an obligation to protect everyone by ferreting out any potential threat that could waylay their group, no matter how experienced they may be, and that he still agonized over not being able to prevent the Bloodsetter ambush that had wiped most of them out.

"Don't call me that, right?" Squirrel muttered, biting his thumb and squinting off into the distance as if he could see what was happening through sheer power of will. "I don't like surprises like this," he said. Squirrel raised a hand before Geru or Darien could interrupt. "I know what you're going to say. I'm just as happy as the rest of you to see Wily alive and well, but it's my job to make sure absolutely nothing catches us off guard and unprepared. Not being able to control these types of situations makes me nervous. Doesn't bode well for the future, right?" he said.

Geru clapped a meaty hand on Squirrel's arm. "Well Ve..., uh, Squirrel, like I said don't let it bother you. It's not like Lockhart gave you much of a choice in the matter."

"Mmmm...right," Squirrel mumbled as he continued to chew on his thumb.

Darien focused his aura energy and brought forth the aura around Squirrel. Bringing the colors of emotion to bear and maintaining control was much more difficult with the link to Koseki muted, but he was able to do so with some effort. This was different from a full aura reading and much easier to pull off on his own as long as he didn't push himself too hard or do it for overly long. Light colors of orange and yellow swirled around the corners of Squirrel's mouth and faint wisps of purple leaked slowly from the area around his heart. Darien could empathize with the frustration and confusion the rodent-faced man was feeling, but at the same time he was happy that there was truth to Squirrel's words about finding Wily alive. The purple wisps of affection were proof enough of that. As Master Kuldari would say, "People often lie truly to others, but cannot truly lie to themselves. Emotions and their manifestations are proof enough of that. Emotions never lie."

Darien allowed himself a small smile at the thought of Kuldari. He had been lucky to receive instruction from such a great teacher. In fact, despite the trials, tragedies and hardships he had experienced since Village Breathwynd had been destroyed, he considered himself exceedingly lucky to have found the amazing people around him. He was especially appreciative of the faith they had shown in him despite his flaws, failings and inexperience. Geru once told him Lockhart saw something in him and that's why the General had refused to abandon him where he might have others in Darien's place. After his time within the Order, Darien felt like he was finally starting to understand part of what his purpose might be and so a great sense of obligation to these people that had become like a family to him had begun to manifest.

Darien *did* wish a certain someone would stop trying to skewer him on a daily basis, but that was out of his control. He frowned as he shook off thoughts about Liana, shifting his eyesight back to the impending reunion with Wily.

His dragon eyes widened in surprise when his ears picked up an enthusiastic whoop from Jack as he leapt from his mount in order to engulf Wily in a massive hug and nearly knocking him to the ground. Darien choked back a surprised yelp at Jack's actions; Squirrel uncovered and raised his bow with blinding speed and knocked an arrow as Geru quickly drew his blade at Darien's reaction.

"What? What is it?" Squirrel asked, his eyes darting in every direction.

Darien paused before laughing. "Sorry, I just wasn't prepared to see Jack jump off his horse to hug Wily like that," he said.

"Are you sure about that?" Geru asked.

Darien nodded as he watched General Lockhart follow Jack's lead with a handshake as he clasped his free hand firmly on Wily's shoulder.

Geru sheathed his blade and smiled as he shook his head. "Haven't you learned anything after all this time? Don't you remember what I said before about how the people of the Order view themselves? Our people here under Lockhart are no different to him. Each one of us is his brother or sister, his family. And nothing causes him more grief and anguish than losing a member of that family. It brings back too many memories of the day the news reached him about his homestead being raided and his family slaughtered. So it's no surprise he acts passionately," Geru said. "He'd even do the same for our resident slow-witted youngster as well," the big man added almost as an afterthought.

Darien wanted to be annoyed at the comment, but he was feeling positive for the first time since they had left the Order so he let the issue slide.

That positivity was short-lived however. "Oh, does someone require a hug? Come softly into my welcoming bosom and I will console you so very gently," a melodic voice sounded in his ear as slender arms sensuously enveloped him from behind and delicate hands began to lightly caress his chest in an affectionate manner.

Darien's chest tightened and he let out a gasp at Liana's sudden touch. But just as quickly as she had Darien wrapped within her embrace she disentangled her arms and distanced herself from the quickly dismounting Geru.

Darien felt himself blushing a deep shade of crimson, not just from somehow being snuck up on, but from the feel of that one brief moment in Liana's arms. In that instant he had been assaulted by a wealth of emotions mixing with her oddly comforting touch as she cradled him in long and elegant arms, pressing her humble breasts against him. Her hot breath on his ear while whispering mocking words hinting at hidden promises of something exotic and forbidden caused a bodily reaction he thought only Wochisa was capable of eliciting.

All sorts of colors suddenly erupted around him in a tidal wave of emotion. His loss of control over his aura energy was so sudden and the colors so vibrant that he almost lost consciousness again. He had to take several calming breaths in order to regain enough control to confine the mists like he had been taught. He supposed bringing out the mists around Squirrel might have been a bit too much for him in his current state. But as he relaxed the colors slowly faded from view. Many of the colors that had suddenly sprung forth were to be expected, but there were a few he most certainly did *not* expect to arise where Liana was concerned.

Why in the Hells was there pink? Darien fought down a surge of panic. Pink and it's various hues usually represented love, lust, and other similar emotions. *There is no reason, by the Godlings above, that those should have been there! What in the Hells?*

Darien took a deep breath to steady himself and Geru quickly stepped between the two of them.

"What in the Hells do you think you're doing? I was led to believe you had reached an accommodation with General Lockhart. Do you mean to break it so soon?" Geru demanded angrily. Squirrel already had one hand on another arrow, his eyes narrowing in suspicion and ceasing their furtive movement. Tartas observed quietly from the rear, presumably to keep an eye on the lady's attendants.

"Geru wait," Darien said quickly. He took note that Liana's retinue had not made any of their usual threatening gestures when he was interacting with Liana, although Marco looked apoplectic as usual. He assumed this had something to do with whatever agreement the General had reached with her, but he couldn't dwell on it further at the moment.

Darien took a step forward and forced himself to look Liana in the eye.

"Just who, or what, are you exactly?" he asked with more confidence in his voice than he felt.

Geru frowned, but allowed Darien to brush past him to stand directly before Liana.

"I hope you know what you're doing," the big man muttered as he folded his arms in a menacing fashion, never taking his eyes off Liana. Even the tattoos on Geru's arms seemed to undulate slightly in response to his ire, but Darien was too focused on his nemesis to notice.

"Just what are you?" Darien asked again. "From the first day you arrived at the Order you've gone out of your way to harm me for no reason. And now you've twice done something that makes my aura dangerously unbalanced. And just the other day your aura…"

"Shhhh, little boy," Liana said, lightly placing a single porcelain finger upon his lips. "Some things you shouldn't look too deeply into unless you're willing to risk much more than one such as yourself can afford to lose," she said with as serious a look Darien had ever seen on her face.

Darien frowned at her demeanor, but worked up the courage to brush her finger aside and press on. "And now you've done something to my sister that has made her too terrified to even speak to me," he said.

Liana frowned and a slight look of confusion and concern flickered across her face; if Darien hadn't been so focused on Liana at the time he might not have noticed the subtle change, but he took it as a sign that what he was saying might actually be getting through to her.

"Whatever your issue is with me is one thing, we'll deal with it as we may, but when it comes to Koseki I won't stand for anyone hurting her!" Darien could feel his blood boiling and he gritted his

teeth in order to keep from losing control of his aura again. His
good mood had completely vanished. "If she has suffered any type
of permanent damage then there will be even more of a problem
between us, your agreement with General Lockhart be damned,"
he growled.

A feral sensation enveloped him and Darien felt his entire body
tensing at the sudden surge of anger threatening to overwhelm his
senses. He had already acted recklessly by confronting Liana while
the General and Jack had gone to greet Wily and the Godlings
above only knew what Marco and Mari would do, but he had
resolved that he would do anything and everything it took to defend
Koseki from threats she couldn't defend herself from. Liana had
proven to be the first such threat and had violently enlightened him
to the fact there were probably more to come. He now felt like he
had a responsibility to resolve this issue with Liana one way or
another before he got caught up in even more dire circumstances.
Clenching his hands into fists he readied himself for Liana's reply.

After several moments Liana softly replied. "I understand. Tell
your...sister...that I apologize and that I meant her no harm."

Darien blinked at her response. He hadn't been sure what to
expect from the enigmatic woman during yet another
confrontation, but the last thing he expected was an apology. Even
if it was just for Koseki.

Liana performed an odd bow, again using the hand on heart
gesture she had used previously. Without another word Liana
elegantly turned on her heel and returned to the protective circle of
her retinue. Marco directed a look of absolute fury at Darien
before turning to fawn over his mistress.

Darien let out an explosive sigh and nearly jumped out of his skin when Geru's large, meaty hand suddenly clamped down on his shoulder.

"You sure have a penchant for causing trouble as soon as the General's back is turned," the big man said. For some reason Darien felt aggravated at his friend's rebuke. He didn't understand why Geru thought his poor relationship with Liana was his fault and he was irritated at the insinuation.

Darien shook off his friend's hand. "I won't apologize for defending and protecting Koseki," Darien said, his mood now distinctively having soured. "Even if dragons physically mature at a faster rate than humans, she's still practically a baby mentally and I won't let anything go unchecked that threatens her well-being. She still hasn't spoken to me since the other night and all I can get from her is a muted sense of terror. I'm not about to let anything happen to someone I care about! Not ever again!" Tears were forming at the corners of Darien's eyes as his voice rose to a shout. His whole body started to shake in anger and frustration built from his time running from and fighting with Liana and the Bloodsetters both.

Geru held up a placating hand. "I know how you feel, but..." he said.

"You know how I feel?" Darien suddenly erupted. The stress of dealing with the uncertainties surrounding Liana and his concern for Koseki had not only wiped out his good mood, but ignited a continuation of his rant from before they had left the Order. "How in the Hells could you possibly know how I feel? What if Liana was trying to kill Koseki? How could I prevent that? Do you know how helpless it feels to want to protect someone and not be able to?

Ever since I met everyone I've always been the one being protected and just when I felt like I had gained enough strength to protect the one thing in my life I should be protecting above everything else that belief gets shattered by the one person I should be most cautious of. I will never forgive myself if something happens to Koseki because I wasn't able to protect her. I *will not* lose any more of my family! Not ever again! Do you have any idea how frustrating this is? I feel like my mind is going to break!"

Panting for breath Darien knew he was out of line, but he couldn't help himself. The same frustrations that had caused his outburst back at the Order had come bubbling to the surface and he felt like he would explode if they weren't let out.

"So don't tell me you know how I feel! You don't know what it's like! You don't know a damnable Godlings thing about..."

His tirade was cut off by a sudden smack hitting him so hard he spun part way around. Shocked and surprised, Darien blinked up at Geru in amazement as the large man sternly folded his massive arms across his chest. Looking severely down on him with a smoldering anger in his eyes Darien had never seen before, Geru made it clear exactly what he thought of Darien's tirade.

"Stop acting like a brat!" Geru growled at him. "You're not the only one here desperate to protect the people you love. That's ultimately the core value behind everything we've been doing, even before we came across your sniveling carcass on the Travel Road. I don't know how you feel? I've lost more and sacrificed more times than days you've been alive boy and I'm not about to let you act like you're the only one with problems. You have a unique situation with your dragon, I fully acknowledge that, but if she's your family then haven't you realized yet that makes her *our* family as well? Are you really that thick-headed? You have no idea how much time and effort the General has dedicated to you and Koseki both. More time than he commits to most and just as much time as he has dedicated to my own situation," Geru said.

"Geru I-" Darien tried to interject.

"Shut your hole!" Geru snapped. "Stop acting like an ignorant brat and focus on what you can do right now and work towards finding a solution so you can be prepared for anything that comes in the future. We won't allow you to wallow in self-pity every time you encounter hardship! You're not the only one with problems! And as to if I know how you feel, I know all too well what you're going through so don't act like you alone have a burden to bear or a heart heavy with tragedy! We all do! It's what has bound us from the start! And that connection has turned into more for all of us. Enough bitching and whining. You want to get stronger to prevent anything from happening to Koseki? Then keep pressing forward and working towards gaining a greater strength and understanding of yourself just like you have been doing. Just like all of us are! Or would you rather run back to the Order and curl up in a corner somewhere and hope this all goes away? You can't act like a child anymore. Your life depends on it. *All* of our lives depend on it!"

Darien stared sullenly at Geru for a few moments before stalking away. He knew Geru was right, but he couldn't bring himself to admit it after his outburst. He was so worried about Koseki that he had gone over the edge and said more than he should have. Standing alone and staring off into the distance his enhanced hearing picked up snickering coming from one of Liana's retainers.

Glancing in their direction he directed a venomous stare at

Marco, who quickly turned to hide his mirth. Liana stood regally among her followers, not even trying to hide the fact that she was studying him closely. The corners of her mouth twitched in what could have been a frown, but Darien didn't care enough to dwell on it.

The sound of approaching horses made him turn to peer off in the direction in which Jack and the General had gone. Seeing Wily with the unidentified man riding along with them he knew he should alert the others that the General was on his way back, but in a fit of pique he chose to remain silent until they reached them.

Eventually the others noticed the riders and Geru and Squirrel warmly greeted Wily with warm embraces and exclamations of relief at his safety. Darien remained a short distance away, unsure of how to act.

Jack, as usual, solved his indecision for him.

"Now boyo, why do you be standin' there with such a dour look bein' on yer face? Wily did just be comin' back from the Next Realm and you do be lookin' like you be shittin' in yer smalls!" Jack laughed.

Darien sighed at Jack's idiotic humor and joined the others.

"Hey Darien, been a while huh?" Wily said as he clasped Darien's hand in greeting.

"Yeah," Darien said.

"Hey come on now! I know we didn't speak all that much, but at least pretend to be excited," Wily laughed.

Darien winced. "Sorry. I really am glad to see you. I am. I guess I'm just out of sorts today."

"Well, that's fine then. Happens to the best of us. And the worst," Wily said with a wink and thumbing at Jack.

"Ah, Wily me lad, you do be a hurtful bastard at times. You do be hurtin' me feelins," Jack said.

"If you had any that mattered I'd take that into consideration!" Wily laughed.

Jack cackled in his irritating way, but the banter failed to lighten Darien's mood like it normally did. His blowup at Geru was already weighing on him heavily, but he didn't know how he should apologize or how to approach his friend.

Lockhart had remained silent during the reunion and Darien noticed the normally stoic General wore the slightest of frowns. The General's eyes were sparkling with such intensity that Darien was taken aback by the sheer force of the sight alone. He would have thought the man would be relieved to have found another member of their group alive and well, but the General was exhibiting none of the expected emotions any normal person would have.

"And who are these people? More new recruits?" Wily asked, openly assessing Lady Liana and her followers. "Wow General, you sure know how to pick 'em! We've been nothing but a bunch of scrubs up until now, but this is definitely an upgrade!"

Darien tensed at Wily's words. There was no telling how Liana would react to that kind of talk and he was sure he would somehow get caught up in the blame if she chose to take offense.

Instead, Liana chose to ignore him completely. Lightly touching a quaking Marco on the head she turned a cold shoulder on Wily in order to speak quietly with Mari. The attendant covered her mouth and giggled at Liana's words. Picking up the topic of their conversation Darien blushed a deep red.

"Well then," Wily said with his smile frozen in place.

Jack cackled even louder.

"It do be good to know you still no be havin' any luck with women!" Jack hooted.

"Shut up Jack," Wily said.

Everyone in their party but General Lockhart paused for a moment before bursting out laughing. Even Darien found himself chuckling at Wily reverting to the commonly used refrain.

"So what's the plan from here?" Squirrel asked, fidgeting in his saddle.

"No changes. And as for that woman, she is the Lady Liana. She will be traveling with us for an indeterminate amount of time," the General said curtly.

The brief moment of mirth dissipated at the General's words. Darien shuddered as the piercing stare swept over him, weighing the value of his soul with that penetrating gaze. Despite his time spent with everyone at the Order he still found himself unable to hold the man's eye for very long.

"Are we done playing with our new toys? I do hope this one has some semblance of charm in him. I don't know what I'd do if I have to deal with yet another incompetent in my presence," Liana's silky voice suddenly cut in.

"Well now Wily lad, mayhaps you did be catchin' the wench's attentions? 'Till now she did be rather fond of our young Darien here. What do you be sayin' Darien? Do you be relinquishin' yer claim on the lithe wench or no?" Jack said with his impossibly wide grin splitting his broad face.

"Shut up Jack," Darien growled.

Jack laughed as he mounted his horse. "I just do be merely lookin' out fer your well-bein' lad!" he said.

"Right," Darien said lightly under his breath.

"Ah well, I'll leave her in your care then. She seems like an interesting one to say the least," Wily said with an uncertain look.

Darien shook his head. "It's not like that really. That woman's been trying to kill me on a consistent basis since I met her. To be honest I'm lucky I'm still alive."

Wily stared at him a moment before forcing a laugh. "Well, that's true for all women if we're being honest. Again, I'll leave it to you so do your best!"

"Oh, does the new toy have something to say to me?" Liana called over her shoulder.

"Ah, never mind," Wily said, the uncertain look still frozen on his face.

Darien sighed. He felt like he was back at square one where the issue of Lady Liana was concerned.

Hopefully I have a chance to explain things in full before Liana decides to have any more crazy ideas, Darien thought as General Lockhart began issuing orders.

"And who is this?" Squirrel suddenly asked while they prepared to move once again.

The man who had arrived with Wily had remained silent during the exchange and now seemed nervous and embarrassed as all eyes turned to assess him. Looking at him closely Darien could see why he had been overlooked. He wore nondescript tunic and trousers of grey and brown with a rope belt and boots of poor cut and quality. His hair was a mop of grey with minor remnants of the deep black it once had been and his eyes were a soft brown creased at the corners with age. There was absolutely nothing remarkable about him whatsoever. Darien felt a pang of sympathy for the man. If things had not happened as they had, he very well could have ended up looking much the same in his future, not that that would have necessarily been a bad thing. Pangs of homesickness welled up within him at the thought. He took a deep breath to calm himself and pushed the unwanted thoughts aside.

The man was nervously fidgeting and looked to be somewhat in pain, but Darien didn't feel it was his place to openly wonder about the man's odd mannerisms. "Oh yeah, he's-" Wily began before the man suddenly elicited a scream so loud it pierced Darien to his core. Everyone instinctively covered their ears against the soul-shattering wailing until the man went silent and sank to his knees clutching his head and whimpering in obvious pain.

An odd fluttering on the wind assaulted their ears in a slow building symphony that suddenly exploded in a crescendo as small winged creatures erupted out of the landscape around them with a myriad of splattering mud and mind splitting cries so loud that Darien was forced to the ground. He was somewhat lucky that he was already covering his sensitive ears, but the cries of the winged creatures were too fierce for it to do much good.

"Hells!" shouted Geru as Squirrel immediately began firing arrows off in rapid succession as best he could in the misty dampness. Tartas and Jack immediately moved into action, fluidly moving amongst the creatures and leaving a multitude of feathered corpses in their wake.

Darien grimaced and forced himself to draw his short blade. Trying to imploringly connect with Koseki, he could feel the young dragon again shy away from his mental touch. Taking a deep breath he thought about what Geru had said moments ago and tried to focus on what he himself could do in this moment despite the eerie screeches from the mass of creatures threatening to rupture his eardrums.

"What in the Hells are these things?" Squirrel screamed as one of his arrows perforated a leathery wing of one of the beasts, causing it to spin wildly out of control until Tartas deftly caught it on the tip of his blade and flung it to the ground.

"Movari," Tartas said as if it should have been obvious.

"Whatever they are, they're better off dead!" Geru spat. Fending off several of the creatures at once, the large man suffered multiple wounds to his bare arms and face as he did so. The muscular man still hadn't changed his style of clothing from the thick green sleeveless leather vest and black trousers he had worn since Darien first met him. Geru was paying the price for that affinity now as blood began to flow down his arms.

Darien didn't hear any more than that as the Movari, as Tartas had named them, continued their assault and drowned out all other noise. He felt slightly disoriented and nauseous from the ear splitting cries coming from all directions, but he managed to keep his wits about him just enough to roll out of the way of several of the Movari targeting him. Coming wobbly to his feet he almost overbalanced and fell as a wave of dizziness swept over him. Thankfully his training from the Order instinctively took over and he decapitated the closest Movari violently hurtling towards him with a single slash. Bile rose in his throat from the sudden movement, but he gritted his teeth and fought to maintain his balance. Several of the Movari blurred in his vision and he had to blink rapidly in order to maintain enough focus on the enemy just to stay alive.

Several times during the onslaught the Movari were able to break through his defenses to rend at his clothes and face until he felt he would be overwhelmed no matter how many of them he managed to slay. The hot tang of blood entered his mouth as more and more of the Movari landed blows with their savage talons. He was beginning to worry that not even his ability to heal at a dragon's pace would be enough to save him from these horrible creatures. His vision filled with blood, feathers and muck while the creatures continued to whirl unceasingly around them. The onslaught was slowly becoming more than he could bear as he sought to fight off the creatures as best he could. More and more the Movari's strikes found their mark and his tunic soon became saturated with blood and gore. Bleeding from several places his grip on his blade began to weaken despite its small size and Darien fought desperately to maintain his defense.

Suddenly Jack was at his side; a hurricane of blade and flesh. Darien would have marveled at the inhuman speed and fluidity of Jack's movement, but he was too busy trying to stay alive. And doubly so trying not to vomit everything he had ever ingested.

The sudden reinforcements, including a grim-faced General Lockhart alongside Wily carrying the slumped and gibbering form of his wild-eyed companion under his arm, caused the Movari to temporarily retreat out of range.

Squirrel, who had quickly run out of arrows, took the opportunity to leap off his mount to gather what shafts were still salvageable from the Movari corpses he had downed. The rodent faced man had a significant amount of blood seeping from the area around one of his shoulders, but he seemed determined to continue to use his bow just the same.

Darien had to squeeze one eye tightly shut in order to keep watch on the Movari circling above while their screeching continued to reverberate incessantly inside his skull. He focused on his breathing and the feel of the damp and muck beneath him in order to maintain his senses.

"You do be a sorry sight me lad. We best be havin' them on the run in a mite, less we be havin' bigger problems to be dealin' with," Jack yelled over the din as he helped Darien to his feet.

Darien wasn't so sure about that, the Movari seemed like plenty of a big problem at the moment, but he took Jack at his word. He tried to will his body to heal even faster than it normally would, but it was doing little good. Hurting all over he took a deep breath. He was beginning to feel light headed from blood loss, but forced himself to focus. The Movari began to uniformly circle above them as their cries continued unabated.

"Now if they do be goin' quiet, then no bets do I be takin'," Jack said under his breath.

Darien wasn't sure if he was supposed to hear that last part or not and was surprised he could still make it out despite the echoing cacophony in his head.

Suddenly, as if in response to Jack's words, the circling Movari all went silent.

"Well....shit," Jack said as he released his grip on Darien and looked around warily.

"Well shit, what?" Darien gasped in exasperation as he steadied himself at the relief from the noise. Touching his ears to make sure they were still intact his hand came away sticky and wet with blood. *Oh that's fantastic! This day couldn't possibly get any worse!*

Lockhart, covered in feathers, blood, and some kind of indiscernible ooze came over to check on their condition during the respite.

"You alright?" he asked Darien curtly.

Darien merely nodded, unable to think of anything to say. *Alright? What kind of question is that when we're all covered in blood? And what in the Hells just happened?* He surveyed the scene around him and nonchalantly wiped his hands on his tunic, hoping nobody would notice the seepage of blood coming from his ears; although the rest of the blood seeping through his clothing was more obvious. "Where in the Hells did those things even come from?" he asked no one in particular. Jack cackled at the question, but no one seemed willing to venture an answer.

Breathing heavily he took in the unsettling sight of his companions, especially the General. There was a light in the man's icy blue eyes that he had never seen before and he seemed to carry his weight in a different manner that Darien couldn't quite describe. He was certain that in this moment the General was a much more dangerous man than he had initially thought. And that thought terrified him for reasons that were unclear; not that anything had been all that clear since his journey started.

Wily's friend was in the worst condition among them. The man had barely moved since the attack had begun and he slumped to the ground whimpering in obvious pain, although it seemed he had miraculously avoided suffering any injuries. He began rocking back and forth oblivious to the rest of them, and Darien didn't blame him. If he had remained the person he was before becoming a Ryudojin he might have reacted much the same.

The iron smell of blood and the even worse odor of offal assaulted his nose while he surveyed the rest of what had suddenly become a battlefield. He scrunched his nose and spit to try and get the taste out of his mouth to no avail. Two of their pack horses had had their bellies torn open and their entrails strewn about haphazardly amongst the muck. The rest of their mounts had bolted out of range of the attack, but he saw they were still close enough they could be retrieved. Taking a quick tally he breathed a sigh of relief at the sight of a wild-eyed Rosy seemingly no worse for wear other than being in a panic. For some reason it seemed the Movari were only interested in the human members of their party as long as the rest of the mounts remained out of the way.

"If you're going to help in any way, now would be an ideal time to start," the General suddenly snarled in a rare display of actual emotion.

At first Darien thought the General's ire was directed at him, but quickly realized he had been referring to Liana.

Glancing in Lady Liana's direction Darien was astonished to see the lithe figure of Liana standing with arms crossed and her retinue pressed protectively around her. At first glance it looked like she had chosen not to partake in the sudden battle and that her retinue was protecting her as human shields.

No, that's not it. Darien squinted and briefly focused his aura energy as best he could under the circumstances without Koseki and tried to assess what Liana was doing without actually trying to read her.

His eyes eventually picked up on a vaguely golden glow bathing the small area around them with Liana acting as the center. The globe of light tapered off into a thin, golden line wildly flickering and trailing off into the distance. It was apparent from the bent and broken bodies of the Movari littering the ground around them that the light was some sort of protective barrier keeping them from harm during the battle.

Darien wished he was capable of something similar; it certainly looked useful. His injuries throbbed as they slowly healed and he continued to control his breathing to help deal with the pain. Having the rejuvenation ability of dragonkind was one thing, but he would rather avoid the pain in the first place.

Liana simply smiled and opened her mouth to speak, but before she uttered a word her smile vanished as a low keening in the air caught Darien's ear. Glancing above, he noticed the Movari had risen even higher into the sky and began to move faster and faster in a widening circle while the eerie keening slowly increased in volume.

"Something's coming!" Darien yelled, taking everyone but Jack and Tartas by surprise.

"What? What do you mean something's coming?" Geru asked. "*What* is coming?"

Jack nodded and grinned his usual grin. "The boy do be right me lumberin' friend. There be only one beastie that do be silencin' a flock of Movari durin' a hunt. The Broodmother do be on her way. Do I be right there Tartas?" Jack asked.

Tartas merely shrugged. "If that's what Darien is talking about. Do you hear her already?"

Darien nodded. "I can hear a weird keening sound," he said between short breaths. "It keeps getting louder by the second. I know my hearing is better than most, but I can't believe you don't hear it yet."

"Are you sure it has nothing to do with the blood coming from your ears?" Geru asked tensely.

So much for hiding that. Thankfully Tartas spoke up before Darien could think of another way to explain what he was hearing.

"Jack and the boy are right. Only the Broodmother could silence such a large number of Movari all at once," Tartas said softly.

"I don't hear anything," Geru grumbled.

"If Darien says he hears it then it's there," the General said curtly, ending the debate.

Jack nodded again. "We do be hearin' her soon enough. 'Course that do be meanin' we might be dyin' a horrific death soon enough, but who do be needin' to know 'bout that!" he hooted with his impossibly wide grin plastered across his face.

Geru and Wily both raised their hands, sending Jack off into peals of maniacal laughter. Tartas, to his credit, simply smiled.

"I think I'd much rather *not* know about my chances for death," Darien said as his vision finally cleared and the initial nausea caused by the Movari's cries receded. The keening of the Movari Broodmother continued to intensify, but oddly it had a calming effect on Darien contrary to the pain caused by the smaller Movari's cries. The sound evoked memories of that night back in the Grove where he had first been entranced by Hosroyu's song. In fact the tone of the keening was eerily similar, although to him it seemed primitive and unrefined in comparison to the elegant and complex symphony of sound and emotion he had experienced that night. Even Liana's melody from earlier had had an elegance to it that was noticeably absent from the Broodmother's discordant keening.

"So just what are we expecting when this thing gets here?" the newly recovered Wily asked with a distinct edge to his voice.

Jack's grin widened even more across his ugly face. "She do be just like these little 'uns, only she be bigger," he said.

"Bigger?" Geru asked, narrowing his eyes.

"Bigger. And she be meaner as well," Jack affirmed.

"Much meaner," Tartas added in his quiet voice.

Wily's unidentified companion's eyes widened in terror as he continued to shake and whimper as if in excruciating pain.

"Great," Darien snorted as he tried to discover from which direction the Broodmother would be coming from so they could at least try to formulate a plan to avoid being disemboweled.

"I can hear it," Squirrel said in a whisper. The Movari above became a whirling blur of feathers, wings and razor-sharp talons as the Broodmother inched ever closer.

"They're frenzied," the General observed. The strange gleam in his eyes seemed to glow even brighter at the prospect of the Broodmother's arrival and Darien shifted uncomfortably at the sight. "And you had better start honoring your words. There's only so much I will tolerate before our agreement becomes null and void," the General directed at Liana.

Darien winced at the acidity of the General's tone and expected Liana to respond in her usual mocking manner, but she merely pursed her lips and shrugged her slender shoulders.

At first Darien thought she was just being flippant, but upon closer inspection his dragon eyes perceived a considerable amount of perspiration on her brow and a slight heaving of her chest and shoulders that belied a labor she was trying hard to conceal while she maintained the soft globe of golden light around herself and her followers.

"She's already near the limit of whatever it is she's doing," Darien said quietly. "I'm not sure exactly what it is, but it's taxing her a great deal," he added in response to the questioning looks.

"Any ideas Jack?" the General asked with an even harder edge to his voice than usual.

Jack shrugged. "Do be tryin' not to die."

Darien couldn't help but bark a short laugh at Jack's blunt absurdity. The wave of dizziness and nausea had all but dissipated and he focused his eyesight on the gloomy horizon ahead. At first he couldn't see anything out of the ordinary, but soon the shadow of a figure began to materialize out of the distant mist. The strange keening suddenly ceased building in volume and instead became a steady rhythm battering the very air around them. Darien shivered at the change in tone as the features of the approaching figure from the southeastern horizon became clearer to his eyes.

"I can see her!" Darien managed to eke out through ragged breaths.

The response from everyone was immediate. Squirrel quickly remounted with his resupply of arrows, although Darien wasn't sure how accurate the man could be with his wounded shoulder, while the rest of them created as much distance as possible between themselves and prepared for whatever was about to happen.

The Broodmother continued her methodical advance and Darien soon became transfixed by her otherworldly appearance. A blackened beak caked with some type of grime centered beneath two intense and rabid eyes, indicating the Broodmother was anything but natural. Heavy feathers of midnight with various hues of tainted blue covered the beast's torso and laced its gigantic, leathery wings. The amount of feathers tapered off towards the rear and Darien couldn't tell if the sparse amount of feathers on the Broodmother's tail end was natural or the result of a fight with some other, unknown predator produced by the land of Pajana. He sincerely hoped it was the former.

Wicked talons extended from the tip and bottom of its wings and from the large claws dripping with the same mysterious grime covering her beak. A patch of feathers around her face were stained with blood and muck, offsetting the fevered yellow of her eyes and creating a terrifying and menacing appearance.

Darien nearly buckled at the sight and gripped the hilt of his blade so tightly his whitened knuckles cracked from the strain. He quickly relayed what he was seeing to the others and wondered just how large this Broodmother must be if the others had yet to even catch a glimpse of it.

"How in the Hells are we supposed to survive an attack from that thing?" Darien asked in a voice hoarse from the unsettling fear gripping his throat.

"That's what I'd like to know!" Geru said tightly. Squirrel nodded his agreement and Tartas' grin grew wider. Lockhart remained silent, intently staring in the direction of the approaching creature as if he could slaughter the Broodmother by sheer force of will alone.

Darien almost believed the man could do so, but he was wise enough to know hoping for the impossible was useless and that they were in dire straits. He tried to think of a solution. Of something that he could do as a Ryudojin, but that would require Koseki's help. He even briefly considered the absurd idea of asking Liana, but any aura energy Liana had was being channeled into maintaining whatever it was she was doing.

He took a deep breath as the terrifying visage of the Broodmother continued her approach. Slowly, tentatively, he reached out to Koseki once more. With Liana occupied and the imminent arrival of the Broodmother looming there wasn't any other choice but to try to coax his sister dragon out of hiding. The conditions were less than ideal, but he hoped she would respond to his desperation and need. Once again he felt Koseki shy away from the contact and he gritted his teeth in frustration.

'*Koseki, please!*' He forced his emotions gently yet firmly through the link hoping to finally get her to emerge from hiding. Darien wasn't sure if she would be willing to listen in her current state, but he was out of options. Their swords and arrows alone would certainly not be enough to take down the approaching monstrosity.

The Broodmother had gotten close enough for the others to get a look at what their immediate future held, causing a varied amount of curses and epitaphs from everyone but the General. Tartas merely whistled at the sight. Jack cackled as usual.

"That's a damnable big bird," Geru said, the strain of the moment evident in his voice. The larger man dug his heels into the muck and shifted his weight more out of habit than any real hope of it making a difference. Once again Darien caught out of the corner of his eye what looked to be unnatural movement from the numerous tattoos encircling Geru's muscular arms. He blinked several times to clear his vision and blamed the odd effect on the dizziness that had been brought on by the Movari. The General made an odd gesture at Geru and the large man relaxed a little, but Darien's attention was already elsewhere.

'Koseki, I need you! We all might die here!' he implored once more.

Finally, slowly, he felt Koseki tentatively establish a complete link and the overlay finally sprang up around him.

Darien breathed a brief sigh of relief until he felt the full brunt of Koseki's emotions roll over him in a tidal wave of color. So many different shades and hues swarmed over and through him at once that he grunted from the impact like he had been struck a physical blow.

"You be ok there lad?" Jack asked, continuing to eyeball the approaching Broodmother like she was no more than a minor annoyance rather than a horrifying atrocity about to rend them limb from limb.

"Yeah. Buy me some time," Darien absently replied.

"Buy you some time? We're gonna get disemboweled and torn apart!" the unidentified man who had arrived with Wily screamed hysterically. Red faced and sweating profusely, the man was doubled over and clutching at his belly like he had been impaled on the point of a sword. Remnants of the man's vomit stained the blood soaked and feather covered ground and his eyes rolled in terror.

"If you don't settle down, Tartas is going to disembowel you right now!" the General said tensely.

Tartas immediately began a slow advance on the man, but he had already resumed rocking back and forth while quietly muttering to himself.

"Squirrel! You and Darien move behind Lady Liana! We'll take this thing head on if we have to while he does what he needs to do! We're counting on you and your friend Darien!" the General barked with authority.

Wincing in pain, Squirrel instantly wheeled his horse around and moved to obey the General's orders. "Let's go Darien!" Squirrel shouted.

Darien barely heard them, but followed Squirrel even while still trying to cope with Koseki's onslaught of emotion.

To her credit, Liana didn't even spare them a glance despite their close proximity to her and her retinue. In his currently linked state Darien could more easily make out the structure of the golden light surrounding them. To him it looked to be made up of millions of tiny golden fibers pulsating and constricting so rapidly the naked eye of a normal person would never be able to perceive it. Darien could tell she was exerting all of her efforts into maintaining the protective light and he hoped he wouldn't be a distraction while he conversed with Koseki. After all, she had demonstrated in the past that she was somehow able to see the overlay.

Darien brushed off his thoughts about Liana and focused on calming Koseki down and getting her to agree to what he had planned. He knew it was reckless and by her reluctance to hear him out he knew she could feel how reckless it was before he had even laid it out for her.

'Koseki,' he began again before his young sister dragon suddenly cut him off.

'No more hurt you Taya,' Koseki said with an imploring and terrified tone Darien had never felt in her before and that threatened to break his heart. He was startled to find Koseki's reluctance didn't stem from fear of Liana or of being hurt herself, but instead from the fear that Liana might use her to hurt him! Instinctively he sent as many soothing and comforting sensations through the link as he could to calm her down. Enveloping those emotions around Koseki in an intangible embrace Darien assured her with feeling alone that everything was going to be ok, that he would always be there to protect her, but right now he needed *her* to protect *them*. He was thankful he had misinterpreted her terror, but he needed her help now more so than ever. What he wanted to attempt could very well cost him his life, or at the least shorten it, and that was also part of the reason for Koseki's terror.

Darien took a calming breath and approached the image of Koseki, still wrapped protectively within Hosroyu's massive claws. Her mother had remained oddly silent while watching their exchange. Darien furrowed his brow in concentration and focused all of his aura energy on Koseki alone, incorporating all the teachings that Kuldari and the others at the Order had taught them. Koseki, for her part, eventually did the same with some gentle coaxing. He knew she was trusting him despite her fears, but he was well aware that the consequences on his end could be dire and that she was extremely worried about his well-being. Liana being preoccupied also played no small role in Koseki's willingness to listen to him and go along with what he wanted.

Once he felt like he was about to burst from the overwhelming tide of their auras he channeled every ounce of that energy onto a single spot on Koseki's ridged forehead, just now starting to change in color from the grey clay-like scales of her birth. To her credit, Koseki actually waited patiently for Darien to finish, even going so far as to extend her neck out from within her scaly cocoon and lower her forehead in trembling anticipation. It never ceased to amaze him how fast her moods could change, especially when she got excited. This was something Darien had long ago promised his young sister dragon when they had begun their training and he knew she had been impatiently waiting for him to deliver on that promise. Even with the threat of the Broodmother imminent he knew he had to do at least this much to fully bring Koseki out of hiding so they could help protect their friends. Despite the strain his efforts were causing, Darien gave a small smile at the sight of the easily distracted Koseki placing her trust in him despite her lingering fear of anything bad happening to him.

After several more intense moments of concentration Darien released all of that pent up aura energy onto that lone singular spot on Koseki's forehead. She took that energy and 'folded' it into her own before sending it back towards the image of Darien. In a space no more than the width of a fingertip he gently placed the tip of his tongue on her ridged brow in what was a traditional greeting among the Elder Dragons known in human terms as 'The Kiss of the Dragon'. For the first time since they had been bound by the magics of the Grove within the confines of the Birthing Circle, Darien and Koseki made physical contact.

Instantly flashes of that night when Darien had saved Koseki from stillbirth flashed through both of their minds and the events of their journey together intertwined their auras even closer. Darien wanted nothing more in that moment than to throw his arms around Koseki and let her know everything would be fine, but that was far beyond either of their capabilities at the moment. It had taken enough of a toll as it was to create even that miniscule amount of physical contact. So much so that he was no longer certain he had enough strength left to pull off what he wanted to do as the shouts of the other members of his party left no doubt the threat of the Broodmother was almost upon them.

Smiling with affection as the varying colors of their emotions continued to swirl and mist around them he formed an image of what they wanted in his mind. Koseki lolled her tongue out in her particular form of a dragon smile and he felt her emotions of trust coincide with his own as her fear of Liana faded. He knew Koseki loved testing the limits of their bond and was often impatient to do so to the point where she would forget everything else when they had an opportunity to try something new. She was wholly placing her well-being in his hands, even though both of them knew there was no telling what would happen from here. They had never tried what they were attempting in such an extreme or dangerous manner before, but their training in secret and melding during the incident with Liana back at the Order had given them the courage to go even further despite the risks.

Stepping away from Koseki, Darien turned to face the now swiftly approaching Broodmother. Behind him Hosroyu lifted her offspring up between two large talons and gently nudged her forward to stand with her Ryudojin.

"I can't wait to see what you have planned Darien," Tartas said quietly, his eyes never leaving the form of the hastily approaching Broodmother.

They could all feel a buffeting wind begin to pick up from each flap of the creature's enormous wings. The remaining horses screamed in terror and bolted in the opposite direction of the Broodmother's approach.

"There goes our supplies," Geru groaned.

"I sure hope you're better in a fight than you were the last time I saw you!" Wily yelled.

"He is! Darien, I don't want to rush whatever the Hells it is that you're doing, but could you please, you know, hurry it up a little before we all die? Right?" Squirrel called.

Darien ignored everyone's comments and again focused on all of his and Koseki's combined aura energy. They were both physically and mentally drained from that one brief interaction of physical contact they had just created, but he knew right now there was no other recourse for their survival. It was a greater risk to his own well-being since he was still partly human and therefore more fragile than a full blown dragon like Koseki; if the risk had been greater to her then he never would have considered such a dangerous course of action. Thinking of the danger involved, he briefly wondered just how much General Lockhart would scold him for what they were about to do. If he survived.

Darien felt amusement from Koseki at the image of Lockhart scolding him, but chose to ignore it. She had earned that much at least. Both of them continued to send every ounce of their remaining energy into the link until their intertwined auras synchronized, causing the same type of vibration as when they had partially melded back at the Order. This time, that vibration intensified even further and the link expanded within both of their beings as two melded into one. The link still had that slippery feel that had been present at the Order, but the intensity of their focus helped them coerce the link into doing what they wanted it to do without losing their mental grip. The swelling of the link made Darien feel like he was overflowing with aura energy. It felt like he was shedding water and his entire being tingled with energy and went cold. It was a terrifying experience, but he knew they would need all the energy they could get in order to pull this off.

The force of the wind from the Broodmother's wings assailed the party with such force that it was all they could do to stand their ground and not get swept off their feet.

"Do no be gettin' blown away on the wind! You do be as good as dead then!" Jack yelled with glee.

"Stand your ground! Be ready to strike at any vulnerable spot you can find!" Lockhart shouted into the squall.

Darien tensed in anticipation of the pain that would accompany what he and Koseki were about to do. Before, they had only shown the beginnings of what they had accomplished during their training in secret and that had been painful enough. But now they were trying to go far beyond anything they had done before and dying from injury or burning himself up with an overabundance of aura energy was a real possibility.

'It okay Taya,' came Koseki's trembling and dulcet voice from somewhere within his own being.

Darien smiled despite the considerable strain they were under. He and Koseki were one. What he thought and felt so did she. He trusted his sister implicitly and knew she felt the same, but he could tell there was still considerable fear remaining.

'We do,' came her voice again. He could feel the trepidation in her own thoughts and knew she was doing her best to be brave in the face of grave danger and that he needed to respond in kind. Taking a final deep breath he took his first step forward.

As soon as he did so, the Broodmother suddenly banked sharply upwards with such surprising agility and force that Darien almost lost concentration. At the same instant the wildly circling Movari above went suddenly still and held their places with only the silent flapping of their leathery wings disturbing the air.

"What in the Hells is she doing Jack?" Geru asked, the strain they all felt evident in his voice.

"She's planning on taking us out all at once," Tartas replied before Jack could answer.

"Explain!" Lockhart barked sharply, his eyes never leaving the Broodmother while she continued her inexorable climb upward. The air around the Broodmother increasingly gained an odd shimmer that rippled as if she was splitting the very air itself as she soared.

"He do be meanin' her attack bein' a mess of violence comin' straight down on our noggins'. And there be no way for us to be gettin' far enough away to be avoidin' it now," Jack said. "First she be gatherin' as much energy from her surroundings as she rises then she do be emittin' a screech so loud you be goin' deaf from the force of her voice and yer eardrums do be burstin' and bleedin' worse than a stuck pig. Yer skull be feelin' like it do be crackin' and yer bones be turnin' to jelly. And that no be mentionin' the grime coverin' her beak."

"What about it?" Squirrel yelled, his eyes furtively darting in every direction.

The grin on Jack's ugly face widened at the question. "While you do be reelin' from losin' yer hearin' she be rainin' that poisonous sludge down on yer head. While you be wipin' that goo off yer noggin before it be meltin' yer face you be blinded and in too much agonizin' pain to avoid bein' torn asunder by her brood."

"Fantastic, can't wait," Geru said.

Wily groaned. "I always wanted to go out being disemboweled while some acid mud melted my face."

The man hiding behind Wily whimpered in pain again while Jack cackled with glee.

"He didn't even mention the force of her impact creates a full blown crater like those we've been seeing here and there along the countryside before her brood begins to tear you apart. Of course, there's usually not much left to tear apart at that point, but they do their best," Tartas said mildly.

Geru, Squirrel, and Wily all looked at each other for a brief moment before speaking in unison. "Shut up Tartas." Tartas grinned and Jack further dissolved into peals of laughter.

Darien barely heard the exchange, so lost in his connection to Koseki that everything around them was like a dream. Holding together the thrumming and fused link they had forged was taking all he and Koseki had. To hold any more aura energy could cause irreversible harm to Darien's body according to Kuldari's instruction during his training sessions, but right now he saw no other choice. From what he understood the risk to Koseki herself was minimal since all of the energy was effectively being transferred one way as she folded and sent back to him what he was sending her. She was not completely clear from danger and would need ample rest to recover afterwards, but Darien had to trust they could pull this off together. With Hosroyu there to protect her offspring Darien felt at least comfortable, if not entirely confident, about going all out. Koseki's faith in him also was a driving force behind his determination to see this through. Besides, they had no other options left. They were simply too ill-equipped to deal with the Broodmother while Liana was using all of her strength to maintain her barrier.

Drawing on the infusion of aura from their combined consciousness they narrowed their focus, this time narrowing it into several different places within Darien's physical body at once. They almost lost control at this point, but Darien and Koseki managed to recover in time to maintain their resonance. Those places where they sent energy with as much strength as they could muster no longer were simply shared between himself and Koseki, but were as one. They grimaced as Darien's physical body painfully contorted while the energy melded new forms inside and out. They gasped for breath as their lungs became one and an odd burning sensation welled up within their throat as their mouth and face all violently twisted into grotesque shapes never meant to be worn by humankind. Scaled ridges rose above dragon eyes and their mouth and nose painfully elongated with popping muscles and snapping tendons while scales of light black and purple began to sprout, mottling their face and throat. Teeth began to grow and sharpen and their tongue elongated and forked.

They felt like they couldn't breathe, but they continued to push their body well past normal limits and with every ounce of strength and knowledge they had accumulated they lunged forward suddenly and with such force a small crater of their own was left behind where they had stood.

As soon as they moved, the Broodmother ceased her ascent and began to turn towards the circle of Movari to begin her dive. Small droplets of grime peppered the landscape, causing everyone but Darien to dance around them.

"Godlings above!" Geru yelled, twisting and turning to avoid the falling gobs of grime.

"She do be gettin' ready to unleash the roar. We do be good as dead if she be gettin' that off!" Jack shouted.

Darien and Koseki's new form could no longer hear them. They broke into a run, feeling like they were on a separate plane of reality from the others. The feeling of the ground beneath their feet barely registered despite the small craters left by the impact of each stride.

Drawing what little remained of their aura energy from their resonance they winced in pain at the melding process accelerating its effects. It took everything they had to remain conscious and aware as they nearly completed the melding of Darien's upper torso. They both knew this was one major downside to melding. Despite the increase in their understanding and ability there was no avoiding the sharing of pain and fatigue that accompanied such a strenuous task. Although most of the aftereffects would affect Darien, Koseki would have her own recovery to endure.

Darien and Koseki screamed together in rage, pain and emotion, desperately forcing even more aura energy then they thought they had left into the melding. To the others Darien was gone, replaced by some unimaginable half-human, half-dragon beast out of a tale of the world before the Unification. Blood and fluid erupted from their back as draconic wings sprouted from their shoulder blades and they screamed an unearthly roar.

Suddenly launching themselves awkwardly and violently into the sky they inhaled a deep breath, deeper than they had thought possible and held it until they felt like they would burst. Pumping their lungs as they held their breath they locked eyes with the Broodmother and knew it would only be moments before she unleashed her devastating roar. When they felt like they couldn't hold the well of energy any longer and their lungs brimmed to capacity, they released everything they had stored within in a violent and concussive blast of purple flame, enveloping the Broodmother and incinerating the circle of Movari in a blinding instant.

The stench of melted flesh and charred bones as the smoking carcass of the Broodmother spun wildly past assaulted their nostrils as Darien and Koseki lost control of their link. The silent concussion from the severing of their connection rattled his already reeling mind and he vomited bile, blood and ash as he fell. His body abruptly, and with more agonizing pain than he thought possible, returned to normal. Darien barely had enough time to glance at his friends below before his eyes rolled back in his head and he freefell to the ground where the others stood in mute astonishment.

Chapter 6

Darien was floating in darkness. He had no sense of direction, no depth, no purpose; nothing but a cocoon of emptiness surrounding him. He tried to flex his fingers and found he had no hands, no feet, nor a corporeal body at all. Weightless, formless, he floated aimlessly in pure oblivion. If he had had a mouth, a bemused and comfortable smile would have formed on his non-existent face. Nothing about his current circumstances alarmed him, although a feeling that he probably should be flitted around his consciousness. The thought quickly dissipated before his formless self; a lone incorporeal being unbound by rational thought and reason. An intangible embrace of love and warmth enveloped him as he floated and all was right in his existence.

If he had had lungs he would have taken a deep breath of relief. His consciousness paused at the thought. Why would he be relieved? There was nothing here. No time, no space, no color or sound; just a placid existence free from fear or worry. The sentiment of comfort enveloping him grew as he continued on this unplotted course. He had no way of knowing where he was or how he had gotten there, or even where he had been. In fact, he couldn't remember *anything*. He had no knowledge of a name to go along with his lack of a physical body or if he had even ever had one, not that it was important. Nothing was important here. Nothing existed here. There was no beginning or end; just an endless space of comfortable nothingness.

Wisps of half-formed thoughts and muddled images bubbled to the forefront of his consciousness and agonizingly slipped away before he could acknowledge them, let alone recognize or interpret them. He idly wondered who he was and what had brought him here, but quickly dismissed those questions as unimportant since he had no cause to search for answers.

A subtle, invisible nudge momentarily startled him as it gave his formless entity the sensation of tumbling through the aether, but he instinctively knew there was no danger here and the sense of panic quickly passed. He absently wondered what had just occurred, but the thought was fleeting and inconsequential. Just as his formless self accustomed to the comfort of his timeless and shapeless state the nudge came again, this time desperate and more insistent. He caught a sense of something vaguely recognized as worry behind the nudge. For the first time since he discovered himself in this formless space he was able to tenuously grasp the concept of what had sent his consciousness tumbling.

Thoughts and images that had evaded his perception until now flooded through him in a vivid cascade of colors and sounds, although he still could not place any coherent meaning to them. A third push came, this one with so much force and determination that he felt his consciousness was having its insides pulled out from within, if he had had insides to be pulled out.

Eventually, after what could have been a minute, a month, a year, an eternity, he became aware of a pinpoint of light that had appeared sometime during his trip. The light grew larger while he motionlessly tumbled and the thought of his journey coming to an end flitted through his consciousness just before all went black.

A searing pain suddenly sprung up behind his eyes as Darien exited the dreamlike void only to find himself still surrounded by darkness. For a moment he panicked, thinking he had gone blind before sheepishly realizing that he had eyes and should probably open them if he wanted to see.

His eyes weakly flitted open and he instantly regretted the decision as the throbbing intensified tenfold. It took some time and heroic effort before he could keep them open for longer than a few moments. After some time passed they adjusted to the minimal light in what he determined to be a darkened room.

Where am I? His dragon eyes focused on the rough canvas hovering inches from his face. A flapping near his head caught his attention and with agonizing effort he rolled his eyes towards the sound to see a small slit in the canvas rippling with a light breeze. He sneezed as a sudden chill shook him and groaned at the pain exploding behind his eyes before it faded back to an aching throb.

Slowly his memories of the battle with the Broodmother returned. He cursed an oath that would have made Oltan box his ears and tried to will his incredibly sore limbs to comply with his brain's instructions. Gently poking and prodding himself he checked for injuries and was surprised to find he was more or less intact, minus the pain and soreness incorporating itself into the very fabric of his being.

He let out an explosive breath and winced in pain. A scratching and burning in his lungs made him feel like he had inhaled the smoke of a hundred campfires. He coughed several deep, throaty coughs and spat out multiple gobs of grey goo and blood that he didn't want to think too much about. Leaning against the blanket covered saddle someone had thrown together he closed his eyes and replayed the previous day's events in his mind.

He frowned. There was no telling how long he had been laying there unconscious, but he supposed he would get his answer once he willed his body to function. He was sure Jack and the others would give him the full details of what happened afterwards and the General was sure to be more than sore with him. Again.

He just hoped this latest incident didn't mean the General finally did leave him on his own. Geru's warnings about being left behind had stayed with him and it was entirely possible his moment of desperation had been the final act that swayed the hard man's decision. He didn't want to think about what he would do if he crawled out and found no one but Rosy waiting for him.

Risking another deep breath Darien again groaned with effort as he rolled over and pushed the saddle out of the tent before crawling out on his stomach. The wounds he had suffered from the Movari during the Broodmother's attack had mostly healed already, but he still felt like his entire body was sore inside and out. The pain behind his eyes was by far the worst, but seemed to be getting better as time went on.

Carefully, and doing his best to ignore the slowly fading pain wracking his body, Darien pulled himself out of the tent to find it was just a large piece of canvas repurposed as a temporary shelter.

Regaining his feet he swayed slightly for a few moments before gaining his balance. He squinted against the pain as he surveyed his surroundings amidst the murky twilight marking the days' end in Pajana. Darien was startled when a steadying hand gripped him by the back of his tunic. As his brief bout with dizziness passed Darien turned to thank whichever of his friends had come to his aid and paused in bewilderment when he came face to face with an unfamiliar figure.

After a few moments of confusion Darien remembered there had been another person who had joined them with Wily, but there hadn't been enough time for an introduction before the Movari and Broodmother had attacked. The newcomer let go, but remained silent, quietly waiting for Darien to speak. The nondescript man wore his stringy and greying hair in a ragged mop above aging and tired brown eyes that had seen too many years of worry and toil. He dressed in a homespun tunic and trousers with a rope belt and his boots of brown leather were scuffed and well worn. The man's entire dress and demeanor indicated he was someone used to a hard life of being overlooked and ignored. Darien felt a pang of sympathy for him. He furiously thought of something to say, but his mind was still somewhat foggy so all he could manage was a weak "Uh, thanks."

"You're welcome young master," the man replied, slightly bobbing his head and avoiding eye contact.

An awkward pause followed while Darien searched for something more to say.

He was saved by General Lockhart's appearance.

"Darien, glad to see you up and moving. You've been unconscious for the last three days and we were beginning to worry," the General said. The unnamed man quietly extracted himself from the conversation at the General's approach and left the two of them to speak alone.

Darien blinked in surprise as what the General said penetrated the fog in his mind.

"Three days?"

The General nodded and waved in the direction where Jack, Geru, and Wily had huddled over a meager fire. "Thankfully Jack was able to piece this together out of some of our remaining supplies. I had hoped a woolen blanket would be among them since you spent a great deal of time shivering, but we had to make do," the General said, fidgeting with the small opening as if trying to find some fault with it.

Now that the pain behind his eyes had faded to a dull ache Darien could focus a little more clearly and could see the canvas had been meticulously stitched together in such a manner that it could just barely accommodate someone of his size.

Part of what the General said registered with Darien.

"Jack made this?" he asked dubiously.

The General nodded again.

Darien toed the makeshift shelter expecting it to collapse at his touch, but he was surprised at just how sturdy it was.

"Jack can *sew*?"

Darien was stunned. He never expected Jack would have a talent for something so mundane.

"The people in our company are capable of many things Darien. We have to be out of necessity. You should be more aware of that than anyone else, especially considering your own situation and what you did to save us the other day," the General said.

"Well that's true," Darien said sheepishly.

As the General's words sunk in, another thought hit Darien.

"Koseki!" he cried.

The General folded his arms and a brief flicker passed across his face, but Darien was too panicked to notice the slight change.

"How is she?" the General asked, but Darien was already immersed in the link trying to get a response from Koseki. There was a change in the feeling of the link as he sought out a response from his dragon sister. If he had to describe it in human terms he would have said that it felt 'wobbly', but he was still able to reach out with some effort. As he sought Koseki, he again could feel her presence, but no response was forthcoming. He did notice one major difference from her previous seclusion and this one however. Her presence didn't seem to be muted by a barrier like it had been before, but somehow he got the impression that she was either unable or unwilling to complete the link at the time. He did get the sense that she was unharmed and was surprised at what felt like he could *feel* each of Koseki's breaths through vibrations in the link. How this was possible he had no idea, but at least she seemed no worse for wear save for some fatigue.

Darien frowned. It was to be expected that she needed sufficient rest after the stunt they pulled, but this was the second time Koseki had ignored him. He worried her seclusion was his own doing this time rather than the fear of Liana harming him.

"Well?" the General asked sharply, quickly bringing Darien back to reality.

"I think she's ok. Something's off though," he muttered.

Lockhart didn't reply, but a twitch of an eyebrow indicated that a more detailed explanation was needed.

Darien sighed with frustration, but knew better than to try to push this discussion off regardless of how little information he was working with.

"She's there, I can feel her, but I can't get any type of response from her. And it's different from before when she was just hiding from Liana. There's no barrier muting her or blocking me. I want to say she's unharmed, but I can't say for sure until she's willing or able to acknowledge a full link again," Darien said.

The General frowned slightly, which is to say the corners of his mouth twitched, but the concern on Darien's face must have shown because after a moment the General spoke.

"You'll let me know when you get a better handle on what's going on with her," he said.

Darien nodded while avoiding the urge to shudder under that piercing gaze.

The General turned to leave and paused.

"And Darien?"

"Yes sir?" Darien yelped.

"Thank you. I don't know how we would have dealt with that monster if you hadn't taken what I assume to be a monumental risk to you and Koseki both. In the future please ensure doing something like that is absolutely necessary. Never forget that every moment of every day you are responsible for two lives. Not to mention the lives of the rest of our companions, just as each of them are responsible for yours. It's a heavy responsibility we all share, but you're unique in that what you do directly affects someone who is literally a part of you. Remember that and act accordingly," the General said.

"Yes sir," Darien replied. He knew the General was speaking the truth. Having Koseki's life forever tied to his own was the biggest responsibility he had ever had to bear and he was well aware that he was somewhat lacking in that department. That was why he had so desperately wanted to get stronger while at the Order.

"Uh, how is everyone else? Everyone seemed pretty beat up from those things," Darien ventured.

"Everyone is alive at least, that's the most important thing. Squirrel got the worst of it and is in a makeshift sling for the moment. The rest of us are going to have several new scars, but we were able to patch ourselves up somewhat with the minor amount of supplies we were able to recover," the General said. Darien took a breath and sent up a prayer of thanks to whatever Godling was listening for the safety of his friends.

"That's good," Darien said.

General Lockhart nodded a final time and with quick, powerful strides made his way apart from the others to stare off through the gloom. Looking at the man Darien wondered if the General was trying to force the land itself to yield to his will.

Darien watched him for a few moments trying to decipher what exactly was driving this man so desperately and what it was that caused people to instinctively want to follow him. Although Darien admitted to himself he had also developed a loyalty to the man despite the General's intense demeanor and piercing gaze. There was just something about the man's intensity, as terrifying as it was at times, that made you believe he would succeed at the impossible.

"Whatever it is, I'm glad these are the people I'm with," Darien muttered as he continued to try to coerce Koseki out of her self-induced solitude.

A short while later, while the peculiar company plodded along through the muck and mire of the less traveled ways of Pajana, Darien finally got a response from Koseki.

Riding comfortably atop Rosy his head began to nod in a losing effort to stay awake. Twilight still had not yet quite melded into evening, but Darien felt a heavy weariness from the events of the last few days. The dreary landscape of Pajana and the steady sucking of the horse's hooves as they picked their way along were also contributing to his wear and fatigue.

A gentle, uncertain nudge probed the back of his mind. Darien almost jumped out of his saddle at the sudden prodding, but a moment later realized Koseki was finally coming around. He smiled to himself before acknowledging his sister dragon. She still had a tendency to be uncertain if she thought he was mad at her. The fact it had been some time since she had initiated the link in such a tentative way told him all he needed to know. His smile turned to a frown as he wondered if perhaps she had been injured and was unable to make a full connection before.

I'll never forgive myself if she suffered some sort of irreparable damage. Darien took a deep breath and coaxed the gentle nudging into the full link. The link was there just like always, but she had somehow been keeping herself distant from him. He supposed he would find out eventually just how that had been accomplished and why, but for now he just wanted to ensure Koseki's well-being.

The overlay sprang to life, but slowly and with a stutter that Darien and Koseki had only experienced once before. Normally the vibrant and vivid representation of Koseki's environment would erupt in an explosion of color that matched the young dragon's excitable and rambunctious nature. The stuttering of the overlay was a concern since it had only happened previously when Liana had gotten involved, but as far as he could tell he and Koseki were connecting. He would need to get answers about the cause of the abnormality eventually, but checking on Koseki's status took precedence.

Locking onto Koseki, he was surprised to see his sister dragon again curled up defensively behind one of Hosroyu's massive forelegs while the enormous Elder black rested casually amongst their rocky surroundings. He tried to get an impression from Hosroyu to see if she was unhappy with his and Koseki's actions, but the majestic black remained silent so he tentatively continued inspecting Koseki's condition.

Darien was surprised that he could still feel Koseki slightly trembling as he sent as many calming and soothing thoughts through their bond as he could. As he approached Koseki and her mother he mentally visualized placing a reassuring hand on the ridge of Koseki's brow and was stunned that for a fraction of a fleeting moment he could feel the still developing scales beneath his palm. It was similar to what they had done three days before, but without the intense amount of energy and concentration they had expended during the confrontation with the Broodmother.

He paused and felt Koseki cease trembling when her surprise resonated in response to his own. Darien's smile widened at her reaction. Her rampant curiosity and amazement at the world around her was one of her most endearing, and sometimes most aggravating, qualities he loved about her.

Koseki slowly and with some trepidation uncoiled herself from her mother's leg and Darien continued to assure her everything was ok. Koseki looked warily around Darien's own surroundings before asking a question that concerned him.

'No lady or scary monster?' Koseki asked in a quavering voice. Darien scowled so fiercely at the mention of Liana that Koseki took a skittish step backwards. He quickly assured her his ire wasn't directed at her, although he did worry about her reliance on vocal communication when they had been working so hard on using emotions and the colored mists.

'Don't worry, I won't let anything like what she did the other day happen again, I promise. I just want to ensure the melding we did didn't hurt you in any way,' Darien told the young dragon as Koseki finally waddled over to his side in an attempt to nuzzle his hand affectionately. Again the physical interaction briefly flared for a fraction of a second and Darien felt an increased surge in the young dragon's jumbled emotions. He was concerned that she had overextended herself to the point where she hadn't been able to calm down mentally yet, but she surprised him as she usually did.

'I ok. Just resting. Taya ok?' Koseki said.

His smile widened at her bravery. He could feel her weariness and worry, but her need for reassurance was greater than either of those and he couldn't help but marvel at her.

'Just no go away again!' she said suddenly and with such anger and fear that Darien was momentarily stunned.

'Go away? What do you mean?'

Koseki stamped both her forelegs in a fair imitation of a child's tantrum.

'Just no go away! Promise Taya!' she pleaded.

'Ok….Ok,' Darien said trying to calm the young dragon by attempting to pat her again. They once again made the briefest moment of contact before it dissolved and Koseki's attitude instantly changed from anger to exultation. He knew no other information would be coming from Koseki while she continued to attempt to nuzzle and nip at his hand in fascination.

'Hosroyu', he asked, turning his attention to the Elder black. *'I have a few questions. How did Liana interact with Koseki the other day without me feeling anything or knowing what was happening? I want to learn how to prevent that type of thing from ever happening again. And what does Koseki mean when she says I 'went away'?'*

Strangely, Koseki's mother paid his questions no heed, instead raising one single, massively ridged eyebrow in his direction.

A brief surge of worry came from Koseki and she momentarily ceased her revelry.

'No more,' Koseki sent.

Darien's confusion grew. *'No more what?'*

Koseki waddled back to her mother and again entwined herself around a massive leg before responding.

'No more voice shared,' Koseki said. Her mother affectionately gave her offspring a lick from her elongated and forked tongue that was mottled with shades of purples and pinks that couldn't be found anywhere else in the world of Taulia.

'What? Do you mean she can't hear me anymore?' Darien asked incredulously.

Koseki, after enduring the loving ministrations of her parent, sadly nodded. *'The lady,'* she said.

Darien blinked in surprise. *'Liana? How?'*

Up until this point Hosroyu had always been able to what she called 'intrude' on their link. She mentioned early on in their relationship that this was a singular occurrence where the Ryudojin were concerned. She had reminded them several times her ability to do so would fade until their link strengthened to the point where it was a specific sharing of selves singular to the two. Since they had been training at the Order Hosroyu's voice had slowly diminished to the point where she had to forcibly interrupt their link, although her presence seemed to fade slightly with each attempt. The point of what they had called 'intrusion training' was so that Darien and Koseki could try to get a feel for what it was like when someone tried to break into their bond and what the warning signs of such an attempt were.

Darien knew eventually they would be able to eliminate the possibility of Hosroyu or anyone else finding a way to use their link against them. However, having the wise dragon cut out so suddenly felt like a personal violation that made Darien's stomach sour.

Koseki briefly nodded her head in another human-like response when his worry registered on her. He supposed he had himself to blame for her human imitations. His sister dragon had proven herself to be impressionable to say the least.

His amusement at Koseki aside, this sudden development worried him. He had known this moment would eventually come, but to have it occur so wildly out of their control was unsettling.

The idea that Liana might be much more powerful than he had thought gave him a chill.

A thought hit Darien as he felt Koseki silently agreeing with his sentiment.

'Koseki, are you still able to talk to your mother while we're linked?' he asked.

Koseki swiveled her head towards her mother in a more dragon-like manner as she considered. Darien would have laughed at the way Koseki transitioned from human to dragon characteristics so seamlessly if the situation had been less intense.

After a moment of concentration Darien was relieved to hear Koseki answer in the affirmative.

'Yes, but is hollow,' she replied with some mild confusion.

'Hollow? What do you mean?'

'Just hollow!' Koseki snapped, her tendency towards impatience bubbling up.

'Alright. Alright,' Darien soothed. He would try to find out exactly what Koseki meant later. Whatever shock Liana and their melding might have had on her made him sure her recovery had not been easy. In fact he wasn't entirely sure he had recovered himself. His body still ached in most places although the scratching in his lungs had all but vanished and he hadn't hacked up any more of that strange bloody grey goo either. Darien fervently hoped there wouldn't be any other unforeseen side effects from their melding that would prove to be a problem in the future.

But he had made it his priority to ensure Koseki's well-being before all else so his own health would have to come later.

'You ok Taya?' Koseki suddenly asked again with concern, still using the shortened version of his Ryudojin name 'Tayabun'.

Koseki didn't always use his name, but when she did she always shortened it to 'Taya' due to her being unable to pronounce it correctly during the early days of her infancy.

Darien allowed himself to briefly get lost in the memory of Koseki as an unsteady infant and again assured her that he was fine.

Darien thought back to the first night in the Grove when he had saved Koseki. From that moment forward he had been irrevocably bound by fate, circumstance, and love to the young dragon. They had come a long way since then, but he knew they also had a very long way to go ahead of them as well and that more dangerous and stressful situations like the Broodmother were sure to come.

Koseki lolled out her tongue in her typical version of a dragon smile when she felt the affection of her brother, but suddenly she sent a staccato of panic and bared her teeth in warning.

Glancing warily to one side Darien realized Liana had silently ridden up beside him. The hood of her cloak had been pulled forward to conceal her face, but as she turned to speak Darien was startled to see tears forming at the corners of her eyes. Even more surprising was the mixture of anguish, anger and doubt etched on her delicate features.

Darien immediately began to disengage the link to Koseki, but Liana shocked him with a subtle, almost pleading gesture she kept hidden from her followers trailing behind them on foot.

"Let me speak to them...please," Liana whispered so softly that even Darien's hearing barely picked out the words.

Darien was stunned. *'Did Liana just ask a question* politely?' He hadn't meant to send the question through the link, but Koseki already wasn't listening.

He was caught so off-guard he couldn't even form a coherent response, let alone disengage the link to Koseki. The change in Liana's demeanor was baffling, but something had been nagging at him since the time he and Koseki had attempted to read her aura. And despite the pain that experience had caused and her fears about Liana, he knew Koseki shared his curiosity about the strange trio of auras mingling within her and which had so violently rejected their touch.

"I will *not* ask a second time," Liana fiercely whispered. A single tear finally freed itself from the corner of one eye to run down her porcelain features. Darien was struck by how vulnerable Liana looked at the moment, but he usually could never tell when the woman was being genuine. However, this time he was able to pick up from the subtle emotional vibrations coming off her that she was grudgingly putting aside her pride. Just the fact he could sense anything from Liana so easily meant at least some of her barriers were down and that she was being sincere.

However, Darien was not about to take anything at face value when it came to Koseki's safety, especially where Liana was concerned. He was about to steadfastly refuse when Hosroyu's giant form suddenly lunged upwards in a startling display of strength and agility. The massive Elder black raised her elongated neck to the heavens and silently roared at the grey sky overhead before settling back to the ground with a showering of dust and stone that seemed so real Darien instinctively held his breath. He knew it was just an image of what was happening around the two dragons, but the majesty of Hosroyu tended to override common sense. Neither he nor Liana actually heard Hosroyu's roar, but her message was clear; get to the point, and quickly.

Koseki slowly and tentatively emerged from hiding and cocked her head to one side as if listening to something.

'She will listen,' Koseki said before settling back within her mother's bulk.

Darien could palpably feel Koseki's trepidation and uncertainty mixing with his own even while she nuzzled worriedly at her mother. He wasn't sure what Liana wanted, but having lost the ability to speak directly to Hosroyu could prove troublesome should things go awry.

The odds of something going awry are high with Koseki as an interpreter, that's for sure, he thought. A spike of irritation hit him and he gulped at Koseki glaring at him in indignation from behind one of her mother's claws.

Liana remained quiet for several moments, the only sounds being that of the mire as they trudged through more of the muck coating the Pajani landscape.

Liana seemed to be gathering her thoughts and lightly bit the side of her lower lip in a minor sign of distress. Darien was surprised the woman could show even that much vulnerability. He was seeing more sides of this woman in the last few minutes than he had during the entirety of his stay at the Order and he was finding it extremely unsettling. Even so, he remained on guard for any surprises and quietly moved his hand to the dagger hidden in his sash.

They rode on and the coiling fog around them mixed eerily with the images of the overlay, giving the momentary silence a gloomy vibe. A sudden dampness accosted Darien's cheek and he looked up to see sprinkling drops of rain falling from the dreary sky above. He sighed. It seemed like even the Godlings themselves were taking a hand in order to make his life as trying as possible.

Darien took a deep breath. "What do you want me to do?"

Chapter 7

"Pay attention!" Liana hissed. Darien sighed. It hadn't taken long for Liana to reassert her proud and overbearing demeanor. "You're distracting the young Elder."

Darien blinked as the rain slightly increased in intensity. He pulled his riding cloak tighter against the damp and chill as he tried to balance his irritation at getting soaked and dealing with Liana.

Young Elder? He purposely ignored the surge of pride coming from Koseki at being called an 'Elder' despite her lingering doubts about Liana.

Darien really wasn't comfortable with Liana having such direct access to Koseki. Especially since he had just promised to prevent anything from happening to her and still had no inkling of how to prevent Liana from causing havoc with their link. He also wasn't sure how Liana planned to communicate with the dragons, but he had no doubt the woman had a way. He wasn't about to question Hosroyu's decision in the matter either. The Elder black seemed agitated, and an agitated Elder dragon wasn't something he wanted to deal with.

He glanced helplessly at Hosroyu as Liana closed her eyes and took a deep breath before performing the same odd hand gestures she had used before.

"Wait..." Darien said as a surge of panic welled up in his chest.

"Quiet. I am concentrating. If my words are not good enough for you then it is none of my concern," Liana murmured.

"Your word? This coming from the woman constantly trying to kill me?" he muttered.

Liana opened her mouth to rebuke him again, but they were interrupted by Hosroyu's gigantic head quickly and lithely lifting from the ground to hover on her elongated neck between the two humans.

Darien could tell even with Hosroyu separated from the link that the Elder black was rather annoyed and he checked with Koseki to confirm his suspicion. He was surprised to see even Liana had the decency to look rebuked and she remained respectfully silent while Hosroyu settled back on her haunches.

Darien tried his best to ignore Koseki's subtle laughter. She seemed to have quickly overcome her concern from just a few moments ago. Darien supposed having her mother so closely involved might have something to do with that, but he brushed it aside and turned his attention back to Liana.

Taking a deep breath Liana continued her gesturing and Darien found if he concentrated hard enough, he could just make out what looked to be faint colors of auras following each movement before dissipating. He was so enamored with this discovery that he almost jumped out of his skin when Liana suddenly, but gently, placed a hand on his shoulder.

Darien felt uncomfortable under her touch not only because it was Liana, but because of the strange tingling sensation suddenly coursing through his body. He could feel a strange energy flowing into him from Liana's hand and he rolled his shoulders in agitation as it tried to thread through the link. Although uncomfortable in more ways than one Darien was most concerned with how easily Liana incorporated her energies into the link, but he had to trust Hosroyu would somehow find a way to intervene if she tried anything harmful.

A strange combination of both awe and of being violated swept over Darien as bright and vibrant images flashed brightly before his mind's eye. The color of auras and energy were so brilliant in their three-way connection that Darien's eyes ached from their beauty. A feeling of shock overcame him as he strained his hearing to the limits and was positive he could barely hear a slight giggling as well as the faint sounds of someone quietly sobbing.

However, as soon as he felt like he could somewhat follow these oddities the images vanished in a jarring instant as if they had been forcibly pulled away.

Liana opened her eyes to direct a venomous scowl in his direction, but offered no explanation before returning her concentration to whatever it was she was doing.

Darien sighed, but steeled himself against any possible hostile action on Liana's part.

A jolt rippled along the boundaries of the link so suddenly it almost knocked Darien clean off Rosy. Hosroyu had always told him eventually no one would be able to intrude upon their link as

they grew and learned together, but apparently they were far from
reaching that stage with Liana so easily integrating herself. Not
even during their training at the Order had they felt such a jarring
sensation where a third party intrusion was concerned. Hosroyu's
interruptions had always had a subtle and gentle touch, but this felt
much more abrasive.

Darien frowned as he reconsidered. *It's not exactly like she's
trying to break in; it's more like she's hovering just above it and
brushing up against it with her own aura. Why would that cause such
a shock? Who exactly is Liana? How does she seem to know so
much about Hosroyu and my link to Koseki?*

Darien realized for the first time that ever since he had met
Liana he had been so focused on staying alive he had never given
much thought to where Liana had come from or what her past
might be.

He would have loved to dwell on what it was driving Liana to
her murderous impulses and erratic behavior, but at the moment
he had to pay attention to what was happening right in front of
him.

The energy flowing from Liana intensified and if not for the
surprisingly firm grip of her hand on his shoulder, not to mention
the copious amount of energy flowing into him, he may have fallen
for real. Instead, he received another shock when Liana's voice
echoed hollowly inside his head. Her voice sounded like an echo in
his mind, like she was speaking from a distance, but if he focused he
found he could clearly understand her words.

'Elders,' her voice echoed along the link. Darien wasn't sure
how to describe the sensation, but her words were vibrating along
the edges of the link where her aura touched instead of being a

natural part of the whole. It was an odd experience he struggled to put into a perspective his human brain could comprehend.

The best he could come up with was that it was like an unwanted cricket crawling on his skin. He shrugged in discomfort and resisted the urge to scratch at the invisible itch.

Liana continued to speak and her voice slowly became indecipherable while echoing inside his mind. He could glean no meaning from the language she had switched to, but the words held something hauntingly familiar tugging at the reaches of his consciousness. Part of him felt he should have a better understanding of what was being said, but try as he might he couldn't glean any coherent meaning.

Koseki was also having a difficult time. Senses of confusion and frustration emanated from the young dragon in undulating waves and Koseki looked and felt uncertain as she haltingly relayed Liana's words to Hosroyu. From Darien's perspective Koseki was able to speak the language with some effort, although she didn't seem to fully understand it and Liana had to calmly repeat herself several times. He was amazed the volatile woman could exercise such patience; it was yet another side of her he hadn't known existed.

Darien continued to warily watch the particular scene play out before him. Not for the first time he wondered what exactly was Liana's interest in Koseki? He had easily determined when they first met that she intended to kill him for whatever reason so he had spent most of his time trying to avoid her. In the last few days their relationship had taken an unexpected turn and somehow had become increasingly more complicated while they traveled.

Not being able to understand the conversation or its scope was making him nervous. No matter what Liana said he did not like her this close to Koseki, especially with Hosroyu disconnected from their link. He gritted his teeth and decided he had to have faith Koseki's mother would have powerful enough magic to counter any aggression on Liana's part.

The odd exchange continued unabated for quite some time while their party plodded through the mire. As usual the De'Segua siblings kept a close eye on their mistress during the process. Marco looked ready to explode with fury as usual, but was being held in check by Mari. Jack loomed close by wearing a leering grin in Marco's direction, but Darien couldn't tell if Jack was looking out for him or just having fun at Marco's expense.

If Darien had to guess, he'd say it was probably both.

The conversation between woman and dragons continued and Darien soon felt like he was being lulled to sleep by the melodic sound of their conversation and Rosy's gently swaying beneath him. The falling drops of rain that couldn't seem to decide if they wanted to come down in force or not added to the dreamy atmosphere. Darien felt his eyelids growing heavy and he had to fight to stay awake.

Just as he drifted to the edge of sleep he was startled by two words he clearly understood. Two words that *any* resident of the world of Taulia would understand. Luxes and Tenebrae. The two Great Gods once known as the Balance and whose fall joined the two peoples of the world into one during the event known throughout history as the 'Unification'.

Just before their party had arrived at the Order of the Fist they had had to cross the Jarabin Plains, an area constantly assaulted by unrelenting sand storms and containing relics rumored to be artifacts of the battle between Luxes and Tenebrae that resulted in the birth of the Godlings. Darien still had a great many questions about that particular part of his journey, but all of his time at the Order had been spent on training and running away from Liana so he hadn't gotten much of a chance to ask Kuldari or anyone else to elaborate on what he already knew.

Another spike in Koseki's fear and uncertainty caught his attention and he soothed the young dragon with calming thoughts even though he wasn't sure of what had just transpired between Liana and the pair of dragons.

What he did know was that where Luxes, the God of Light and Tenebrae, the God of Darkness were concerned nothing was ever a small matter.

Darien could sense Koseki begin to flounder even deeper in confusion despite his attempts to calm her. Whatever had happened it had unsettled the skittish young dragon and Darien felt like communications were about to break down.

I need to end this right now.

Again as if in response to his thoughts Liana abruptly thanked both Hosroyu and Koseki in the common tongue before withdrawing her aura energy as well as her hand from his shoulder. The look on her porcelain features betrayed nothing of what had been conveyed, but he did notice the slightest sign of hesitation linger in her eyes before vanishing. Without another word Liana calmly slowed her mount and rejoined her companions.

"Hey!" Darien called after her. "What in the Hells was that about? You didn't do anything to Koseki did you? Answer me!" He hadn't meant to snap at her, but his worry for Koseki and his uncertainty about what had happened was putting a strain on him. Liana paused momentarily in her saddle before deciding to ignore him completely.

"Hey!" he called again, moving to bring Rosy closer. Instantly Liana's followers moved to block Darien's advance with the air of some sort of muck-covered honor guard.

He brought Rosy up short and sighed in frustration. He tried to reach out to Koseki to see what she could tell him, but the young dragon had already fallen asleep and Darien could feel the exhaustion deep within both of their very bones. Hosroyu cradled her young charge in a surprisingly gentle manner for a creature so large and Darien allowed himself a tired smile before relinquishing the link. The overlay instantly vanished and he blinked in the sudden gloom.

He sighed again and Rosy whickered slightly at her rider's change in mood.

"Sorry girl," he said softly. Darien gently patted Rosy as they plodded along in an eerie silence. He could feel everyone still on edge even days after the Broodmother's attack. Just like Rosy Darien couldn't seem to settle, especially after the exchange he had just witnessed.

He wasn't sure exactly what it was he had just experienced, but that wasn't surprising. When it came to Liana he was never sure what was happening around him at any given moment.

The only time I'm positive I know what's happening is when she's trying to kill my ass. That's usually pretty clear. I almost wish we were still at that point. At least then I'd be a little more confident about what she intended.

He paused in his saddle at another annoyed whicker from Rosy and he shook his head to clear it of unreasonable thoughts.

Well, maybe not.

Rosy snorted at her rider's indecisiveness and Darien gave her another gentle pat.

It wasn't long after his exchange with Liana before the newcomer who had joined them with Wily approached Darien again.

Slowing Rosy's pace Darien turned in the saddle towards the man. He seemed to have something on his mind, but for a few minutes he simply walked next to them with a conflicted look on his face. Darien felt like he should perhaps say something to lessen the awkward tension, but he couldn't think of anything.

After several more minutes of the odd silence Darien finally cleared his throat.

"Is there something you wanted?" he asked more brusquely than he intended. Darien inwardly sighed at the harshness in his voice, but the strain of the last few days was weighing heavily on him.

The man winced and began to wring his hands in worry.

"Ah yes, young master. You see, uh..." the man stuttered.

Darien looked the newcomer over as he stumbled over his words, but this only seemed to agitate the man further. Darien was confused by his nervousness, but considered for a moment that his first impression of Darien had been him sprouting dragon wings and breathing purple fire so maybe his reticence wasn't all that confusing.

"Um, You must have something you want to say... Uh, I'm sorry I don't think I ever got your name," Darien said.

The man bobbed his head at the question. "Ah yes, my name is Gelas young master," he replied in a slightly quavering voice.

Darien thought back to the incident with the Broodmother and remembered the man had seemed to be suffering from a great deal of pain even before she had attacked. "Nice to meet you. Have you recovered from earlier?" Darien said politely, trying to ease the tension.

Maybe my eyes are reminding him too much of the Broodmother. He broke eye contact in the hopes it would put Gelas more at ease if he wasn't staring into the eyes of a dragon.

It had the opposite effect as Gelas bobbed his head again and began to wring his hands so fervently Darien was afraid he might rub the skin right off.

"Or is there something you needed maybe?" Darien ventured.

A loud laugh from nearby came as answer. "Don't worry about old Gelas, Darien. He's always so nervous that you might have to shake him to get a coherent answer," Wily called.

Gelas winced at Wily's words, but he did stop wringing his hands.

"Ah yes, forgive me young master. I am just unsure of the proper way to approach you," Gelas stammered in his alto voice.

Darien blinked in confusion. "What do you mean? Just talk to me like you would anyone else."

Gelas immediately averted his gaze and Darien silently cursed himself. He almost wished he had taken Kuldari up on his offer to help teach him how to temporarily shield the true nature of his eyes from others. At the time he had felt like doing so would somehow be a disservice to Koseki and he had gotten oddly offended. Even now he found himself getting irritated by the memory, but he had to admit learning it might have been useful.

His agitation must have shown on his face as Gelas began bobbing his head and furiously wringing his hands again.

Darien took a deep breath and wondered why he always made such an awkward first impression on people. He *was* grateful Gelas hadn't tried to murder him within the first thirty seconds or so after meeting him like a certain someone else he knew. He glanced sidelong at Liana in irritation. Liana must have felt his gaze on her again as she slightly turned in her saddle and directed a small self-satisfied smile in his direction.

Turning the troubling thoughts of Liana aside Darien decided to try a different tact.

"So Gelas, how did you end up traveling with Wily?" Darien asked, scratching absently at his cheek.

Instead of drawing the nervous man into conversation Darien's question again had the opposite effect of what he intended. Gelas' face blanched white and he began to stammer even more.

"Well ah, young master, that is..." Gelas mumbled.

"Why so nervous Gelas?" Wily laughed loudly. "You see Darien, believe it or not old Gelas here ended up saving my ass after that Bloodsetter ambush. We've pretty much been stuck together ever since."

"I see," Darien said.

Gelas still seemed to be on the verge of terror so Darien decided to let the matter drop until the man built up the courage to speak.

The awkward silence continued until General Lockhart sharply called for a halt. Darien assumed it was a chance to rest the remaining horses, but when Squirrel's furtive figure emerged out of the mist of gloom he learned otherwise.

After the Broodmother's attack Squirrel had vehemently argued with the General to be allowed to finally scout out ahead on his own. Darien had never seen Squirrel so animated nor the General so hard pressed to change an order. Despite his injured shoulder being wrapped in a makeshift sling Squirrel was adamant he be allowed to do his job as their scout and that he would be much more comfortable knowing what lay ahead of them.

"After all, we don't want anything like the Broodmother showing up while we're unprepared again. Not being ready for anything is going to get someone killed real quick, right?" Squirrel had said.

I guess it comes from the trust he's earned from serving the General for so many years that he can be that way, Darien had thought during the exchange.

In the end the General had surprisingly relented, but with the stipulation should he encounter even the slightest suspicion of danger he would return straight away without further investigation or delay. Jack and Tartas had both offered to go with him, being native inhabitants of Pajana, but Squirrel had said it would be better to keep everyone else in a group than to split off more personnel from the main party than necessary.

The General hadn't spoken a word since Squirrel had vanished into the Pajani countryside and Darien noticed the slightest softening of tension around the General's eyes that belied his worry and relief at Squirrel's return.

That relief would prove to be short lived as Squirrel reported.

Squirrel shifted uncomfortably in his sling for a moment before asking something odd. "Sooooo Jack, Tartas, you're both native inhabitants of Pajana right?" Squirrel asked.

Jack turned his head cockeyed at the question. "You do be knowin' that be true," he said. Tartas just nodded.

"So in an offbeat and murky area like this, there shouldn't be any sustainable homesteads or the like, right? People like that should be concentrated more south than here, right?"

Both men nodded. "Anybody that do be choosin' to live 'round here do be interested in not livin' much of a long life," Jack said.

"So why would there be some fancy mansion deep into this uncharted area? I'm guessing that's not normal, right?"

Darien had begun gnawing on some dried jerky during the exchange and almost choked at Squirrel's words. *A mansion? There's no way that's possible!*

Jack gave a low whistle and Tartas' eyes opened wide in surprise.

"What is it?" the General asked harshly. The man was apparently in no mood for any more delays or surprises.

Jack held up his hands defensively. "It do be unusual that be true, but it be by no means unheard of," he said.

Tartas nodded again at Jack's words.

"If there do be this mansion you be speakin' of then there do be only one explanation," Jack said.

"And that would be what?" the General asked through gritted teeth.

Darien was getting the sense he was about to witness the rare event of General Lockhart losing his patience and his unease forced Darien to concentrate in order to keep the colored mists from springing up from everyone around him. Even so a small amount of orange mist leaked from the General and Darien sincerely hoped Jack and Tartas could keep the man's irritation to a minimum.

He was sure he didn't want to witness what the General was like when he truly lost his temper so he felt it best to remain silent. Darien continued to chew his jerky for what felt like the thousandth bite and waited for a better explanation.

It was Tartas who replied.

"Little Maiani's," he said in his soft voice.

"I see," the General replied. Darien was shocked at the General's lack of reaction. He had no idea how the man could remain so calm in such an odd situation.

"Little Maiani's?" Darien asked quietly, glancing at Wily in the hopes the experienced mercenary would have some sort of an idea what they were talking about.

Wily shrugged. "Seems Jack and Tartas are both familiar with it so let's see what they have to say."

"You do be goin' right on ahead Tartas me friend. She do be yer kin do she not be?" Jack said.

Tartas shook his head and took a lazy swipe at Jack that was easily ducked.

"Just because they say she's of the Bowali like me doesn't automatically make her my kin. She's a myth even among our own people. There are very few who can even claim to have encountered her," Tartas said. "And it's said there are even fewer that make it back alive after paying her place a visit," he added as an afterthought.

He has a really bad habit of doing that, Darien thought.

"So what exactly is this Little Maiani's?" Geru asked.

The muscular man crossed his arms in annoyance and Darien was again struck by how oddly the intricate tattoos encircling his arms seemed to subtly gyrate along the contours of his muscles. It may have been because of the multiple scrapes, scratches, and gouges littering his arms from the Movari attack, but for an instant they looked alive, undulating in agitation like serpents made of ink and flesh. Darien blinked a few times to make sure his eyes weren't playing tricks on him and the movements ceased.

I must not be fully recovered yet. He chewed some more before finally swallowing the mush of jerky. The tattoos had gone back to normal and Darien wondered what meaning the odd designs might have. If it had been Jack he could have shrugged it off as one of his whims, but Geru was a serious man for the most part so Darien doubted they were a frivolous accessory.

He shifted uncomfortably in the saddle as he thought on a way to apologize to his large friend about his outburst the other day before he could ask about something that was probably very personal.

The General's eyes narrowed and Tartas hurried on with his explanation.

"The best way to explain would be to say Little Maiani's is there, but not there. In fact she's nowhere, but she's everywhere," Tartas said.

"What in the Hells does that even mean?" Geru asked in exasperation.

"It do be meanin' her location always be changin'," Jack interjected.

Tartas nodded in agreement and continued. "That's right. It's never been reported to have been seen in the same place twice. There are rumors of a time when two members of the Order encountered her place at the same time, in two wildly different locations, and simultaneously held a conversation with the woman herself without knowing the other was even there. It wasn't until they reached the safety of the Order and compared stories of their experience that they realized what had happened," Tartas said.

"How is that even possible?" Darien asked.

"No one really knows, although Kuldari seems to have some knowledge of her. He does seem rather taciturn on the topic though," Tartas said.

Jack grinned a wide, mocking grin across his lantern shaped jaw. "It do be no more surprisin' than some brat with glitterin' eyes bein' bound to a precocious young dragon," he said.

"Shut up Jack," Darien said.

Darien knew Jack had a point, as much as he didn't want to admit it. There was so much more to the world than he could ever have imagined; so much more than what he had encountered even within the library back home. It was overwhelming to know that he could have spent the entirety of his life poring over the knowledge stored there and never come close to understanding as much of the world as he did right now. And if he was being honest with himself, he knew he still didn't really understand all that much.

Thinking on the library back at Village Breathwynd, what he and his caretaker Oltan had often referred to as the vaults, caused a twinge of homesickness in his stomach. During his travels he had adapted to both his situation and his physical changes as best he could, but there were still moments that brought up happier memories of his past. He had to be careful not to depress himself too much by dwelling on them.

"Can we avoid it?" the General asked sharply, startling Darien out of his thoughts.

Squirrel shrugged. "I'm not sure. Once that fancy manor materialized out of the mist I high-tailed it out of there, right?" Squirrel paused for a moment as his eyes darted nervously in all directions like he was unsure of where this mysterious manor would appear next. "I *can* say that there was a sort of...pull when I saw the place."

"A pull?" the General asked, his ice blue eyes glittering fiercely.

Squirrel's eyes momentarily ceased their rapid assessment before continuing on, considering his words carefully.

"A pull, right? It was like an invisible tug pulling me towards it. My itch to explore the place grew the more I tried to leave it behind. Even when I forced myself to head back I wasn't happy about it. If I had stayed for more than a moment I may not have been able to tear myself away even with my shoulder like this. It's that beautiful a sight, right?" Squirrel said.

Darien could hear the General's teeth grinding during the exchange.

After the Broodmother and now this, he knew the General would be less than pleased at his plans being so wildly derailed. Darien instinctively wanted to move Rosy further away from the General, but steeled himself to remain still.

"Tartas, what more can you tell us?" the General asked.

Tartas rubbed his chin thoughtfully. "I'm not too sure to be honest. Then again no one is too sure when it comes to Little Maiani's. I can say that I don't think I've ever heard of something like an invisible pull drawing people in, but I do know when it comes to her then almost anything is possible."

Darien felt a tired Koseki rousing from her nap and nudging at the back of his mind, but with something so important being discussed he chose to ignore her. He sighed at Koseki's indignant pout while she pulled back from her pestering. He sent some of his aura energy through the link to appease her for the moment. Darien knew better by now than to completely ignore the young dragon and he smiled despite the lingering traces of Koseki's sulking wafting through his being.

The General continued his line of questioning. "And if we can't avoid it? How dangerous is she?"

Tartas spread his hands wide. "Hard telling not knowing as they say. Even those who did come back after visiting her weren't too coherent in their explanation. All I can say for sure is that some come back while others do not and those who do return are far, far fewer. What happens to those that do not is still a mystery, although we all generally assume the worst," he said.

Darien could tell the General was less than pleased with Tartas' explanation, but he assumed the man would decide to press on while hoping to avoid any more unnecessary danger.

Darien shivered at the explanation of this Little Maiani. The Broodmother had been enough of a terror for one lifetime and he fervently hoped to be far removed from such horrifying experiences in the future. Darien prayed to any Godling listening to help them avoid the possibility of encountering something else so terrifying so soon.

"Lady Liana, you've been especially quiet during the course of this conversation. Do you have any information to add about this Little Maiani's?" the General asked.

Liana, who had been whispering with her subordinates off to one side, smiled at the General in her condescending way and very slightly shook her head in the negative.

"Squirrel take point and lead us away from this Little Maiani's place as best you can. I don't like wasting any more time than we already have, but I will not risk such an uncertainty. Especially not now," the General barked.

"Right," Squirrel said. Everyone collectively took a breath and prepared for whatever lay ahead on the next leg of their travels.

"I wonder what this Little Maiani's place really is," Darien wondered aloud.

"Well hopefully we won't have to find out anytime soon. Sounds like more trouble than it's worth," Wily said. "Although I do wonder just how good looking this Little Maiani actually is though," he added.

Both Jack and Tartas laughed at the comment before stifling their mirth at a withering look from General Lockhart.

Darien prayed they would never have to find out as they continued on into the gloom of the Pajani countryside.

Darien wiped the moisture from his face. The mist and rain had steadily increased since Squirrel's discovery of Little Maiani's and their chosen route of travel had become even more of a muddy and sodden mess. Darien shivered and pulled the hood of his cloak tighter against the damp as Rosy whickered slightly in protest of the cold.

After another hour or so General Lockhart again called for a halt to wait on an update from Squirrel. By now the mist and rain had increased to the point where seeing more than several feet in front of you was nearly impossible. At least that's what the others claimed. Darien wasn't having the same severity of issues as the rest, but he tried to be sympathetic to their complaints.

It wasn't long before Squirrel again returned out of the mist.

"Are we still heading away from that place?" the General immediately asked.

Squirrel nodded. "As far as I can tell we're still heading around the area I ran into it, but it's slow going, right?"

The General gripped the reins of his mount so hard the charger whinnied.

"Continue picking a trail as best you can. I do not like all these delays, but I want all of us to be prepared for the possibility of encountering another hostile entity. We will not be caught off guard like with the Broodmother again. Is that understood?" the General said.

Although the General's icy gaze never left Squirrel's face the rest of them knew his words were meant for all of them.

"So timid for one who acts so brave," Liana murmured quietly from the rear.

Darien was pretty sure he was the only one to hear her words, but he chose to ignore them. He got the sense the normally composed Liana had become concerned once Little Maiani's had been mentioned and that made him uneasy. Darien was certain the woman was more worried about their circumstances than she was letting on. Her unease rattled him as it wasn't an emotion he was used to sensing in someone normally so composed. It spoke volumes that he was able to glean anything from her at all since it was nearly impossible to do so under normal circumstances.

Absently rubbing Rosy's mane to distract himself from the uncomfortable feeling creeping over him Darien kept one eye on the newest additions to their group. Wily and Gelas had been sticking close to him since Gelas' awkward introduction and he hoped the strange man's nervousness would fade so they could have a normal conversation. The way Gelas had acted during the incident with the Broodmother concerned him, but he couldn't dwell on it at the moment. He couldn't dwell on *anything*. Darien frowned. *What was I just thinking about?*

His thoughts were becoming muddled and trying to think straight was getting more and more difficult. The air around him was becoming heavier and heavier and he began to feel more and more drowsy with each passing moment. His skin lightly tingled with his increasing lethargy and the hairs on the back of his neck stood up. This odd confusion continued to grow with each step Rosy took and he lightly gasped for breath as it was becoming more and more difficult to breath.

What am I doing?

It was a strangely familiar sensation he knew he had experienced somewhere before. The heavy air continued to be infused with an ethereal feel and the mesmerizing sensation sent chills up his spine.

Eventually he was barely able to grasp that what he was feeling was the same type of entrancing magic Hosroyu's song had lulled him with that had led to his bonding with Koseki. Unlike the discomforting and distorted feel the Broodmother had exuded, this felt like the same hauntingly beautiful magic Hosroyu had infused into her song on that unforgettable night.

"About time you noticed," Liana murmured so softly that only he could hear.

He drunkenly rolled his eyes back at Liana and couldn't be sure through the fog filling his mind if the look of worry etching itself across her face was a trick of the mist or a legitimate expression of concern. She seemed just as unsure about what they were experiencing and had he been in full control of his faculties that revelation would have terrified him. There was no doubt in his mind now that it was too late. They had already been caught up in the same type of magic that had been contained within Hosroyu's song and only the Godlings knew what that foretold. If he had been able to function normally he might have worried about just how often this type of thing had been occurring lately.

"Wait," he managed to slur in a daze. The pressure in the air suddenly dropped and a shimmering sheen warped the landscape, causing a wave of disorientation in all of them and the horses to rear in panic.

It took all of Darien's remaining ability to focus on keeping Rosy from throwing him off and from vomiting the meager travel rations they had been surviving on since losing so many of their supplies during the Broodmother attack. He was thankful he was able to maintain control since he didn't think his body could take much more abuse after his melding with Koseki and the odd exchange with Liana. After a few more moments of feeling like his insides were roiling in agitation the sensation passed and he dismounted on rubbery legs, calming Rosy as best he could and leaning on her for support.

"Poor girl, you've been through more in the last few days than most horses experience in a lifetime haven't you?" he slurred softly as the dizziness ebbed. The intoxicating magic lingered in the air,

but had lessened to a degree where he could begin to function
somewhat normally.

"I think we have more important worries," Liana said with
contempt, striding past on slightly staggering steps. Darien guessed
even she was having a difficult time with whatever had just befallen
them, but apparently she had already mostly regained control of
herself. Gelas, who was noisily retching into the dew covered grass,
seemed to be the worst off out of anyone.

Darien paused.

Dew covered grass?

During their trek through Pajana there hadn't been much
semblance of grass or any other type of healthy fauna once they had
turned southwards towards Het Tapas.

Darien, still holding Rosy's snout in a trembling hand, took a
look around and was stunned by what he saw. Gone were the muck
and mire of Pajana and in its stead stood a lush and meticulously
maintained landscape dominated by an enormous stately manor.
Pristine white paint shone brightly everywhere he looked,
accentuated by the clear starry night sky above. Large ornate
columns carved with precision stood like massive sentinels to either
side of a large double door made from some unknown reddish wood
and polished to a magnificent sheen. Fantastic rainbows of light
danced from panel to panel amongst the long vertical windows
cross-sectioned with panes of thick glass. The roof of the manor
slightly overhung the porch and was made of a hard black material
reflecting each pinpoint of light from the stars above in a stunning
display.

Darien had to call upon all of his training in order to keep from
becoming overwhelmed by all the colored mists springing up from

everyone around him all at once. He was having more and more trouble keeping the mists suppressed and under control while he tried to grasp what in the Hells was happening this time.

Taking a deep breath his already reeling senses were assaulted by an aromatic scent he assumed was being produced by the strange berries hanging delicately from the abundant foliage adorning the entryway. Darien was awestruck not only by the absolute majesty of what he was witnessing, but also by how more and more similar this experience felt to the night when he had first bonded to Koseki.

Koseki tiredly nudged lightly at the back of his mind again. Darien got the sense from her that she had also been somehow affected during the strange transition to the manor's grounds and that she was looking for comfort just as much as she was checking on him. Darien assured her he was fine despite his disorientation and that he would try to explain exactly what happened after he knew what was happening himself. He gently pushed Koseki away without complaint from the young dragon for once. Darien didn't want to risk any more harm to her on top of the exhaustive experiences she had been forced to endure recently.

He curled his toes at the feeling of the lush grass beneath his feet and some of the dew managed to seep into his leggings through the leather soles of his boots. Were it not for the sound of Gelas retching nearby Darien felt like he could drink in the sight of the manor grounds forever.

Even Jack gave a low whistle at the majesty of the place. Geru and Tartas stood in mute astonishment while Squirrel, to his credit, recovered quickly and moved to inspect the grounds.

"Hold a moment, Squirrel," the General said, his hand never straying from the pommel of his sword.

"Oh, too scared to even move now are we?" Liana lightly mocked.

Liana's words rang hollow in Darien's ears as he felt her continued unease even without having to exert his own aura energy.

The General ignored Liana and scanned the area around them assessing just how much of a threat the place might pose.

Squirrel's eyes darted about rapidly and his free hand twitched unconsciously at his inability to investigate the phenomenon.

Liana's followers huddled closely together around their mistress. Marco had crouched low with a feral look in his eyes like a rabid animal on the verge of attack. The fact the man's gaze was fixated on Darien made him more than a little uncomfortable. Marco had always worried Darien. One time he had read Marco back during their stay at the Order and had almost been knocked senseless by the intensity of the colored mists swirling around him. Red mists of anger mingled with ones tinged with undulating edges of blackness indicating a strong desire to kill. The only other recognizable mist Darien had seen was a deep lavender representing lust. Darien hadn't dwelled too deeply on if that lust was associated with Liana or for his desire to kill. He wouldn't have been surprised if it was both. Since that time Marco had proven to be volatile and unpredictable and if it hadn't been for Liana keeping him under control who knows what the man would have wrought by now? And given what Jack and Tartas had said, it wasn't an absolute they would even survive their coming to this place so he hoped the man could reign in his emotions enough in order for them to discover a way to escape with their lives intact.

Darien shook his head to try to clear it of the intoxicating scent, but his being was becoming more and more saturated with whatever magic and energy fueled the manor's existence. It was akin to the time when Geru and Jack had forced several mugs of whiskey on him in order to get him drunk enough to where they could stitch up a wound he had received in the back of his head.

He reconsidered and decided that this was far more pleasant despite being so unsteady. The whiskey had tasted awful. In direct opposition to then, the feel of the magic infusing him now was euphoric, but he was definitely feeling more intoxicated and sluggish with each passing moment.

Mebbe I havensh recovahd that mush...

His eyes slid over from Marco to Liana and she also seemed to be struggling, but seemed to be handling it much better than he was. The others had more or less recovered from their arrival and didn't seem to be experiencing the same effects. Darien couldn't understand why only he and Liana had been oversaturated in such a manner.

He never got an answer as they were all struck by a formless wave confirming Squirrel's description of an 'invisible pull'. Darien felt strongly compelled to follow this pull back to its origin and he stepped towards the manor despite the General barking orders to resist and stay their ground. He understood the General's orders, but his body wouldn't obey his brain's commands and Darien could see the others also trying to fight the urge as he staggered on unsteady legs towards the manor. Squirrel had clenched his hands into fists so hard that blood dripped out slowly from his palms and even Jack and Geru were having trouble following the General's command.

A bemused smile spread across Darien's face as the pressure in the air increased even more and small pinpoints of light arose all about them. It took Darien's eyes a moment to register the tiny creatures at the center of these miniscule balls of light, but in his dazed state he didn't dwell on this revelation any more than he would a common housefly.

Gurgling sounds came from Liana's attendant Mari and she began to move in strange halting motions towards the manor. Darien bemusedly watched her take several jerking steps before the wide wooden doors slowly creaked open. The faint sound of chimes echoed melodically throughout the grounds and the strange small balls of light flared in resonance with the melody.

Nothing emerged from the darkness within and no-one appeared to welcome or chase them off, but the opening of the doors served as a breaking point for the De'Segua siblings, even Marco, and he began to quickly approach the manor without exhibiting the strange motions as Mari.

Darien heard Liana sigh.

"I suppose we might as well, seeing as someone has taken so much trouble to welcome us. And you should be embarrassed by how drunk you are. It's disgusting," she said.

When she spoke Darien noticed a flash of light and could again see a golden rope connected to Liana glittering beautifully in the night air and stretching off into the distance. The rope flared brightly in concert with the light creatures upon the door's opening before quickly fading from view. Even though it was the second time he had seen this peculiar phenomenon his befuddled state prevented him from thinking too deeply on it.

Had he been in full control of his mind he might have risked commenting on it, but his attention quickly shifted back to the manor and he slowly began to involuntarily follow in Liana's wake.

The others also took this as a cue and started to follow suit. Darien thought he could hear the General speaking, but his words sounded muffled and obscured as the air became heavier and heavier with each step bringing him closer to the manor. Approaching the entrance he climbed the five small steps leading to the porch. His legs felt rubbery and he got the sensation of slogging through sand with the same dreamlike quality he had experienced the night when Hosroyu's song had infused every ounce of his being.

The floorboards creaked beneath his feet and the sound echoed in his mind in a cacophony of joy at their use. Darien dreamily smiled at the sensation of the very floor being alive. It was like centuries of august dignity was infused in every aspect of the manor, which only sufficed to further remind him of the confines of the Birthing Circle. He was now mere inches from the entrance and still could not see anything within the beckoning blackness even with his singular eyesight. This should have alarmed him, but he could no longer even think of fighting the irresistible compulsion drawing him into the manor's interior.

He again vaguely heard the General's voice while Liana and her followers had disappeared ahead of him into the shadow beyond the door. They had been absorbed into the blackness as they passed over the threshold and Darien quickly found himself face to face with a vaguely undulating void beckoning him further.

With a bemused smile plastered on his face Darien stepped into the unknown in a stupor.

Philip Lockhart cursed. Then took a deep breath. Then cursed again in a few different languages for good measure. He had never been a man prone to outbursts, but seeing every one of his men behave like mindless marionettes infuriated him. Had even one of them been able to resist the manor's allure he would have been able to keep his composure, but the force Squirrel had termed 'an invisible pull' had easily claimed them. The corners of his mouth twitched in a frown and he resisted the urge to let out an aggravated sigh. He had made a mistake by not trying to physically restrain at least one of them and hoping their experience would be enough to keep them in line, but the magic of the place had proven too much for them to handle.

Lockhart gritted his teeth and tried to at least be thankful some of the various items he kept on his person at all times allowed for a certain level of protection from the arcane; most of which had been gifts from the old man during his childhood. He stared hard at the manor in front of him as if he could force it to submit to his will. The small points of light floating about the grounds dimmed and the manor began to subtly shimmer. He took that as a sign the manor's time in this place was at its end. Lockhart ground his teeth in irritation and with long, powerful strides quickly crossed the meadow. Climbing the creaking wooden steps without hesitation he passed into the blackness.

Chapter 8

Darien shivered at the sudden change in atmosphere. Gone were the lush manor grounds and saturation of magic that had lent an uncomfortable heaviness to the air. In its stead was a large hall furnished like an upper scale tavern or inn, if such a thing existed. He and the others stood in a small foyer with a single door leading to a larger area dominated by what looked to be a large counter intricately carved with symbols and pictures Darien couldn't even begin to guess the meaning of.

A man even more muscular than Geru blocked their path and stood with arms folded while assessing them through hooded eyes. The man had dark olive skin weathered with age and was draped in fine robes of purple and orange. A strange wrapping of white silk covered his head and a glittering jewel of burgundy rested upon his forehead. Well-worn sandals with supple leather straps crisscrossed his feet in contrast to the rest of his attire. Behind him they could barely make out the silhouette of someone angrily arguing in a loud voice.

Marco was already growling like a feral animal at the silent sentinel before them. Darien was sure the elder De'Segua sibling thought the man was responsible for some imagined affront to his mistress, but Liana just stood quietly off to the side with Mari. The woman's tear streaked face was an obvious sign of her discomfort and she clung nervously to her lady while Liana coolly assessed their new locale. Jack and the others looked about them in wonder at the intricate and obviously old and expensive furnishing and decorations covering the walls and ceiling.

Just the foyer alone must have cost a fortune, Darien thought as he tried to adapt to the abrupt change in surroundings.

His inspection was interrupted by the increasing volume of the angry man shielded from view by the one in robes. Darien blushed at some of the man's choice of words for whoever he was speaking to. Oltan would have boxed his ears if he ever had dared to speak in such an ill manner. The man continued his verbal tirade for several minutes while Darien and the rest stood in awkward silence. The robed man made no attempt at explanation or conversation and Darien for one wasn't going to ask.

Darien noticed Liana lightly touch Marco on the neck before moving to inspect the carvings covering nearly every inch of the walls and floorboards with a puzzled look on her face.

Liana's indifference to their newfound situation made Darien nervous. Only the Godlings knew what kind of trouble her aloof attitude could land them in right now. The last thing they needed was for her to cause some kind of disturbance like the agitated man ahead of them. It didn't take much longer for the man to show them just how much of a folly such a thing would be.

The unknown man's anger suddenly exploded in such a rage

that Darien took a step back in surprise. The man screamed "I'll kill you, you tiny bitch!" with such animosity his words reverberated loudly in Darien's sensitive ears before cutting off with a sickening gurgle. He was about to whisper to Wily if he knew what was happening, but the one in robes finally stood aside to reveal a horrifying display. What they bore witness to stunned all curiosity out of them.

A man of medium build and wearing a nondescript dark grey tunic and green trousers hung suspended in the air before them. Short blonde hair cut close to the skull framed blue eyes and a straight nose that was currently twisting in agony. Normally a person's features wouldn't have made such an impact in Darien's mind, but what happened to the man next etched them into his memory forever.

A wave of nausea swept over Darien as without warning the suspended man vomited a violent fountain of bile, pus and blood. His eyes began rolling fervently in his head and an accompanying stench indicated he had defecated. Blood slowly seeped from the man's eyes, ears, nose and mouth and his skin quickly changed from a healthy pink to deep red as his insides were rapidly overcome with infection. It looked like the man was trying to scream but was unable to due to his tongue slowly stretching out from his mouth until it was dismembered with the sickening sound of tearing flesh that echoed in Darien's ears.

The General gritted his teeth and gripped the pommel of his sword so hard his knuckles cracked. Geru moved to assist the victim in some way, but for the first time the tall, silent man in robes reached out one of his massive hands to bar Geru's advance. Geru obviously wasn't happy at the interference, but didn't argue or try to force his way past.

Darien assumed that meant they wouldn't be allowed to
interfere. He had a sickening feeling in his gut. The battle with the
Broodmother had resulted in a horrifying experience Darien never
wanted to go through again, but at least at the time it was a battle
against a maddened creature that would have killed them had they
not defended themselves. This man was being wantonly murdered
right before his eyes. An internal struggle wrenched at Darien's
heart. The strange, silent man obviously did not want them to
interfere, but this was a murder no matter how Darien looked at it.

"No!" he shouted. His body began moving before his mind could
comprehend what he was doing.

"Stop!" he vaguely heard everyone say at once although an
accompanying "Oh my," came from Liana, who didn't even bother
to look away from her inspection of the foyer.

He had no idea how he was going to help the poor man, but he
instinctively knew he couldn't just stand by while someone was
being killed. He was only able to take a few steps in the victim's
direction before the large meaty hand belonging to the man in
robes swiftly gripped Darien by the face and easily lifted him off his
feet.

Instantly all the energy drained from his body and he went limp.
He didn't even have the strength to make fist, let alone defend
himself, but the man didn't seem to bear him any malice; he just
shook his head.

The others in the room, besides Liana and her retainers, tensed
at the odd situation, but Darien found enough strength to weakly
wave them back by wagging the tips of his fingers. The man
nodded and gently dropped him to the floor, even supporting him

until Darien could steady himself.

Darien gasped as his energy rapidly came back like he was an empty mug filling up with ale. The others relaxed, but Darien knew the General would have some strong words for him later. It seemed the robed man would not initiate any physicality unless one of them tried to get actively involved. Darien would hate to see what would happen if they tried anything else.

"Godlings above Darien! Geru *just* showed us that we wouldn't be allowed to interfere! Don't do anything like that without warning! We don't even know what we're dealing with yet and you're charging in headfirst without thought! We talked about this!" the General said with such quiet tenacity Darien nearly cowered at the force of his words alone.

The man suspended in air continued his violent and rapid deterioration while they watched in awe. Darien squeezed his eyes shut as the man's face sunk into itself and blood began to seep from under his fingernails to drip to the floor in a slowly widening pool. Bones cracked and the snapping of muscle and sinew made Darien wince as the man slowly and painfully turned into a lifeless bag of meat. Mercifully it wasn't much longer until his arms and legs gave one last spasm before his body went still and heavily slumped to the floor with a sickening squelch.

What remained in place of what was once a living human being was a hollow husk of skin and bone laying in a disjointed heap atop a crimson pool of blood. Darien risked opening his eyes and swallowed the bile rising in his throat as panicked nudges from Koseki assaulted the inside of his mind.

Darien tried to assuage Koseki's concerns while the others in the room stood in shock at what they had witnessed. Except Liana of course. Not even the instant vaporization of a man's insides was important enough to tear her away from the miniscule carvings she had been studying since they arrived.

Darien didn't know what to do or what to expect next. He hoped he never had to witness such a horrific experience ever again and that the same fate wouldn't be in store for him because of his attempted interference. For several moments no one spoke a word and Darien was finally able to get Koseki calm enough that she stopped mentally throwing herself at him. He was worried the impulsive dragon would accidentally hurt herself due to her worry so he made a promise to fully link once he was more sure of their situation. He got the impression his young sister dragon was not happy with this, but he felt her withdraw all the same.

Waiting nervously for whatever would happen next Darien sighed. *I never imagined having a dragon for a sister would be so exhausting.*

Darien and the others turned to General Lockhart for direction and he could tell the man's mind was working furiously on a solution. He also noticed the General no longer gripped the pommel of his sword and instead stood with arms folded much like the robed man had been.

Their collective indecision was solved for them by a lilting voice spoken slowly with a slight drawl.

"No worries, sha. As long as you are sure to be mindin' your manners in Maiani's place you shan't have a worry in the world. Unlike this moppet who thought threatenin' Maiani would be gettin' him somewheres."

The voice itself was odd but not too remarkable, especially after spending so much time with Jack, but the owner of the voice was not at all what Darien expected. Sitting on several cushions piled high atop an ornate marble counter was a child. Or at least she *looked* like a child. She couldn't have been more than three feet tall at best in Darien's estimation. Skin the color of midnight shone under the lights hanging from the ceiling in upside down flower-shaped candelabras. Her hair was coiled elegantly atop her head in a mass of braids and adorned with an exotic flower the soft color of cream. A small nose and mischievous set to her mouth only served to enhance her childlike appearance. She wore robes in the same cut and style as the silent giant, but hers were of a light blue accentuated with numerous white birds and flowers of no species Darien had seen before. The child was idly cooling herself with an ornate hand fan as an attendant appeared to begin removing the 'moppet's' remains.

Was that little kid the one talking just now? He was more than bewildered at everything happening around him at the moment.

The child spoke again as if she could read his mind. "Maiani ain't no small one. This is Maiani's place and Maiani is I," she said.

Darien inwardly cringed. This person was apparently no child. Her demeanor alone made that apparent now that he got a better look at her. But it wasn't just her demeanor that belied her age, it was her eyes. For the first time since his own transformation into a Ryudojin he was staring at another person with eyes as unique as his own. He idly wondered if she had also had her eyesight altered by magic. That was the only explanation he could come up with as he locked eyes with the tiny figure while she finished speaking. Tiny pinpoints of colored light dotted her pupils and flowed in and out of golden irises lightly pulsating with power.

Darien felt ill at ease despite her assurances. He got the impression she was someone whose bad side he definitely did not want to be on. And for some odd reason he was struck by memories of how Corly used to look while berating him for whatever it was she had decided to get angry with him for at the time.

Darien's chest tightened at the memory and the small figure who had named herself Maiani softly laughed. Her laugh mingled with the sudden echo of light tinkling bells that sounded hauntingly similar to the chime they had heard back on the manor grounds.

The General saved him from further scrutiny by striding confidently up to the counter, his hand still noticeably removed from the weapon at his side. This time the silent man made no move to bar his advance and the rest of them relaxed slightly.

The diminutive woman's eyes slid over to the General before quickly assessing him and the rest of the individuals now in the room. Her gaze lingered on Liana for a few moments before settling back on Darien, but when she spoke next her words were for the General.

"Well Philip sha, you seem as if you may be out of sorts. What can Maiani do for you and why is it you all have come to pay Maiani a visit?"

The General pulled up short of the counter and paused a moment, carefully considering his reply.

"I apologize for not clearly understanding your question," the General began slowly. "We had no intention of..."

"Oh?" the one calling herself Maiani interrupted in a loud voice, snapping her fan shut with an ominous click. "No one arrives at Maiani's without reason Philip Lockhart. No one."

Darien swallowed hard at the miniscule woman's strange reaction. *What is she talking about?*

He was positive the General, who hated delays and unforeseen trouble more than anything, would have every reason to follow his initial plan to avoid this Little Maiani's place. And he was even more certain not one of them would willingly cause such a delay.

Except... His eyes rolled over to the crouching Liana, still engrossed in more of the small carvings.

"Oh, don't go accusing me brat," Liana murmured softly.

Marco took a menacing step in his direction with such a look of hatred that Darien involuntarily flinched.

Before Marco could do anything rash the robed man again moved more quickly than one would guess and placed a restraining hand on Marco's chest. Strangely enough Marco didn't seem to suffer the same effects Darien had and tried to swat the large man's hand away in a rage.

"Let go of me you Godlings forsaken desert breeder," Marco snarled.

Marco's words proved even less effective than his attempt to disengage himself. The robed man quickly grabbed him by the front of his tunic and effortlessly threw him to the far side of the foyer with one hand. Marco hit the wall with a resonating thud and slumped unconscious to the ground. It all happened so quickly Darien wasn't sure what had happened at first.

"Maiani would appreciate no violence in Maiani's home," the childlike form of Maiani said lightly, the lights in her eyes flaring in concert with her words.

"Sorry about that," Liana murmured, still engrossed in her own investigation. Darien went wide-eyed not only at the immense strength the man had just exhibited, but at Liana's reaction.

Did Liana just apologize?

Jack whistled softly and the stoic man in robes lifted the corner of his mouth in a small smile before taking his place by the counter.

"Why thank you, sha. Perhaps Maiani should be introducin' you to our current guests in the queue. This man is Ahaan al Aman. He is Maiani's current protector and keeper of Maiani's hall. Say hello Ahaan," Maiani said.

Ahaan simply nodded his head.

"Oh yes. Forgive Ahaan for his lack of speech. He is missin' his tongue due to some bit of misbehavior when first arrivin' here at Maiani's so do try to be patient with him," Maiani added lightly.

The corners of the General's eyes hardened at the implied threat and Darien fidgeted nervously. He sensed the conversation could take a dangerous turn at any moment and fervently prayed it wouldn't come to that.

"Now then sha, why is it you came to pay Maiani a visit?" she asked again.

All eyes turned to the General. For several moments all was still and Darien felt himself holding his breath. After everything he had witnessed he didn't think he was prepared to try to fight his way out of this place. It hadn't gotten the man Maiani had referred to as a 'moppet' very far.

Darien felt his whole body go flush from the tension in the room. It felt like the saturation of magic he had experienced on the manor's grounds was flooding back and filling him to the brim.

But as soon as that first tingle of oversaturation began Darien noticed the slightest relaxing of muscles in the General's stance. Had he not spent so much time around the man he might not have noticed even with his enhanced vision. The sensation passed as the General spoke.

"Forgive my ignorance, but please allow us a moment to confer so we can discuss amongst ourselves what may have brought us here as we simply do not know at this time. We had just been attacked by a creature known as the Broodmother and were trying to leave the country without any more undue notice," the General said carefully.

Maiani snapped her fan open and lazily waved her acquiescence, turning towards Ahaan and conversing quietly with him. That is, Maiani spoke and Ahaan listened, occasionally nodding at her words. Oddly enough, Darien couldn't seem to pick out the words even with his ability to hear most things others would miss. He was at a loss as to what they were going to do next. As far as he could tell they had no way of knowing who exactly had pulled them into Maiani's residence or if Maiani was even telling the truth. She *did* just violently liquefy someone's insides right in front of them. It wasn't like they had much reason to trust her.

General Lockhart gathered them all together away from Maiani and Ahaan and even Liana joined them with a small sigh after the General shot her a pointed glance.

"I don't think I need to tell everyone we have found ourselves in another extraordinary situation," the General began. "We need to find an answer as to why we're here. I would rather avoid any type of confrontation, especially so soon after surviving our encounter with the Broodmother, and doubly so in a place where we have no inclination as to how things operate. It should be obvious after what we've witnessed so far that the normal properties of the world don't apply here so be ready for anything and everything,"

"I do always be ready for fightin', drinkin' or fornicatin', whatever the situation be demandin'," Jack said. The broad smile on his face melted at a withering glance from the General that Darien felt would have caused his heart to stop had it been directed at him.

Jack cleared his throat and the General continued to speak as if he hadn't been interrupted, but Darien's attention was focused on assessing the diminutive form of Little Maiani. His chest constricted tightly again at the memories of Corly constantly bubbling to the surface. Now he understood why he felt so uneasy in Maiani's presence, the murder notwithstanding. Despite the woman's size and lax appearance she exuded an iron will and expectation of having things go her way that forced the memories of Corly into his head. The similarities were unnerving, minus the clothes, skin, and apathy towards wanton violent murder of anyone who displeased her of course. That last thought worried Darien, not so much for himself, but for Koseki. She had been through even more than him the last few days and was physically and emotionally exhausted. She needed to rest and recover, but Darien wasn't sure how he could protect her in a place where he didn't even know what rules applied. The last thing he wanted was to get his sister dragon hurt while he stood by helplessly.

Maiani must have felt his eyes on her, ceasing her conversation with Ahaan and sweeping her gaze across their group until again locking eyes with Darien. He got a sinking feeling in his gut as a slight frown creased the smooth lines of her face.

"Come here sha," Maiani said softly.

Everyone in the group froze at her words and Darien let out a deep sigh. It was obvious to all of them she was talking to him.

"Why is it that you always attract the attention of the most troublesome women?" Geru said quietly.

"How in the Hells should I know?" Darien muttered.

"Be courteous, but be careful Darien. There's still too much we don't understand here," General Lockhart said.

Darien nodded. He squared his shoulders and nervously approached the counter. He could feel everyone's eyes on him as Maiani studied him in silence for a few moments. Darien swallowed hard under her scrutiny and resisted the urge to scratch the fading scrapes and gouges on his arms and chest he had suffered while fighting the Movari. Thankfully they had almost healed completely otherwise he would have been scratching up a storm in his nervousness. He did idly wonder why they hadn't already healed since he had spent the three days after the encounter unconscious, but he dismissed it as unimportant.

I wish I knew more about how I usually heal so quickly; no one in the Order seemed to have an answer for it, Darien thought while he waited on Maiani. Ever since he had met Hosroyu and Koseki any physical ailment he suffered healed much more quickly than the average person and no one seemed to know why. The abilities and characteristics of the Elder dragon race were still relatively unknown to humankind so there hadn't been much to go on. Koseki had never spoken about it and Hosroyu had always remained relatively silent on the matter, seemingly preferring Darien to discover the answers on his own. None of his teachers, even Kuldari, had been able to provide much in the way of guidance, but there had been plenty of theories. Not that theories had ever done him much good. He had simply started calling it 'dragon recovery' and hoped it was just another one of those things that was locked away in his head to be discovered at a later date.

He felt a shift in the air as the sparks of light in Maiani's eyes flashed and swirled in a beautifully dazzling display and Darien again felt that heavy saturation of magic pressing down on him. Maiani slowly spread her fan out even wider and Darien picked up subtle ripples in the air around the folds of the fan as they expanded before she emphatically snapped it shut. Her eyes slowly returned to normal, or as normal as was possible for the owner of this bizarre place.

"I see now, sha," Maiani said.

Darien blinked. *What? She sees* what? He was completely confused.

"Now Maiani knows which of you pulled Maiani's place to you," she said.

Darien was stunned. "What! I swear to the Godlings above that I had nothing to do with that!" He was so shaken he was starting to panic. The last thing he wanted right now was to cause a problem like the moppet before them had done.

Maiani thrust her fan out so that it was mere inches from Darien's face. His breath caught in his throat as the vivid memory of the man who had been there when they arrived flashed through his mind. None of the others moved and Darien wasn't sure whether to be grateful they weren't escalating the situation or to despair over no one coming to his aid. He risked taking a short breath and inhaled a sweet smelling scent from the closed fan that caused him a brief moment of euphoria. The scent wrapped around him and clung to his clothes. It wafted through his nostrils and mouth, settling on his tongue. It perforated every pore of his skin and set his blood tingling as it passed through the very fabric of his being. He could inhale that scent for hours on end and be content. It was intoxicating. It was glorious. It only lasted a few seconds. Maiani abruptly withdrew her fan and the scent and euphoria immediately vanished. Darien gasped. He felt like a loved one had just died and fought back tears welling up in his eyes.

"Not you, sha. The child you carry with you," Maiani said as if that explained everything.

"What? The boy do be pregnant? You do be a rare sort boyo!" Jack hooted.

"Jack, you say another word and I'll cut you into so many pieces you'll be a pile of pink mist by the time I'm done," General Lockhart growled.

Jack snapped his large jaw shut and even had the good grace to bob his head in apology.

"No sha. I speak of the blood of the Elders this one carries. The blood that connects you brought you here through her own fear and worry." Maiani paused for a moment. "It seems she felt the 'nice place' would be much safer for you than wherever it was you were and her mother lent her aid to make it happen," she said.

"Koseki did?" Darien asked.

Maiani unfolded her fan with a delicate snap of her wrist and brought it back up to her face, concealing all but her eyes. "Yes sha."

"That's impossible! She's nowhere near strong enough for something like that and she's exhausted! How could she possibly be the reason we're here?" Darien started shouting. He knew he was panicking, but his feeling Koseki might be in danger from yet another source he was incapable of defending against was enough to break him. Confusion and despair washed over him in equal waves as he sought some sort of answer to Maiani's claims.

"Darien, calm yourself!" the General barked, but Darien didn't hear him. He had to restrain the inclination to reach out to Koseki and complete their link, but he knew from her presence in the back of his mind she was in no state to do any type of melding. She needed rest and there was no telling what could happen in this place or what more Maiani was capable of.

Maiani raised her fan for silence and the General clamped his jaw shut so hard Darien could hear the man's teeth grinding.

"Did you not hear Maiani? Her mother helped greatly in accomplishin' this feat. Do not worry sha; no harm will come to your siblin'. Maiani simply chose a more...tactful way to approach your situation than some other clumsy and impulsive children of the Early Dawn," Maiani said.

Darien's brain slowly began to function again, but what Little Maiani said bewildered him. "Early Dawn?"

"Yes sha."

He had no idea what the woman was talking about, but he was too tired, confused and scared to press for an answer.

Before he could form another cognizant thought Maiani called out to another of their group.

"Come here child of the Early Dawn," she said.

For a few brief moments no one moved. Maiani snapped her fan shut again and the sparks in her eyes flared in annoyance. "Do not force Maiani to ask a second time, sha. It will be *much* less pleasant."

Darien started as Liana calmly took her place next to him with another sigh. His hand unconsciously went to the blade at his hip. Some habits were too ingrained to break.

He glanced sideways at Liana and was surprised to see that her demeanor seemed not to have changed in the slightest. Despite their circumstances she still held herself as elegantly and regal as an empress. Back straight and head held high she met the gaze of Maiani evenly and without fear. Darien *did* briefly pick up on some uneasiness from her, but the sensation vanished so quickly he thought it must have been his imagination. He was also surprised to see she seemed no worse for wear from maintaining that strange golden dome that had protected her and her followers during the Broodmother's attack. He still had no idea what magic she had used or what that golden rope attached to her had been, but those were questions he could save for later. Or for when he wanted her to try to murder him. Again.

"Well sha, have you discovered the true source of your unease yet?" Maiani suddenly asked.

Darien felt Liana slightly tense at the question, but he thought better of taking another appraising glance at the woman since there was no telling what would set her off and make her want to kill him again.

Several tense moments passed before Liana finally framed a reply and Darien got the distinct impression Liana herself was not very happy about the words she spoke.

"I have yet to fully discern exactly what flows through the minds of the Great Elders and I may have been...hasty in my initial approach to the circumstances," Liana said.

Maiani raised an eyebrow at her response and surprisingly a frustrated sound escaped from Liana's lips.

"I should not have immediately made an early assumption and tried to harm the brat, but I will not apologize for my actions. If anything he has become somewhat stronger due to my decisions. Elders know he needs it," Liana added.

Darien avoided the impulse to roll his eyes at Liana's interpretation of 'helping' him.

"Oh? Is this so?" Maiani asked. It took Darien a moment to realize the question had been directed at him.

He wasn't sure how he should answer and was just as sure he needed to answer both carefully and truthfully. The still unconscious form of Marco slumped in the corner served as a stark reminder that he should consider all of his actions with great care.

"I admit there is still much I don't understand," Darien answered slowly. "Ever since my village was taken from me, I feel I have learned a great deal about the world and I am extremely grateful to the people in my life who have helped me despite my inexperience and tendency to make mistakes. As for Liana I don't necessarily agree with her, but it's not uncommon for us to disagree."

Maiani had the decency to laugh lightly at Darien's words, those softly tinkling bells sounding again and tickling his ears and invoking a warm sensation of joy that quickly faded.

"Oh sha, you both are so far from who you were it is clear neither of you even know who you are in this very moment. Maiani may be of some service to you both," Maiani said. "And to your adorable siblin' as well," she added as the lights within her eyes again flared brightly.

Darien wasn't sure he wanted another person of unknown abilities gaining access to Koseki in any way, but they were all seemingly at this woman's mercy at the moment.

"However, nothin' at Maiani's comes for free," Maiani said.

Darien was even more confused. Not only was this woman saying she could help both him and Koseki in some way, but that it would come at a cost. He wasn't sure if having someone's help forced on him and then charged for it was ethical, but he had spent enough time around the General to know when he wasn't being given a choice in the matter.

Darien felt an ominous premonition come over him at the mention of nothing being for free and got a sinking feeling in his stomach that things were about to spiral out of control even further.

Liana remained silent at his side, apparently content to let Darien continue to fumble his way through the conversation.

"Maiani hasn't forgotten about you, sha. You still seek what you once desired although your true goal has now changed. Your confusion stems from your own frustrations at encounterin' new elements of the Early Dawn all at once. Not to mention your own greed is finally beginnin' to catch up to you," Maiani said to Liana.

Liana continued to remain silent, but Darien could tell it was taking quite a bit of effort on her part to remain cordial. Had this been when he first met her Darien was sure Liana would already have exploded in a violent rage at this point. Several more tense moments passed before Liana finally answered.

"Just a short time ago I would have dropped to my knees in blind reverence of you and this place both, but these recent events you speak of have raised many questions within me that I have yet to find adequate answers to. And as to what you call 'greed' I call survival at any cost, but this brat is only a part of one and has no business with the other. Neither do you," Liana said.

Darien was amazed Liana was able to keep any sort of defiance out of her voice despite her words. She made it sound like she was stating facts and wasn't under the scrutiny of someone who was capable of making her insides become her outsides without much effort.

The lights in Maiani's eyes flared even brighter and an oppressive aura of menace briefly filled the room before Maiani again smiled behind her fan.

"Oh sha, you speak so many lies. Not to me, but to yourself. Maiani's place will indeed be very beneficial to you. Whether you believe in those benefits will be up to you. All of you," Maiani said.

Liana frowned at Maiani's words, but chose not to answer.

Darien resisted the urge to step away from Liana in case Maiani decided someone else needed to be liquefied.

"Let us continue this discussion later. There are things that must be discussed with the others in your party before Maiani continues with the rest of those waitin' in the queue. If you follow Janare here, she will show you to a place where you both may rest for a time," Maiani said.

A woman in colorful livery appeared from somewhere behind the dais and gave a stiff curtsy before quickly turning and heading down a dimly lit corridor that Darien was sure hadn't been there a moment before.

"She expects us to follow brat," Liana said. She strode away confidently in Janare's wake without a second glance.

Darien remained rooted to the spot before another small tinkling of laughter from Maiani got his feet moving. Following hesitantly behind Liana Darien's ears were able to pick up a few more of Maiani's words before he was suddenly cut off from the rest of those remaining in the foyer.

"Well Philip sha, you seem to have gotten involved with an intriguin' group, two children of the Early Dawn and even the Shadowbearer walks unerringly by your side," he heard her say.

This was the second time Darien had heard someone use that term. The first had been when they had been interviewed by Speaker of the Wind Anawo before they had been allowed refuge within the Jarabin encampment. When Anawo had spoken the term he had been referring to Geru, but Darien had forgotten about that particular exchange up until now.

However, he didn't have any time to dwell on the matter as Liana pulled up short in front of him so abruptly that he almost walked into her. A doorway had appeared seemingly out of nowhere and Janare had stopped suddenly before entering. Liana frowned at the woman as she stepped into the room, but after inspecting their surroundings for a few minutes seemed satisfied.

Liana sat on the edge of the large and ornate bed dominating the center of the room. "Calm yourself. We were told what to expect on our way here were we not?" she said.

"What do you mean?" Darien asked. He shifted his weight in such a way that he could feel the hidden dagger in his sash, just in case.

Liana again frowned slightly, giving her a pouty look that Darien might have found attractive if it belonged to anyone else.

"Do not presume to play games with me. This Janare person made it explicitly clear about what is expected of us until we are again summoned by that Maiani," Liana said.

Darien was confused. Janare had done nothing more than show them to their room and had remained silent until just before leaving them. She hadn't given them any sort of instructions as far

as he knew, but Liana seemed convinced the woman had said
something important while escorting them here.

Darien considered his words before answering. This is where an
argument would usually start and who knows what that would lead
to where Liana was concerned. He thought back carefully about
anything that may have happened on the way to the room or if he
had missed some sort of obvious sign, but he couldn't recall Janare
speaking or giving any sort of indication about what was expected
of them. But since they were currently in such a strange place
where the normal rules of the physical world didn't seem to apply
he decided to answer as truthfully as he could.

"I don't know what you remember, but as far as I know Janare
didn't speak a single word until just now," Darien said. He
expected Liana to become furious with him and to begin making
threats or accusations, but her response surprised him.

"I see," was all she said. Darien waited for some sort of verbal
barrage to follow, but Liana remained quiet and lost in thought.

Darien still felt on edge being alone in the same room with
Liana, but he thought that maybe Maiani's earlier display would
keep the volatile woman in check. At least as far as one could hope
to keep someone like Liana under control. And Godlings only knew
how long that would last.

"Are you positive you do not recall anything?" Liana suddenly
asked.

Darien nearly jumped out of his skin at the sudden question, but
again answered in the negative.

"No, but what about you? You seem to remember things
differently." He really had no idea what Liana was talking about
and was having a hard time determining exactly what was going on

with the woman. Ever since she had spoken with Hosroyu she had been fluctuating between her previous self to someone trying to find common ground with him and back again. It felt like she was trying to change but trying to keep herself from changing while she did so. It was making things even more stressful than helping if anyone asked him.

Darien waited patiently for her response while trying not to let his own agitation show. He quickly checked his link with Koseki and was relieved at the reassuring nudge he received in return.

Darien was relieved that Koseki still seemed safe enough for the moment. He was sure this Little Maiani knew everything about the situation where Koseki was concerned and she seemed to have indicated the young dragon was doing just fine, but he still felt better verifying her safety himself.

Liana's eyes narrowed, but whether that was due to his question or to his reaching out to Koseki he couldn't be sure. She always seemed to get offended whenever he and Koseki interacted. How she could tell when they did so was still a mystery to him however.

Liana remained silent and Darien tried his best not to fidget under the enigmatic woman's scrutiny.

Liana was slightly confused and more than a little annoyed. The brat seemed to be so clueless about everything around him at all times, but if he truly did not remember what had occurred as that Janare creature had guided them then it might explain the sudden change in his demeanor she had experienced.

When they had first been drawn into this place Liana had been struck by an intoxicating and overwhelming sense of the old magics that were so abundant in her home. The brat had noticed as well, but was so weak that it had nearly overwhelmed him. Typical. She had learned much from her conversation with the Great Elders about the boy and had stunningly been rebuked for her actions for the first time in her centuries of existence. Even now she still could not fully comprehend why this particularly weak and pathetic human creature had become worthy of the Selected, but the young Elder's genuine affection for him had forced her to consider changing her tactics yet again. She figured their current situation would be a perfect opportunity for implementing her new approach to the problem. At least that was what she had thought before their interaction with Janare. Once she had begun to explain what Maiani expected of them the brat's personality had morphed into something unexpected.

Gone was the weak and confused creature she had always known and in its place was a confidant, arrogant, and dangerous being that spoke freely in a rough and brusque manner. His aura energy and magics from her home had resonated more strongly than ever before and he seemed comfortable and in control of such immense power that it was awe-inspiring even for her. When Janare had been giving her instructions he had even gone so far to grope the woman while demanding to be referred to by his title as a 'Ryudojin'. Liana had been surprised by the sudden change, not to mention a little aroused, but had decided not to interfere until he had addressed her in a way that would normally have gotten him immediately killed.

"You. Liana. Be sure to inspect everything is as it should be for ones such as us. I will not tolerate anything less than what is worthy of the Early Dawn. And be sure you are ready to appease me should I require it. It has been a tiresome few days," the brat had demanded. Liana had been stunned at his words and actions, no small feat for a human. Her first thought had been to reach out and destroy this human thing that dared treat her in such a manner, but something about his demeanor caused her to hold back. Before she could make a decision however, the woman named Janare had responded.

"Your lodging is adequate to your station. Be pleased that Amet Maiani has even allowed you to remain here beyond normal circumstances. Those such as your companions are normally expelled quickly and without mercy. Show some gratitude for your fortune and for the Amet's grace," Janare had said.

Before Liana could redirect her steadily increasing wrath onto Janare the boy had reacted even more quickly and violently than she could have anticipated.

Moving with blinding speed the brat had grabbed Janare violently by the throat and lifted her off her feet, slamming her into the nearest wall. He had squeezed her throat so hard her tongue had protruded from her mouth, which he then grabbed with his free hand. At this time Liana had felt an astronomical shift in the atmosphere around them and the brat's aura energy and magics went berserk. So much so that even one such as she stumbled and almost lost consciousness.

"And *you* be pleased and grateful I do not rip your tongue from your head girl. You walk among deities more than on par with your precious Amet. I only do not do so because dealing with the tiny wench afterwards would be more trouble than it is worth to myself and my companion. You *will* show us the deference and respect we are due or I will erase your very existence from the annals of these halls. Do not think we are not well aware of the laws this place operates under. We are more than capable of disposing of trash such as yourself from the very fabric of the universe," he snarled with such ferocity that Liana had actually taken a step back. That was when she had suddenly found herself pulling up short as Janare entered the doorway that had appeared out of nothingness.

Now he stood looking as nervous and vulnerable as ever with no indication of the dangerous being she had seen.

What happened within that space of magic we were escorted through? It seems anything may be possible within this place. I must be even more cautious as to how I proceed with the brat while here. Although it does offer some intriguing possibilities.

Liana studied Darien some more. He was trying to hide the fact there was a dagger within his sash and doing quite a poor job of it. The boy was still as skittish as ever and the sight of him exuding such weakness, especially compared to the massive strength and confidence he had just displayed, threatened to make her nauseous.

She wished to leave him and his cowardice behind and to explore their host's abode some, but Janare had been emphatic that they were to remain in their room until an as yet undetermined time. What this Maiani truly wanted was still a mystery, but her centuries of existence had taught her that sometimes it did pay to be patient, although it was not her preferred approach.

Liana lied back leisurely on the bed and briefly reveled in the exotic scents and tactile feel of the numerous linens and pillows. The mattress had been stuffed with some unknown material, but by its pleasing scent she guessed it had been created from the same natural resources as the rest of their surroundings. At least this Maiani had regard for the origins of the natural world, unlike the

rest of those she had been forced to associate with recently. Her
present company was irritating enough, but she was more than
ready to finish this business and move on to direct her wrath onto
those who had chosen to bargain their way through the Grove some
months prior and who had subsequently come up short on
payment. That would be a moment to relish in and she lightly
licked her lips in anticipation of when that time would come.

She allowed herself a small sigh before popping one eye open to
focus on the brat. He was still clinging to the far wall so hard it was
as if he was trying to sink into the stone. She bit her lower lip as the
events of the last few days played out in her mind. Combined with
some of the other things Janare had said before the brat's
personality had changed she was now sure that he had some sort of
role to play in the future events of this current world.

She supposed it was beneficial that she hadn't killed him yet.
What she now needed to do was ensure his part in the reshaping of
the world she so desperately longed to return to was a positive one.

Her frown upturned into a smile as she thought of how useful
Darien and his connection to the Great Elders could be in the
remaking of the world that had been shattered so long ago. She
begrudgingly admitted he might indeed even have a place in the
reshaped world, but only insofar as the Great Elders allowed.
Should he ever fall out of favor with them then she would be sure to
be the one to end his existence, but for now she needed to begin to
incorporate him into her plans now that she was allowing him to
live.

"Stop cowering like a child," she snapped.

The brat visibly winced at her tone and she resisted the urge to
grimace at such an open display of weakness. She again wondered

exactly what had caused such a drastic change in him back in the corridor, but she chose to dwell on this interesting dichotomy later and to focus on the task at hand instead.

A wave of incomprehensible emotions surged within her and she emphatically stamped them out immediately. That was another problem she would have to address eventually, but for now the brat held greater importance.

"Come here and sit with me awhile. I have a feeling we may be waiting quite some time," she said.

Darien blanched at her words and almost reached for his blade. Liana sighed again. "Have I not kept my end of the bargain with the Great Elders? You should be more trusting of one of your companions," she said. She knew that preying on his sense of companionship was one way of exploiting that particular weakness and she needed to lay the groundwork of trust if she was to use him in the future.

He slowly made his way to the bedside and tentatively sat down. He kept one hand on the small blade at his hip and the other not far from the dagger in his sash, but she had at least gotten him close.

Liana suppressed another wave of strange emotion as she struggled to keep her irritation from rising any further.

Putting on a smile she gently placed one hand over the brat's own and held firm when he tried to pull away. This also kept him from doing something as foolish as drawing his blade in her presence as well as conveying a sense of intimacy between the two.

"Let us get to know one another shall we?" she purred in a silky voice.

Lockhart drummed his fingers against the wooden arm of his chair in irritation. He, along with Jack, Geru and Tartas, had been taken down a strange hallway by some servant of Maiani and left to their own devices. They hadn't been precisely ordered to remain, but based on what he'd seen so far he felt it was strongly implied for them to stay put. It seemed the Godlings themselves were taking a hand to delay him even further. He needed to get into Het Tapas as soon as possible and meet with his contacts waiting there for him. Although he had to admit their current predicament could in fact aid his initial plans of laying a false trail for any pursuers since he was sure Bamaul had someone following them. Stopping at the Order had been necessary after crossing the Jarabin Plains, but he knew Bamaul would eventually figure out they had gone into Pajana instead of heading directly into Het Tapas and would have set someone to watch the place. At this point he wouldn't be surprised to find that even the volatile Lady Liana had been sent by that madman. Being swept up in yet another event outside of his control grated on him and his planned time frame to meet his contact was becoming less and less feasible with each passing moment.

There had been far too many unknown variables that had come into play ever since he had set his sights on Village Breathwynd, starting with not arriving in time to prevent the Bloodsetter attack. That matter still rankled him and always gave him an uneasy feeling. There was no method the Bloodsetters should have been able to employ in order to evade the forces he had chanced entrenching in the Grove that cut off Breathwynd from the rest of Katama.

His mind rapidly sifted through his years of experience and

knowledge to try and discover a logical and conclusive answer, but nothing came to mind. It was a bad habit of his to brood over past events for far too long, at least that's what his father used to tell him. He would also always tell him to try to find the advantage in any situation and he had to admit that despite the ensuing devastation the Bloodsetters had caused the Village he had at least come away with the boy in tow. This had proven to be problematic at times due to the boy's confusion and inexperience, but he also had proven himself quite invaluable as well. He *did* wish both the boy and his young dragon were less impulsive than they had proven themselves to be so far. That's how they had gotten into their current situation if Maiani was to be believed, but also how they had survived the Broodmother's attack so he supposed he had to thank Atera, the Godling of Chance, for at least evening things out a little.

Then there was the boy's relationship to the old man. If he had truly been living in obscurity for so long it would prove to be a boon should they be able to locate him. He had no doubt now the old man was still alive, whether in hiding or in capture. Bamaul would revel in lording over his old nemesis had he indeed been captured, but if they were lucky the old man would have escaped the raid on Breathwynd and having the boy among his men would provide an opportunity to draw him out to join the fight against the tyrant.

The only problem was that if the old man was indeed in hiding, then why hadn't he made himself known? His old teacher was surely capable of finding a means to contact him even after such a long time. Lockhart had to admit it was far more likely the old man was being confined at the Castle of the King and was being subjected to the Godlings knew what at Bamaul's hands.

Why the old man had sat in seclusion for so long was beyond his comprehension, but he was sure it must have something to do with Darien. He must have some strong ties to the lad since as far as Lockhart could tell he had been just a normal boy until he had morphed into a Ryudojin. What those ties were was a mystery to him even after speaking with the boy several times on the subject, but if providence someday came then perhaps he would have his answer.

Jack and Geru were currently inspecting their luxurious lodgings and engaging in their usual banter while Tartas quietly dozed in the corner. He had learned long ago to generally ignore Jack and Geru's behavior in situations like this, but there was a sort of comfortable familiarity about their presence in such an extraordinary place. Despite the overwhelming amount of irritation they often provided he thanked the Godlings those two were still with him. And having the calming presence of Tartas along as well was an unexpected benefit that he would have to thank Kuldari for in the future.

Lockhart knew he could use some of that calm himself, but wishful thinking had never gotten anyone anywhere so he dismissed the thought. What this extraordinary place actually held in store for them was another unknown quantity that was threatening to wear his already waning patience even further. His rhythmic drumming picked up speed and intensity as recent events filtered through his mind. He went over every scenario he could think of to prepare and plan for any outcome of this newest obstacle.

Lockhart closed his eyes to calm himself as a decorative, and obviously very expensive, vase was launched across the room to be deftly caught in midair by Tartas. The man hadn't even opened his eyes.

"Please try to refrain from breaking anything. Godlings only know what kind of backlash that could cause," Lockhart said absently.

Some semblance of an apology was uttered by his second-in-commands, but his mind was already back to assessing their situation. No matter what the future held in store for them, the only option they seemed to have at the moment was to wait on Maiani's pleasure. He disliked not having more options available to him, but it was completely out of his control at the moment so all he could do was plan for any and all eventualities as things progressed.

Then there was the spectacle the boy had unveiled during the Broodmother's attack. Not a lot in this world shocked him, but the boy had a knack for unnatural and heart stopping surprises. He supposed he had to allow some leeway due to the unknown nature of a Ryudojin and the boy's inexperience as such, but those unknowns were vexing to say the least. It was possible he got the knack from the old man as well, which would explain much. Still, Darien was honest and determined, if not overly talented, and Lockhart had noticed a tendency in others to gravitate towards him.

Add in the fact the boy had been separated from them and paired somewhere within Maiani's Halls with the enigmatic Lady Liana caused an uncomfortable feeling to creep up his spine. Godlings only knew what mischief she would cause if left alone unsupervised with the boy. He wanted to believe that even she had been cowed enough by Maiani's demonstration to behave herself, at least as far as Liana could bring herself to behave. The woman

seemed to operate on an obscure set of principles Lockhart had yet
to fully understand. Even after their private discussion that had led
to their agreement, which was tenuous at best, he was still no closer
to discovering just what motivated the woman. He knew that her
ultimate goal, whatever it happened to be, involved Darien in some
way and he wasn't sure if that boded well for the boy's future or
not.

Lockhart paused in his drumming and fought down feelings of
frustration and uneasiness. He maintained his outward composure
despite the troubling circumstances and despite Jack and Geru's
never ceasing raunchy exchange. By this time in their relationship
the banter between the two had come to serve as a soothing effect
when his mind began to cycle through so many problematic
elements at once. Lockhart picked up his drumming again. He
needed to focus on what they could do in the moment and on what
they could control in their current environment so that they could
be prepared for any eventuality. Getting everyone back together
and finding a way out of this Little Maiani's place as soon as
possible was their utmost priority. And he still had no idea what
had happened to Squirrel. Or Wily and his friend, not to mention
Liana's retainers. Once they were able to leave then he could
refocus his efforts on making contact with his agent in Het Tapas.
Keeping a handle on Darien as a Ryudojin and Liana's ulterior
motives would be secondary, but he hoped they were both out of
surprises for now.

The sound of shattering porcelain brought him out of his
reflection and his drumming ceased. The corners of his mouth
twitched downwards in a frown. He reached for the corded rope
hanging from the ceiling to summon a servant to clean up the mess

as Jack and Geru exchanged guilty glances. Tartas opened one eye briefly before deciding to ignore the two and go back to sleep. Lockhart suppressed his irritation.

At least some *things are constant and predictable in this world,* he thought in consternation.

Chapter 9

Darien didn't know how much time had passed since they had been left to their own devices. Janare had not made another appearance since showing them to their room, nor had anyone else come to give them an indication of what to expect. Liana had been acting oddly ever since mentioning 'getting to know each other' and her shift in demeanor was making him skittish. It was becoming more than what his heart could take.

One positive that could be said for their situation was that it was providing some benefit for Koseki. The sense he was getting from her was hard to interpret even for him, but she seemed to be getting the rest the young dragon sorely needed. Darien and his sister dragon had both been pushing themselves and each other past their boundaries physically and emotionally too much lately so any time spent where she could rest and recover without fear was a positive.

He checked on her again for what must have been the hundredth time. The slow and relaxed thrum lightly reverberating across the link assured him she was sleeping and comfortable, wherever she and Hosroyu happened to be. With everything that had happened since leaving the Order he hadn't had much of an opportunity to ask about where the two dragons had relocated to or why they had done so. He supposed it didn't really matter as long as they were safe, but he *was* curious about the barren and rocky terrain where they had settled.

Long and slender arms suddenly encircled his neck and a silky voice tickled the inside of his ears.

"Lost in thought are we?" Liana whispered, biting him lightly on the ear.

Darien yelped in surprise and pulled away from Liana, but she held firm.

A sultry and seductive pout formed along Liana's porcelain features.

"Come now, shouldn't we take this *wonderful* opportunity to strengthen our bonds and become closer to each other? Much closer," Liana cooed.

Godlings no, Darien thought as he eyed Liana warily. He could never keep up with her wild swings in personality and attitude, especially when it came to how she interacted with him. If he didn't know any better he would say she was vying with herself to determine what her true personality actually was.

The Liana before him seemed much different than the one who had left the Order with them such a short time ago. He supposed her interaction with Koseki and Hosroyu had something to do with her changes, but not being privy to what had passed between them he was left to wonder what the scope of that conversation had encompassed. Having lost the ability to directly speak with Hosroyu he was going to have to go through Koseki as an interpreter and only the Godlings knew how accurate or coherent that would be.

Darien shook his head to clear it and a flash of anger crossed Liana's features. Darien's hand went unconsciously to the hilt of the small blade at his hip and he quickly assured Liana he wasn't shaking his head at her.

"Sorry," he mumbled. "I can't figure you out and I can't bring myself to trust you even after speaking with Hosroyu. You *did* spend an inordinate amount of time trying to kill me."

A mock expression of disbelief played out on Liana's face and she lightly placed a hand against her chest in feigned astonishment.

"My, my. What vile accusations you levy against me. Whenever have I done such a horrid thing?"

Darien's eyes narrowed and an uneasy feeling swept over him.

"Nearly every day," he said.

"Oh? Is that so? I believe that was purely nothing more than training was it not? Aren't you so much stronger than before?" Liana said. "Even if you are still so inconceivably weak," she added.

Darien was exasperated. Running away from Liana was all he had done and he was tired of her aggression, her antics, and her condescending attitude. However, she *did* have a point about his gaining in not only strength, but experience as well. Melding was still a process he and Koseki were far from perfecting, but they were getting closer every day thanks to what they had learned at the Order from Kuldari and the others. Darien knew this was an important moment in their development and that he eventually had to face Liana in his own way before they could truly come to an accord. He took a deep, stabilizing breath and slowly exhaled as

Kuldari had taught him. As he did so he envisioned he was releasing all his tension and worry and could feel those emotions slowly melt away. He continued to exhale and a sense of calm enveloped him with each breath. Deciding he would no longer play this game with Liana by her rules any longer he came to a decision. He would no longer worry about what her motivations were and would deal with things where Liana was concerned as he saw fit. Starting now.

He exhaled fiercely through his nostrils in a very dragon-like manner and adjusted the sash at his waist. This was more to keep his hands close to his weapons more than anything, but he doubted Maiani would tolerate him picking a fight. He was sure the diminutive woman had the ability to act upon any one of them at a moment's notice should she desire based on what he had seen of her so far. Squaring his shoulders with more confidence than he felt, Darien faced Liana and forced himself to look her in the eye.

"Fine. You want to get to know each other? Then let's do that. What exactly did you have in mind? And don't think for a second I trust you, but I'll play along," Darien said. He was just glad he was able to get all that out without swallowing the nervous lump in his throat. His heart was thumping so hard he was sure that Liana could hear it and he had to take measured breaths to keep from panicking.

Liana's eyebrow rose in surprise at his change in attitude and for a few moments seemed unsure of what to do, but she shrugged and moved much closer to him than Darien would have preferred. She leaned in so close he could feel the heat emanating from her body and his eyes were inevitably drawn to the slight rise and fall of her chest as she lightly grasped his arm. With her free hand she seductively traced along the back of Darien's head and down the side of his face.

"What did I have in mind? What indeed I wonder?" Liana said. Pressing herself against him Darien tensed as he fought against how alluring the sweet earthy scent of her hot breath was. It reminded him strongly of the Grove and more specifically the type of intoxicating magic he had experienced there. Liana reminding him of that night again made him uneasy, but he held steady despite his sudden attraction to the volatile woman.

Darien wanted nothing more than to pull away from Liana, but that would mean going back on what he had just decided. He knew that he was going to have to deal with Liana and others like her on his own if he really wanted to be able to protect Koseki and the others important to him. Darien steeled himself to see this odd situation through no matter what, but he was uncertain where this sudden unexpected desire for Liana would lead.

Liana moved closer until her lips hovered a microscopic distance from his own. Their eyes locked and Darien's breath caught in his throat as Liana's crystalline green eyes captivated him. His heart started pounding even harder and his throat went dry as all thoughts of pulling away from Liana vanished. His body was screaming for him to react, but he still forced himself not to do anything too reckless, regardless of what the lower half of his body was aching to do. Liana's breath continued to infuse itself into his being and she slowly moved her hand down along his leg, inching closer to places he would rather she not have access to under normal circumstances. She stopped short of her goal and lightly sighed. The two of them continued to stare at each other for what Darien felt like was forever. They were frozen in time, neither willing to close the infinitesimal distance between them.

Darien was outwardly maintaining his composure as best he could, but inwardly was panicking. His hands were so clammy he had to wipe them on his trousers and he didn't know how to keep the rest of his body from reacting to both her proximity and her touch.

What in the Hells is she doing? What in the Hells am I doing? Darien thought in a panic.

Try as he might Darien couldn't help but feel aroused in the heat of the moment. Despite everything that had happened between the two of them he felt an overwhelming desire to complete the connection being offered and take her into his arms and fall into bed together. Fleeting thoughts of Wochisa, the Jarabin princess he had fallen in love with back on the Jarabin Plains, flitted through his mind. Thinking of the dark-skinned beauty, and of the knives she had so expertly wielded, caused him to slowly and agonizingly pull away just a fraction of an inch. Liana quickly moved in anticipation of this and her lips just barely brushed up against his at the same moment Janare reappeared in the doorway.

"Amet Maiani will see the two of you now that she has graciously allowed a few moments of her time," she said coldly before turning on her heel and stalking back into the strange blackness beyond the door.

Darien jumped out of Liana's embrace at the interruption, embarrassed at Janare having been witness to the odd moment. Liana sighed and stretched languidly.

"My, what terrible timing these people have. I wonder just what you would have done had we not been interrupted?"

Before he could answer Liana placed two fingers on her lips and then lightly pressed them upon his own.

"A promise to revisit this again in the future," she whispered seductively. Liana sauntered past him following in Janare's wake and Darien had to again convince himself not to act on how his body was still reacting.

Darien shook his head to clear the fog in his mind from the strange interaction with Liana. He had never felt such an array of emotions from her before and all of them had actually seemed genuine. Trying to calm himself he could feel Koseki snorting while she slumbered. If she wasn't already asleep he would have been positive she was laughing at him again.

"Godlings above, what was that all about? And what exactly was I about to *do*?" he groaned. Thinking about what would happen to him should Wochisa ever discover what had just occurred a chill went up his spine. She had *really* seemed to like that knife she kept hidden away within the folds of her Jarabin garb and she definitely knew how to use it. He took a deep, shuddering breath and tried not to think about the amount of bodily harm he would have to endure should that ever come to pass.

"Well, it's not like she'll ever know about it. And it's not like anything happened. I probably have nothing to worry about," he muttered. Stepping out of the room to follow after Liana he paused. "Probably."

Stepping into the hall, a lurch in his stomach made him sway slightly on his feet. He looked to the left and right and seeing Liana hurried to catch up. She turned at the sound of his footsteps and an emotion he had never seen before etched itself onto her face. Darien was so stunned he stopped in his tracks and his mouth dropped agape in astonishment. It was a look of absolute worship. Pure and unadulterated adoration flooded every aspect of her delicate and porcelain features. The impact of her emotion was so strong he was almost knocked off his feet and it took an incredible amount of self-control to keep the colored mists from springing up all over the place. He could physically feel love, lust, desire and excitement oozing off of her in palpable waves. It was highly unnerving.

"Lord Darien? If we don't hurry the Amet will be unhappy with us. If that's ok with you of course. We can always just kill her if that's what you want to do! I don't really mind and I bet Lady Koseki would think it was fun too!" Liana said in a breathy, but excited voice.

Darien frowned in confusion at her subservient tone and demeanor and slowly approached Liana and Janare, who was impatiently tapping her foot in irritation.

What in the Hells?

It seemed every few minutes Liana's personality was changing wildly in ways he never would have imagined possible. He wasn't sure what she was up to now, but she knew better than to speak of Koseki in such a way, especially after her 'talk' with Hosroyu. Darien also felt irritated at the insinuation of his sister dragon finding amusement in killing someone and that must have shown on his face. Liana blanched and took a step back from him in obvious terror and confusion.

His mind raced with how to respond. It was possible this was just another way for her to mock him, but something seemed off. That was when he noticed Liana was wearing different clothing than just a few minutes ago and was missing her trademark golden ringlet she always wore to keep her light red hair swept back away from her face.

There was no way for her to have changed so quickly and Darien was at a loss as to how to respond to her change in both clothes and demeanor.

He was in such a state of shock the only tact he could think to take was nod as he approached the two women.

"Oh! Is that so? Should we start with this one then?" Liana said eagerly in response to his nod.

Shit. "Ah, no. Let's see what Amet Maiani wants with us first," Darien said.

A look of disappointment flitted across Liana's face, but was quickly masked as if she were afraid he would notice.

Janare quickly turned and again began leading them down the hallway, her sandals making clapping sounds against the peculiar shiny black material coating the floor. Darien was lost in thought as they traveled. He noticed there were no doorways or other exits that he could see and this worried him. It made him feel like they were trapped and were completely at Maiani's mercy.

His silence seemed to worry Liana and she would often take a tentative step towards him to grab onto his hand or arm before stopping herself.

Darien decided the best thing he could do was go along with the moment and see what happened next. He knew the General would expect him to make the right decisions while they were separated and he had to properly assess everything around him in order to do so. He certainly didn't want to repeat any of his past recklessness in a place where anything seemed possible and people were torn asunder for giving offense.

Darien felt like he should be used to abnormal circumstances being outside his control, but it still made him uncomfortable to have no clue what was happening around him the majority of the time.

"Lord Darien?" Liana asked quietly, her voice rife with worry.

He held up a hand to forestall any more questions that he wouldn't know how to answer.

"Let's follow Janare and leave our decision after we speak with Maiani again," he said.

Liana looked perplexed, but again hid her confusion quickly. She took the opportunity to finally grab his arm and let out a contented sigh. Darien was so startled by her gentle display of affection that he instinctively pulled away.

Liana pouted at his reaction, but didn't make a move to get close to him again. She did let out the occasional sigh and her eyes practically never left him as they walked. Her behavior was making his shoulders itch and was bewildering to say the least. Was this what she meant by getting to know each other better? But if so, why so many drastic changes? She had never before shown she knew how to interact with someone without using them or trying to kill them.

Darien supposed it was just another tactic trying to build off what had just happened when they had been summoned. His frown deepened and Liana took a step away from him at the change in expression. *Calm down. Just wait to see what Maiani has to say about all this. Maybe she can explain what's going on with Liana. And hopefully General Lockhart and the others will be there as well so we can work on leaving.*

After a few minutes of walking in silence they emerged into

another room and Darien again felt that peculiar lurch in his stomach at the transition. He wasn't sure what had just happened, but he was certain they hadn't taken any door or deviated from the hall in any way. They were just suddenly in another place. He found the entire experience extremely disorienting.

Little Maiani again sat atop her ornate cushions piled upon her dais with Ahaan standing in silent vigil by her side. Both wore robes similar to earlier, but Maiani had chosen one a pattern of green with white clouds and Ahaan wore ones of purple with lavender slashes dispersed throughout.

Darien's heart sank at no sign of the General or the others and he nearly jumped out of his skin as Liana appeared behind him. How she had gotten behind him was baffling in of itself, but now she was back to wearing the same clothing she had been wearing earlier. Her attitude and demeanor had reverted back to normal and she frowned at his obvious scrutiny, but the smoldering look in her eyes warned him asking about it would bring nothing but trouble.

"Ah children of the Early Dawn, there you are. Allow Maiani to formally welcome you to Maiani's home. Maiani trusts you have many questions, but first it must be asked if you found your lodgins' adequate? It is a pride of Maiani to ensure guests are never left wantin'," Maiani said from behind her ever present fan.

With a sidelong glance at the already fuming Liana Darien assured her everything had been fine.

"Everything was great. It was much more than anything I've ever had before so thank you for that, but can I ask what happened to General Lockhart and the others? We haven't seen them since earlier," Darien ventured.

"No worryin' for you or for your companions so far, sha" Maiani said.

'So far' Sounded a little ominous to Darien, but he tried to ignore the feeling of unease creeping over him.

Maiani smiled from behind her fan and Darien wondered again just who, or what, this Little Maiani actually was.

He supposed he could have asked Liana if she knew anything, but he had been a little distracted. Based on what Liana had said when they first arrived she must have some idea about what Maiani was, but he had been so overwhelmed by the circumstances around their arrival he hadn't thought to ask.

"Now sha, you should be focusin' on the here and now rather than the could have beens, although those are not exactly off the table. However, your abilities are as far from that as can be right now. Perhaps in the future Maiani can be of help with that as well. Or will Maiani be?" Maiani said.

"Uh, ok?" Darien said. He got the distinct impression Maiani was having a lot of fun at his expense. Liana was having none of it however.

"Can you cease the pointless gibberish now? I do not have the time that the bra...boy does to wait any longer on your leisure. I have already waited too long. State your business with us or provide an exit, less I provide one for myself," Liana snapped.

Maiani lowered her fan and all traces of mirth left her while she stared coolly at Liana for several tense seconds; the flaring sparks in her eyes reminding Darien of the starry night sky above Breathwynd that Corly used to force him to look at with her.

To her credit Liana remained uncowed. Maintaining her regal demeanor Liana met Maiani's gaze without flinching or giving an inch.

"Well sha, it seems you have already progressed much in the short time you have spent at Maiani's. At least that is what you want Maiani to think. Why so desperate to leave Maiani's care? Could it be the variations of your young interest that has you so eager to leave? Not so long ago you would have spoken only of 'me', but now you speak of 'us'. Why is this so Maiani wonders?"

Variations? Darien opened his mouth to question what Maiani meant, but was stopped by a worried nudge from Koseki.

'Taya, are you you?' Swirls of light yellow accompanied her words. If Koseki was so worried that she was letting the colored mists leak through then something about their current situation must have triggered her concern now that she was awake.

Why she was asking something so strange confused Darien and he wasn't sure how to respond. An even stronger nudge prompted him after his silence. She was more insistent than usual and was attempting to open the full link in somewhat of a panic. Darien knew he had to respond as he definitely did not want to deal with the overlay, Koseki, Maiani and Liana all at the same time.

'Yeah? Why would I not be me?' Darien asked. He was startled by another swirl of yellow being sent off back through the link to Koseki.

I guess I'm not that in control either.

He was having a difficult time keeping up with Koseki since she had a tendency to become somewhat incoherent and relied heavily on the mists when upset in what Darien had termed 'dragon babble'. He knew learning to communicate with his sister dragon in all sorts of situations would prove worthwhile in the end, but right now she was testing the limits of his current abilities.

Eventually he knew they would be able to work past situations like these as long as they worked tirelessly at improving their bond, at least that was what Kuldari had always said during their training sessions, but Darien couldn't help but feel a little overwhelmed.

Darien got a strong sense of frustration, worry, and annoyance from the young dragon and he braced himself for further onslaught of colors and weight of emotions, but Maiani pointedly interrupted.

"You may connect, child. No harm will come to either of you or to your variations so long as you are behavin' within Maiani's home," Maiani said. She folded her diminutive arms within the confines of her robes with a mischievous smile.

Liana's jaw tightened at being ignored, but thankfully she chose not to make a scene. Godlings only knew what would happen then.

"Are you sure about that? I am not quite ready to trust you or anybody else when it comes to Koseki and her well-being. She's been through more than I can bear recently and I won't do anything that puts her in harm's way," Darien said. He was *not* about to take any chances when he wasn't totally convinced she had fully recovered from her recent ordeals. "Except for your stunt with the Broodmother," Liana angrily commented.

Maiani continued to ignore Liana and smiled at his words. "Your concern for your siblin' is admirable, sha. But in this place she is safer than most anywhere in this world. Maiani's home is tied to your siblin's own in an intimate way. To cause her harm would be a violation of nature itself. But you will have to take Maiani's word for it. Your siblin' grows impatient it seems."

Darien frowned, but Maiani was right; Koseki was getting more and more insistent. Taking a deep breath, and readying himself for the worst, he and Koseki opened up to each other and the overlay sprang up. Thankfully it seemed the small dragon had gotten sufficient rest to recover from the events of the past week. There was no stuttering or any other noticeable problems so he was grateful for at least that much.

Darien blinked while the image of Koseki bounded about in joy and relief at their contact. He felt they had only been at Maiani's a short while, no more than a few hours at best, but he inherently felt the change in time through Koseki.

"Time flows in many ways here at Maiani's. You and all your variations take up quite a bit of energy compared to most so it is no surprise at the time difference you feel. Be not worryin' child. It is the nature of Maiani's home," Maiani said.

Koseki stopped her prancing and lifted her head at Maiani's words. Her tongue protruded from between her not yet sharpened teeth and she used it to 'sniff' the air in a way Darien had come to understand was her way of identifying and processing new smells and experiences. Why she needed to use her tongue for this had initially been a mystery until their training at the Order. He had come to understand it was the dragons' way of storing these sensations within their internal memory so they could be more easily identified later on.

Maiani's eyes flared again as her stern expression softened and she let out one of her tiny laughs like a myriad of tinkling bells that Darien found mesmerizing.

Koseki happily ambled up to Darien and nudged him before approaching Maiani and laying on her belly at the foot of the Amet's dais. Koseki cocked her head up at Maiani in her usual way when questioning a new experience that Darien always found endearing. He was curious why Koseki seemed so interested in

Maiani. Just moments ago she had been in a near panic when connecting and now her focus was entirely on the diminutive woman. He sighed. He supposed he should be used to Koseki's lack of attention span and wild swings in emotion by now, but it still frustrated him at times. Koseki swiveled her head towards him and her tongue lolled to the side in her version of a smile before turning her attention back to Maiani.

"Hello sha. Are you satisfied that your beloved siblin' is just as he has always been in your knowledge?" Maiani asked the young dragon.

Koseki's tongue lolled back and forth before she lowered her head to the ground and closed her eyes to rest.

'Koseki! Don't sleep here!' Darien sent. It was just like her to demand to connect and then do whatever she pleased after she got her way. Darien was exasperated and more than a little nervous about keeping a full link active here, but Koseki seemed disinterested in letting the link go. She opened one eye and focused on Darien; daring him to sever the link without her consent.

'More pretty women,' she said before closing her eye and settling in.

Darien's face went flush. He thought he had gotten past that. *'You're not being fair.'* Koseki just ignored him.

He decided to let the matter go. He could feel the young dragon's tension and unease she had been trying to keep in check ebb away while she dozed. He couldn't believe how resilient the young dragon had become since the night of her birth and he knew he needed to improve his own abilities if he was to make good on his promise to protect her no matter what dangers they faced. Of course, right now that meant both of them not doing any of the reckless and dangerous things that were always getting them in trouble.

Liana moved to sit next to Koseki, but a look of fury came over her and she moved as close as she could to Maiani without Ahaan having to restrain her. He put his hand out just in case and the furious woman stopped a hair's breadth from his outstretched palm. Darien was stunned by Liana's sudden and unexpected display of rage.

Darien idly wondered if the same thing that had happened to him would also happen to Liana; or worse what had happened to Marco. He decided to not get involved and listen to what the seething Liana had to say.

"So what happens now? Was it always a part of your machinations to bring the young Elder here? She is not a thing to be owned and used by others! You should be aware of that just as much as I!" Liana shouted. Liana's usually porcelain features had reddened and clouded over with rage. Darien was shocked to see that Liana was actually quaking in anger as she continued her belligerence.

Darien took a step back at Liana's eruption. He had never heard her really even raise her voice, let alone shout, but now she was apoplectic. Maiani calmly faced the indignant woman, but he wasn't so sure a brawl wasn't about to erupt right then and there. He doubted even the stoic Ahaan would be able to handle the two of them should it come to that. He silently prayed it wouldn't.

"This little 'un was concerned for her beloved siblin' and Maiani had no reason to deny her a place in Maiani's home. After all, a child of the Early Dawn is just as much a part of this place as Maiani herself, even one such as you," Maiani said.

Darien had no clue what Maiani was talking about and her constant riddles were giving him a headache. He went and sat cross-legged in the Jarabin style on the floor next to the dozing Koseki and took a deep breath to calm his thoughts. Darien also wanted to be close to the image of Koseki in case things got out of hand.

"Can you please be a bit more clear about why exactly we're here?" Darien cut into the conversation. He felt de-escalating the situation before Liana tried razing the place to the ground would probably be best.

"Because you are not yet ready to leave child," Maiani answered as if that should have been obvious.

Darien resisted the urge to sigh in frustration. He felt like everything and everyone around him enjoyed toying with him and making things as complicated as possible. It was like trying to unravel one of Kuldari's riddles the man loved to ask.

"Sha, your tension is palpable. Did Maiani not tell you your presence here would prove to be a benefit to us both? You have already encountered several experiences that will prove helpful to attainin' your goals should you choose to understand what it is you have already seen," Maiani said.

What in the Hells does that even mean! he thought in exasperation. Darien was lost. He had no clue what Maiani was talking about, but that hadn't changed since the moment they arrived. Before he could ask another question Liana interrupted again.

"I assume you are referring to the shifts in the corridors that connect the rooms of this place?" Liana asked through gritted teeth.

Maiani's fan suddenly reappeared in her hand and she again hid a smile behind its folds.

"Maiani is not surprised one such as you picked up on the flow of the shifts and the change in variations, sha. You are a singular variation in itself with your particular choices during your most recent migration. Perhaps Maiani should allow you to leave if you truly are not interested in learnin' more about what benefit we here at Maiani's can be to you? Of course Maiani would insist that those from your migration be left behind. It would be only fair wouldn't you say?"

Darien was even more confused. He had never heard Liana speak about a migration or anything of the sort and couldn't begin to guess what it meant.

From the look on Liana's face she wasn't pleased with Maiani's words and Darien worried about what the volatile woman would do. This was the last place he would want to pick a fight, but Liana was never one known for backing down. She did seem to be having difficulty coming to a decision, which mildly surprised him.

For as long as he had known her Liana had always been decisive and unapologetically direct in both her words and her actions, but since she had spoken with Hosroyu she had seemed somewhat unsure of herself. She was still as intimidating as ever, but something had felt off about her over the last few days. And then there was how she had acted when Janare had led them here. He wondered if that was what Maiani was referring to.

"Or perhaps Maiani should be sendin' you back to your room so you may think more upon your circumstances. Or maybe Maiani should be sendin' this other child back with you so you may continue with what you were doin' prior to comin' before Maiani?"

Maiani said with a small, mischievous smile.

Darien's eyes snapped to Liana's face as the fresh memory of the odd moment between the two of them replayed in his mind. He felt the heat rising in his face again and had to take several breaths to get himself under control.

As he continued taking controlled breaths he nervously waited for what Liana would say next.

Liana, for her part, didn't seem interested in discussing the matter. "What I do, where, and with who is my business and mine alone. As to what you said a few moments ago, that is also none of your business, nor does it have any bearing on the brat, the young Elder, or anyone else for that matter. I have said this before. I will not renounce any action I have taken to survive no matter who I stand before. Those involved should be thanking me rather than resisting. *You* should be thanking me for taking them in. Now explain your own actions. I grow tired of your game of riddles."

Darien absently placed a hand on Koseki's head in order to calm his nerves and the young dragon lightly snorted in happiness at his touch. He was positive Liana was going to be the death of him in one way or another. She had absolutely no filter and no fear no matter what situation she found herself in. He had to admit he admired her fearlessness and wished he had the same confidence, but even so her unpredictable nature caused him nothing but anxiety. Ever since he had left Village Breathwynd he had constantly been wracked by doubt and indecision while consistently relying on others to see things through. If he had Liana's ferocious tenacity he wondered what he would be able to accomplish?

There was still just so much he didn't understand. Coming to this place had yet to seem beneficial in any way despite Maiani's assurances, but that was assuming the diminutive woman was even telling the truth. Darien still hadn't decided whether or not the woman could really be trusted and speaking with her like this wasn't making it any easier on him to make a decision.

He tried to sort through everything that had happened since they arrived at Little Maiani's as the conversation between Liana and Maiani slowly began to fade. His breathing began to match the rhythmic rise and fall of Koseki's abdomen with each breath. He found himself absently reflecting on everything that had happened in his life to bring him to this point. Thinking of Oltan and Corly he found the old feeling of homesickness begin to return, but that feeling was replaced by others as he re-lived his experiences in bonding to Koseki, meeting Wochisa, and spending time at the Order of the Fist. He could feel Koseki's consciousness watching these memories with him just as she had done soon after their initial bonding. He felt a sense of renewal wash over him and Koseki lightly nudged him with her snout at his memories of all those he missed and all those that had helped him along the way. He smiled and was about to open his eyes when a discordant note struck both him and Koseki like a concussive blow. He gasped as the memories rewound in an explosive flash and he began to relive them a second, then a third, then a fourth time.

Darien was suddenly experiencing memories in which he never met the General and the others that night in the Grove and had only met Hosroyu instead; using his knowledge gleaned from ancient documents stored in Oltan's library to force a bond with the weakened dragon's unborn child and violently ripping Koseki's body from her mother's womb. His stomach churned while he watched violent and remorseless versions of Koseki and himself wreak havoc throughout Katama, leaving nothing but blood, destruction and ashes in their wake. He witnessed his first meeting with Liana and utterly crushing her to the point where she begged for her life and swore everlasting fealty to him. He turned red at the passionate nights he and Liana shared afterwards and wished he could look away, but his consciousness was glued to every intricate detail as they played out before his mind's eye.

He and Koseki, flanked by Liana, Wochisa, and others unrecognizable to him razed Katama to the ground in a display of brutality that obscured the reason why he had started his journey in the first place. His heart sank at the sight of meeting Bamaul and wiping out the Bloodsetters at his command. Instead of exacting revenge on the tyrant king of his country Darien spared the man, deeming the destruction of his home village to now be inconsequential. At first Darien was sickened by the events unfolding before his eyes, but as the chaotic chain of images flashed through his mind he found himself agreeing more and more with his actions. He was more than justified. All had been taken from him so he would take all in return. There was no one who could stand in their path and nearly none spared in their wake. The world was his and he would burn it to the ground if he damn well pleased!

He reveled in the charnel accompanying them wherever they went, their strength and power expanding exponentially. Smoke filled his nostrils and the tang of blood coated his tongue as his physical body shook in resonance with this newfound feeling of power, rage and bloodlust. His blood was pulsing so hard in his veins they expanded and grew tight against his skin. Rushing air filled his ears and the iron taste of blood increased tenfold as myriad colors of mists associated with death and destruction coalesced around him. His breathing became ragged and shallow and his eyes snapped open wildly and rolled in his head. Darien mentally reached through the mists to embrace this violent entity unbound and unchained by petty emotions such as concern and compassion. He reached out and his fingertips fleetingly brushed up against what he sought to obtain. A spark ignited at his touch and he clenched his hand to claim it. What he desired was within his grasp. Not just Bamaul, but all of Katama would fall before him. He would destroy it all and rebuild it in his own image. He would be all and all would belong to him. All he had to do was take it.

In a trance Darien slowly clenched his fist to grab hold of this newfound power until a violent and panicked mental shove rocked him to his core. For an agonizing moment Darien was suspended between two realities and was unsure of which was real and which was imagined. His mind felt like it had split in half and the only thing real was the throbbing and agonizing pain in his shoulder. It took more than a few moments for his mind to process this last fact.

Why does my shoulder hurt so much? Through the fog of memories and visions the slow realization he was in pain sunk in. Quite a bit of pain. Quite a *lot* of pain. Slowly, agonizingly, these new memories faded and he opened his eyes to his own reality. Looking down he found the source of the pain. It took his brain a few moments to process the absurdity of his current situation. A dragon claw had pierced his shoulder and Koseki was in a panic as she clawed at him with one of her free legs and butted at him with the crown of her head. Darien had left his hand on his young sister dragon during the terrifying experience and had gripped her crown with such rage and strength that she was crying out in pain. A sea of colored mists swirled around them both. Emotions of indescribable depth and color cascaded around and through them and his mind slowly began to comprehend what Koseki had done.

In her desperation she had pierced him clean through the shoulder with one of her razor sharp claws. He could feel the blood soaking into his tunic and he let out a primal scream when his mind finally registered the full sensation. Through the fog of excruciating pain he could feel Koseki's own pain, worry, panic, and guilt at what she was doing. Taking a deep breath, he released his grip on her crown and instead held her gently in place to keep her from assaulting him any further. A tough task for someone with a dragon claw stuck in his shoulder.

'Taya! Taya!' she kept crying hysterically as crystal tears formed at the corners of her eyes to fall and shatter on the brightly lacquered floor.

With slow and measured breaths Darien tried to cope with the pain and calm Koseki. Both were proving to be problematic.

Thankfully Ahaan came to his side and gently gripped Koseki's foreleg before quickly pulling it free from his shoulder. A wave of dizziness came over him but he focused on the worried face of Koseki to keep himself conscious. Janare appeared at his side and ripped open his tunic to apply pressure to the wound and began to bind it with a peculiar bundle of thick cloth. He thanked the Godlings above for the ability to heal quickly, but the pain was still nearly unbearable and he had to fight to keep from falling unconscious.

Once Janare had finished her ministrations Darien agonizingly reached out with his good arm and gathered the still sobbing dragon into his chest. Or at least as much of her as he could gather. Breathing in short, gasping breaths and holding firmly to Koseki Darien tried to reclaim a hold on his own sanity; terrified of what he had seen, of what he had almost become, of what he still may one day be.

That's when he noticed a strange golden glow surrounding Koseki while unintelligible words flowed from Liana much as they had when she had spoken with Hosroyu. The glow softly pulsed as the thin miasma coating the young dragon from crown to tail slowly faded as Liana ceased her chanting at Darien's recovery.

Panting heavily, Liana's face was fury incarnate.

"Just what...in your Hells...are you *doing*?" she spit out, each word coated with rage and venom.

Darien didn't need to read any of Liana's aura to know she was angry, and lethally so, but his first concern was Koseki, who was still considerably upset.

'*You were scary. And mad. You were very bad. Not Taya,*' Koseki sent between intermittent sobs.

'*I don't know who that was, but I'm back now. I promise,*' Darien sent.

'*Promise?*' Koseki asked in a warbling voice that threatened to break Darien's heart.

Despite the throbbing in his shoulder Darien weakly smiled at his sister dragon and nodded. Koseki looked up at him like she was unsure, but ultimately took him at his word. She lightly nudged his injured shoulder with a small, apologetic grunt.

'*Sorry Taya,*' she said.

'*No, I'm the one who should be sorry. I don't know what happened, but you saved me. Thank you for looking out for me.*'

Gently gripping her head in his hands he lightly placed the tip of his tongue on her forehead in a Dragon's Kiss before cradling her head into his lap.

Darien's mind was reeling. Not just by Koseki's appearance, but also by the nearly overwhelming kaleidoscope of emotion barging in on his consciousness. Apparently the effects of their bond as Ryudojin were amplified by being in such close proximity to each other. Or it could be just another effect of Little Maiani's. Darien didn't have the energy or mental faculty to decide which.

The mists were a sea of emotions. Nearly palpable colors of all sorts clung to the both of them like ethereal garments and his eyes unfocused at their number and scope. Koseki for her part was having little trouble once she calmed down. He had no idea how the little dragon could be so resilient, but he supposed he had Liana to thank for protecting her during, well, whatever it was that had just happened.

"I should incinerate you where you sit! Do you have any inclination of how much danger you just put the young Elder in? Perhaps I was right about taking your life and returning the magics you stole to their rightful place! There is no excuse for placing yourselves in such a position! What in your Hells were you thinking?" Liana seethed.

Uh-oh. Darien wasn't sure what Liana was going to do next, but he was sure it probably wouldn't bode well for his health.

Before she could act any more impulsively Koseki slowly unfolded herself from Darien's arms and tentatively walked over to Liana before rearing up on her back legs and extending her neck to place the tip of her tongue upon Liana's forehead in greeting. Instantly the volatile woman dropped to one knee and a look of awe spread over her face.

I thought she said she was past that sort of thing, Darien thought.
Koseki gingerly walked back to his side before entwining herself
around him and resting her head upon his non-injured shoulder.
He was effectively pinned in place, but he didn't think he had much
of a right to complain.

Darien gasped for breath and tried to maneuver himself into a
more comfortable position with the young dragon's bulk weighing
heavily on him.

He looked askance at the dragon wrapped around him and tried
to concentrate on the real and concrete experiences that had shaped
them since the night he left Breathwynd. His mind continued to
revert back to normal and he assured Koseki that he was fine to
ease her worry.

Catching his breath and waiting for the pain in his shoulder to
dull Darien took a moment to look at Koseki as she lightly trembled
against him. He was amazed at how much the young dragon had
grown and how her scales were beginning to harden and develop
the magnificent colors of midnight like her mother.

That was when the realization finally hit him. He should have
known it right away when she had nudged him earlier. Or when
she had pierced his shoulder. He was holding Koseki. Not making
contact through the link like when they melded, but physically
holding her.

The colored mists continued to swirl as Koseki nuzzled against
him to reassure herself the Darien she knew was back and he
couldn't help but let out a shuddering breath at what he had almost
done.

Maiani's melodic laugh again filled the room.

"Well child, Maiani did not expect such a desperate act. But it was you who truly desired to be by your siblin's side so earnestly was it not? Although it seems things didn't quite go as you expected did they?" Maiani said.

It took a few moments for Darien to realize she was addressing Koseki. Koseki slightly raised her head and bobbed it in Maiani's direction before settling back in. Darien picked up on Koseki's feeling of embarrassment at being chastised, but he pretended not to notice.

"You are here now of your own volition child, so allow us to welcome you to Maiani's. Perhaps it was the triplet Godlin's of fate that brought you here in your beloved siblin's time of need. Or maybe you came to bridge the gap between these two children? Maiani does not believe your siblin's quest will be fruitful should they not quickly do so. It may be they are both too stubborn to realize this themselves without your presence. Especially this one here," Maiani said with a slight nod at Liana.

Liana took a deep shuddering breath and regained her feet. All traces of fury were gone, but she looked drained and somewhat unsteady. Darien never expected to see Liana in such a vulnerable state and found it just as unnerving as when she had requested to speak to Koseki and Hosroyu.

Gritting her teeth Liana took another menacing step in Maiani's direction which caused Ahaan to quickly reassert himself as a buffer between the two. She stopped short, but her eyes screamed murder in stark contrast to the weak and vulnerable look she had worn moments before.

Marveling at Liana's uncanny ability to change emotions so rapidly he slowly acclimated himself to the numerous swirls of mist filling the room. She normally presented such a controlled demeanor that to see her rapidly exhibit so many different emotions was a shock to his senses. He was sure there was something unique about Liana's aura energy although he was in no condition to even think about trying to read her. However, as he looked at her through the mists enveloping them he was able to momentarily see a light and nearly invisible aura layered over Liana much like Koseki's surroundings would be overlaid when they completed their link. Shaking his head and blinking a few times the odd imagery vanished. He wasn't sure if his mind was playing tricks on him due to the shock of the last few minutes, but he figured it was something he probably shouldn't ask about.

Koseki was studying Liana very closely and Darien was amazed at her apparent lack of trepidation at being so close to the woman, not to mention her greeting Liana with a Dragon's Kiss a few moments ago. Just a short while back Koseki had been absolutely terrified of the woman and had relied heavily on her mother for comfort, but now she seemed comfortable in Liana's presence. He would even say Koseki was enthralled.

That was until the odd fluctuation of energy laying over Liana ceased and she returned to normal. Darien was struck by an emotion of sadness and worry from Koseki when the fluctuation dissipated. He was surprised to find Koseki felt sympathy for Liana and he wasn't sure how to react to that. Darien supposed he should be used to how dynamic and spontaneous Koseki was both physically and emotionally by now, but her showing concern for someone like Liana was unexpected.

Darien reached up and placed a hand gently on Koseki's ridged brow. She tensed and he winced at her reaction, but she didn't shy away. He wasn't sure if the contact was to reassure himself or Koseki, but after a moment she trembled happily at his touch.

Liana took several moments to stare a hole through Ahaan before turning her attention to Darien and Koseki. Sweat beaded on her forehead and she took a deep breath, pausing a moment to readjust her ever present golden ringlet.

"Well brat, now what are your intentions? The young Elder was brought to such a place for what reason? Do you even have any understanding of how vulnerable the young Elder is here? How vulnerable we all are?" she snapped.

Darien took a deep breath himself before replying. The mists had faded somewhat and he was finally able to concentrate. Even now Liana had the habit of assuming he was at fault for everything when it came to Koseki. Although she may have a point this time considering what had just happened.

"I'm pretty sure Maiani mentioned this was Koseki's idea. Even I had no warning she was going to do this. I don't even know *how* she was able to do something like this, much less why. For all I know she just did it on the spur of the moment," he said.

Koseki snorted in indignation, but she seemed too content with their contact now that the danger had passed to take offense at his comment.

He resisted the urge to rap her on the head and instead directed his next remark at Maiani. "Liana does bring up some valid points. How exactly is this possible and could Koseki have suffered any adverse effects? Was she able to do this on her own or did you have a part in it? I don't like Koseki being exposed to anything dangerous that could cause her harm," he said.

"Like when you stole her appearance at the Order?" Liana

interrupted again.

Darien scowled at her, but Maiani answered before he could reply.

"Is this because you are too powerless to defend against such things?" Maiani asked. The diminutive woman lazily waved her fan to cool herself, but her eyes never left Darien's face.

Darien bit back a heated reply. He wanted to say her words weren't true. He wanted to refute what Liana had said. He wanted to say he and Koseki had worked extremely hard to achieve the results they had and that he could shield her from any threat. No words were forthcoming because he realized coming here had proven once again just how many unknowns there were in the world and how unprepared he was despite all he had learned. He now realized why Kuldari had wanted him to stay longer at the Order of the Fist.

Maiani pointed her fan at him for emphasis. "Did Maiani not say comin' here would prove a benefit should you allow it to be? Did Maiani not say anythin' was possible in this place? It seems the younger siblin' understands the workin's of this place much more so than the elder. Maiani finds this curious," she said.

And I find it curious how you constantly refer to yourself in the third person, he thought. Darien continued to pat Koseki on her head in order to concentrate. He could feel Koseki's joy and had to admit for the first time since leaving Village Breathwynd he felt a sense of completeness. Now if only they weren't trapped in some sort of mystical house of fun and horror he might feel somewhat at ease.

He tried to speak to Koseki through their completed link, which was curiously still active despite the two of them being physically together, to try to discover what the young dragon had been thinking by initiating this chaotic chain of events. He doubted he would get a coherent response, but he figured he should at least try.

He let out an explosive breath as Koseki's body tightened around him when he asked her about her motives.

"Ok, ok! I'm sorry!" he gasped. Loosening her grip with an offended snort Koseki quickly went back to dozing. Apparently his sister dragon didn't like being questioned. A brief image of Corly flashed through his head again and he took a few deep breaths before being able to breathe normally. If Koseki started taking on the characteristics of his deceased friend then he was in for a lot of trouble.

Regaining his breath he lightly rapped Koseki on the head. *'Don't do that. You could have crushed me. You're really strong,'* he sent. He knew massaging Koseki's ego was usually the best way to get her to both focus and cooperate and it was no different in this case.

Koseki opened one eye to stare balefully at Darien, but the sense of satisfaction and pride emanating from the link told Darien all he needed to know. Despite the lingering pain he wanted to laugh at Koseki's reaction. He could tell she wanted to be irritated with him for his reasoning behind the compliment, but she enjoyed being praised too much to have it matter.

Maiani's laugh lilted throughout the room. "Well sha, it seems there are no issues with your relationship with one female in your life. Now if you could maintain such calm relations with the others then mayhaps you would have far less worries," Maiani said. "Although some may prove more intractable than others," she added, pointedly glancing at Liana.

Darien didn't respond and felt his face go flush again. It wasn't his fault that most of the women he encountered ended up causing some sort of problem was it?

Koseki laughed at him in their link so the others wouldn't hear and he could feel the rumble of her mirth run through her elongated neck. *'At least you* tried *to hide it,'* he sent.

Koseki pretended not to hear him, but her tongue lolled out of her mouth and she nuzzled contentedly at him. He sighed. There was no way he could stay mad at her. She always knew exactly how to get him to forget his irritation when she did what he called 'Koseki things'.

He turned his attention back to the matter at hand. "Anyway, shouldn't we be given a little bit of direction here? If you're waiting for us to figure out what it is you expect then I'm afraid you're going to be waiting a while," Darien said.

"Is that so?" Maiani responded, continuing to lazily fan herself.

To Darien's eyes the folds of Maiani's fan were weaving through the mists of color still swirling haphazardly around the room. The mists were less intense than their initial onslaught, but the sight was still a lot to take in. They caught at the edges of the fan like fine sand for an instant before slipping away and Darien was struck by the odd memory of Mistress Wavely mixing batter at the sight. The sad memory aside, he was starting to find it difficult to focus on the conversation. Having a dragon wrapped exuberantly around you while colored mists of emotion swirled and filled the air tended to have that effect.

Trying to glean any helpful information out of the woman was proving to be an exercise in futility. His own irritation at their current situation aside, he was more than amazed at the restraint shown by Liana despite her outbursts. Had she been the same Liana from when they had first met it was more likely she would have already gone on a rampage and killed everybody in the place or gotten all of them killed.

Still, there was no question now this place did hold some answers pertaining to his bond with Koseki so he knew he needed to remain patient despite his frustration.

Another low rumble from Koseki indicated she shared his sentiment. Maybe his sister dragon was more aware of the nuances of their bond than he thought. Maiani *did* say Koseki had been the one to initiate their coming here.

However, Darien also knew Koseki was prone to both distraction and whims without thought of consequence so it fell to him to bear the responsibility of deciding if this place was truly as safe and beneficial for them as Maiani had indicated.

Maiani coolly eyed him while she continued fanning. Liana's face was a mask of barely controlled outrage and Darien got the sense so much had happened so quickly and so far out of their control that she probably didn't even know what she was outraged about, Koseki's presence aside. He supposed it didn't really matter considering Ahaan's ability to keep order, but he did consider himself lucky she hadn't completely lashed out yet.

Almost in concert with his thoughts Liana spoke.

"I have had more than enough of this charade," she hissed angrily.

Darien sighed heavily. He needed to stay calm and find another reason to intervene before Liana decided the best way to deal with her anger was to take it out on him like she usually did.

He closed his eyes to think, his breathing continuing to match the rhythmic rise and fall of Koseki's belly. *Think!* He tried to analyze each detail of their visit so far up to this point from the moment they arrived. His memories of the meadow outside were hazy and disjointed from when he was affected by that oversaturation of magic, but he forced himself to remember every detail he could.

"At least one of you is attemptin' an effort," Maiani murmured.

Liana looked about to explode at the comment, but noticeably relaxed when Koseki opened her eyes and lolled her tongue out in the same manner she used with Darien in the volatile woman's direction.

Darien fought down a surge of jealousy at the interaction, but chose to ignore it while he searched for an answer as to what Maiani expected from them.

He vaguely remembered the small creatures scattered about the meadow and how they had resonated with the magic and energy of Maiani's mansion. Then there was the curious change earlier in Liana's dress and demeanor. There was also Maiani's display of power from when the previous visitor had found himself pulled inside out after becoming agitated and violent. A display that had horrified Darien, but he forced himself to analyze even that.

Slowly, agonizingly, he began to weave together the invisible threads of information that had been shown to them. He didn't understand the why or the how, but he was certain this place was connected to that strange pocket of nothingness he found himself floating in after their fight with the Broodmother. Both places had the same feel to them, an intangible quality he couldn't describe but inherently knew to be true. And in contrast to the nothingness of that space Maiani's might be the opposite. He had already seen one alternate possibility so who knew how many more there might be? What he had experienced a few minutes ago was the final piece of the puzzle he needed to make a realization.

He opened one eye and glanced at Maiani to see if he could get any reaction to his line of thought. At this point he assumed she could read his mind, or at least have some way to tell exactly what he was thinking.

Even from where he sat he could still see the lights in Maiani's eyes flare up through the haze of fading colors filling the room.

"Almost child of Early Dawn, but not quite the truth you seek," Maiani said.

Darien closed his eye again and fought off another surge of frustration. Try as he might, he couldn't come up with any other conclusion despite wracking his brain. He could feel his caretaker Oltan shaking his head in disappointment as Darien came up empty again and again just like he sometimes would back home when he failed to grasp the meaning of a particular lesson. Thinking of Oltan, he furiously concentrated even as far back as his time spent studying back in Village Breathwynd despite the depressing memories, but not even the massive amount of information he had digested over the years held even a hint about Little Maiani's. Maybe if he had more time, or more information, or more of a clue in general then he might be able to form a cohesive answer. He sighed and opened his eyes.

"Ah sha, you disappoint me, but yet you were so close," Maiani said.

Maiani snapped her fan shut and Darien found he and Koseki lifted into the air by an unseen force. Not bothering to resist, or even be surprised, Darien and his sister dragon floated in mid-air until they were 'sitting' in front of the dais at eye level with Maiani.

"Allow Maiani to somewhat walk you through things, sha. Then perhaps you will gain greater understandin' of what you have chosen to involve yourself in my young Ryudojin," Maiani said.

Darien wasn't sure he understood what Maiani was talking about, but he didn't have time to think as he was again brought within a strange vision encompassing yet another form of magic he had never experienced before. The energy and magic infusing Little Maiani's began to fluctuate and undulate around them, giving an odd bend to the air. The colored mists brightened before fading and mixing with these strange undulations warping the air. Thankfully neither he nor Koseki seemed to be suffering any negative effects from the sudden change, but the sensation still made him uncomfortable.

"Be at ease, sha. No harm will come to you or your beloved siblin'. Pay close attention to what Maiani has to show you and mayhaps you will gain more of an understandin'," Maiani said.

Darien was having a difficult time adjusting his eyes to what he was looking at as the warping in the air coalesced into something more tangible. Usually his vision went beyond that of a normal human thanks to his bond as a Ryudojin, but in this instance it was like looking through clear jelly. He was able to make out some movement, but all he could see was a rapidly moving black mass within the strange vision and with no coherence. He concentrated as hard as he could, straining his eyesight to the limit, and began to acclimate himself to the change in atmosphere. Slowly, details began to take shape from the formless mass.

'Use more than just your eyes child. As a Ryudojin you have the ability to see that which others cannot. Especially in a place such as

Maiani's,' Maiani's voice sounded in his head.

He should have been startled when Maiani's voice sounded in his head, but by this point he had decided to just roll with whatever absurdity came next within Maiani's walls.

Darien frowned and focused on the scene slowly emerging from the chaos. He was surprised the normally skittish young dragon draped around him was not only composed, but was taking a keen interest in events. It seemed Koseki had also made strides during their time at the Order and he felt a sense of pride at her growth.

Koseki aside, his mind and eyes did not want to comprehend the chaos unfolding in front of him, but he tried his best to pick out anything recognizable among the million tiny strings of rapid movements. He also strained his hearing to its limits to try and pick up any intelligible sound from the loud buzz assaulting their ears.

With considerable concentration and effort, he was eventually able to understand a little about what he was looking at as shapes and images slowly separated from the writhing mass. It was a mash up of people overlaid one over another over and over again in an infinite pattern. Slowly and painstakingly deconstructing the mass he was able to pick out a scene. Then another. And another. He continued until he understood how to separate each piece of the mass from the rest. Darien had to use all of his concentration to hold a stable vision apart from the others and perspiration beaded on his brow from the effort. Koseki also seemed to be having the same sort of struggle. Darien mentally pushed comfort and support in her direction and immediately the scene taking shape disintegrated back into the maelstrom of energy. He gritted his teeth in frustration.

'*Try once more, sha,*' Maiani's voice came.

Darien felt exhausted to the core of his being and knew that he couldn't spend this kind of energy much longer without suffering ill effects. Nor could Koseki, if the tiring feeling coming from the young dragon was any indication, but he pressed on to find answers and see what these versions of himself and his friends were doing within the vision.

It took some time to separate an individual scene from the rest a second time, but what awaited their efforts was a terrifying vision.

He could inherently tell, whether by chance, luck or fate that the version of himself he was witnessing was the same as the one from earlier that had nearly consumed him. Thankfully he seemed to be immune to the negative effects he had experienced earlier, probably thanks to Maiani's doing. Looking down at the alternate version of himself, Koseki, Liana and the others he could only describe the scene as an absolute bloodbath within Little Maiani's halls.

Liana's retainers, along with Ahaan, Janare and others he didn't recognize had been hewn to bloody pieces and strewn about. The floors and walls were slick with blood and gore that covered everything. Chunks of mutilated meat stuck to the ceiling, occasionally falling to the floor to land with a sickening plop. His heart tightened at the damage Koseki had sustained all over her body. Everywhere he looked he and his companions were locked in battle with various denizens of Little Maiani's and he was baffled as to how such a tragedy could happen. He watched in silent horror as he, Koseki and Liana finished their respective engagements and advanced in unison on Maiani herself, who still sat calmly on her dais much as she was in Darien's own reality. As the three of them drew closer to Maiani the scene melted away and

Koseki quailed in fear, finally losing her grip.

'*Calm, sha. For every swing of the pendulum of fate it must swing back the other way. Try again and seek other than what your worries have guided you to as so far,*' Maiani's voice sounded in a calm, but strained tone.

Darien felt his eyes and limbs grow heavy with exertion and Koseki was unwilling to even try, but an influx of energy that could only have come from Maiani boosted the young dragon's spirit and Darien began to seek out a scene less horrific than the one they had just witnessed.

Their persistence was rewarded as a new and more peaceful scene slowly coalesced out of the madness. In this scenario he lay comfortably in the same room he had shared with Liana while Koseki contently rested coiled up in the corner atop a mountain of cushions. He blushed at the sight of not only Liana, but Wochisa both resting comfortably in their own way. Unlike the first scene Darien felt a sense of peace and calm emanating from the people like there were no troubles or worries in their world.

The group was calmly and idly discussing something and the current sense of urgency and worry he felt was non-existent. An unknown person lay on the side facing away from view. He paid little attention to the figure at first, assuming it was just a person he hadn't met in his own travels. That immediately changed when Oltan limped into the room. The unknown person jumped up and flew into the old man's arms with an exclamation of joy. Darien's mouth fell open and his mind refused to acknowledge the tiny figure of Corly as she happily guided Oltan to an ornate chair. Tears welled up in his eyes at the sight of his long dead friend happily engaging with those who had become an important part of his life since he left Village Breathwynd, other than Liana of course. How she could have survived in this version of events he couldn't begin to guess, but the fact she existed somewhere lightened his heart, if only a little. The scene suddenly melted away as the emotional shock of seeing Corly proved to cause too much strain on his concentration.

Darien felt Maiani sever whatever connection she had provided and blinked while his eyes adjusted to the light. They settled back to the floor with a gentle thud. Koseki still had her neck coiled around him and seemed no worse for wear, although he did get the sense she was extremely tired.

"What *was* that? I can't believe there are so many possibilities about everything that's happened to me," Darien said in awe.

Maiani sighed lightly. "Ah sha, you were so close to an understandin'. Now Maiani knows why this Oltan was always so frustrated with your lack of progress in certain matters. What you bore witness to was not possibilities, but *actualities*. They are not what *could* occur, but what are occurrin' even in this very moment," Maiani said.

Darien was stunned. "How is that even possible?"

"Did you seriously not discover this? It was obvious from the shifting imagery adorning the foyer," Liana snapped. "Young Elder, just *why* is this brat amongst the Selected? Surely there must have been much better options than he," she almost pleaded.

The exhausted Koseki only snorted, but Darien was suspicious she was laughing at him. In fact he *knew* she was laughing at him.

'*Shut up,*' he told her via the link. She snorted again.

He decided to ignore Liana, who had completely reverted back to her old self at this point, and instead tried to understand what

Maiani was showing him and why.

"Several variances just occurred, if that fact helps you any. Do you truly still not understand sha?" Maiani said with a small smile.

Darien thought some before answering with a question of his own.

"You've mentioned these 'variations' a few times now. Just what are these variations you've been speaking of?" he asked.

"Are you an absolute idiot?" Liana spat in exasperation.

He continued to ignore Liana and the snorting Koseki.

"Ah sha, perhaps there is some hope for you yet," Maiani said.

"So you say," Darien said. He waited for further explanation while Maiani continued to fan herself. Janare appeared out of nowhere with a cool drink for the Amet. Darien noticed the green liquid was in a crystalline glass; an expensive luxury few could afford. He also noticed nothing was brought for the rest of them.

Maiani took a long sip from her refreshment and looked down at Darien. She lifted the glass in her left hand and asked him the single strangest question he had ever heard.

"Is the glass in my left or my right?"

Darien raised a skeptical eyebrow, but decided he should probably answer truthfully.

"Your left."

"Correct. However, you would also have been correct if you had said the right," Maiani said. The glass vanished from her left hand and appeared in her right.

"What?" Darien blurted. His first thought was that she must have used sleight of hand like the trickster visiting Village Breathwynd some years back with Hulgar's traveling troupe, but Maiani quickly disabused him of this notion.

"Of course you also would have been correct if you had chosen to say both," Maiani said as another glass materialized in her free hand.

Darien was stunned. Even Koseki perked up and began to pay attention.

The drink in her left vanished and she took another long sip of the light green liquid from the glass in her right.

Darien was confused. There didn't seem to be any way she could have been hiding them in her robes, but then where did they come from? He wished Oltan was there, then maybe he'd have a chance of understanding what exactly Maiani was trying to show him.

He felt like he was in the middle of one of the old man's lessons that he didn't quite understand. Oltan had always been patient with him and would always find a way to get Darien to think on the lesson at hand in order to come to a conclusion. Right now he felt in desperate need of Oltan's guidance while he wracked his brain trying to come up with an answer to the riddle. Old and familiar frustrations began to creep up on him and he had to force those feelings aside and concentrate.

He could feel a keen sense of anticipation from Koseki as she waited for her human brother to figure it out.

'You could be trying to figure it out yourself you know,' he sent.

She merely bumped her head against his in a gesture that meant 'hurry up', but he was at a complete loss.

"That's too bad, sha. Maiani had hoped you would have been able to decipher this particular lesson on your own. Perhaps Maiani has put just a touch too much faith in your abilities," Maiani said as the remaining glass also vanished.

"Typical," Liana muttered.

Darien took a deep breath and closed his eyes. He tried to ignore the irritable women surrounding him. So much had happened in such a short amount of time he felt like he couldn't keep up. What Maiani was trying to show him was tugging at the corners of his mind, but he couldn't quite grasp the truth of the concept she was showing him. Even more importantly *why* was she trying to teach him anything at all? She had mentioned earlier there was a mutual benefit to them being drawn to this place, but so far all he had encountered was confusion and riddles. Liana did seem to have an idea about the nature of the place, but she wasn't someone who was usually forthcoming with much information. And he was clueless as to how to read the strange images and symbols back in the foyer that Liana claimed formed words. He had never encountered such a thing even in all his years of studying back home.

He was sure Oltan would have known something about it, he always did, but right now he was lost. Koseki butted him again, but more gently this time. He laid his cheek to rest on the crown of her head while he concentrated and felt a sense of calm at the contact. What was it about the magic of this place that could help both he and Koseki in their bond as Ryudojin? How was what Maiani was showing him connected?

So far he had seen a man violently and mercilessly twisted inside out, wild changes in Liana's attitude and personality, and disturbing visions of a distorted and ruthless version of himself. Hardly what one would call a cohesive pattern, but his instincts told him otherwise.

All those years in the library studying and learning under Oltan had ingrained in him a sense of where a lesson lay, even if he didn't always understand the meaning of that lesson at first. This situation fit right in with all those other times, albeit on a much larger and more terrifying scale. Maiani would not be so persistent and patient with him if there wasn't some truth to her words about these actualities. And he knew he was just being stubborn, but he refused to ask Liana for help. Not that she would be willing to do so anyway.

He replayed everything he had seen in his head and felt Koseki's tired consciousness watch along with him. Apparently she was interested enough in his own memories, but had lost interest in the outcomes Maiani had shown them. He needed to get her back to their room so she could rest. This was tiring her out much more than he, but he pressed on and forced himself to review as much as he could remember.

He couldn't help but return time and again to his original thoughts while he unraveled the nature of Little Maiani's. If what he had seen was what would have been the result of different choices and experiences then what was the point of the demonstration with the glass? It was almost as if...

Darien's eyes snapped open at the realization and he stared open-mouthed in astonishment at the Amet.

"Ah sha, it appears you may have uncovered some semblance of an answer," Maiani said with a small smile.

"About time," Liana said. Crossing her arms in irritation she turned away from him.

There was only one other explanation Darien could think of. The more he thought about it the more sense it made. It would explain the chaotic black mass he had had to sort out and what Maiani had meant by 'variations'.

"Do you mean to tell me all of these things aren't just happening on their own, but are actually happening all at once?" he asked. Maiani's smile widened. Even Ahaan grinned.

"In one form or another child. There are not only an infinite number of possibilities in this world, but realities that both exist out of and within your own. Here at Maiani's it is possible for those with ability to peer into each of their realms and see what becomes of you," Maiani said.

Darien's eyes narrowed in suspicion.

"Is it possible for you to manipulate them as well? Is that how you were able to do the thing with the glass?" he asked.

"No, sha. Such a power to manipulate the realities of others is beyond the power of Maiani," she said.

Maiani's wording confirmed Darien's suspicions.

"But you *can* manipulate your own can't you?"

"In a way, yes," she answered with a small smile.

"So that means when you said actualities these things really are occurring all at the same time?" He wasn't really asking questions, but was rather thinking out loud as his mind raced to keep up with the implications of this revelation.

Were there other beings who could manipulate their own realities like Maiani? And just how far did those abilities go? Based on her answers and her demonstration with the glass she could only affect her own realities, but what if there were others who could do more? Was Maiani herself capable of more and just not telling them? She *had* turned a full grown man into a pile of goo pretty quickly.

Darien shuddered at the thought. Anyone with that kind of power would be akin to a Godling. Maybe even on par with the

Fallen Great Gods. He silently prayed that no such being existed in this world. If there was, he was sure there would be no way to stop such a creature unless someone like Maiani decided to get directly involved. Darien felt that wouldn't be very likely unless she and her own were directly threatened based on what he had seen of her so far. It was entirely possible Maiani's abilities and influence were limited in other ways as well. If they weren't then she could easily have found a way to rule over the entire world if she had chosen to do so.

"You think in such simple terms child, but be not wary. Maiani has her place and this place has Maiani. What others choose has no bearin' here," Maiani said, interrupting his thoughts.

Darien was beginning to suspect Maiani enjoyed speaking in a way that left unsaid her words had more than one meaning, but he supposed someone constantly swimming in a stream of her own realities might have a good reason to do so.

"Maiani was beginnin' to become concerned you weren't going to grasp what your irritable companion was able to discover so easily, but now you have listened to Maiani and Maiani says learnin' from this revelation will be of great benefit in the future against foe and friend alike."

"I'm not sure I understand what you mean," Darien said as Koseki elicited a very human-like yawn. He got the impression she had lost interest in the topic for the moment and he resisted the urge to sigh.

"You will in time, child. Know that our promised transaction has been completed and you may return to your room. Maiani needs to finish discussions with the others in your party. Some are provin' to be less tractable than others and Maiani may have to evict some forcibly should they persist."

Darien blinked. "Do you mean to say you've been speaking to the others at the same time you've been speaking to us?" he asked.

Maiani smiled and the lights in her eyes brightly sparkled. "Janare, please return them to their room. And perhaps this other one can resolve her own internal turmoil before they depart."

Liana scowled at the diminutive woman, but chose not to respond. A choice Darien was forever grateful to the Godlings above for.

Janare guided them back to their room without incident and without any of the abnormalities Little Maiani's enjoyed throwing at them. Darien decided not to dwell on it and was just thankful for the brief respite. He *did* want to know how the others were faring and he worried over which one of them was the 'less tractable' one Maiani had mentioned.

Chapter 10

Lockhart stood stoically before Little Maiani and tried not to let his annoyance show. She had done the intelligent and strategic thing by dividing their forces and separating the one who was always a catalyst for these events from his sight. It was a standard practice that gave her a monumental advantage so he wasn't going to begrudge her for it, especially since he would have done the same, but it irked him nonetheless. He disliked being in such a disadvantageous position and effectively held hostage in such an unpredictable situation. His face betrayed none of these thoughts while he engaged in a silent stand-off with the diminutive woman. She seemed to be in no hurry despite having been the one to summon them. Lockhart wanted this finished without any further delay before the boy, or the Lady Liana, ended up getting them all into a greater predicament.

Despite Tartas and Jack's knowledge of the place, they knew nothing more than the rumors they mentioned earlier and the lack of information was hindering his decision making. He resisted the

urge to grip the pommel of his sword. The Godlings only knew
what this Maiani would consider a threat and he had no intention
of engaging in a place where the very rules of common sense and
predictability were non-existent. If this were Two-in-the-Hole, a
game of cards popular among taverns throughout Katama, they
would be facing a stacked deck from the dealer with little chance of
success.

So he decided the best course of action would be to wait out
Maiani despite the time constraints he constantly felt pressing on
him. He had ordered Jack, Tartas and Geru to remain silent unless
spoken to directly by Little Maiani or himself. So far they had
obeyed without incident. So far. He narrowed his eyes as he
analyzed the woman sitting on the dais without giving away the fact
he was doing so. She appeared much as she had earlier, but this
time she was slightly unfocused, almost distant. If he didn't know
any better he would say her mind was somewhere else entirely and
that she wasn't yet aware of their presence. He doubted such a
thing was possible, but he refused to discount anything in this
place; he had seen too much already to do otherwise. All he could
do was wait and see what was next in store for them and respond
appropriately.

Suddenly Maiani's eyes changed. A subtle shift he would have
missed had he not been scrutinizing her so closely. Her eyes
suddenly gained a sheen to them as if only now becoming aware of
them and she finally addressed the four men.

"Step forward Shadowbearer," she said without preamble.

Lockhart's jaw tightened. That was something he had not
expected. The number of people who should know of that name
could be counted on one hand and still have a finger or two left

over. And they had already met one back on the Jarabin plains. This was now the second time she had mentioned the term and that made him nervous. Just how much did this woman know?

Geru glanced at the General and stepped forward at a slight nod. Geru noticed the telltale tightening of the General's jaw that was one of the few very signs he ever exhibited of irritation. This was proving to be even more of a delicate situation than any of them had expected.

"First of all Maiani will say right out that Maiani cannot relieve you of your chosen penance. However, Maiani can briefly relieve you of some of your sufferin' for a short while should you choose," Maiani said.

Geru wasn't expecting such a direct approach to something only a handful of people in the world knew about. He hadn't told Darien yet and not even Squirrel and Wily knew, although he was sure Squirrel had his suspicions. He would rather avoid the subject all together, but he doubted that would be an option considering their circumstances.

He bowed his head and thought carefully before answering. "I believe in accepting the consequences of my choices and I will not ask anything of you, but should you choose to follow through with what you just said then know I would be grateful. However, I also cannot afford to be put in a position where I might become a liability to my friends. If your aid means becoming a slave to a set of conditions or trade then I will decline," Geru said. As tempting as her offer was he wasn't naive enough to believe she would do as she said for free.

"A very noble response. Worry not sha, for Maiani has already completed her desired transaction from another of your party.

Ease your mind and close your eyes for a moment," Maiani said.

Geru glanced again at the General and for once got no inkling as to what his leader was thinking. This meant this decision was his to make alone and that he was expected to make the correct choice. He supposed he should have expected as much. It had been years since he or the General had last broached the subject, aside from that one incident with the Bloodsetters a while back, and he had always been left to make his own decisions when it came to that particular matter. Still, this was an extraordinary set of circumstances and he knew any misstep could cost them dearly.

Moving closer to the podium he took a deep breath and closed his eyes. Like earlier he could hear a light tinkling of bells as Maiani softly laughed.

"Be at ease sha, this will take but a moment in time," Maiani said in a quiet tone.

Geru already couldn't hear her words. He felt weightless as his body rose from the floor and a soft white glow enveloped him. A pleasant and warm sensation suffused his body and a feeling of contentment welled up within him. Memories of a time long past came unbidden to his mind and he smiled at some of the faces he saw within the vision. Especially one.

"Ameila," he whispered softly. Tears formed at the corners of his eyes as the glow intensified around him. Geru let out an explosive sigh as emotions he usually kept in check ran rampant, but not in an unpleasant way. But the pleasing sensation lasted only a few more moments before being suddenly and violently shattered by liquid fire coursing through his veins and burning the very air from his lungs. He tried to gasp for breath and found he could no longer breathe. He tried to move his arms and legs and found them paralyzed. Geru tried to scream in agony and found he had no voice. His throat was raw and felt like it had been sliced with a thousand blades. The more he tried to scream the greater the pain intensified. His entire being was being incinerated from within and he felt like his skin was blistering and cracking from the pressure. Sweat and tears began to pour down his face and he couldn't even blink away the sting.

He tried not to panic, but he could feel his body giving out and was sure he was finally and mercifully about to die. Geru let out an explosive silent scream as the intensity of his agony increased thousand fold and he prepared to meet his end. Oddly, a feeling of relief mixed in with the unbearable pain and his tears continued to run unabated down his cheeks. *At least I got to see you again.*

And just as soon as he felt his turbulent existence would finally be extinguished an audible crack reverberated loudly throughout the room. Geru's eyes rolled back in his head as he slumped to the floor and landed in the arms of Jack, who had appeared just in time to keep his oversized frame from slamming to the ground. Light wisps of smoke wafted off his skin and trailed off to disappear among the frescoes coating the ceiling above. Jack checked Geru's vitals and nodded at the General. "He do just be nappin'," he said with the scent of lightly singed flesh hanging in the air.

"Tartas me friend, can you be givin' me a hand with this gigantic beastie?" Tartas nodded and helped him ease Geru to the floor off to the side.

"Does he always snore like this?" Tartas asked in his soft voice.

"Of course! Geru do be capable of wakin' the Fallen Great Gods themselves with his nasal cavities alone!" Jack hooted.

Lockhart shot Jack a look that would have withered stone. Both men instantly went quiet and with guilty faces took up places to either side of the snoring Geru.

Lockhart didn't know what had just happened, but it appeared Geru would be asleep for a while. He only hoped the others would get through this without something so dramatic occurring.

"Let Maiani again assure you those others for whom you show concern are well and have their own interviews with Maiani nearin' completion. There is one however, who is provin' to be quite problematic and should that one continue with this variation then Maiani will be takin' appropriate action," Maiani said.

Lockhart's mind raced. Who could be so foolish to cause such a problem in this place? The boy might be naive, but he should be smart enough to understand their situation. That could change if he felt Koseki was in some kind of danger, but Lockhart felt instinctively that wasn't the case. Liana or one of the De'Segua siblings? Maybe, but Maiani had said 'he' which left all but Marco as candidates. And *he* had learned a very painful lesson about crossing this woman. By process of elimination that left Squirrel, Wily and that Gelas fellow.

Squirrel more than likely was not comfortable with the decisive lack of information available to act on his own. Lockhart resisted the urge to clench his jaw even tighter. That left Wily and Gelas. He knew nothing of Gelas other than that Wily had vouched for the man. There *was* something vaguely familiar about him and it rankled Lockhart that he couldn't quite discover why. As far as Wily was concerned the man had always been somewhat rash and had been separated from the rest of them for an extended period of time. Lockhart had not had much time to assess Wily's state of mind with all the issues the boy and Liana had presented since leaving the Order.

That was his own mistake. He took pride in knowing everything there was to know about the men and women under his command. Dealing with all the boy's unknowns as a Ryudojin had seemingly clouded his ability to do so. Lockhart had no one to blame but himself. He had been far too focused on the one instead of the whole recently. Lockhart only hoped Wily would have enough sense to not cause a disturbance that would get all of them killed before they could find a way to depart Little Maiani's in peace. The man should be aware of this already, but emotions were a fickle thing. He was stuck in his current situation and in no position to either aid or chastise the man. Having no leverage in these discussions annoyed him, but he would do everything in his power to ensure they all survived. Lockhart silently prayed to whatever Godling above might be listening that both Wily and Gelas wouldn't do anything to turn the denizens of Little Maiani's into their enemies.

His prayers went ignored as a discordant gong echoed loudly in the chamber and Maiani's eyes went distant again while her face clouded over with rage. It may have been a trick of the lighting, but Lockhart was positive the woman flickered briefly. She raised one arm and violently brought it down in a chopping motion aimed in their direction. She made a sound Lockhart couldn't decipher, but the power in that word struck all of them like a physical blow. The world twisted around them and Lockhart's stomach lurched sickeningly.

He closed his eyes to steady himself and took several calming breaths. Once his gut stopped churning he took another deep breath. When he next opened his eyes he was in complete and utter darkness.

Now what?

Bamaul was giddy. Not everything had gone exactly to plan, but his beacon and the fool accompanying it were making good progress. The failure of the Broodmother had enraged him at first, and many had paid for that failure with their lives, but things had turned around. After what the boy had pulled off in that particular battle Bamaul wanted him for himself even more. And with the weakened state the boy must be in the timing for his next strike couldn't be better.

Regam, his ever present Chief Bloodsetter, stood attentively by his side awaiting his liege's next command. He had many more interesting obstacles to throw in front of Philip Lockhart and the boy with the dragon eyes, but the next trap he had laid for them at the border of Het Tapas and Pajana was absolutely awe-inspiring. His emotions began to stir and the bells in his mind slowly began to ring. The giddiness passed as soon as it had arrived and he had to adjust his mentality to calm the bells before they became a tempest devouring his mind.

"Regam," he said evenly.

"Yes, your Majesty?"

"I take it everything is ready for when our friends make it to the border towns of Het Tapas. I'd hate for them to arrive only to feel un-welcomed," Bamaul said. He resisted the nearly uncontrollable urge to stroke the bracelet that had fused to his wrist over the last few years.

"Yes, your Majesty. All is as it should be. Those in place have been counseled...appropriately as to how to proceed. They have been made more than aware of the consequences should they fail to act in accordance with your wishes," Regam said.

Bamaul could see Regam's eyes gleam with excitement. The man could be exceptionally one dimensional at times, but his loyalty and fervor could never be questioned.

"Good. Now then-" Bamaul stopped suddenly and his eyes narrowed in suspicion. He licked his lips and brushed his fingertips across the filament of silver embedded in his onyx bracelet. The bells went from a mild ringing to an eruption of sound and fury so quickly he had to bite his tongue to keep from going mad at the onslaught. His vision blurred and he gripped the arms of his throne in order to remain upright.

"My Lord?" Regam ventured.

Had it been any other man Bamaul would have massacred him on the spot for such insolence, but Regam was allowed more leeway than others for a reason.

Bamaul tried to contain his rage and fury. The beacon had suddenly and inexplicably vanished.

"Find them! Find them immediately! What have you done this time Philip? How dare you continue to defy your King, Master and God! I want them found. I want them found right away! I don't care how many lives you have to use, find them!" he screamed.

Bamaul was teetering on the verge of unintelligible ranting as the madness of the bells threatened to swallow him whole. The only thing keeping him grounded to reality was the burning iron taste of blood in his mouth. He spat a gob of the stuff onto the floor and heaved himself to his feet. Wobbling slightly as his head swam an overwhelming urge to kill radiated within him so deeply he shivered in ecstasy. Bamaul needed to vent this offensive frustration on someone, anyone.

"Regam!" Bamaul said, his voice cracking under the strain of the symphony of clanging bells in his mind. "Throw him," he said, pointing to the nearest guard kneeling in reverence along the near wall.

"Very well," Regam replied, the wrinkles at the corners of his eyes hinting at the cold smile under his Makavai coverings.

Bamaul stalked from the throne room, letting the screams of the jumper soothe his nerves. He paused just long enough to take a deep breath and revel in the satisfying squelching thud echoing up from the courtyard below. The bells receded somewhat and he was able to focus his eyesight. His rage slowly subsided while his vision cleared and his mind eventually began to function rationally.

Neither his beacon nor the wretch would betray him, he was more than sure of that, so what had occurred? Philip Lockhart wouldn't have it in him to kill them even in the unlikely event he was able to discover the identity of their true master. He also doubted the boy would have the ability to overturn the elements Bamaul had instilled in the beacon in the first place. That unknown woman however, she bothered him quite a bit. She was unpredictable and his lack of knowledge about her origins infuriated him, but the boy also had shown himself to be unpredictable at times as he had shown with the Broodmother. The loss of such a strong weapon was...disconcerting to say the least. Many had died as a result of his anger that day. Maybe it was time to again visit his dear old friend Oltan. The old fool *surely* must know something more about the boy and his friends that he hadn't yet told. And tell it he would.

"If he values his life he will tell us all he knows," Bamaul

growled to no one in particular. With his destination decided
Bamaul made his way through the castle halls with purposeful
strides.

It wasn't long before Regam caught up to him. The man had an
uncanny knack for reading his lord's moods. Bamaul expected no
less from his most trusted subordinate. While he walked Bamaul
forced himself to maintain the precipitous balance between his
inner rage and anger while maintaining an outward calm. It was a
balance easily broken by the slightest provocation and he had to be
careful lest he lose control and the bells consume him.

Before long he found himself standing in front of the great
locked door guarding the place where his 'special' guest was held.
Regam initiated the complicated process of releasing the locks and
wards and Bamaul restlessly tapped his heel on the stone floor in
irritation.

"What is taking you?" he growled.

"The locking mechanism fluctuated briefly. It shouldn't be
much longer than a moment or two before..." Regam said just as
an intense blast of energy erupted from the door and hurled Regam
backward into a startled Bamaul. Both men landed with a decisive
thud several feet from where they had stood and now a smoking
crater of wood, metal and other valuable materials that had gone
into the door's construction marked where it had stood. Despite
being dazed by the blast and the collision Bamaul could just make
out sparks of energy leaping from one point to another and swirling
throughout the corridor with wild abandon before fading away.
The knowledge that valuable materials and magic had just been
destroyed and released into the world almost drove him to complete
madness, but his anger at the absurdity of what had just happened

barely kept him in check. The air felt heavy and as he inhaled, a strange metallic tang coated his tongue.

He sputtered in outrage and heaved the unconscious Regam off him with disgust. Bamaul quickly regained his feet, ready to massacre whatever or whoever was responsible for this affront. Oddly the bells within his mind were unusually silent when they normally would be going berserk, but he wasn't focused on that; he only had one thing on his mind. The old fool had chosen a poor time to attempt an escape and would soon be subjected to the most brutal, painful and agonizing retribution. He had to remind himself to try not to kill the decrepit old fool once he emerged; he was still a valuable piece to Bamaul's ascension. But Bamaul did have some *very* proficient men and women at his disposal that specialized in inflicting pain and torture without incurring loss of life. He would enjoy introducing his old friend to them all in an intimate setting.

Aware of the constitution of his most important guest, Bamaul simply waited. He had no blade on him, not that he needed one, but he was more than confident he could handle things as they were. Even unarmed he was more than a match for the weakened, malnourished old man and even if Oltan had some sort of trick up his sleeve that allowed him to destroy the door he must have nothing left in reserve. On top of that, Bamaul knew that rushing into a darkened room where an enemy lay in wait was the height of foolishness; and he was never a fool.

He absently kicked Regam in the ribs a few times and his chief Bloodsetter's eyes flitted open. Regam quickly regained his feet and gave his master a nod of apology before drawing his sword.

Regam cautiously advanced on wobbly steps to the door's

shattered remains when an unexpected figure suddenly burst forth
with a loud cry and carrying the beaten and broken Oltan on his
back.

Even Bamaul took a step back in shock before he could recover
from the sight of Philip Lockhart suddenly appearing within the
bowels of his domain.

Regam aimed a somewhat sluggish blow to Philip's head and
was parried surprisingly quickly for someone carrying a decrepit
old man on the cusp of entering the Next Realm.

Instead of engaging them as Bamaul had expected Philip simply
ran towards the stairs like a man possessed and with the purpose of
someone who knew where he was going. It took only a moment for
Bamaul's initial surprise to wear off and he bellowed in rage at the
sudden realization his most prized possession might be getting
away. The bells began to ring in earnest and he gripped his
bracelet so hard he could feel it burning into his skin. The veins in
his forehead pulsated with each bell resonating within his mind.
His blood burned hotter and hotter and his breathing became more
ragged. Bamaul knew losing this much control could end with him
killing a valuable piece to his plan, but his rage was leaving all
rational thought behind. Regam had already begun pursuit and a
raging Bamaul followed closely on the Bloodsetter's heels while
trying to maintain a shred of sanity.

The bells were ringing so furiously his vision again blurred and
everything around him took on a darkened and saturated hue.
Various shades of color swirled, shifted and swam before his eyes.
He wanted nothing more than to unleash the untold power he had
accumulated over the years with the bracelet he had sacrificed so
much for, but that small sliver of sanity desperately reminding him

to cling to his final goal kept him from doing so.

He could vaguely hear Regam giving orders in a loud and commanding voice free of strain or excitement. Taking command when the bells were consuming his master was one of Regam's most important duties and why Bamaul almost always kept the man close at hand.

The castle staff and soldiers were in complete disarray while Philip continued his mad dash through the halls, only stopping long enough to defend against the few soldiers competent enough to act upon Regam's orders. The man never even broke stride.

"Kill that motherless atrocity!" Bamaul bellowed as the chase continued. One soldier misinterpreted this order and took an awkward swing at the old man on Philip's back, narrowly missing severing Oltan's head from his shoulders. Philip never even looked back, but instead increased his speed. Bamaul passed by the confused soldier and cracked the incompetent fool in the side of the head with one meaty hand. He made sure to use just enough strength to crack his skull without killing him. That would come later.

He somewhat heard Regam give the calm order to hold the man for throwing. Such a coherent order was beyond Bamaul at the moment.

The chaotic game of cat and mouse continued out into the open air of the courtyard where a small company of soldiers had managed to gather in formation to cut off Philip's escape. Philip seemed to hesitate momentarily before veering off in another direction at a whisper in his ear from Oltan. The startled squad of useless fools turned to give chase, but were getting in one another's way and were causing confusion amongst themselves. Bamaul was seething in incomparable anger and could feel his tenuous grasp on reality slipping.

To make matters worse just as the squad seemed to get its act together they were assaulted by three unknown men who Bamaul had never seen but inherently knew very well. They were three of Philip's surviving companions, but the boy was not among them. Bamaul gritted his teeth and the familiar taste of blood filled his mouth.

Philip yelled something at the three men over his shoulder as he continued to get further and further away from his pursuers, but Bamaul was too enraged to comprehend the words.

The three men crashed into the soldiers' ranks with the practiced skill of men used to fighting alongside each other. The same should have been said about the soldiers in question, but mock battles hardly had the same ebb and flow of an actual battle where fear of death and the stench of blood and offal permeated the field, and these fools had never done more than drill sporadically and serve as a token force. The Bloodsetters under his command were his true soldiers, save for a few others, and the difference in experience and ability couldn't be more obvious. If only the majority of his Bloodsetters weren't away from the castle at the moment purifying the country then it might have been a fiercer battle, but things were decidedly one-sided as the three men cut a swath through his soldiers.

Regam moved to join the combat and engage the three new invaders.

"No you fool! Follow Philip at all costs! These replaceable pawns do not matter in the slightest. Retrieving the old man and taking Philip Lockhart's head is all I require!" Bamaul screamed.

Regam didn't respond, but merely nodded and silently veered back onto his original course in pursuit of Philip Lockhart and the old man.

In his current state, the only thing keeping Bamaul's mind from completely shattering under the strain of the raucous sounds of the bells was his singular focus on retrieving the old man and throttling Philip Lockhart with his bare hands.

Just the thought of peering into those ice cold blue eyes while all life left them was enough to make Bamaul giggle with maddening glee. Suddenly, mixing within his insane giggling and the tempest of bells, the hints of a whisper appeared, caressing the outer reaches of his mind. A whisper he had never heard before and one that threatened to swallow all of him whole, bells and all. It teased and tantalized with promises of mysteries and power unimaginable. Had Bamaul been in control of his faculties he may have been able to grasp a sliver of meaning to what the whisper foretold, but his mind was far too gone at the moment.

He felt his grip unwillingly intensify on his bracelet and the whisper turned to mocking laughter barely heard above the thrashing torrent of sound assailing his mind.

His breath still heavily laboring, Bamaul used all of his considerable will to stay sane. He could no longer speak, let alone give orders, but Regam understood his current state and was acting accordingly; he always did.

The colors and shapes around Bamaul took on an even darker hue and the edge of his vision darkened. His fingers twitched in anticipation at the glorious image of Philip Lockhart's death replaying over and over again in his mind.

He followed closely on the heels of Regam more on feel and

instinct rather than anything else and the feeling of finally
cornering one of his most hated adversaries was almost as arousing
as it was satisfying. With that thought, the whisper returned with
words of quiet promise creeping into every corner of his soul while
the bells continued to clang ever more furiously.

Bamaul and Regam kept pace with their prey through all the
twists and turns Philip took throughout his mad dash and easily
avoided the obstacles he knocked into their path. Eventually Philip
made his way back into the castle proper instead of trying to escape
into the outlying areas and that was where he finally made a
mistake. A glorious, fatal mistake.

In his panic Philip had ascended a rarely used staircase leading
to a corner of the castle that hadn't been utilized in years. Bamaul
was vaguely aware of some sort of storage room at the top of the
winding stairs, but there was nothing of use left there and more
importantly, nowhere to escape to.

Bamaul's eyes gleamed in delighted madness and a bloody grin
split his face as Regam bounded up the stairs after them. It
wouldn't be long now before this futile game of chase came to an
end. Perhaps with Philip's death the bells would grant him some
respite from their assault. The whisper in his mind gently caressed
him in concert with his wish and he almost lost consciousness at the
touch.

Only his years of training and sacrifice kept him upright and
mobile. He had a moment of confusion, but managed to get a hold
of that tiny bit of sanity in time before the bells took everything
from him. Bamaul barely felt the stone steps underneath his feet as
he pounded his way upwards after Regam. Philip may be able to
stay them for a time should he turn and fight from higher ground,

but with carrying Oltan as a handicap he would soon tire and their numbers would overwhelm him.

The body of a soldier suddenly came clattering and tumbling down towards them with a scream but Regam easily avoided it by deftly leaping into the air and kicking off one of the stone walls. Bamaul simply grabbed it with both hands and used the soldier's own momentum to toss him overhead with astonishing strength. He accidently leaked just a tiny fraction of the bracelet's power in that moment and the whisper encouraged him, enveloped him, and promised him even more in its quiet, mocking laughter as the soldier's body landed heavily and his armor crumpled upon the force of its impact. Bamaul screamed in inarticulate rage and desperation. He *had* to ignore it. It was vital to ignore it, but it was so, so tempting. But again that fraction of sanity he had spent so long honing for when the bells assaulted him urged him to refrain from accepting the whisper's invitation. At least for now.

Finally reaching the apex of the stairs Bamaul slammed his head sideways against the wall to gain control of himself. Regam had burst into the room ahead of him and he took a moment to compose himself while a rivulet of blood trickled down the side of his face unnoticed.

He calmly entered the circular room and took inventory of their surroundings through the darkened haze clouding his vision. Numerous shelves wrapped themselves around the room in a pattern of three rings. It was obvious this place had once stored a great many volumes, but now they stood mostly empty. Two other small rooms were adjacent to where they now stood and dust and debris blown in through the open window littered the floor, shelving and few remaining pieces of furniture left behind. Motes of dust thickened the air and glittered like tiny jewels in the filtering sunlight streaming through the lone window.

Following Regam as he stalked his prey Bamaul's grin grew even wider in a horrifying mess of blood and teeth. Philip's boots had left obvious impressions in the dust coating the floor leading into one of the rooms, not that there was anywhere else for him to go.

Bamaul almost walked headlong into Regam upon entering the adjoining chamber. The man had stopped short and was warily assessing their cornered prey. Philip had backed himself into a corner with nowhere left to turn, but was still a dangerous and cunning man to deal with nonetheless. Philip had moved a bookcase from along the far wall, but this detail failed to register on Bamaul as he relished in the sight of his cherished prey finally within his grasp. With the old fool clinging helplessly to his back they formed a pitiful display that disgusted Bamaul to his very core.

Still barely in control of that tiny bit of sanity Bamaul shoved past Regam and began to stalk unsteadily towards his intended prey; the clanging bells and whisper forming a rising symphony of madness with each step. Philip stood poised and ready for a fight, his sword raised and that annoying look of excitement Bamaul had always hated in his piercing blue eyes. Scores of lesser men had fled from Philip Lockhart at the sight of those eyes, but not Bamaul, no longer. He was now so much more than the weak and talentless peons infecting the world and no mere mortal man could sway him.

Bamaul could almost taste the years of frustration and anger coming to an end as he continued his methodical approach. He was not so foolish as to rush at his enemy without caution and was ready to react to anything Philip or the old fool might try. His eyes rolled back into his head and he reveled in the scent of the fresh blood dripping from Philip's blade. Resounding echoes hollowly beat into his mind with each drop as it hit the floor, adding to his madness. Bamaul slowly raised one arm behind him and Regam immediately placed his own weapon into his king's hand in a practiced motion he had performed many times.

He had already forgotten his desire to throttle his foe due to new visions of Philip Lockhart's head rolling at his feet and his lifeless body clattering to the ground swimming before his eyes. He licked blood from his upper teeth and raised the blade overhead to strike down the hated adversary who had eluded him for years.

The fact Lockhart never once moved from his position to engage or defend despite his situation never registered on Bamaul until Oltan mumbled something into Philip's ear. Quickly Philip spun and with startling energy slammed his palm into the wall behind him. A single stone instantly sank into a hidden recess and with a loud creak a section of wall quickly swung away into the open air. Without a hint of hesitation Philip Lockhart spun on his heel and leaped out into the world below.

Even in his enraged state Bamaul was too stunned by what had happened to move for a few moments. *The fool just leapt to his death!*

The clashing sounds of insanity in his head were near to overwhelming and even that fraction of sanity he had left began to fray when the realization hit that his prey had deprived him the satisfaction of killing him himself. The whisper laughed again before morphing into a primal howl ripping through his mind and culminating in the back of his throat. Bamaul was just about to

release this shriek of absolute madness upon the world when a
soldier appeared in the doorway behind them panting out of
breath.

"Y-Your Majesty! Lord Regam! Another enemy has appeared!
We need new orders and more reinforcements before we can
approach!" the soldier nervously reported. He knew very well he
could be killed by either man just for reporting to them while they
were busy, but he had been given no choice by his superior.

Fortunately for him, the soldier's presence at first never
registered on Bamaul. The King was so lost in rage and madness
that there was an impenetrable miasma covering his consciousness
cutting him off from the outside world.

"Y-Y-Your Majesty?" the soldier stuttered. Fear and
trepidation that his life might be about to come to an end caused his
voice to quaver. It was Regam who answered.

"And what *single* enemy is so ferocious that a change in
defensive strategy and this pathetic display is so warranted? Have
those three others been killed or detained yet?" Regam snapped.

"Well, no, it's just that a sentry reported that a boy appeared in
the rolling hills area and..." the soldier stammered.

"A boy?" Regam's eyebrows rose in disbelief. Had Regam had
his sword in hand he would have struck the fool down where he
stood.

"That's not all!" the soldier quickly replied. "With him is an
actual dragon! We don't know how to approach them! We've
never received training for something like this!"

The bells and whispers enveloping Bamaul vanished. His vision
cleared and his self-control returned. He was finally able to loosen
his grip on the bracelet and gasped in pain as skin from his palm

tore away as he steadied himself against the dizziness and nausea washing over him. This had been the closest the bracelet had ever come to claiming him, but it was far too soon to allow that to come to pass. Bamaul shook off the unsettling thought and the soldier's words finally registered on him.

He slowly turned to face the soldier, each one of the wretch's features an affront to his senses. "Regam," Bamaul said, his voice betraying no emotion.

Without a word Regam swiftly grabbed his blade from his King and removed the soldier's head from his shoulders. A fountain of blood and gore erupted from the man's neck as his body spasmed to the ground in a clattering heap. None were allowed to live who bore witness to the effects of the bells in his mind. Especially not the mortal fodder that were not of the Bloodsetters under his command. Regam cleaned his blade on the dead soldier's cloak and tossed the man's head out the hole in the wall after their quarry in a rare fit of pique.

Stepping over the already forgotten corpse, Bamaul's smile returned. Calmly making his way back to the castle proper Bamaul could guess who the boy who had appeared could be.

"Come Regam. Let us welcome young Darien to his new home here at the Castle of the King."

Chapter 11

Darien vomited into the grass. Profusely. Heaving heavy breaths as his stomach emptied its meager contents he was amazed his boots hadn't gotten covered in the stuff. Weakly leaning against Koseki with a shuddering hand he felt just how much she was also struggling to deal with whatever in the Hells had just happened. Darien wasn't sure what a dragon vomiting would look like and was doubly sure he didn't want to find out. The link told him she was just as exhausted as he was. They both felt like the rest they had received at Little Maiani's had been ripped away from them and their bodies and minds were protesting against the extreme strain.

The last thing either of them remembered was returning to their room with Liana. A few minutes later a strange gong had resounded and next he knew they were atop the small knoll he was violating with bile and vomit. Darien likened the sensation of leaving Maiani's to being forcefully ejected through a barrier. It was no wonder his stomach felt flipped upside down.

I wonder if that's what it feels like to be tossed through a door?
Jack would probably know. I'll have to ask him.

His thoughts were jumbled and making little sense so he tried to
gain his bearings as best he could. Sinking to the ground in tandem
with Koseki, his vision swam sickeningly. Koseki's labored breath
matched his own and her legs gave out underneath her as she
thumped heavily to the ground. A cloud of dust arose underneath
the small dragon's girth and Darien had to fight the urge to gag at
the musty smell. They had both used far too much of their aura
energy lately, not to mention the strain on their physical bodies,
and now that the rest they received at Little Maiani had either
worn off or been taken away he wasn't sure how much more they
could take.

With a grimace Darien wiped away the stubborn strands of bile
and goo doggedly sticking to his chin and tried to get his bearings.
He blinked several times to clear the tears from his eyes in order to
survey their new surroundings. Nothing in their immediate area
looked familiar, but an ominous feeling crept over him at the sight
of a nearby castle and the faint sounds of clashing swords and
angry shouts. He rested his head on Koseki's flank and began to
gently mentally check her condition. Darien could tell how
exhausted she was not only through their connection, but by her
lack of exuberance. If she had been at full strength she would
already be frolicking amongst the knobby hills and trees
surrounding them with her curiosity raging.

Running his hand over her scales he smiled. The grey scales of
her birth were finally beginning to mottle with soft shades of black,
grey and purple. At first they had seemed to be gaining solely the
lustrous onyx sheen of her mother, but now that he looked closely

most were taking on a deep purple hue instead. He ran his hand along her neck until it came to rest on the crest of her head, each taking solace at the physical contact. A sense of weariness continued to sift through the link along with her happiness.

'*So tired,*' was all he could get out of the normally excitable dragon. As far as he could tell neither of them were physically injured in any way, save for where Koseki had pierced his shoulder. That had already begun to heal back at Maiani's, but they were suffering from exhaustion, disorientation and muscle fatigue from the extreme pressures they had been put through. Kuldari and Tartas, among others, had warned him against burning himself out if he pushed too far past his limitations and both he and Koseki were paying the price for that now. Closing his eyes Darien calmed his breathing and tried to ignore the rawness of his throat. Once he was able to get his breathing and nausea under control he thought about what to do next.

It wasn't long before he realized Koseki had fallen asleep. He didn't blame her; he wanted nothing more than to lie down and forget about the world for a while himself. Unfortunately, he knew that wasn't an option. He took several more deep breaths to calm himself and thought about what else he could see and hear with his dragon senses.

A somewhat overgrown path picked its way through the surrounding trees to slope downwards towards the castle in the distance, but looked to be rarely used. Darien shielded his eyes against the sunlight and took a long look at the foreboding structure looming a ways away for any clues as to where they might be.

Several pennons atop multiple towers flapped lightly in the

breeze and he could just make out figures scrambling furtively about atop the castle walls. He squinted in concentration as he tried to identify the flag's crest and nearly swallowed his tongue at the realization he had seen the sigil before. A white hourglass depicting falling black sand supported by two black circles rested on a field of crimson. Three crooked lines also the color white rose in ascending height from the hourglass with the middle line ending in an odd hook. It was the mark of the tyrant Bamaul. He was back in Katama. And not only that, within the stronghold of the very man he and the others had been seeking to overthrow. He groaned. It was the worst possible time for them to be anywhere near the Castle of the King. Especially with Koseki in such a weakened state.

He didn't know what had caused their sudden expulsion from Little Maiani's, but the problem of escaping had been solved for them only to be replaced by a greater one. And he had no idea what had happened to the others. As far as he knew they could be scattered all across the world.

He blew a stray hair out of his eyes and continued to inspect their surroundings. The sounds of skirmish continued to carry on the wind and he wondered exactly what sort of a situation they would find themselves in this time.

"Nothing's ever easy is it?" he muttered. Darien pondered what his next move should be and came up empty. He would rather not leave the exhausted and sleeping Koseki alone if he could help it so he decided his best course of action was to utilize caution and simply wait. It was entirely possible the others could be close by and would come looking for them. If enemies appeared instead he wasn't sure what he could do. He and Koseki were in no condition to attempt any type of melding and he still wasn't confident his skills with the short blades would be enough to hold off multiple attackers. He wasn't even sure he could fend off *one* enemy at the moment.

Darien took a quick inventory of his supplies and found a sizable piece of dried jerky remaining in his pouch. Feeling forlorn he tore off a chunk and began chewing. He left the larger piece out for Koseki, but doubted it would do much to sate her hunger once she woke. That thought troubled him. Exactly how *was* he going to get Koseki fed now that she was physically here? It wasn't like he could let her loose to go hunting in her exhausted state and besides; she couldn't even fly yet so how would she hunt?

Frowning, he looked more closely at the area around them. They were on an elevated hill surrounded by sparse trees and several smaller hillocks covered in short blades of grass. The trees were far less intimidating in scope and number than those of the Grove back near Village Breathwynd, but an ominous feeling in his stomach kept him on edge all the same. He didn't know what to expect, but he was sure it would be something he wasn't prepared for.

In contrast to his inner turmoil, sunlight gently filtered through the sparse trees and a light wind rippled the leaves and grass with the subtle touch only Turae, the Godling of nature, could provide. Unlike the murky, damp and foreboding countryside of Pajana the climate here was temperate and he took a brief moment to thank the Godling for at least that much.

He took a quick walk around their perimeter, never leaving Koseki out of his sight, and noticed the remains of several stone and wood structures haphazardly scattered among the knolls. From what he could tell they had been abandoned a long time ago and were in varying states of disrepair. None were taller than a single story and most were crumbling and falling in on themselves.

Charred timbers and jagged stones littered the structures both inside and out. Darien's curiosity made him wonder what these buildings had once been used for and why they had been abandoned. He felt the familiar itch to learn that had always driven him during his studies back home and his eye twitched at the prospect of investigating further.

With a glance back at Koseki Darien pulled up his hood to conceal his eyes from any who might be watching. He didn't hear anything unusual, but he couldn't be too careful. Walking towards the nearest structure, he told himself he was just going to check to make sure there was nothing dangerous hiding nearby while Koseki slept. He didn't want to leave Koseki's side, but he was able to figure out a route that allowed him to keep her within his sight while still being able to inspect a few of the buildings. Darien didn't know why he felt these ruins were so fascinating, but he just couldn't dismiss the familiar tug calling for him to explore.

Coming within a few steps of the closest building Darien glanced back at Koseki to make sure she was still in sight and smiled at the image of the excitable young dragon in such a state of repose. Still feeling somewhat wobbly he kept his senses strained to the limit in order to pick out the sounds of anyone approaching as he turned back to the ruin before him.

The sounds of the skirmish at the castle still carried to his ears, but they were too jumbled at this distance for even him to identify individual voices. Besides, his focus was on Koseki and these interesting ruins.

Kneeling in the soft earth he ran one hand along a rotten timber laying across the entrance. The damp and rotten wood easily flaked away at his touch and he absently rubbed the detritus between his thumb and forefinger. His mind wandered as he thought about what these ruins could mean. It was probably nothing, but Oltan had ingrained in him long ago a sense of curiosity of anything new and interesting. He always felt a need for it to be fulfilled to the point where he couldn't just walk away without answers. Darien had to admit that he and Koseki were a lot alike in that regard, although he wouldn't want to let her know that.

He inhaled the rich and earthy scent of the area and sighed. The peacefulness of everything around him, minus whatever was occurring down at the castle, was in vast contrast to what his life had become lately. Even his time at the Order of the Fist had been chaotic considering the nature of the place. Not to mention his constant problems with Liana.

Sighing again, he stood and brushed the blackened remains stuck to his finger on his cloak before stepping into the ruin. There were more than enough gaps and broken sections of wall for him to maintain a visual of Koseki while he scanned the inner remains for clues as to what this building might once have been.

Darien decided to stay away from the interior walls for the time being in case anything decided to come tumbling down without warning. He began searching the open area for anything of interest while maintaining his vigilance on the sleeping Koseki and keeping an ear out for any changes. He was surprised at how faint she seemed through the link despite her being so close in proximity. It was the exact opposite of how it had felt at Little Maiani's and he wondered if it was a side effect of her falling into a deep sleep or because of the strain they had been under lately.

Not noting anything of worth he was about to leave and head to the next tumbled mess when the corner of his eye caught something that he had overlooked. Had he not had the eyes of a dragon he would never have noticed the small corner of stone etched with indecipherable sigils and mostly covered in debris, detritus and nature's reclamation. Darien didn't know why, but he got the feeling these sigils were important. Or at least had been at one time.

Cautiously examining his new discovery, Darien began to carefully clear away the rubble in order to discover what lay beneath. He knew he was probably wasting time and that it was most likely part of a design for decoration or something of the sort, but his curiosity was getting the better of him.

Kneeling, he inspected the stone mound more closely while gently clearing away the overgrowth. Lightly running his hands over the emerging, but still faint, designs in the stonework he found a surprisingly sturdy wooden door wedged tightly between the sections of stone. A wry smile formed on Darien's face. It was oddly reminiscent of the library entrance he had passed through uncountable times while growing up in Village Breathwynd.

Darien had been stunned that he had never noticed the contraption Oltan had rigged in case of emergency and even more so at how he had to discover how the contraption worked. He wondered if there was a similar mechanism rigged here much like what he had discovered during his escape from the library the night his village had been attacked.

That smile quickly turned to a frown as he continued clearing away the remaining debris. He noticed the wooden hatchway did not quite match the rest of the damp and rotting wood strewn about the area. It was far too well maintained and seemingly in working order for it to have been an original part of the building. Lightly pulling on what he was now convinced was an entrance to a lower level he found it locked tightly shut. Someone had taken great care to conceal this place and Darien never would have noticed it had the stonework not caught the attention of his dragon eyes.

Still thinking about his experience with the library he began to look for a way past the barrier. He supposed he could try to break through with a piece of the rubble littering the area, but for some reason he felt using brute force would be disrespectful. Darien was so engrossed with his discovery that he didn't notice or even hear the soft yet hurried footsteps behind him until it was almost too late.

Just as his brain registered the sound of someone coming up from behind he half-turned before a small force barreled into him and a blindingly sharp pain erupted in his lower back. He screamed as both he and the small ball of violence exploded through the wooden hatch that had been concealing time-worn stone steps leading down into darkness.

Pieces of wood and stone peppered him and his unknown assailant as they tumbled down into a darkened room and landed in a disheveled heap. The air exploded out of his lungs at the impact of hitting the floor and the assailant landing on top of him. He felt the wound in his shoulder reopen and shuddered at the sensation of tearing flesh as fresh blood stained his tunic. Trying to ignore the pain of both wounds and the lack of breath in his lungs Darien's training from the Order took over and he kicked off his attacker.

Quickly moving to the far end of the room he rapidly took stock in what in the Hells was going on now. His opponent must have been of the same mind and moved just as quickly to block the exit, cutting off any chance to escape.

Hells. Darien gasped as he caught his breath and checked the throbbing pain in his back; his hand came away sticky and wet with blood. He stretched his shoulder slightly and could feel the muscles and tendons already at work trying to repair themselves. Darien was sure to end up with some scarring, especially since it was a wound received from a dragon, but he forced himself to ignore it. He grimaced and wiped the blood from his hand on his tunic before drawing his short blade with his good side. "I'm getting too many extra holes put in me today," he grumbled under his breath. His opponent hissed at his words with such venom that Darien was taken aback. The unknown assailant was seething with such anger that a cloud of red billowed off him in undulating waves. Darien took a measured breath to control his reeling senses. Whoever this person was, he had made his intentions clear by attacking, and more importantly, stabbing him.

Darien was more than a little worried. He wasn't sure how capable he really was in actual combat against an opponent truly bent on killing him. Especially now that he had sustained two serious wounds in short order. His ability to heal was taking longer than normal and he swayed a little due to all the blood loss. The hollow feeling he had in his gut was a far cry from the frustration he often felt during his training with Tartas. At least then when he failed it was just painful. Here, he was sure failing would prove to be much, much worse.

He was well aware he had gotten lucky when he and the others had been ambushed by a Bloodsetter raiding party a while back. He had not only been able to survive by the Godlings own luck, but had actually killed one of the Bloodsetters that had attacked them.

This was the first time since then that he found himself in actual armed conflict against someone trying to murder him. It felt much different to him than during all those confrontations with Liana. Liana had always been up front about the fact that she intended to kill him and he had wholeheartedly believed her, but this was on another level. There was so much anger and hatred in the uncontrollable mist that it was practically oozing off his opponent like sludge. Darien felt sick to his stomach again, but if he didn't have the nerve to face an enemy here then what would become of Koseki should he die? It was a terrifying feeling.

Gritting his teeth against the pain in his back and the ache in his shoulder he took a moment to warily study his opponent.

What in the Hells?

Darien was bewildered. It was a Bloodsetter, but the oddest Bloodsetter he had ever seen. For one thing he was extremely short compared to the ones Darien had encountered before and had a very slight frame. Penetrating eyes full of anger stared menacingly out from his Makavai and he looked to have his hair in a topknot judging from the bulging mound underneath his ceremonial garb.

What really concerned Darien though was the blood soaked dagger in the Bloodsetter's hand and the low growl of rage building in his throat. Darien's senses were assaulted by another sudden surge of color as his control over the mists generated by others weakened even further. He was stunned at the variety of emotions in the span of such a brief moment. It was like the Bloodsetter was unconsciously switching emotions from one moment to the next.

This definitely isn't a normal Bloodsetter. Hells, he thought as he grimaced at the throbbing in his back. He tried to will his body to heal faster, but he knew that was just wishful thinking.

Confident that talking his way out of this was not going to be a viable option he readied himself the best he could despite the pain. Given the chance, he'd rather avoid killing the Bloodsetter and get back to Koseki so he could try to awaken the sleeping dragon. He reached out to her and only got a sluggish and undecipherable response before she quickly faded back into the recesses of his mind. He didn't know why, but he got the vague sense his sister dragon was irritated.

Darien resisted the urge to sigh. Now that he got the sense his sister dragon was mad at him he had something else to worry about, but he would have to figure out how to deal with that problem later. If he was still alive later.

He didn't know what was suddenly bothering Koseki so much, but his first priority was getting back to her. He'd figure the rest out afterwards since right now he had more important things to worry about. He took a deep breath to steady himself and let out a hiss at another surge of pain. Darien assumed a defensive stance to compensate for his wounds and dug in for the fight of his life.

Philip Lockhart didn't hesitate. When the old man told him to jump, he jumped. Even if he was leaping into thin air several stories high.

He had been amazed to find the old man actually alive. From Darien's disjointed narrative about his past Lockhart had had his suspicions, but he never would have guessed to have them validated in such a way.

He and his companions had been in the middle of discussions with Little Maiani when they had abruptly and definitively been interrupted by a gong sounding deep within the mansion that had sent him spinning off into blackness.

After a period of confusion and nausea quickly tempered by sheer force of will, he took a deep breath and waited for his eyes to adjust to the darkness surrounding him. He tensely waited for his eyes to adjust and strained his other senses to their limit to not only be on guard for anyone or anything hostile, but to get a sense of where he had ended up.

Lockhart resisted the sudden urge to gag at the musty and damp smell of mold, mildew and unwashed skin assaulting his nostrils and he got the impression he was somewhere underground. He shifted his feet slightly, never losing the perfect balance of his combat stance, and felt rotting straw shift on the dirt floor beneath his boots.

After some time standing in vigilant silence his eyes finally adjusted to the point where he could more easily make out the room's contents.

Scanning the room as best he could in the darkness he made out what looked to be cages or cells. Lockhart assumed he had ended up in some kind of prison, but if so then it was the oddest prison he had ever seen.

Why are there only four cells?

He supposed the number of cells didn't matter and that he should be grateful he at least didn't end up on the other side of the bars.

Lockhart remained still while he listened for any signs of life from the cells surrounding him. At first there was nothing, but after a few moments he caught the very faint sounds of weak and labored breathing.

Lockhart gripped his scabbard in anticipation of some sort of trap. It wasn't impossible for him to still be within the confines of Maiani's so he couldn't let anything else catch him by surprise. Too many people were depending on him for that.

Making a decision he slowly spun on his heel and stalked through the darkness to inspect the source of breathing, keeping an eye on the other cells in case of anything unexpected. Quickly reaching his target, he maintained some distance from the strong iron bars and took in the mass of sunken, shriveled skin and bones hanging from shackles on the wall.

Lockhart had been through too much in his life to accept anything at face value so he didn't move or speak for a time; instead he chose to silently scrutinize the cell's lone occupant. The prisoner's head hung limply against his sunken chest and greasy, ragged grey hair matted itself to his skull. His body was emaciated, covered in sores and looked like he had undergone his fair share of torture. The stench of his unwashed body radiating out in waves would have made most gag in disgust, but Lockhart had seen far worse. Had there not been a slight rise and fall of the man's chest with each labored breath one would not have been remiss thinking the prisoner deceased.

Lockhart continued to study the man for a time, not making a sound and barely daring to breathe. The prisoner certainly looked close to death and Lockhart wondered if he should leave things as is or if it would be more merciful to release the man from his chains to ease his suffering. Lockhart ground his teeth in frustration at his lack of information. It *was* entirely possible this was a just punishment for whatever crime the man had been imprisoned for. Of course, it was also just as possible the prisoner was being held captive unjustly and if so then Lockhart felt a duty to either end his suffering or find a way to release him from his chains.

While Lockhart was deciding on the best course of action the prisoner finally reacted to his presence by weakly lifting his head. At the sight of Lockhart the man's eyes widened and he flashed a crooked grin before weakly dropping his head back into his chest. The man whispered something that sounded like a name, but was spoken so quietly Lockhart couldn't make it out. However, that wasn't what had caught his attention. His eyes narrowed in suspicion at the shocking sight hanging before him. Despite the prisoner's weakened and emaciated appearance he could never mistake those eyes or that grin for anyone else. He had seen both uncountable times during the days of his youth, but he still didn't move or speak. It could still be a trap or another of Maiani's tricks. There were too many unknowns to be sure, but he had to make a decision and quickly. The more time he took meant the longer it would take to regroup with everyone and take stock of their situation. Then maybe they could piece together a coherent narrative as to what had happened.

He used everything he had learned over the years, every trick and nuance made available to him, to assess whether what he was seeing was real or imaginary. His mind whirled furiously with possibilities and his jaw clenched tightly. Knowing it could prove foolish to delay his decision much longer Lockhart took a few cautious steps up to the bars of the cell and peered closer at the man; his sword ready to be drawn and strike in a single motion if need be.

The man struggled to lift his head again. A spark of life briefly ignited in his eyes and a weak smile creased his filthy and haggard face. The man whispered again and this time Lockhart clearly heard "Philip..." The prisoner's efforts lasted only a moment before his head again sagged with a low sigh.

Lockhart immediately chose his course of action. He fervently hoped the bars of the cell were of the standard variety and not something greater enhanced by magic. It would be refreshing to encounter something relatively mundane after all the extraordinary events he had been exposed to lately.

He doubted he could do much more than chip away at the iron bars until they were sufficiently weakened, but he couldn't think of another approach. He drew his sword and positioned himself to strike, breathing deeply and calmly as he focused on the bars in front of him. He had to be methodical and deliberate in his swings if he didn't want to shatter his blade. Chipping away at the bars would ruin it beyond repair, but that couldn't be helped.

Not knowing where he was meant he had little time, but if he didn't approach the problem carefully his efforts would go for naught. Blowing air through his nose like an enraged bull Lockhart began his strike hoping he had judged his strength correctly and that things would go better than he expected them to.

Just as his blade was about to connect he was stopped by an unexpected audible crack and a squelching that made him grimace. The ear shuddering sound repeated itself and Lockhart was surprised to find the odd sounds were coming from the prisoner. The old man lifted his head again and with some effort spit a stream of blood and goo with a throaty cough. Lockhart sheathed his blade and squinted at the three small blood covered objects rattling to his feet.

Squatting as he retrieved the objects he ignored the blood and stringy substance adhering to them and inspected what the old man had given him. In a rare display of surprise his eyebrow twitched.

Teeth. The old man had just removed three of his molars and spat them at Lockhart's feet. He began to clear away the blood and gore when he heard another soft whisper.

"Need them...to activate."

They were so softly spoken that if he had not been in such an eerily still and quiet space Lockhart never would have heard him.

"The blood?" Lockhart questioned.

"No...the strings."

"Strings?" Lockhart looked more closely at the small pieces of enamel in his hand that had been a part of the old man's gums until a moment ago and carefully cleaned the viscous fluids away. That was when he noticed the small stringy goo was not muscle tissue or parts of the teeth, but something artificial. Each tooth had two small strings at opposite ends. Knowing the old man as he did, Godlings only knew what these were for.

"And what would you like me to do with these?" Lockhart asked while trying to keep the creeping feeling in the pit of his stomach at bay. The prisoner quietly chuckled a weak rasp into his beard and Lockhart's stomach tightened at the sound. He lifted his head to look at Lockhart sideways as if he didn't have enough strength left to lift it all the way and smiled that crooked grin again. Blood and spittle ran unabated down his chin, mixing with the dirt and grime of his matted and scraggly beard in a grotesque display. Others may have shrunk back from the sight, but Lockhart was very familiar with the old man's tendencies and refused to show any surprise.

"So what do I do with these?" he asked again more calmly than he felt. The old man's penchant for mischief was showing, even in such a precarious position. Lockhart guessed the old man must be the source of Darien's streak of impulsiveness that always reared its ugly head at the worst of times. The prisoner spoke again in a strained voice.

"I should have known," Lockhart said.

Oltan always had a penchant for tricks like this. In the past he had often reveled in his own cleverness and at the struggle of his students and colleagues alike who attempted to unravel one of his many riddles. One of the reasons Lockhart hadn't been entirely sure Darien's Oltan had been the same man was the absence of this character trait from the boy's descriptions. Darien had always portrayed the man as warm and friendly, but strict when it came to being studious. Perhaps Oltan had hidden that side of himself or maybe the boy just accepted who the old man was without question. Lockhart's guess was that Darien never noticed the contrast compared to the rest of the old man's traits. To him, it was an odd affliction to the personality of a man so obsessed with the concept of learning and imparting knowledge, but Lockhart knew Oltan had never shirked his duties and had been respected by the entirety of the castle staff, including the former king Tammaz.

He listened carefully for several tense minutes while Oltan struggled to wheeze out instructions. After Oltan had finished Lockhart repeated back what he had heard verbatim to ensure he hadn't missed anything important. Oltan gave out another sigh, but didn't give any indication that Lockhart had gotten any of his instructions wrong.

He was stunned at what Oltan was telling him to do, but he had no reason to doubt the old man's words. Lockhart let none of his surprise register on his face as he wedged one of the molars into the tiny space between the cell's middle hinge and the stone wall.

Pulling one of the small strings attached to the tooth he ran to the far end of the room as he had been instructed. Pressing up against the large and rather ornate door that, according to Oltan, was their only avenue of escape he tensed for whatever came next. He didn't have much time to wait as a small explosion erupted outward from Oltan's cell. Lockhart silently prayed to the Godlings above for the old man to have survived that. It would be in line with his current run of luck to have Oltan perish just before he was rescued, but his fears were allayed when he picked his way back to the cell. Motes of dust and dirt floated haphazardly about and the smell of damp mildew intensified as spores exposed to the small blast were released into the air.

If this place wasn't enough of a health hazard before it sure as the Hells is now, Lockhart thought as he covered his face with part of his tunic and took shallow breaths to avoid inhaling too much of the sickening miasma thickening the air.

Approaching the cell he could see the hinge had been blasted off the wall and the other two had come loose as well, allowing him to maneuver the cell door to the floor with some effort. He didn't know how Oltan had created such a device out of his own anatomy and wasn't sure he really wanted to know, but now he had a way to enter the cell and get Oltan loose.

Getting Oltan down from his chains proved to be less of a problem than Lockhart had anticipated. They proved relatively easy to pick with one of several tools he kept on his person for emergencies such as this.

Oltan mumbled something about Lockhart's penchant for having sticky fingers, but he chose to decidedly ignore the commentary on some of his more youthful indiscretions. Hoisting Oltan's frail body onto his back Lockhart again listened to the next set of instructions being weakly whispered into his ear. He rolled the two remaining teeth in his hand and couldn't help but wonder if they were really capable of what Oltan claimed. Not that he had any reason to doubt the old man, but he had gotten the sense this imposing door looming up in front of them had some sort of magic property imbued in its construction. Getting past something like that seemed like it would take more than what they had available to them at the moment. On top of that, his most recent experience with magic had been less than pleasant thanks to Maiani and he would rather not tempt fate more than once in a day when it came to the arcane.

However, their options were limited. No, he had no other options. It was this or nothing and if it failed then even he had no inclination as to what to do next.

"Don't worry so much..." Oltan wheezed in his ear.

It took Lockhart a moment to realize the old man was trying to laugh, but was in such a pitiful state it only came out as a rough wheeze. More blood and spittle came drooling down his chin and soaked into Lockhart's tunic. He chose to ignore it.

Lockhart sized up the door in front of them with a frown and thought on what Oltan had said while he had been picking the locks on his chains.

"We can get out that door. The magic of its construction focuses on keeping others out more than to keep 'guests' inside. Bamaul could never conceive of anyone being in any condition to leave their cell, let alone attempt an escape. I'm sure those last two fragments I gave you will at least do enough damage to allow us to leave," Oltan had told him.

Placing the remaining molars in position Lockhart quickly pulled all four tiny pieces of string and hurriedly ran back to the cell. He leapt back inside just as another explosion, larger and louder than the first, rattled the room so hard he felt like his bones were shaking. Sparks and magic residue filled the air and Lockhart had to hold a deep breath in order to avoid inhaling anything potentially dangerous. Tiny pieces of stone, dirt and metallic debris peppered them and he tried to shield the old man as best he could from the fragmentation. Oltan, for his part, seemed to be enjoying himself, softly wheezing in glee at the explosion. Lockhart idly wondered if the old man had completely lost it during his incarceration. The softly laughing old man with blood and spit plastered to his grimy face was a far cry from the wise teacher and investigator Lockhart had known in his youth.

Ignoring the trauma as best he could, he drew his sword and quickly made his way out of the cell. Taking another breath to steady himself and preparing for the worst Lockhart unleashed a battle cry and leapt through the small hole that had blasted outwards like the skin of an orange peeled back. The scene awaiting them was one that even Philip Lockhart could not have imagined and the timing of it couldn't have been worse.

Bamaul stood before them in all his madness and his chief Bloodsetter Regam was already advancing on them with groggy steps. Had Lockhart not despised these two men more than anyone else in the world he would have been amazed at their resiliency to recover from being exposed to that blast so quickly.

Every fiber of his being screamed for him to strike down the two men who had caused so much pain and misery over the years and to finally end Bamaul's reign of terror. Regam was vulnerable and the tyrant was unarmed. His goal was right there within reach! Unfortunately carrying Oltan on his back put him at a clear disadvantage and he knew the old man would be the first of their targets in his weakened state. Additionally, he knew it was foolish to presume Bamaul harmless and incapable even unarmed. There was no telling what the man was truly capable of and the info he had gleaned from various informants over the years indicating the tyrant's true level of strength was varied and lacking.

Oltan whispered in his ear again and Lockhart nodded in agreement. There were too many unknown variables in this insane situation for him to complete his mission despite being so close. He admitted to himself he wouldn't present much of a threat against that monster in his current state anyway. It was another reason why he had spent so much additional time at the Order and why he had wanted to get into Het Tapas before stealthily sneaking back towards Katama. So he made his decision quickly and decisively as soon as his boots softly landed on the floor. He parried Regam's blade as the Bloodsetter seemed somewhat unfocused and even with Oltan on his back Lockhart was able to keep his balance enough to where he could propel himself forward.

Lockhart began trying to recall the layout of the castle's interior in order to plan out his next move as he made his way to the only exit he could see. He wasn't sure exactly where in the castle they would emerge, but Lockhart was confident once they were free of this Hell he would be able to navigate his way around. His first priority was now to escape the castle with Oltan. Second was to find if his companions were also in the vicinity and rendezvous with them as soon as possible. Third was to get the Hells away from the Castle of the King. He ground his teeth in frustration. It was much too soon for them to be there and they had far less knowledge, manpower and leverage than he had hoped for.

Lockhart's immediate problem was that he had no prior knowledge of this obscure prison ever existing under King Tammaz, but that didn't necessarily mean it hadn't always been there. As they ran upwards his mind was furiously trying to come up with a plan for any number of places in the castle they could end up when Oltan again whispered in his ear. The old man had to repeat himself twice more to be heard over Bamaul's insane roars emanating from behind as the madman gave chase.

Lockhart flung open the wooden door at the top of the stairs and found himself in a long and narrow hall. The guards kneeling along the wall on either side were slow to react to Lockhart's sudden emergence from the depths of the castle. Lockhart was past them and gone before they could even rise and draw their weapons. Shouts followed after them as he weaved through the halls of the castle he had once spent so much time exploring in his youth, startling soldiers and servants alike.

He considered it lucky he hadn't had to engage anyone too seriously while he still had the element of surprise on his side. Alarm bells began ringing in the castle, but Lockhart was sure the reason for the alarm itself had yet to be communicated to most of the castle personnel.

That feeling lasted right up until he reached the open courtyard located in the heart of the castle interior. He needed to reach the other side in order to access the particular part of the castle Oltan had insisted on visiting, but their way was barred by a combined squad of nervous castle guards. Their formation was lacking and their equipment was a mismatch of weapons and armor that looked to be suffering from a lack of proper care on a regular basis. By the way they were standing, fidgeting and glancing at each other for any inclination as to what was happening they were no more used to actual armed conflict than a newborn babe.

The alarm bells finally began to ring louder and more insistent as Lockhart narrowed his eyes in a minor sign of irritation. He knew these men were now more ceremonial in nature so they shouldn't pose too much of a threat, but their obvious lack of discipline rankled him. This token force was a practice put in place by the current 'ruler' of Katama. Before Bamaul's ascension to power only elite soldiers who had proven themselves several times during the course of their service were allowed such a position, but now they were no more than living decorations in honor of Bamaul's self-styled aggrandizement.

Lockhart also knew most of these men were only here because of the protection and financial security the position afforded to their families despite the constant danger of being in close proximity to an insane madman who might disembowel them on a whim. He would rather not harm men who were more or less still loyal subjects of King Tammaz and were just trying to live the best they could under the circumstances, but he was out of options.

Just as he was about to jump into the nervously arrayed squad he was saved by a roar indicating the arrival of Jack, Geru and Tartas as they slammed viciously into the guards' flank.

"Try not to kill anyone!" Lockhart barked, immediately

changing course to avoid the eruption of fighting while the startled and panicked guards attempted to defend themselves from the three seasoned fighters.

Please forgive me. Lockhart knew the three must still be suffering ill effects of their forceful expulsion from Maiani's, especially Geru, but he had to believe they would be fine as long as they worked together. He sent up a silent prayer to the Godlings above for the men he was leaving behind on both sides. The item Oltan was sending him to fetch had to be removed from the castle and out of Bamaul's reach at all costs if the old man was to be believed. And he had never had a reason to doubt Oltan's wisdom before. He was sure Jack and the others would be fine against those frightened and inexperienced guards, but he was still worried.

There still hadn't been any sign of Darien and his dragon or Squirrel. Wily and his nervous friend were also unaccounted for, not to mention Lady Liana and her retainers, but the fact those three showed up indicated the others were probably close by as well. His foremost priority right now was finishing this errand and escaping as quickly as possible. Such a thought irritated him, but he knew they were underpowered and overmatched at the moment despite their advantage in terms of experience. It was like the Godlings themselves were taking a hand in trying to prevent him from succeeding at dethroning Bamaul.

He chided himself for cursing his own luck; luck and favor had nothing to do with his situation. Once he finished this errand that Oltan had been so insistent on then he could focus on the next step. Leaving the shouts and sounds of battle behind Lockhart picked up his pace even with the decrepit old man on his back. He could feel Bamaul and Regam closing in on them and the incoherent screams originating from behind gave him even more incentive to move quickly. Only the Godlings knew what that madman was actually capable of thanks to the strange artifact he wore strapped to his wrist.

Lockhart bounded up another stairway, startling a maid in the process. The woman yelped in surprise and dropped the bundle of linens she had been carrying before ducking into an alcove in terror. He was confused why there was still staff going about their duties while the alarm bells were furiously ringing, but he didn't have time to dwell on it as another guard appeared on the stairs ahead of him. Oltan had mentioned there probably wouldn't be anyone stationed here, but unfortunately the old man was wrong for once. Lockhart expertly parried the man's strike and sliced into his arm with a flick of his own blade, causing the guard to lose his grip on his sword. It wasn't a mortal wound, but the man probably wouldn't be able to swing a sword for a while.

Slamming the man against the stone wall Lockhart then sent him tumbling down the stairs below. Lockhart half hoped the guard would fall right into Regam and Bamaul, but instinctively knew he would have no such luck. He hated putting one of Katama's inhabitants in such a position, but he had no other alternative.

Sweating from his concerted efforts, Lockhart finally reached their destination, Oltan's old secret study. According to the old man, no one but he and King Tammaz had known of this room's existence. Apparently he had used some method to conceal access to the top room from others and if someone did notice anything awry in that particular small space of the castle they would 'forget' by the time they descended the stairs. He had no idea how such a thing was possible and he didn't really want to know, but now that he stood within the study himself he could tell why Oltan had taken measures to keep others from finding it.

Old and brittle volumes and scrolls sparsely littered the shelves lining the walls of the circular room, but it was obvious much more had once been stored here. Three continuous shelves ran in complete circles around the room, only broken at even intervals by four heavy wooden bookcases. A light wind rippled through the air from the lone window to their left and Lockhart fought back a sudden urge to sneeze at the thick layer of dust coating everything.

There must have once been thousands of rare and valuable tomes of knowledge here, but now it was a shell of its former glory. Two separate doors opened on the far side of the room into additional chambers and Lockhart hoped at least one of them would have an escape route. He thought Oltan would want one or several of the few items remaining, but the old man directed him to the door angled off to their left. He could hear Bamaul's incoherent screams edging closer and once in the next room he methodically began searching according to Oltan's instructions.

The room had no windows or source of light, which made searching for one particular item vexing, but Lockhart remained calm. Following the old man's instructions being lightly breathed in his ear he moved without hesitation. Finding his way to the far side of the room he came across a series of wooden bookcases that looked much like the ones in the previous room, only these were packed with artifacts and items of curious origin that Lockhart couldn't even begin to guess the purpose of. "Decoys," came Oltan's labored explanation like he could read Lockhart's mind.

Decoys for what? he wanted to ask, but refrained. Patiently following Oltan's whispers he selected the center bookcase and gripped it by its edge. Pulling with some effort he moved it several inches away from the wall and again resisted the urge to sneeze at all the dust it kicked up. Running his hand along its backside he found an odd depression in the wood and used the tip of his index finger to press on the small opening.

Oltan mumbled something about pockets, but Lockhart ignored it. *His mind is starting to wander. It's a miracle he was able to even guide me this far, but we can't afford to waste any more time.*

Lockhart plunged his hand into the opening, scarcely believing it as his hand vanished into the wood and an odd tingling sensation crawled up his arm. He glanced at the front of the bookcase to see if his hand had gone clean through and wasn't surprised to see that it hadn't. According to what he could glean from Oltan's tired mumbling his hand was apparently occupying another space separate from the room. Lockhart decided not to think about it. This was the sort of thing Oltan reveled in and would spend hours on the subject if he really got going. It just gave Lockhart a headache, which in retrospect is probably why the old man enjoyed talking about it so much.

Fumbling around blindly in this 'pocket' Lockhart was finally able to grasp what felt like a small leather pouch bound with thick, heavy straps. He grabbed it and felt the hard resistance of cut stone beneath the leather. Quickly removing the pouch, he stuffed it inside his tunic just as Bamaul and Regam caught up to them.

Furtively scanning the room Lockhart made note of the lack of escape routes. There were no windows and just the one doorway leading to and from the room. He hoped the old man hadn't sent them to their deaths by insisting on this errand or at least had another trick up his sleeve like with the molars, but he prepared himself for the worst case scenario.

He gritted his teeth and made ready to force his way through the lunatic and his henchman when Oltan again mumbled in his ear. Lockhart instantly whirled and palm slapped a stone in the exposed wall behind the bookcase. The odd sound of something moving sibilantly through the walls softly resonated in the chamber and a few seconds later a portion of the wall swung outwards. Ignoring whatever Bamaul was screaming Lockhart leaped out the opening at Oltan's behest despite being several hundred feet above ground.

He knew better than to trust either in luck or the Godlings' favor so he kept his eyes open and his senses sharp in order to react to whatever came next. What did come next was apparent as soon as Lockhart looked down in order to judge their descent. Multiple stones below their feet protruded from the tower wall in a staggered fashion spiraling down to the safety of the ground below. Lockhart used the momentum of their descent to leap from one stone to the next as they fell. It was as treacherous an escape route as he had ever taken; one wrong step would send the both of them tumbling to their death. It took all of his considerable skill, effort and concentration to accurately judge the distance between each stone and to land and leap off towards the next in one fluid motion. Lockhart couldn't spare a glance to see if they were being pursued or even to check on the old man's condition. He heard a soft moan from Oltan as the wind whistled past his ears so he took that as a sign the old man was at least still alive.

He didn't have time to consider how they would land when they reached the ground, but he would figure that much out once they made it down alive.

Escaping the castle grounds was still his top priority. Jack and the others should be fine and know what to do in this type of situation, so he wasn't going to worry about that at least. After he made his escape it would only be a matter of time before he could focus on meeting up in the countryside. He fervently hoped they could shake any pursuit in time to accomplish that.

What they did from there largely depended on the old man clinging to his back. Whatever it was that he had insisted on retrieving was obviously of some importance, but Lockhart had some reservations about whether it was really worth the risk.

Still, he had absolute trust in the old man that had been earned many years in the past. He knew Oltan wasn't someone who made rash decisions or wasted time on the unimportant. Lockhart forced himself to believe the errand had been necessary, whatever it had been for.

Their momentum continued to increase as he leapt deftly from each step and a frown creased his face as the wind buffeting them intensified with each passing second.

He began to formulate a new plan as they descended and again cursed the unpredictability that had been ruling over them lately. If he ever saw Little Maiani again he would have some choice words for her, regardless of the outcome.

Ever since they met Darien the unexpected had occurred seemingly at every turn. It was one of the many factors that went into his decision to keep an eye on the boy whereas he may have abandoned another. The boy had proven to be full of surprises and Lockhart had seen enough in his lifetime to recognize Darien just might be the catalyst for a major event and was worth keeping close by despite his inconsistencies and inexperience. What that event might be he had no idea, but he could feel it in his bones that the boy and his dragon would prove important one day. Additionally, everyone had taken quite a liking to the lad, despite his aggravating impulses, while he grew under their watch. He was far from the terrified child they had met back in the Grove, but the remnants of the villager he had been still sometimes bubbled to the surface and usually at the most inopportune times. Lockhart also wished the boy would be more open about his situation where being a Ryudojin was concerned.

The boy had promised to do so, but then the incident with the Broodmother had occurred. Even if his actions did save them, the General didn't like the strain it had put on Darien's body. Worst case the boy could end up killing both himself and his dragon if he wasn't more careful.

Even worse than worst case would be for him to lose himself to the Darksouled. Lockhart definitely didn't want to think about what would happen then, but that would be a bridge to cross should it ever appear. Lockhart shifted his focus back to their current agenda since the ground was swiftly rushing up to meet them. Luckily no soldiers appeared within their vicinity, but Lockhart was sure some form of opposition would be arriving soon. He would rather not have to fight his way through any more soldiers since doing so without dealing lethal blows was just as exhausting mentally as it was physically.

Lockhart absorbed the impact of the ground meeting the heels of his boots with a grimace and a loud crack accompanied a searing pain shooting up his leg. Using his momentum to awkwardly propel himself forward he ignored the pain. Had he not been carrying Oltan he could have tucked and rolled in one fluid motion to prevent most of the damage, but that wasn't an option. His ankle was on fire from the sudden impact and he was pretty sure it was broken, but he did his best to ignore the excruciating pain and put all his effort into moving his legs as fast as he could as he hobbled his way towards the outer reaches of the castle grounds. He sincerely hoped the chaos caused by their sudden arrival would be enough that not all gates and escape routes would be blocked off just yet.

Loud shouts of pain and confusion accompanied the echo of steel on steel reaching his ears, confirming that Jack, Geru, and Tartas were still engaged with the soldiers. He hoped they would cease their distraction quickly now that he had neither the time nor ability to give them any orders. Not only that, but only the Godlings only knew what had happened to the rest of the party, not to mention Lady Liana and her retinue.

In this scenario he knew he had to trust his subordinates would know escape was now paramount. They had always kept a time limit on these kinds of battles and once that limit was reached everyone would do everything in their power to regroup. Darien might be the lone exception, given his unpredictable nature, but he had to trust the boy would have enough sense to at least look for the others should he be alone.

He fervently hoped that Squirrel or Wily was with Darien, but with the way things had been going lately he doubted that to be the case since it would make things a bit easier once he and Oltan made good on their escape. Of course, the Godlings being as fickle as they were, that hope would probably prove to be wishful thinking. Still, he fervently hoped this situation would somehow work itself out without any of them losing their lives, but he wasn't going to rely on luck and the Godlings alone. He had learned that particular lesson a long time ago.

Right now I need to focus solely on escaping as quickly as possible and to set my ankle. I'll worry about the rest once we get out of here safely. Once we're clear of the castle I'll head towards the tumbled ruins of the old outbuildings and take shelter in the tunnels underneath them.

With a set destination in mind, Lockhart continued his labored pace despite the agonizing pain in his ankle and relayed his intentions to Oltan between breaths. He felt the old man's grip tighten slightly at the mention of Darien and realized Oltan would have had no idea the boy was among his company.

He was sure the old man was shocked at the news, but right now there wasn't any time to explain; that would have to wait until they were free and clear of this nightmare scenario. The escape route he had chosen was based on their location and what area of the castle would be the slowest to react to their arrival. The supply gate he was aiming for was usually minimally staffed and little used during this part of the day. Add in the fact the men stationed there were usually assigned as a form of punishment and as a result were often lax in carrying out orders. Rounding a corner Lockhart thanked the Godlings above that the supply gate remained open.

He slowed as he approached the gate and assessed a scene of panic and confusion unraveling before his eyes. The gate stood partially open as a rather large wagon had somehow gotten itself stuck while trundling through. Giving the situation a cursory glance, the corners of Lockhart's mouth twitched up in a smile. The drivers sat upon the wagon arguing in loud and obnoxious voices with the flustered soldiers about the broken wheel that had gotten them stuck. The wheel had partially shattered and the hub had miraculously gotten itself wedged into one of the ruts in the packed dirt that had been created by thousands of wagons passing through over the years. The two atop the wagon didn't seem to be overly concerned about finding a solution and were more interested in hurling insults to enrage the men stationed at the gate. One of the men was wearing a sling supporting his shoulder and was screaming about the inherent value of their goods and how desperately the king wanted to get his hands on them and that anyone who interfered was sure to be punished by the tyrant himself.

The fear and uncertainty that Bamaul's name had on the castle's regular soldiers was obvious since no one wanted to take charge of the situation in all the chaos. Of course, no one wanted to be the one to incur the king's wrath and no one wanted to volunteer to find him or one of his officials for fear of being turned into a jumper. Lockhart felt it would have been a hilarious cycle of repetition if all of their lives weren't at stake.

"Hey you! Wait! What are you doing?" someone yelled. Ignoring the soldier and squeezing between the wagon and gate, he nodded at the red faced and yelling Squirrel sitting atop the wagon next to Wily.

Leaving Squirrel, Wily and the confused soldiers behind Lockhart made a quick review of what he had seen. Gelas had been among the people gathering around the wagon, apologizing profusely to the flustered and angry guards as Squirrel and Wily continued their charade.

That just leaves Darien and his dragon to account for.

Of course the boy would be the only one he wasn't able to locate.

Lockhart swore the Godling of chance and trickery had one eye on the boy at all times. He didn't spare a worry for Liana or her followers since he was sure that wherever Darien was, the volatile woman was sure to be close at hand.

Lockhart tried his best to pick up his pace despite the worsening pain in his ankle while he awkwardly ran. He needed to find a place where he could put the old man down for a minute and get some much needed rest for the both of them.

Now he wished he had thought to steal one of the horses at the gate, but it was too late to go back for that. He gritted his teeth and forcibly shoved his moment of regret aside. Lockhart took a deep breath and doubled his efforts on reaching the tumbled ruins littering the hillocks north-west of the castle grounds. As far as Lockhart understood it, no one knew what purpose the stone and timber buildings had actually served in the remote past, but he knew from his childhood they were an excellent place to hide. Brief memories of time spent in these tunnels playing with other children of the castle staff intruded into his thinking, but he forcibly put them out of his mind. Although he didn't like to dwell on past memories it was those times spent with his few friends that had led to the discovery that many of the buildings had basements and sub floors connecting via a network of hidden tunnels. They were often cleverly disguised, but they could be found if one looked carefully enough. It was now his hope to use these tunnels to vanish from pursuit once they had all reconvened.

The original plan he had made long before meeting Darien was to search out where the other end of the tunnels were and use them to launch a subterranean surprise attack on the castle before Bamaul was even aware he was under siege. Lockhart had made painstakingly slow progress with that over the years, but he had been able to cobble together small supply depots in a few of them. He had hoped there would eventually be many, but the chaotic turn their journey had taken drastically changed those plans. He was sure the others would be smart enough to head in the same direction as he was now, but he doubted Darien would understand to do so. It was his own fault for not thinking far enough ahead.

He had seen enough in his lifetime to know anything could happen at any time, no matter how unbelievable or outlandish so he should have gotten the boy more up to speed on his plans. Add in Darien's tendency to panic and Lockhart wasn't sure exactly what the boy or his dragon would end up doing in such a dire situation. He hoped Darien had enough sense not to do anything as life threatening as his transformation during the battle with the Broodmother, but Lockhart knew despite his hopes the boy was sure to surprise again no matter the situation. He just prayed it wouldn't be anything too extreme.

Chapter 12

Breathing heavily and with sweat pouring down his face
Lockhart silently cursed. He disliked the majority of events that
had unfolded since stumbling upon Darien, not that he blamed the
boy for any of it, but he also understood they had received several
boons as well. He just wasn't sure how most of them would work in
their favor at the moment. This unexpected rescue of Oltan
however, was one that he knew how to make use of without
question. Had they never met Little Maiani or spent time in that
odd mansion they would be in a more advantageous position
strategically, but he inherently felt he had received Oltan as
compensation for those plans unraveling. Lockhart just hoped
Maiani wouldn't consider it to be some sort of warped favor to be
returned later. He hadn't been able to get any type of read on the
woman and that bothered him more than he cared to admit.

Lockhart was thankful he had found the old man alive, but what
did they do from here once they had lost their pursuers in the
tunnels? Oltan needed rest and some semblance of medical care

more than anything and none of Lockhart's men had much skill past field dressings. Blinking away the sweat stinging his eyes as he ran Lockhart pushed his worries aside and put all his effort into reaching the ruins. Once they were able to get the rest and care they both needed then he could put together a plan of retreat.

Hells, we all need some respite after dealing with the Broodmother, Maiani's and now this.

Wishful thinking aside, Lockhart risked a glance behind him and was relieved to see no signs of immediate pursuit. He had no doubt Squirrel and Wily were doing their best to delay the castle soldiers and he prayed they would be able to follow in his wake before they lost their chance to escape after him. He was more worried that Gelas would prove to be a hindrance to them than he was about Squirrel's injured shoulder. The man had lost his mind during the Broodmother attack and didn't seem much suited for physical combat, or for any type of conflict for that matter. Lockhart couldn't puzzle out why Wily was so steadfastly attached to the man. Despite Wily's claims that Gelas had saved his life, Lockhart couldn't see someone with Wily's temperament tolerating him for long. There was something off about Gelas, like he was unused to or incapable of thinking for himself. He knew a man as volatile as that could become problematic the longer time wore on, but he would address that issue when they weren't running for their lives.

Taking controlled breaths and trying his best to ignore the excruciating pain in his ankle Lockhart doggedly continued his trek towards the ruins. If his memories were correct there were actually few usable tunnels accessible from this end, but there was a very good chance that number had dwindled even more since his childhood. He was just glad Oltan had always encouraged his curiosity and tendency to explore while everyone else had chastised him for it. Had the old man not done so then Lockhart may never have found the ruins or the tunnels underneath them in the first place.

It wasn't much longer before he found himself approaching the area where the ruins lie. Forcing down a wave of nostalgia Lockhart slowed his pace now that he was sure he was free of pursuit. Making his way among the less traveled areas he began creating markings for the others to follow after leaving the worn pathway. No one but his own men should understand the subtle changes made to the landscape while he wended his way up to the ruins, but there was always the chance someone could get lucky.

Finally reaching the crux of the area he stopped short at being greeted by the sleeping form of a young dragon. As Lockhart slowed at the sight Oltan wheezed in shock and surprise at the docile form of the dragon resting soundly upon one of the many small hillocks dotting the area.

Lockhart was stunned. This was the first time in his life he had seen an actual live dragon in the flesh. Even in a state of calm repose the small dragon was still a majestic sight; just being in her presence was awe-inspiring. Such a rare event would have been something to celebrate had they not been escaping from a raving lunatic intent on executing them. Lockhart stopped to think for a moment and quickly came to a conclusion. Long ago he had learned that when faced with something unexpected or unexplainable the most obvious answer would be whatever was left over after eliminating every other possibility, no matter how unlikely. He eliminated most other explanations before coming down to two possible answers. Either this was a young dragon separated from its mother alone and vulnerable in the wild, which would be improbable, but not out of the realm of possibility, or this was Koseki.

He considered everything that had been happening to him and his men lately and concluded this being Koseki was the most likely scenario since it would fit with all the other madness they had endured since leaving the order. If true, Lockhart counted this a blessing since it meant Darien had to be close by. He decided to ignore the how and why of the young dragon's appearance for later. Taking another moment to catch his breath Lockhart inwardly winced at the pain shooting up his leg and into the base of his spine.

A strange gurgle coming from Oltan made Lockhart look over his shoulder to see a look of amazement and wonder etched onto the old man's filthy and haggard face. For the first time since Lockhart had been transported to Oltan's prison a spark of life ignited in the old man's tired eyes as he drank in the sight of the sleeping dragon.

"I believe she's Darien's dragon. I'll explain later," Lockhart said. He would be lying if he said he didn't get a small amount of enjoyment at seeing the incredulous look spreading across Oltan's face, but he didn't have time to relish the rare moment. Wincing in pain now that his surge of adrenaline had worn off Lockhart hobbled over to who he assumed must be Koseki. As he looked over the small dragon for once he was at a loss as to what to do next.

How exactly does *one awaken a sleeping dragon?* Lockhart paused a moment to consider the oddest question he had ever asked himself. *The answer is most likely 'carefully'.* Lockhart considered his options before deciding letting her be was probably the best course of action for the moment, especially since being wrong about the dragon's identity would most likely end up with him being incinerated.

Oltan spluttered in his ear and was making an obvious effort to be let down as spittle splashed over the back of Lockhart's neck. He tried not to let it bother him too much; the old man was like an excitable child living his dream at the moment. Lockhart just wished it could have come under more favorable circumstances.

There was much to fill Oltan in on once they got the chance. He wasn't quite sure how to explain Darien's unique situation to the man who had raised the boy. Oltan must have thought Darien safely far away from any of the conflict ravaging the country of Katama and discovering he was part of Lockhart's company and connected to a dragon must have taken the old man for quite the loop.

Lockhart slowly eased Oltan to the ground before walking around the dragon to see if she had been harmed. He was relieved to find she appeared no worse for wear, at least as far as he could tell. *If Darien had been so worn out from their tricks that he slept for three days then Koseki must be just as exhausted, maybe even more so.*

He could only imagine what kind of a toll it had taken on Koseki. According to Darien she wasn't much more than a toddler in terms of dragon maturation so he had to trust the boy would know what to do should she require assistance.

She didn't seem to be suffering from any physical damage, but she did present another problem entirely.

That problem being that her size may make his plans of utilizing the tunnels underneath the ruins null and void. Even though she wasn't yet terribly large, at least as far as dragons went, Lockhart wasn't sure the small tunnels would be wide or stable enough for her to navigate. He knew Darien would refuse to leave her, not that he wouldn't do the same; Koseki had become just as much a part of their party as Darien and had perhaps given the most out of all of them lately.

He was relatively sure the humans in their party would fit, if not altogether comfortably, but his memories were the hazy ones of a young boy so the tunnels could be much smaller than he remembered. However, their options were severely limited at the moment and he needed to be decisive as to his next course of action and quickly.

Oltan had weakly pulled himself up to a sitting position and was swaying somewhat unsteadily. The old man reached out and gently placed a shaking hand on Koseki, slightly shuddering with each deep breath the sleeping dragon took. Lockhart didn't blame him. Despite everything he had seen and done in his lifetime the old man had never realized one of his biggest dreams as head of the Interspecies Relations Development Department - Mythical Division; that of meeting an actual dragon. Such an event had been one of Oltan's underlying goals in much of his research and Lockhart knew the moment must have been bittersweet due to the circumstances surrounding them.

Koseki softly snorted and let out a small sigh at the old man's touch. She lazily opened one eye and raised her head to bump against Lockhart's chest. He took that as a positive sign confirming this was indeed Koseki and tentatively reached out to place a hand upon her forehead. Not even he would go so far as to assume familiarity with a dragon had he not been interacting with a Ryudojin for the past few months so he was relieved when the young dragon seemed to take no offense at his gesture.

"I'm going to assume you're Koseki?" he asked. The young dragon again bumped his chest and he took that as an affirmative. "I'm glad to see you're alright. Is Darien close by?" Lockhart wasn't sure if she could fully understand him or not. It was entirely possible Darien spoke to her in a language incomprehensible to normal humans. The boy had never mentioned anything of the sort, but it would fit in with his character to neglect to mention something like that. Not that he would withhold such a thing on purpose, but he did tend towards the oblivious where those matters were concerned.

Koseki slowly swung her head towards one of the dilapidated ruins nearby and Lockhart took that to mean Darien was inside and unharmed. Now that everyone but Liana and her retainers had been accounted for they just needed the others to catch up with them to move forward from here. He wasn't sure if Liana would care enough to join up with them again, but he suspected she wouldn't let Darien get too far out of her sight.

He hadn't taken more than a step towards the ruin before a low rumble filled the air. The rumble slowly grew in volume until it shook the very trees, forcing several panicked birds to take flight. He had to brace himself against the trembling ground and Oltan toppled into Koseki at the unexpected noise. The young dragon snorted in surprise and indignation, but didn't seem any worse for wear. Just as it had started the rumble suddenly ceased and the landscape grew eerily calm. Lockhart drew his sword as an uneasy feeling crept over him. He couldn't tell which direction the sound had come from as it had permeated the air around them and infused itself into every rock and tree. Gooseflesh prickled all up and down his arms and he resisted the urge to shiver. He knew both from instinct and experience that whatever it was, it was something major. It had the same feel as when he had first seen the Broodmother, but felt only slightly less ominous. It had even torn Oltan's eyes off of Koseki. The dragon herself seemed to recover from her sluggishness and lifted her head again to sniff curiously at the air.

Lockhart spun on his heel and almost collapsed from the pain in his ankle when the sounds of someone approaching in a hurry reached them. Several someones. The corner of his mouth twitched down in a grimace. He had hoped the others would catch up to him before any organized pursuit could give chase, but he prepared himself for whatever the Godlings decided to throw at him next.

The eerie silence allowed him to easily distinguish Jack's distinctive brogue among the others not known to him. Those unfamiliar voices were tinged with a desperate terror that Lockhart found strange.

"What are they so panicked about? Those token guards shouldn't have even left the castle proper! Why are they so worked up?" he wondered.

He got his answer when a scream of incomparable rage and madness pierced the odd stillness around him.

"Shit."

Lockhart avoided the impulse to swear several more times and chastised himself for expecting Bamaul to follow the same rule of order that King Tammaz would have. The madman himself had decided to join his troops on the ground. Lockhart had hoped he and Oltan's escape would have driven the madman so far into delirium he would be unable to recover or at least enough to discourage pursuit. From the reports he had garnered over the years it was rare for the tyrant to ever leave the castle interior, leaving most of the affairs of the rest of the kingdom in the hands of that abomination of a man Regam.

The shouts and cries coming from further down the path made it clear Jack and the rest were having some difficulty in following Lockhart's orders not to kill any of the token force from the castle. He knew it had been an unreasonable demand based on their circumstances, but he had made the assumption a minimally trained force such as they would not be forced to chase after far more skilled opponents despite their advantage in numbers.

Lockhart clenched his jaw in irritation again.

This is my own fault for underestimating Bamaul's insanity.

The fact Bamaul himself was bringing up the rear was a testament to how badly the tyrant wanted them dead.

Lockhart tried to prepare his mindset for combat, but the odd silence surrounding him was making the hairs on the back of his neck stand up. It felt like the entirety of the sparse woodland was holding its breath while it waited for something to break the silence.

It wasn't too much longer before the familiar faces of Geru, Jack and Tartas appeared at a run up the old pathway.

So much for those markers, he thought in annoyance.

Following behind them were very exhausted, and obviously very terrified, soldiers from the castle.

Lockhart stamped out another surge of irritation at the soldiers' lack of discipline and broken formation; he understood they were not the ones at fault for their ineptitude. What did give rise to his ire was the man stalking behind the soldiers in measured strides. A normal man wouldn't have been able to keep pace with running soldiers, despite their armor and arms, but Bamaul had morphed into something much different than human over the years.

The three men crested the last rise and Squirrel and Wily finally made their appearance; crashing loudly through the ruins off to Lockhart's left.

Did anybody even look *for those markers?* He would have to speak to them about that later. If there was a later.

The squeamish and obviously scared out of his wits Gelas was stumbling along behind them, but was acting strangely. The man seemed even more agitated and terrified than during the battle with the Broodmother. He was muttering incoherently to himself and was clutching his head as if in pain. Lockhart still had a great many questions to ask the man, but Darien's stunt during that fight and their subsequent trip to Little Maiani's had delayed them.

Lockhart was revisited by the unsettling feeling that something was off about Gelas, but he was well aware of how stress and fear could change a person from moment to moment. Still, he felt there had to be something more where Gelas was concerned. He took a breath to steady himself against the pain in his ankle and put those thoughts aside as he drew his blade in one swift, fluid motion. Philip Lockhart had endured far too much adversity in his lifetime to let it all end here for nothing. He would love to take the opportunity to bring down Regam and Bamaul right now, but there was still too much uncertainty as to what kind of strength Bamaul possessed and what Regam himself was capable of. Lockhart had found gathering information on the two men to be nigh impossible over the years. Add in the fact Oltan had wheezed into his ear that escaping should be their only priority and Lockhart knew he had to take advantage of the opportunity rescuing Oltan had given him. Escaping would also give him the chance to discover what recovering that strange artifact had been about.

His friends finally reached him and he gave Geru and Tartas a nod in Oltan and Koseki's direction. They were obviously confused by the decrepit old man and startled at the young dragon, but wordlessly took up positions to defend them. Geru's breath was somewhat labored and Lockhart wasn't sure he was one hundred percent after his strange experience back in Little Maiani's halls, but the man made no complaint so Lockhart chose to assume all was well unless Geru spoke up and said otherwise.

The muscles and tendons in Lockhart's neck bulged at the tension in his body. Unlike the altercation with the Broodmother this conflict elicited no excitement or fervor. These were residents of Katama; King Tammaz's people. He knew Bamaul was demanding they complete an impossible task and that they were being herded to their deaths. Before them was a small, but lethal and experienced group of fighters, and behind was a psychopathic and homicidal madman forcing them onward. Had Koseki not been in such a sluggish state they could have made a play for the tunnels, despite Lady Liana's absence, in the hopes that the dragon would somehow manage.

Sweat continued to pour down his face as his body went flush from pain, fatigue and frustration. He could hear his blood pounding in his ears and his heartbeat increased a thousand-fold as the soldiers approached. Lockhart took a deep breath. He knew he couldn't afford even a moment's distraction where Bamaul was concerned, but this was a situation he had desperately wanted to avoid. The approaching soldiers slowed to a cautious approach at the sight of Lockhart and his men when they were all suddenly thrown violently to the ground by an unexpected blast of pressure that came out of nowhere, breaking the silence of the woods.

Lockhart's battle instincts took over and he tucked and rolled with the blast, quickly recovering on slightly wobbly feet. His men were much quicker to react than Bamaul's, that was to be expected, but they all froze in shock and awe at what blotted out the sky above them. It was like night had suddenly usurped the day and a low, despairing wail rose from the castle soldiers.

Even Tartas let out an astonished "I'll be damned!"

An enormous Elder black dragon had appeared out of nowhere in concert with the explosion of air that had knocked them to the ground. Lockhart had had the briefest of glimpses at its arrival, as he had been the first to come to his feet, and would later describe it as having 'unfolded' from the very air around them. Black scales deeper than the depths of midnight covered the dragon from its thick ridged brow right down to the very tip of its tail and scales of indescribable shades of lavender mottled her underbelly. Uncountable rows of razor sharp teeth bared menacingly at them before the dragon slowly and elegantly raised its head to the sky and unleashed a roar so powerful Lockhart felt the Godlings themselves must be quaking in fear.

Koseki, for her part, slightly flexed her fledgling wings and weakly let out a small roar at the larger dragon's arrival. The black dragon beat her wings a few times, buffeting the humans with a wind so strong Lockhart had to shield his eyes and squint through

the dirt and grit pelting his face. The castle guards who had
regained their footing were sent tumbling backwards again by the
force created by her wings alone. The dragon then drifted lightly to
the ground with more grace and dignity than Lockhart would have
thought possible for a creature of such enormous size, but a large
plume of dust still rose around them. The soldiers began to cough
and choke on the debris and many no longer even tried to regain
their feet. The scent of bodily waste assaulted Lockhart's nose,
indicating many of them had lost control of their bowels.

Lockhart didn't blame them. This dragon imposed a much
more terrifying, yet beautiful, presence than Koseki did. If this was
what the young dragon would one day become then Lockhart
counted every blessing the Godlings could give that she was on their
side.

For several tense moments no one moved or even dared to
breathe. Even Lockhart found himself holding his breath. Then
the dragon bellowed at the sky so violently the trees shook and
several of the dilapidated buildings collapsed in on themselves.
Gelas dropped to his knees, gripping the sides of his head in agony
and letting out a soul wrenching scream. Oltan, who had luckily
been shielded by Koseki's bulk, rolled several feet and lost
consciousness. Lockhart hoped no more harm would come to the
old man than he had already suffered, but there was nothing he
could do at the moment. Geru staggered to his feet and went to
check on Oltan, giving Lockhart a slight nod that he was alive.

Lockhart locked eyes with the only other man in the clearing
who had been able to remain upright. Bamaul. Standing his
ground the tyrant king was violently shaking with rage and his eyes
looked ready to pop out of his head. One hand tightly gripped the

wrist where he wore that strange artifact he had acquired during his exile. Regam was groggily coming to his feet and seemed overly focused on Bamaul.

Lockhart clenched his jaw in frustration. He and his friends were completely at the mercy of whatever fate the Godlings had in store for them now. Unsure of which course of action to pursue, Lockhart doubted any man in existence had ever been presented with such a scenario. He doubted any would ever again. He knew he had originally committed to focusing purely on their escape, but Bamaul's insanity had provided a temptation Lockhart was finding difficult to resist. Should he try to take out Bamaul while he was distracted even knowing that he was far weaker than whatever the madman had become? Or should he grab Oltan and take the opportunity to flee and risk leaving Koseki behind? Darien's dragon had slowly come back to life during the Elder dragon's display and not having the boy there to interpret was handcuffing his ability to make an appropriate decision.

After several more tense moments the two dragons made the decision for him. Koseki rose on unsteady legs and lazily wobbled over to the larger dragon. The Elder dragon used one of her giant claws to grab Koseki gently by the scruff of her neck and deposit the smaller dragon onto her backside with more grace and care than Lockhart thought possible for such an immense creature.

The Elder dragon lifted her head to the sky and again loosed an earth shattering roar so ferocious Lockhart felt like his eardrums would burst. Gelas was babbling incoherently with tears streaming down his face and the soldiers, as well as Lockhart's own men, were in obvious pain as they tried to cover their ears. With incredible speed and power the dragon lifted off the ground with several beats of her enormous, leathery wings. For a few moments the dragon hovered in place looking down upon the humans before the space around it again folded and bent with a sharp inrushing of air. Lockhart had to fight against the pull of the suction with all his might before it stopped as suddenly as it had begun.

The dragon and Koseki disappeared without a trace, leaving behind toppled buildings and terrified, whimpering men as proof of their passing. Lockhart immediately made a decision now that the problem of what to do about Koseki had been solved. He assumed Darien would have an idea what had happened to the young dragon. The massive Elder black didn't seem to have acted in a hostile manner towards Koseki; not that he was any kind of expert on the relationships of dragons. But now that the most recent bit of absurdity in his life had vanished he chose the most obvious course of action.

"Run," he barked. Tartas picked up the unconscious Oltan and the others followed his orders without hesitation. Lockhart led the way for the others in the direction that Koseki had indicated Darien had gone. If his hazy memories were correct then this particular building would have an open access point to the network of tunnels underneath the ruins. According to the information he had been able to acquire over the years combined with the disjointed memories of his youth he was sure most of them would have a hidden entrance point, but whether they remained accessible or not was the question. It was entirely possible some of them had rotted and collapsed over the years, but they had little choice at the moment if he wanted them all to escape together.

He risked a glance over his shoulder and saw Wily scoop up the sobbing and stammering Gelas like a sack of grain as he ran. Just before Lockhart turned away he noticed Wily looking back at Regam and Bamaul with a sour expression. He hoped Wily wasn't thinking about trying anything under the cover of the chaos the Elder dragon had brought, but thankfully his brief moment of hesitation passed and he quickly followed after the others.

With everyone gathered, the Lady Liana was the only member left unaccounted for. Her retainers remained absent as well, but he doubted they would be far from their mistress. He didn't like what problems leaving her would most likely cause in the future, but they couldn't afford any more delays. This worried him more than he cared to admit. It was entirely possible the Lady would interpret his actions as a breach of their agreement despite his not knowing whether she had actually been sent to the same area as them.

He shook his head to clear it of any uncertainties; there wasn't time to dwell on that right now. Keeping his tense gaze on the soldiers haphazardly trying to regain some sense of order his worries about Liana were solved in spectacular fashion. A shimmering and sparkling wall of light suddenly rent the ground between them with such force that chunks of earth, timber and stone erupted in every direction. Everyone stumbled and pulled up short at the unexpected explosion and many of the castle guards who had finally regained their feet simply slumped to the ground in terror and exhaustion at the newest bit of insanity the day had wrought.

"What in the Hells is it now?" Lockhart growled.

He got his answer when Liana suddenly materialized out of thin air, startling everyone but Lockhart; he was far too used to these kinds of surprises by now. The soldiers all wore a look of astonishment as Lady Liana sauntered past and gently ran one pale hand across Lockhart's cheek.

"Shall we go? That won't last forever you know," she said.

Liana's retinue also emerged from a nearby ruin and hurriedly joined their mistress. Apparently helping them in any way hadn't been part of their agenda as they huddled close to Liana.

"Then move!" Lockhart said through gritted teeth.

He could see the few soldiers who had regained control of their faculties cautiously approaching the shimmering veil of light. No sound from Bamaul or his soldiers penetrated the barrier, but it was clear from the spittle and blood running down the tyrant's chin that the man had lost his senses even further while he screamed obscenities at his subordinates.

Lockhart took a quick appraisal of Liana's creation and could see no end in sight to the barrier in either direction, not that there was much for him to see as he stepped inside the ruin. *What in the Hells* is *this woman?*

Following the others as best as he could with his broken ankle he immediately veered towards the shattered entrance in the corner that Darien must have uncovered. How the lad had known it was there was a mystery, but the sounds of an intense fight coming from below gave him a sinking feeling in the core of his gut. Hopefully their arrival would help Darien bring to a conclusion whatever trouble he had found himself in this time so they could make their escape and bring down the tunnel behind them before Bamaul recovered from his trance. He wasn't going to count out the chance Bamaul would know of the tunnels already, but even if the tyrant hadn't been aware of them before he was sure to know about their existence now.

There was no telling where some of the tunnels would end up

since there wasn't an accurate account or detailed map of every tunnel, not that he expected to ever find one, but most of the tunnels should empty out into the same general vicinity. He was positive there were also others connecting to any number of various places based on his years of painstaking research. Wherever they ended up, it couldn't possibly be worse than their current situation. Especially with a raving lunatic screaming for their heads. Additionally, he wanted to escape before their exhaustion and injuries became a fatal hindrance.

Making his way down he quickly took account of their numbers. All of them were present save Darien, but he could hear the boy down below still engaged in a struggle. Lockhart tightened his grip on his blade.

He entered the underground chamber and it took a moment for his eyes to adjust to the dim amount of light, dust and debris still swirling about from the Elder Dragon's display. Reaching the bottom of the stairs he paused at the sight of the oddest stand-off he had ever witnessed.

The tension in the room was so palpable Lockhart could feel it pressing down on him like an immense weight. The others also seemed to be at a loss as to what to do; even Jack had the sense to remain silent.

He thought for a moment, but he couldn't tell if their presence even registered on the two other people in the room. Darien was bleeding through his tunic on one side, but the blood looked to be clotting to his clothes already. Both parties were breathing heavily and were drenched with grime, blood and perspiration. Neither took their eyes off the other despite Lockhart's appearance.

Geru made as if to intervene, but stopped at a curt gesture from

Lockhart.

"Something feels off," the General said quietly.

Lockhart had lived through more than his fair share of combat experiences so he could tell when the subtle signs of something abnormal were involved. The posture of Darien and his opponent, the obvious intensity of their fight and the heavy charge to the room that practically crackled around them lent credence to his assessment. It wasn't normal. This was something personal. Perhaps something even more.

After several stunned moments Darien finally spoke, never taking his eyes off his opponent. "What happened? Koseki disappeared for a few seconds. Is she alright?" he quietly asked between heavy breaths.

Lockhart wasn't sure how to answer since he didn't know exactly what had happened himself. He also didn't know what Darien meant by 'disappearing', but if the boy was asking what had happened to Koseki then it meant something had interfered with their connection.

Lockhart thought for a moment. Since it seemed Darien wasn't even taking the time to connect to Koseki then he must be taking this fight more seriously than anything Lockhart had seen from the boy so far in the relatively short time they had spent together.

"I can't be sure, but I'm going to assume she's safe. A much larger dragon showed up and took off with her. Right now I know nothing more than that. I'm guessing you re-established some contact with her after she left?" Lockhart said.

Darien nodded. "I felt her vanish for a moment before she came back to where she usually is in the back of my head."

Lockhart had no idea what the boy meant by 'back of his head', but chose not to question it. "More importantly do you need any help here? An escape path should be somewhere nearby," he said.

Squirrel had already begun to move about the dimly lit room. Lockhart was sure Darien wasn't having any issues with the darkness, but he was confused as to how Darien's opponent had been able to injure him when the boy should have such a clear cut advantage? Not only that, but Darien's opponent was much smaller than him, especially for a Bloodsetter. Lockhart twitched a frown as he analyzed Darien's opponent. Most Bloodsetters had skin a deep suntanned brown and were generally of a lanky yet toned build. This particular one was shorter and much slender than any Bloodsetter he had ever seen. Lockhart knew that size was relative and anyone could be capable of amazing feats, Darien was living proof of that, but it was just another factor adding to his feeling of unease.

There was one more glaringly obvious factor that set this Bloodsetter apart from the others as well. "What in the Hells?" he began before Darien cut him off.

The boy took a deep breath and winced in obvious pain before spitting a gob of mucus and blood onto the dirt floor. "I'll catch up. Please don't interfere."

Lockhart heard Liana sigh dramatically. "Stop dawdling and kill this thing already and let's get a move on. Or should I just do it for you since you're so woefully incapable?" Liana said in her usual arrogant tones.

Darien's face twisted in anger. "No!" he said emphatically. It might have been Lockhart's imagination, but the room seemed to flicker briefly with the intensity of Darien's response. Even Liana seemed shaken for a moment. Looking at the others Lockhart guessed he was the only one besides Liana to have noticed. Liana quickly masked her surprise and put her normal haughty expression back in place. She imperiously smoothed her reddish gold hair back and adjusted her circlet. She turned to stare intently at Lockhart.

"This agreement is starting to wear thin my patience General, but very well. Brat, do whatsoever you please. However I do not give you leave to die just yet, it would bring too much shame upon my shoulders for you to lose your life to such a weakling," she said.

Darien muttered a response, but Lockhart couldn't pick out the words. Darien's opponent however, had clearly understood him and the mask of rage contorting the Bloodsetter's face was murderous.

Liana sauntered over to Darien and unabashedly brushed her lips against his cheek with a whisper. The Bloodsetter tensed and elicited a guttural growl that Lockhart was sure boded none too well for Darien's immediate future. She directed a mocking look at Darien's opponent before languidly stretching with a light yawn. "Shall we go then?"

Out of the corner of his eye Lockhart noticed that Squirrel, who had been completely ignored by Darien's opponent while he searched the room, had suddenly vanished. The furtive man must have found an entrance into the tunnels and several seconds later a whistle indicating the all clear reverberated throughout the chamber.

Thankfully the entrance was located much closer to them than to the Bloodsetter, but Lockhart doubted this particular Bloodsetter cared about anything other than Darien. However, where those who served willingly under Bamaul were concerned rationale and sanity were often questionable.

Lockhart got a very bad feeling about what might come from this, but he had made a promise to Darien just before they left the Order about mutual trust and that promise was coming due.

He gave the others leave to exit after Squirrel with a silent nod of his head. As his friends filed into the tunnel Lockhart felt he should at least tell Darien about the old man, still unconscious and carried over Tartas' shoulder, having been found alive. He opened his mouth to speak, but the set and determined look on Darien's face told him the boy was no longer listening.

Had the old man been conscious maybe he would have known how to extract Darien from such an intense situation, but Lockhart wasn't sure if that would have been a good thing. Even a moment's lapse in concentration could be fatal in a situation such as this.

Following after the others into an even deeper darkness Lockhart looked over his shoulder one last time at the two figures in the room. The look on the Bloodsetter's tear and blood-streaked face was one he committed to memory. Lockhart wondered what could drive one of Bamaul's henchmen to exhibit such obvious anger and hatred for the boy. He regretted leaving Darien, but he had to trust the boy would be able to resolve things in his own way.

Lockhart shifted attention to those ahead of him in the tunnel. Darien's eyes would have been helpful, but Lockhart had made the decision to let the boy handle his problem on his own and hoped he would find a way to follow after them.

Just how much more of this insanity are we going to have to overcome to free this nation from Bamaul's tyranny?

The knot in his stomach tightened at the thought. Philip Lockhart decided he'd rather not have the answer.

Chapter 13

Lockhart gasped and swore at the pain in his ankle. His mind whirled with all the events that had spun wildly out of control since leaving the Order of the Fist that had left him and his companions in such a precarious situation. Not that events both foreign and dangerous were anything new to them, but this time there were far too many variables involved for his liking.

Discovering Oltan had been a small blessing, and whatever the old man had insisted on retrieving before their escape was obviously important, but he had essentially traded away his best element of surprise and perhaps even Darien in the exchange. Not to mention Liana's theatrics and whatever in the Hells had actually happened to Darien's dragon.

He and his companions hurried along the tunnel and the dim light from behind began to fade the further from the entrance they got. Liana, for her part, provided them with a small globe of light held delicately in one hand without even having to be prompted.

It irked him that his initial plan of using these ancient tunnels to launch a surprise attack on Bamaul was gone forever. It had taken him and countless others years of effort to put a small number of waypoints in place with the miniscule amount of information he had acquired. That had all just gone to waste.

Now that the opposite had happened and they were using the tunnels as an escape route he would have to find a way to collapse what tunnels he could once Darien caught up. Bamaul was certainly not the type of man who would allow such a vulnerability to remain now that he was aware of its existence. Even worse, he could use them to increase his stranglehold on the country. He gritted his teeth both in annoyance at their situation and at the pain throbbing in his ankle.

Leaving Darien in his predicament was weighing heavily on him. However, if he was going to back up his words of trust with actions then now was the time to do so. Plus the whole situation back at the ruin still seemed off to him. He searched his memory and as far back as he could remember he had never witnessed such an emotionally charged scene. And he had seen plenty in his lifetime. He just prayed the boy would finish it quickly and hurry after them. He didn't want to think about what might befall Darien should they need to collapse the tunnel before he arrived. Lockhart had a fleeting thought that he could leave a tunnel open just in case so Darien could try to follow after them, but summarily dismissed it. The risk was too great.

He fought the urge to curse in every language he knew. He had to focus on the ones around him at the moment, especially the old man. No one had complained about their injuries save for Gelas, but he was sure the others had gotten even more banged up during the conflict and needed rest as well. He also wanted to ask the old

man about the bauble he had retrieved once Oltan regained
consciousness and had been given some medical care. What they
had almost gotten killed retrieving while blindly jumping out of a
tower several stories high was he had no idea, but he was sure it
would prove vital in the days to come. If they lived that long.

Bamaul was apoplectic. Not only had Philip now twice slipped
from his grasp, but Oltan had been taken from him as well. His
seething anger rolled along with the torrent of raging bells in his
head and for a moment his tenuous grip on reality was swept away.
Regam had to forcibly remove his hand from the bracelet before he
lost all control. He had been gripping the thing so tightly it had
begun to fuse to his palm and a few more layers of skin tore away
when Regam separated them. For any other man such an act
would have meant instant obliteration, but this was one of Regam's
many duties as the one closest to Bamaul.

Such an allowance was necessary. He was not so foolish to
assume he could handle all of the power his bracelet contained. At
least not yet. The few charred and mangled bodies of soldiers who
had gotten too close to him and now lay smoking on the ground
gave testament to that. He wrinkled his nose at the charred stench
of flesh, metal and bone as he growled in protest at the offending
corpses. Bamaul ignored Regam's administrations as his chief
Bloodsetter applied a special salve to his palm.

The pain of skin tearing away had barely registered and now his
eyes rolled into the back of his head as it ebbed. He exhaled a long,
slow breath as the ocean inside his mind receded somewhat. Had
he not released a minute amount of the power stored within the
bracelet at the moment of the Elder dragon's arrival then who

knows what might have happened? Bamaul knew he couldn't afford to risk losing any more of the energy he had painstakingly cultivated over the years and to recoup even the minor amount he had expended would take considerable effort even for him.

The shimmering sheet of golden light blocking them from their quarry remained even after the strange woman vanished into the ruins. Bamaul intently watched the veil of light undulating and shimmering under the sunlight. Hues and shades of color refracted off the wall in every direction like a summer festival's fireworks. The king of Katama found the sight enchanting, which only served to infuriate him further.

His eyes rolled over to Regam and his vision swam for a moment. Taking another steadying breath he gave a command in low tones.

"Throw one of these wretches into that thing," he uttered. Watching the shimmering veil he could feel the hairs on his arms stand up and an indescribable itch crept over his entire being.

His eyes narrowed in suspicion. *This...could prove useful.*

A maniacal grin formed on his face while he relished in licking the blood from his teeth. Ever one to seek an advantage where one may not be apparent, Bamaul had already begun making preparations for whatever results this new obstacle may provide; no matter how many pawns needed to be sacrificed.

Regam, for his part, remained silent and moved to pick up the nearest corpse.

"No, one of the live ones," Bamaul said quietly. He continued to stare intently at the veil of light and possibilities began cycling in his head.

Regam immediately changed course and picked up the nearest

dazed soldier. Dragging him towards the shimmering light, the soldier barely had enough time to realize what was happening before eliciting a short scream that cut off when his body sheared apart once Regam forcibly tossed him into the barrier of light. The momentum of Regam's throw nearly carried the soldier's entire body through the veil, but fell short just below the neck. The now former soldier of Katama's head rolled slowly down the slope to rest at Bamaul's feet, leaving a trail of gore in its wake. Bamaul grimaced in disgust and rage that even in death this *thing* would dare to touch his person. He reared back and violently punted the head away with a sickening squelch.

Regam stood by, quietly waiting for his next order with a fervent light in his eyes. The creases underneath his Makavai gave away the head of all his Bloodsetters was clearly enjoying this.

"Another," Bamaul said.

Regam grabbed another soldier still barely holding onto consciousness. Bamaul's small, wicked smile broadened. Regam had bypassed several unconscious and deceased soldiers in order to get to this one. The soldier had seen what had just happened to his former comrade and desperately tried to crawl away, but Regam lifted one leg and with a powerful downward thrust stomped on the soldier's spine.

The combination of the man's screams and the sound of his spine severing were a glorious anthem to Bamaul's ears. The result was the same as the first, but this time Regam was sure to throw the entire thing all the way through the barrier. Nothing remained of the man, not even the lingering stench of charred flesh, blood and defecation that normally would accompany the thing's passing. But Bamaul's attention to detail paid dividends when he noticed a slight fluctuation in the veil's constitution. His grin widened even further. A modicum of understanding was slowly taking shape and he felt giddy at the possibilities coming to him.

"Regam, continue until you are told to cease," Bamaul said.

Regam continued to work in earnest. The few soldiers still holding onto their wits began to scream and crawl away from the Bloodsetter, but their pleas fell on deaf ears. Regam spared them not a moment's mercy.

"This is just punishment for your ineptitude and your ancestor's cowardice," Bamaul said more to himself than as an answer to the screaming soldiers. His eyes never wavered from the veil of light as one sacrifice after another vanished.

Bamaul's eyes unfocused and he risked opening a gate in his mind so that the tiniest fragment of power from his wrist would enable him to stare even deeper into the make-up of the unnatural sheet of light. It was a terrible risk after having just accessed that power already, but he deemed it necessary despite his earlier reluctance. After a few more sacrifices vanished into the veil Bamaul gave another order.

"Throw one of the unconscious ones, then one of the dead ones," he said.

Regam immediately dropped the terrified soldier he had been carrying and picked up the nearest motionless body. After quickly checking to see if the man was dead or simply unconscious Regam then grabbed another. With more force than necessary he tossed one, then the other through the veil. The result was the same as the others. Bamaul's heightened state detected the same slight fluctuation, but somewhat different and to a lesser degree. Had he not risked leaking power from the bracelet again he would never have noticed the subtle difference. This time he was able to release his hold on the bracelet and its intoxicating power on his own. Feeling the surge of the other-worldly power leech away he briefly got a sense of Lockhart and Oltan moving slowly away from him amongst a spider-web of tunnels in a massive network underneath his feet.

"Run little rabbit. Now that I know about these precious tunnels there is little you can do in my country from here. Enjoy the limited time you have left. I will relish dissecting you piece by piece the next time we meet," Bamaul growled.

The last vestige of power dissipated and Bamaul felt like he had just suffered an insurmountable loss and had to forcefully stifle an overwhelming sense of grief. He shuddered in both ecstasy and despair at the sensation before regaining his composure.

"That's enough Regam. Send for my shamans at once. And get this worthless fodder back on their feet. Their incompetence today was disgraceful."

"Yes your majesty," Regam immediately replied. The chief Bloodsetter instantly began kicking men awake and yelling commands for them to stop acting spineless and get to their feet.

Bamaul watched Regam work with detached interest and pondered what this fluctuating veil of light could portend for his future and his eventual ascension.

Whatever this is, I will be sure to utilize it to the utmost of my advantage.

A feverish shiver ran through him.

"Things are going to get much more interesting from here! Run while you can Philip Lockhart! Run Oltan my old friend! I'm sure I'll be seeing you again much, much sooner than you expect!"

Bamaul shouted in defiance at the sky.

Bamaul abruptly spun on his heel and briskly walked back towards the castle with the moans and cries of the castle soldiers ringing merrily in his ears.

The undersized Bloodsetter continued his inhuman acrobatics, always managing to remain just out of range of Darien's short blades. If it weren't for his dragon eyes and the rigorous training he had received at the Order he wasn't sure he would have been able to track all of his opponent's movements. He *was* sure his old self wouldn't have stood a chance and the fight would have been over before it had even begun. The mist roiling off the Bloodsetter wasn't helping much either. The colors of mist were rapidly changing in a kaleidoscope of color that bewildered his senses. Additionally, his own exhaustion and inexperience were making it impossible to subdue any of the mists while under the strain of fighting for his life. The colors of pain, rage and grief were the most prominent, but there were other alarming colors as well which quickly overlapped and changed at random. His physical and mental limits were too strained at the moment for him to control such a whirlwind and Koseki was being no help at all.

Not that Darien blamed her. He had put far too much strain on the young dragon and he knew asking for more right now could prove to be far more dangerous than not. Right now she was getting some much needed rest up above and he didn't really want to risk her safety if he could help it. Also, she was being exceptionally cranky.

Darien didn't have any more time to dwell on Koseki or the mists; he needed to focus on staying alive as he parried another of the agile Bloodsetter's attacks. His shoulder was still sore from where Koseki had impaled him; that and the wound in his back were slowing his reaction time to the point where he had suffered several gashes already.

If this keeps up, I really will end up dead. And I still don't know what happened with Koseki, but she felt exhausted so there's no way I'm asking her for help. I'm going to have to do this myself.

Not that she would listen right now anyway. He was sure something must have happened to the both of them once they had been forcibly ejected from Little Maiani's, but the Godlings only knew what that was.

'What in the Hells is your problem?' he sent to the dozing Koseki. Barely parrying another strike he decided if he survived this they were going to have a long talk afterwards. But that was a very big 'if' at the moment. After a few more moments he did get the sense from Koseki that someone had arrived up above, but she wasn't panicking or sending mists of fear so he had to assume one of their friends had finally made an appearance. That was one worry from up above off his mind, but right now he had far more to worry about right in front of him.

After what seemed like an eternity of exchanging lethal strikes and slashes the Bloodsetter finally leapt back to create some distance and presumably catch his breath. Both were taking heavy, uneven breaths and were soaked in perspiration, grime and blood. Darien took the opportunity to check his wounds and was relieved to find the one in his lower back was finally healing now that he had a second to catch his own breath.

Staring intently through the haze of mist undulating and raging around the Bloodsetter he was again struck by how abnormal this particular Bloodsetter appeared.

"Who are you? It's obvious even to me you're not a normal Bloodsetter. Why are you helping that madman destroy this country?" he panted. Darien was more stalling for time than anything, but the odd feeling he had wouldn't go away.

Darien shrugged off the feeling as inconsequential as the only answer the Bloodsetter gave was a low guttural growl that was getting louder by the moment. If he let something that small distract him, he'd be dead before he knew it.

The Bloodsetter suddenly elicited such a scream of pure rage and anguish that Darien was momentarily stunned. The Bloodsetter hunched back on his heels as if on springs and launched himself across the room with his blade aimed squarely at Darien's chest. Darien was so shocked by the sudden attack and its simplicity that he almost didn't react in time.

Sidestepping at the last moment he winced and grunted in pain as the Bloodsetter's blade ripped through his tunic and sliced open his side rather than skewering him through his middle. Forcing himself to ignore the excruciating pain Darien swung blindly in a reverse slash. He had been hoping to make a lethal strike or at least return the injury, but he would settle just for creating some room to move. The Bloodsetter had come at him with such speed and ferocity that it was the best he could hope for at the moment.

Because of the Bloodsetter's short stature Darien ended up swiping across his face as he twisted mid-air at an impossible angle to avoid the sudden strike. Darien felt the slightest impact on the tip of his blade as it left a thin red line of blood across the Bloodsetter's face and ripped free his Makavai. The mass of hair that had been tied in a bundle atop the Bloodsetter's head came loose and a complex double braid tied at the ends tumbled free to cascade down his backside.

Darien needed a moment to think this through, but his opponent was hardly giving him any leeway to do so. There was something unnatural and unsettling about this particular Bloodsetter. There was so much anger and hostility emanating from him it was like fighting another Liana, not that he wanted to be reminded of *her* at the moment. He had been caught off guard on that last attack and was sure he wouldn't be so lucky next time.

Whirling away from his foe Darien jumped back to create the distance he needed, intending to use the shock of losing his Makavai against the Bloodsetter. But before he could take advantage he locked eyes with the person who had been so obsessively trying to kill him and froze in shock. None of his muscles would work. His mouth twitched spasmodically, but no sound was forthcoming. His chest constricted so tightly he could barely breathe and his heart was pounding so loudly he could hear it echoing in his ears. Darien's entire body shut down from the impossibility of what he was looking at. Of *who* he was looking at. His brain refused to form any coherent thought as he took in the face of the person standing before him.

Staring back at him, with tears flowing from eyes of the deepest brown and mixing with blood seeping from the Bloodsetter's wound, was someone he never expected to see again in his lifetime. A face that gave rise to all sorts of emotions and memories he had been battling continuously since the night his village had been set ablaze and his life drastically altered forever. A face he had once loved, although he hadn't known it at the time.

It was Corly.

Here ends Volume II of the Dragonsouled Chronicles

Made in the USA
Middletown, DE
15 November 2020